FROM THE EDITOR'S TOWER

Greetings Dear Readers,

It's been almost two years in the making and with a cast of dozens!

The waiting is finally over.

The *Weirdbook* annual!

This is a goody. What we have here is a superabundance of zombies, which is a good thing considering that this is our **ALL zombies issue**.

We have horror zombies, fantasy zombies, and even science fiction zombies. Hell, we even have a zombie guinea pig! What we don't have this time around though are George Romeroesque Plague/Apocalypse Zombies. I think that that brand of zombie has been run into the ground. And if you want to be a stickler for details, I wouldn't even call them zombies anyways.

So I'm very confident that this special issue will scratch that zombie itch and satisfy your Jonesing for things undead.

We have wonderfully weird stories from Lucy Snyder, Adrian Cole, D.C. Lozar, Angela Yuriko Smith, John Linwood Grant, Erica Ruppert and many other talented story tellers.

> *All things undead and decaying,*
> *All Revenants festered and foul,*
> *All things moldy and slaying,*
> *Even the Devil fears them all.*

(With apologies to Mrs Cecil Alexander and the Monty Python troupe.)

—Doug Draa, *Editor*
Nuremberg, Germany
August 1, 2021

Staff

PUBLISHER & EXECUTIVE EDITOR

John Gregory Betancourt

EDITOR

Doug Draa

CONSULTING EDITOR

W. Paul Ganley

WILDSIDE PRESS SUBSCRIPTION SERVICES

Sam Hogan

PRODUCTION TEAM

Sam Hogan
Karl Würf

THE MEDDLER
Matthew John

Three knocks at the door broke the night's long silence.

"Don't open it!" Shel's brother whispered, his eyes wide. Shel had seen fear in him before but never like this. She felt it too, but kept it buried, averting her eyes for fear of returning that haunted gaze.

"Listen, Cam." Three more thumps at the door. "It's not one of them! Maybe it's Redgar." She faked a smile to hide the lie.

"He's dead. You saw!"

Shel couldn't be certain what they'd seen the previous night, but it had looked like Redgar. She peeked through a gap in the shutters. Across the field, at Redgar's house, all was black. As she pressed her face against the wood, trying to see who or what was at her door, a muffled voice came from the other side, "Open the door, children. I've come to help." It was a man's voice—old, deep, unfamiliar.

"I'm opening it, Cam. Hold the axe in case—"

Shel's whispered words broke off as she gripped the iron handle. She took a deep breath and tried to imagine what her mother and father would have done. Father probably would have just smiled and invited the guest to dinner. Old fool. Gods, how she missed him, how she wished they were here.

She tried to open the door slowly, but the howling wind pressed hard against the old wood, almost knocking her back. A man clothed in black barged in and pushed the door closed.

"As I said, I've come to help, but we must douse these lights. Quickly!" The man was tall and slender like a blade. His white beard was stained yellow from pipe smoke, his hooded robe tattered and filthy. He didn't have the look of a friendly stranger, but when Shel considered all that had transpired, she knew they needed all the help they could get. Cam backed away, stunned, the woodcutter's axe gripped in his shaking fist.

"Put that down, boy," the stranger commanded, "and blow out the candles! It's a marvel they haven't been drawn to the light. What do you think brought me here?" Cam's bottom lip quivered and his eyes glistened. For months, he had been constantly on the verge of tears—ever since their parents had left that night. Shel's heart ached for him. She wanted to wrap her arms around him, kiss him on the top of his head the way her mother

Weirdbook

Features

Short Stories

Continued on next page

Poetry

Artwork

used to, but instead she picked up a lantern and blew out the flame.

"Who are you? How did you make it here?" she asked, still not meeting the stranger's eyes.

"I have ways…but if we want to escape this valley, we must work in concert."

Once all the lights had been snuffed, the old man hobbled about the room, opening cupboards, peering into the small rooms. One of his legs must have been injured or lame, for his gait was uneven and slow. In the dim moonlight, Shel watched him pause at the cold hearth and again at her parents' bed in the alcove behind the kitchen. Then he pulled a chair from the table, sat down and retrieved a long black pipe from his sleeve. He pressed the pipe to his lips and snapped the fingers of his opposite hand. Miraculously the pipe began to glow and a thin wisp of smoke snaked up to the rafters. Shel had seen magic tricks at the solstice fair, but never without pageantry. This man was a meddler! She'd thought them myths—naught but phantoms from children's stories. If the tales were true, this man was dangerous. *Never trust a meddler*, they said. Fear gnawed at her. She wanted to grab her brother and run. But, meddler or no, this man was surely no worse than the horrors they'd glimpsed from their window.

Surely…

"Come. Do not fear me. I've come to help you, but I'll admit this old wretch needs your help, too. Shall we help each other, then?" The stranger flashed a thin smile and waved them over with the smoking pipe, beckoning them to sit. Cam stood like a statue, axe now sagging in his arms. Shel strode over to her brother, placed a gentle hand in his and urged him forward. The two sat before the stranger as he sent puffs of fragrant smoke dancing about their moonlit home.

"You saw the fire in the sky, I trust?"

Shel nodded. Cam remained silent.

"And surely you've seen shooting stars before?"

Of course she had. She and her father used to watch for them on summer nights out on Braga's Point, overlooking the lake. At the sight of one, her father would always tell her to make a wish. Once she had, he'd ask what it had been. And always he would smile and tell her it wouldn't come true since she gave it voice. Every summer the joke was the same; so was the smile.

"What you saw in the sky was not unlike a shooting star, only it landed here, in these lands. Normally, these *stars* are benign. Dead. Useless." He paused and took a long draw from the pipe. Then as smoke escaped through his rotten teeth, he went on. "But this one brought *passengers*."

Passengers? What could survive an impact that had shaken the very bones of their house?

"I'm sure you have seen nests? And I'm sure you have seen what happens when you disturb one. Now, imagine the star is like a shell—like a… like a walnut!" The stranger snapped his fingers when he found the right comparison and smiled again. The crooked grin dispelled some of the stranger's mystique, and Shel relaxed her guard. This man wasn't a meddler. Not like those from the tales, anyway.

"When the star lands, the shell is shattered, but the nut—the nest, in this case—remains. But now…" the man's tone darkened suddenly. "Now that they're here, they cannot stay in their nest. Our world is not like theirs, so they must find a new home. And these *wasps* prefer to make their homes… inside us."

Shel waited for the man's lips to split into another smile, for the laughter to come. But the stranger remained solemn. Cam gasped and the man puffed more of the strange smelling smoke and seemed lost in thought.

Inside us? Shel's stomach heaved.

The stranger continued, "I'm sure you've seen them out there, wandering the dark. I'm amazed to have found you two alive. For most, it is already too late.

As you can see," the man tugged his robe up to his knee, revealing one leg that resembled a withered branch, thin and grotesque, "I am in no condition to go back out there. My wards and mixtures allowed me to make it here, to you, and I hope my efforts have not been in vain."

The stranger leaned forward, and Shel met his gaze for the first time. What she saw left her both horrified and amazed. The whites of his eyes were nearly eclipsed by his pupils. From these black pools, tiny specks of light shone like stars, producing their own radiance. Her mind and body froze like her blood.

"Do not be afraid. I realize it may seem strange, but know these eyes have beheld the wonders beyond and that I am the only one who can face the horrors that have come." Mercifully, he broke his stare. But next he seemed to appraise her body, as if she was a prized horse. "You look strong, girl. Capable. You've worked these fields and brought in the harvests. Can you be strong now for your baby brother? Will you do as I ask?"

The outer dark was a monster in her mind—a looming, overwhelming shadow. Next, the stranger would insist she venture out into the blackness, for what could be done from here? How could she help her brother by staying? How could she do as her mother had asked? Hoping to seize what little of her courage remained, she snuck a look at Cam. He sat cross-legged beside her, his face in his hands, silvery tears falling from his fingers. He still hoped Mother and Father would return, but Shel knew better. She was all he had left.

"What would you have me do?" She whispered.

He leaned back in the chair and smiled. His strange eyes made it difficult for her to tell if the grin was of mirth or malice, but in this moment, as the dark waited for her—seemed to call her by name—all was mired in dread.

"You must cross the field and take the northern trail to my home. You've been there before. Don't think I've never spied you and your brother throwing stones outside my grounds, trying to knock the noses from those old statues."

The smile on his face now seemed genuine. Cam peeked out from the cover of his hands and Shel flashed him a knowing grin. They'd always wondered who lived in the tower. And they always suspected a meddler.

"Inside, you will find a talisman. It looks like a simple necklace, but it's much more. With it, I can send these poor souls back to rest and contain the infestation. I know you've been told that we *meddlers*, as most like to call us, are wizards or sorcerers, and though magic may be the right word for the unexplained, we most often deal in science." The stranger paused and picked at the wooden armrest of the chair. "Now, I'm afraid you won't like what comes next. You can plainly see that my body is failing. I haven't the speed nor the fortitude to do what must be done. But you, girl—you have youth, and youth is power. I was unable to return to my home, for the wretches had already entered my grounds. They could smell me coming. You see, I have the reek of magic on me. And the *wasps* are more attracted to my scent than to others. So it must be you. But this..." he paused, reached into his robe, pulled out a black pouch, and tossed it to her. "This will protect you. You must apply this substance around any areas of your body the wasps might enter—nose, eyes, mouth, ears… you can imagine the rest. This will help mask your scent as well as form an unseen barrier. It is not a perfect shield, but if you're fast and careful, you should be able to avoid them."

Shel tried to force the images from her mind, but the horrors flashed in vivid detail. She tried thinking of Cam—of what Mother and Father asked her to do. But her mind's eye remained fixed on the shambling figures she'd glimpsed in the fields surrounding her home. Even from a distance their aspect had been revolting.

"You must not dally, girl. If we wait much longer, I will not be able to contain them."

"No, Shella! Don't go! Don't go out there!" Cam shrieked. He crawled over to her and placed his head in her lap. Shel stroked his golden hair in silence and, looking at the stranger, nodded in affirmation.

"I won't be long, Cam. Remember how quickly we'd make it to that old tower? There and back before Father knew we'd abandoned our chores. Remember?"

"It's dark, Shella. You won't find the way. You won't—"

"Shush, baby brother. I'll be fine." Shel leaned into his ear and whispered, "I'll steal you a meddler's trinket while I'm there."

Her brother flashed a thin smile and relaxed his grip, allowing her to rise.

"I shall protect him, fear not," said the stranger, refilling his pipe. "Your sister will be back within the hour, boy. Come, let me tell you about a meddler's work. Do you know of the fairies that inhabit the Lonewood?

How the man knew of Cam's obsession with imaginary fairies was beyond Shel's knowing, but she was glad of his intuition. Cam remained sitting on the floor, but his head perked up as the old man broached the topic.

"Girl..." the stranger paused and smiled. "Shella," he corrected and nodded. "You will also need this. He bit down on the pipe, securing it between his teeth and fetched something else from his robe. As Shel rose and approached, she saw a large silver key poking out from his gnarled hand. As she reached for it, he held it tight and fixed her again with his strange eyes. Up close she saw the deep lines of age, mottled skin, and his long and hairy nose. A hideous man. But she was convinced of his benevolence, nonetheless.

Still holding the key firmly, he used his other hand to retrieve the pipe from his lips and continued. "This key will open the door to my study at the top of the stairs. What we need lies on a pedestal. Before you touch it, you must feel underneath for a switch. Press it, or..." His faced pinched into a baleful mask as he released his grip on the key, letting her take it. "Be quick and cautious, and you will succeed. And do not—absolutely do not—take the door to the lower levels. It is not safe there."

Shel slipped back to her parents' room and applied the strange blue chalk as the stranger instructed. On the bed she saw one of her mother's scarves. They were the most expensive items she'd owned. Every year, when the trader from Pathra visited town, Father would buy her a new one with what little extra money the harvest afforded him. Shel picked it up, admired the rich green, the shining gold trim, and pressed it to her face. Tears tugged at her lids as she breathed her mother's scent, but she wouldn't allow them to fall. Instead, she exhaled a heavy breath, wrapped the scarf around her neck and thought of her brother. He was all she had left.

She strode back to the main room and embraced Cam, who sat listening to the stranger's story about yellow fairies. As she tousled her brother's hair one last time, the old man cleared his throat suggestively. When she looked at him, he nodded his head toward the woodcutter's axe Cam had left on the floor. She whispered a goodbye in Cam's ear, retrieved the axe, and strode toward the door.

* * * *

In the howling wind, the forest seemed alive. Branches swayed and creaked and rogue gusts snapped her garments like a sail. She stopped often, scouring the shadows for movement against the wind. As the trail ended, the trees cleared and she saw the grey of the coming morning staining the black of night. Ahead of her, the tower stretched above the remnants of an old fence. Like a black sword, it seemed to threaten the very sky. For a moment she lingered before the broken, moss-covered tiles of the courtyard, recalling the adventures she'd had with Cam. The statues guarding the tower, once so familiar, now seemed menacing in the pre-dawn gloom. She counted five of them, but it looked as though a sixth had collapsed.

Had there always been six?

She could not trust her ears but was fairly sure of her eyes, so she proceeded to the tower door. But as she drew within twenty paces of the crumpled statue, she knew they'd failed her. The dark lump was not the remains of a broken sculpture, but a human figure kneeling and curled up in agony. She bristled and froze, straining her eyes, attempting to make out the details. She couldn't tell if it was a man or a woman; all she could see was the hair on its head, the slope of the back, and sides of its arms. Shel stepped to the right, planning to walk a wide circle around the figure. But then it moved. At first it seemed to vibrate and then began shaking like a dog fresh from the pond. Instinct took over and she fled to the entrance. Arriving at the steps, she reached for the silver key, but then noticed the door was already ajar.

Glancing back, she saw the figure had risen and turned away from her, head whipping from side to side as if trying to shake something from its face. Her nails dug into the wooden haft of the axe. The fear of what she saw conquered the fear of what she didn't, and she pushed past the door and peeked inside.

Darkness greeted her. The only light came from the open doorway in which she stood. Seeing no other choice, she pressed against the heavy wood until the door touched the interior wall. Another look back and she saw the figure had returned to its hunched position, still as a statue once more. She waited a moment for her eyes to adjust and entered the tower.

Only the most basic composition of the room was visible as most of the details were lost in the murk. Her feet met stone tiles, but the wind whistled through the doorway, muting her steps. A mixture of pungent smells rode the air—ginger, sulfur, mint, mold. The curious shadows of furniture, trinkets and various tricks of the light kept her on edge as she followed the wall to the first of two doors. It was splintered at the bottom and didn't seem to have a lock. As she passed it by, seeking the door that led to the stranger's study, a loud rasp sounded from the main entrance. The heavy door groaned on iron hinges and as it increased in pitch, the light began to fade. Darkness spread, metal clicked…

And the room went black.

In the talons of panic, her body seemed to melt away. She became a weightless, thundering heartbeat. Breaths escaped in rapid succession, as if she'd fallen into a winter lake. She gripped the axe in sweaty, shaking fists. Though the light was gone, so too was the wind, and a pregnant silence settled over the darkness.

A few more measured breaths and she regained control of her limbs. Once her eyes adjusted, she noticed a subtle glow pulsing through the cracks of the splintered door—the door she was certain led to the basement. The very door the stranger had warned her about.

She weighed the implications. Perhaps a torch burned just beyond the ragged wood; she could snatch it and be out before any harm could befall her. But as she considered her options, a faint humming came from somewhere in the vast chamber. She froze. After a still, breathless moment, it grew louder. And then—

Footsteps.

Something approached.

Without thinking, she backed away and brushed against the basement door. The footsteps drew closer and the vibrating hum became a chorus of a thousand haunted voices, buzzing… like wasps.

One of *them* must have found her.

In the faint, hellish glow she could see a moving figure. With it, the cacophony seemed to amplify—seemed to accost her—as if she was a thief discovered in the marketplace. Reaching back she pushed against the old wood. The door creaked and warm light poured into the chamber, revealing the horrifying details of what advanced from the darkness. In a flash she saw a man's frame, pallid flesh, legs moving in stiff, erratic jerks like a marionette dancing on invisible strings. But worse than its surreal movements was a face resembling a rotten pumpkin, hollowed and carved for harvest celebration, eyes and mouth scooped out, sockets widened—all human features replaced by clusters of swarming insects.

Shel stifled a scream as its mouth split open and scores of winged shadows poured out. She slammed against the door and it gave way. Stepping through, she flung it shut and threw her weight against it, bracing her feet on the stone tiles of the new passageway. Not ten paces away a torch burned in a sconce at the end of the narrow hall. Beside it another door barred her escape, this one composed of iron and bearing a lock. The thin wood at her back rattled as the horror scraped against it from the other side. The air around her began to hum, and tiny shadows danced in the ambient light. A few of the creatures had entered through the cracks and she could see now they looked more like winged spiders than bees—bodies of deep purple with black wings and limbs. Terrified to move, she could only watch and endure the awful buzzing, the brush of tiny wings against her cheeks. Tears streamed down her face, salting her lips as she prayed for the gods to intervene. And miraculously, seconds later, the swarm disappeared.

The stranger's chalk! It must have worked. The buzzing persisted behind the wood. She could still feel the scraping on the other side, but the door remained closed.

Her shattered nerves took over. She secured the axe in her belt, ran toward the light, and snatched the torch from the wall. Drawing the key from her pocket, she peered at the iron lock. As she fingered the cool metal and recalled the stranger's warning, the wooden door protecting her from the thing on the other side exploded from its hinges, slamming into the hallway in a cloud of dust and debris. At the other end the creature stood like some contorted, grotesque scarecrow, its infested mouth splitting into an awful, mirthless grin. Again, instinct propelled her and she jammed the key into the lock. A flick to the right and she felt the bolt turn over. After retrieving the key, she pulled the brass handle and the door swung open. She didn't spare a look back, but the shadows told her the horror hadn't been far from the door when she stepped through and slammed it behind her.

Shel found herself in a small circular room, lined by shelves carved into the brickwork. In the center was a pedestal of stone, topped by a massive slab of wood, stained like a butcher's block. Bolted to the sides were manacles for hands and feet, and a series of leather straps and brass buckles. The air reeked of old death. Sinister shadows seemed to retreat up the grimy walls. Such was Shel's fear of the thing from the hallway that she hadn't considered what the stranger might have warned her about. Was the place trapped? Was it guarded? She stood in place, scanning the room, reluctant to take another step.

The room was a chaotic spread of bowls, cages, strange instruments, broken jewelry, scraps of metal, parchment, and chain. One of the stone shelves was heaped with potions, cups, and containers filled with unknown specimens, dead and preserved. To her immediate right were piles of clothing—boots, dresses, belts and…

A scarf.

Shel felt her stomach sink as the suspicion entered her mind. She reached to her neck and tugged free her mother's scarf for a closer look. But it was a needless inspection. The one she wore was green with gold trim; the one not five paces away was crimson, lined with silver. She'd seen it before. It was the last one that Father had given her mother.

But she had to be sure. Ignoring any potential dangers, she strode over to the shelf and drew the scarf from the heap. She brought it to her face, paused, and inhaled.

Her mother's scent.

Never trust a meddler.

She looked once more to the grim slab of wood, the manacles, the straps. She considered the deep grooves, the red and brown stains marring the surface. Tears crawled down her cheeks as she imagined the suffering her parents endured. Why had they given themselves to him? Why had they abandoned her and her br—

Cam! She'd left him alone with the fiend!

In an instant her body galvanized. A protective instinct crushed her fear and for the first time in her life, truly violent thoughts entered her mind. The meddler had taken her parents, made them suffer, but he wasn't getting her baby brother.

Not if she could stop him.

She stuffed the second scarf beneath her tunic and strode toward the heavy iron door. She moved in haste, worried her brazen resolve might fade. The shambling thing beyond now seemed a small matter. Before retrieving the axe from her belt, she placed the torch in an empty sconce beside the door. But then something caught her eye.

Adjacent to the nearest shelf was a cabinet. Though subtle, something glowed within. She approached, and seeing it had no handles, but a keyhole, she retrieved the silver key from within her pocket. Carefully she ran her hands along the surface of the cool black metal, feeling underneath for any switches. Finding none, she placed the key into the hole. It fit. She turned it to the right and the door clicked open far enough to pull it wide. Her breath caught in her throat as she beheld the contents. She never imagined a tool for killing could look so beautiful. A dagger composed of some bluish silver metal shone like it caught the summer sun. In this grim and dreary chamber, it seemed a divine gift—an outstretched hand, offering to pull her from these hellish depths. The blade bore etchings of a kind she'd never seen, but something about them—the precise yet elegant curl of the characters, too perfect and beautiful to be the work of human hands—made her think of the Ancients. The Shapers. All the tales that religion tried to silence. All the stories of wonder that informed the childhood games she'd played with Cam.

Wasting no more time, she grabbed the dagger and pulled it from the cabinet. It seemed almost weightless and warm to the touch. She strode back to the iron door and gripped the handle. A deep breath. A firm tug.

And the door swung open.

At the other end of the hall the thing stood like the work of some deranged sculptor— crooked and contorted in ways no man should bend. The wasps seemed to mark her presence before the host, and a dreadful hum filled the chamber. It turned to face her, smiling, swarms of insects billowing from its mouth like smoke. She pulled out the axe and simultaneously raised the dagger with her right hand.

Then, as if lightning suddenly struck the hallway, it lit up in flash. A loud crack followed and the dagger sent a single pulse through her hand. For a moment she saw only white light. As her eyes adjusted, at the other end of the corridor she saw nothing but smoke. Stunned, she looked to the dagger. It seemed to glow a little brighter than it had, and seconds later, it faded to a dull luminescence.

Despite her circumstances, she found herself smiling, for what foe could stand against this weapon? But the grin melted as she considered her next move. Freeing her brother was all that mattered, but how best to do it? Perhaps in the meddler's study she'd find nothing but a trap.

What if he'd already gotten what he wanted?

* * * *

During the journey home, she spotted more of the infested wretches, but the wind and chalk allowed her to slip by without notice. The morning sun crept above the hills to the east and painted her home in golden light. No signs of life could be glimpsed from the exterior, no sounds heard above the wind. She blew out a deep breath and told herself Cam would be alive and well, and that the meddler would have no knowledge of her discovery. She strode to the front door and knocked three times.

A moment later, she heard footsteps and the meddler spoke. "Is it you, girl?"

Shel knew he'd already seen her coming when the door popped open and his strange eyes stared down at her.

"Yes, it's me. Where's Cam?"

"Did you retrieve what I asked?"

"No…I could not. They were everywhere. I couldn't make it inside."

The meddler, still barring the door, peered at her for an uncomfortable moment, his expression impossible to read. At last he said, "It is regrettable," and stepped back, pulling open the door. "We will have to go about this another way, then. Come, your brother sleeps."

Shel tried to maintain her composure. She knew desperation would lead to suspicion, so she entered the room casually and approached her sleeping brother. He lay on the floor by the fireplace, his old blanket wrapped tightly around him, his chest swelling and sinking with the breathing of deep sleep. Careful not to startle him, she kneeled, and as she was about to give him a soft nudge—

"Girl," the meddler said, his tone darkening, "you must not wake him."

Shel craned her neck and saw his stature had changed. No longer did he have the aspect of a feeble old man. He was taller, bigger, and his eyes blazed like torches.

"You won't like what you see," he warned. "Your failure means we must do this another way. I don't need you, but your brother is mine."

Shel's heart pounded, her fingers fluttering in anticipation. She had to be patient, had to get this right.

"Shel—Shella." Cam's voice was faint, barely audible. She knew it would be a mistake to take her eyes from the meddler, but—

She turned to see Cam floating above the floor, drifting, as if on an unseen current, toward the meddler. Her brother's eyes snapped open and she was almost sick at the sight. No longer were they a familiar shining blue; they were the eyes of the meddler, black and riddled with strange lights.

"Life is the ingredient for most spells, I'm afraid." His aged voice boomed now, as if five men spoke in unison. "My work is more important than that of mere farmers—more important than that of kings! I must persist!"

"Shella, I can't see!" What's happening?" Her brother's voice quivered as his limp form sailed closer to the meddler.

It was time to act.

Shel rose and charged toward the fiend. She bellowed and raised the axe above her head. The ruse worked. With his concentration broken, the old man's eyes dimmed and Cam's body dipped toward the floor. But it was only temporary. The meddler raised an arm, and though she remained out of reach, an unseen force ripped the axe from her hand. As it sailed above his head and lodged into the wall, he swung his arm as if to punch an invisible foe. The air burst from her lungs as a phantom force knocked her into the table. Dishes crashed. Chairs scattered. She whooped and coughed, trying to catch her breath. Reaching to her belt, she loosened the green scarf she'd tied there. The old man grinned as Cam drifted within reach, but the smile sank when he saw the dagger in her hand.

A flash. The crackle of thunder.

Smoke and silence.

Cam groaned. She saw him rocking gently on the floor and ran to him.

"Cam!" she shrieked. "Baby brother, are you alright?" She winced as he turned to face her, then nearly burst into tears when she saw his familiar blue eyes.

"What happened, Shella? Where is the meddler?" Her brother rubbed his eyes and scanned the room. Clearly, he remembered little of what had happened.

"He's gone, Cam. And now we too must go. It isn't safe here," she paused and smiled, "but I think we'll be alright." She raised the glowing dagger, and her brother's eyes widened. "I told you I'd bring you a meddler's trinket."

"Can I touch it?" he said, as if she held a puppy.

"Not now, brother." She tousled his hair. "We must hurry. Pack your things as if we were off for a hunting trip."

After a few moments they had all they needed. Shel peeked through the shutters and saw nothing stirred, save for the fields of golden wheat. As they took a last look at their home, she leaned over and tied the green scarf around Cam's neck. Then she drew the red one from inside her tunic and wrapped it around her own. Finally, she pulled the axe from the wall and handed it to Cam.

"Now, baby brother, let's try this again."

✗

NECROPHILIC SIN

Ashley Dioses

Her waxy flesh, so blue and cold,
Enticed my finger's touch.
I slid inside her stiffened fold—
Then felt her sudden clutch.

Her milky eyes then opened up
And gazed into my heart.
The ice I felt within her cup
Then pierced through like a dart.

Her nails had sunk into my skin,
Yet I was frozen there.
My nightly necrophilic sin
Had led me to her lair.

She pulled me close to blackened lips,
And penetrated me
With teeth so dull it took more rips
To make a bloody sea.

The laughter of a mad vampire
And giggles from a ghoul
Resounded while I sought desire
On zombies, much more cruel.

TIGER GIRLS VS. THE ZOMBIES
Lucy A. Snyder

Eight months into the Apocalypse and we were all transformed: the living kept dying and the dead got no rest. The America of sitcoms and white-collar cubicles and Happy Meals had burned up like Los Angeles when the wildfires tore down from the hills. It burned up like my momma's brain after she caught the fever. It burned like the clove cigarettes we found in the pockets of the biker death cultists who tried to murder us in Reno.

Being good was the same as being dead. We were all gonna burn, either in this life or the next. But Tura? She knew how to live on fire.

Just a year ago, she was a researcher at UCLA, doing capital-ess Science by day and running triathlons on the weekends, casually busting down barriers just by living her life. I never had a chance to meet her there—I went to the university on a judo scholarship and meant to get a degree in nutrition. But I dropped out after two semesters when a guy at my gym recruited me for MMA. I couldn't turn down what seemed like an easy way to make some cash and get myself on TV. I can't kick worth a damn, but I'm good on the mat, and I won my share of prize money de-prettifying other girls' faces with your classic ground-and-pound. I always felt bad about that, afterward, and wondered what my life would have been like if I'd chosen brains over brawn. Heck, the zombie outbreak might have saved me; if I'd stayed in the game, sooner or later someone was gonna mess me up bad. And even if I didn't get my brain pulped in the ring, what would it look like at 40?

When I first laid eyes on Tura at the refugee camp, I thought she was a fighter like me. She had a warrior's walk and wary eyes. When I found out who she really was, I knew she'd been a great role-model. Way better than someone like me. Most any girl would see her and want to be her. Girls would want to be like her so bad that they'd stand up and blow off all the jerks who said girls couldn't do the math, couldn't crack the code, couldn't get strong, couldn't be people who mattered in the world.

I hoped some of those girls she'd inspired were still alive, and the jerks weren't. But like my daddy said: hope in one hand and spit in the other, and see which one gets wet first.

Now Tura was standing at the side of the road, staring out at the Rocky Mountains across the plain, dressed in oil-stained roughneck jeans and grimy boybeater and a pair of black leather chaps she'd taken off the skinniest dead guy in the Reno cult. Hands that used to carefully dissect brain tumors were now rough, calloused, her knuckles scarred like she'd been in more matches than I had. She kept our hair short with a gambler's straight razor. Months of hauling bodies and engines and fighting for our lives in the hard sun had given her a pair of guns she'd have never gotten on a Nautilus machine.

"You don't need him," I said.

She turned her hundred-mile stare on me. I could see her intellect like a vast, hot desert behind her stone-gray eyes. But not so much as a shadow of sanity seemed to soften her obsession.

She grinned at me, fresh bleeding cracks opening in her chapped lips. "I don't *need* him. That's a dead-cat fact, Johnnie. But I want that man so bad I can't think of anything else."

I squinted at her "You figure he's really still alive?"

She pulled her satellite smartphone out of her pocket and brought up a text message: *OK 4 now. Nbdy hurt. Soldrs fled. Trapt at mtn lab. 2 mnths of food lft.*

"You sure that's Mickey?" I pressed.

She nodded. "I'm certain. He and his labmates are surrounded by zombies. He thinks maybe a hundred shamblers, a couple runners. He got his family in there before the soldiers who were supposed to protect them abandoned the place. They took all their weapons but a couple of .45s."

I sighed. We were supposed to be getting *away* from the damned undead, not heading straight for them. If I had any sense I'd have left right then, grabbed my bike and my half of the food we looted from the Safeway and kept on heading East.

The truth was, I needed Tura. She'd saved my butt more times than I could count. I'd only been able to repay the favor twice, and the idea of leaving our equation unbalanced like that just didn't sit right.

And, if you scratched past that skin, the truth of it was that I loved her like she was family. More, maybe; I never got the feeling I was what my momma was hoping for when she birthed a girl. I never had a sister or a best friend growing up but I dreamed about that plenty. Never had much use for makeup or shopping or all that other girly stuff but it would have been nice to have someone to run around with. Someone to share my secrets with. Someone who made me feel like I belonged in the world.

When you spend your whole life out in the cold and finally find a nice warm fire, you want to stay near it, even if it stands a good chance of burning you.

"You in, Johnnie?" she drawled.

"You got a plan?" I replied.

She laughed that amazing cool laugh of hers. "Of course I have a plan, girl!"

Of *course* she did. And once she told me about it, I knew I'd be all in.

* * * *

We zig-zagged across the landscape, gathering supplies and equipment, guided by the information she was able to pull down from the satellites that floated above all the dirtbound death and chaos like titanium angels.

Her plan started to go off the rails at a National Guard armory hidden up in the hills. The place was locked up tight, but once we broke in, we found the soldiers had stripped the place clean before they bugged out. Not so much as a shotgun to be found, much less the grenade launchers or M230 chain gun we'd been counting on scoring.

"Is there another place we can go for weapons?" I asked her.

She shook her head. "The talk on SurvivorNet is that all the other armories and bases in this half of the country have been looted. We'd have to steal weapons from a gang or militia, and I don't like our chances."

She thumbed through web pages on her phone, scowling. Then her frown changed to a look of intense calculation; it was an expression that simultaneously filled me with hope and worry.

"What is it?" I asked.

"There's something else we can try. It worked in Texas, and if those crazy rednecks pulled it off, I think we can, too."

* * * *

Our first stop was a hardware store, where she loaded us up on rope, duct tape, sturdy canvas drop cloths and a couple of extra utility knives. Then we back-tracked to a Microcenter we'd passed in another town. The front windows had all been busted and the aisles were completely trashed. Unfazed, Tura grabbed her crowbar and headed straight to the back storeroom and started scanning the place with her flashlight.

"They usually keep the really good stuff locked up someplace secret." Her light lingered on what looked like nothing more than a custodian's closet. She stepped forward, tried the knob, discovered it was locked.

"Hmm." She knocked on the door, and I heard the solid rap of bone on steel. "I think we have a winner."

"What are you looking for?"

She stuck the crowbar's chisel tip in the door crack by the knob and started heaving. "You'll probably sleep better tonight if you don't know the details."

"I ... can't say I like that answer."

"Didn't expect you would." She winked at me. "You just have to trust me for now."

The door gave with a squeal of metal and slammed open against the cinderblock wall. Tura shined her light inside. The first things I saw were racks and racks of custom-made gaming PCs, screaming fast monster computers with cases sculpted to look like alien beasts.

I cocked an eyebrow at her. "You planning to challenge the zombies to a Halo deathmatch?"

She laughed, stepped into the closet, and plucked a bright yellow software package off a lower shelf. I caught a glimpse of the words "HüDü Linux: Smartphone Edition" on the box before she shoved it into her rucksack. Tura grabbed some other boxes that looked like they contained some kind of wireless cards and stuck them in her bag as well.

"Let's roll," she said.

* * * *

The next day, we pulled up in front of the Tranquility Creek Wildlife Center. The place was abandoned. Through the front gates, I could see dozens of empty animal cages, their galvanized steel doors swaying gently in the hot breeze.

"Lions and tigers and bears, oh my!" Tura clapped her hands like a little girl.

"Okay, seriously, what are you planning?" I asked.

She pulled one of the .22 rifles off the rack behind us and pressed it into my hands. "We're hunting big game. *But.* I don't want you to kill anything we find. We need to bring 'em back alive. Well. *Undead.* Shoot only if you have no choice; better to run first."

I followed her into the abandoned wildlife center and we began to sneak around, looking for … well, I still wasn't clear on that.

But when we came across a tiger pacing back and forth in a concrete drainage ravine, it was clear from Tura's reaction that we'd found it. The tiger was *huge.* She looked to be six feet long, not counting her tail, and close to 300 pounds. And her fur was in great shape. You wouldn't have known she was a zombie, except for her gray tongue and spoiled-milk eyes.

"Perfect." Tura gestured for me to follow her back to the truck, and we snuck away before the big cat had a chance to spot or smell us.

"Perfect for what?" I whispered back.

"Did you know that Siberian tigers prey on bears?" She had the serious tone of a nature show narrator.

"I did not know that, no."

"Truth. They eat the Russian version of grizzly bears. There isn't a land predator a tiger can't kill. And that especially includes humans."

Her plan was starting to take fuzzy shape in my head, but it still didn't make any sense to me. "So … you want to use that tiger to get rid of the zombies surrounding Mickey's lab?"

"Exactly," she replied. "And the tiger won't run out of ammo."

My face grew warm with frustration. "How in the name of sweet buttered corn are we going to keep that thing from killing *us* instead?"

Tura smiled in a way that a lot of folks might have found scary. "One thing at a time, doll."

Once we were back at the truck, Tura pulled out thetre yellow HüDü Linux box and the other stuff we'd gathered the past few days. She spent a good hour or so thumbing through the manual from the box and fiddling with her phone.

"Okay." She reached into the software box and pulled out a silvery metal rod, maybe six inches long and a half inch in diameter. Then she paused, turning the rod over in her hands. "I think this is doable."

"What happens now?" I asked.

"Well, now you get to dust off your judo skills and shove this rod down the tiger's throat."

"… What? N-no way."

"Now, Johnnie. Don't be a fraidy-cat." Tura gave me a look that was one part *I dare you* and two parts *You owe me and you know it.*

Crap. I did owe her, and I did know it, but I wasn't suicidal. Or stupid. "What about that part where you said that tiger could kill a grizzly bear?"

"You just have to get it a couple of inches down her throat. Easy-peasy considering she'll be trying to eat you, right? Shouldn't take you but a few seconds."

"She'll tear me to pieces in just a few seconds!"

Tura sighed and pointed at the pile of canvas and the duct tape. "Johnnie. You'll be protected, don't worry."

Tura had me put on a set of the spare motorcycle leathers we'd salvaged—they were too big for me, but at least the pants stayed up—and then began to mummy me with wide strips of canvas and duct tape. By the time she was done, I was sweating buckets inside the leather and more than a little dizzy from the heat. But now I was wearing a pretty passable replica of a padded tactical training suit. I had a glimmer of hope it would survive ten seconds with a tiger.

"Are you gonna pass out?" she asked, peering at my face. It probably looked like a stewed tomato.

I shook my head.

"Can you bend your arms? Can you walk?"

I did an awkward macarena and waddled forward a few steps.

"Looking good!" She plopped a motorcycle helmet onto my head and cinched it under my swaddled chin. "Let's go."

* * * *

As I waddled down into the ravine where the tiger paced, I felt like I was wading into the shark-infested water at Smyrna Beach wearing a chum bikini. But, as Tura had explained it, there wasn't any other way. We had to get the rod down the tiger's throat or we'd have no way to control it. And tranquilizers didn't work on zombies, and we didn't have any tranqs anyway. Nor were either of us good enough with a rope to do the cowgirl thing.

I stepped on a twig, and the tiger's head jerked around toward me, her black lips skinning away from algae-greened fangs the length of my fingers. Her pebble-rattling growl made me wish I'd taken a moment to go use the ladies' room, but it was too late for that now.

"Here kitty kitty kitty …." I flipped my helmet's visor down.

The tiger—I was starting to think of her as Fluffy—sprang at me with speed I hadn't imagined. Three hundred pounds of fanged, clawed undead cat tackled me, and the air woofed out of my lungs as she slammed me down on the concrete. Fortunately I held onto the rod.

I'd been in this position before, back when super-heavyweight Amazonia Kartovsky took me down to the mat in our fight in Mexico. I wrapped my legs tight around the tiger's midsection so she couldn't rip my belly open with her back claws. And then before she could chomp down on my helmet I grabbed her snout with my left hand and pushed her away.

Fluffy roared at me and began to rip into the canvas on my shoulders with her front claws. The air filled with a flurry of canvas shreds. The blast of her breath seeped into my helmet and choked me. Cats don't have sweet exhalations at the best of times, but take the worst rotten-toothed, putrid-tuna, paint-peeling stink you've ever smelled and take that to a level that threatens sanity and you'd have some idea of what that tiger's tonsil gas smelled like. In a word, *gross*.

I gritted my teeth against the bile rising fast in my throat and thrust the rod down Fluffy's slimy gullet, shoving my arm in all the way to my elbow. She buzz-sawed at my padding for another minute and then just stopped, her body going slack. I let go of the rod and squirmed out from under the big cat. I was sure I'd be sore tomorrow, but for now the adrenaline had me feeling no pain.

Tura whooped and ran down into the ravine to help me to my feet.

"That was stellar!" She slapped me on my back. "I just have to get the antenna software configured and run the OS installation and probably download some patches for her species and—uh oh."

She was looking down at me, wincing. I followed her gaze. The canvas on my right forearm was stained with blood around a puncture hole.

I'd been bitten.

I was all kinds of dead meat.

* * * *

I started getting the chills as Tura helped me back to the truck. I knew from watching other people turn what would come next: terrible fever and thirst, convulsions, and then, finally, my eyes would go white and I'd pass into ravenous undeath.

"You should just kill me," I told her through chattering teeth.

She shook her head and began to cut the canvas, tape and sweat-soaked leather off me with a box knife. "I need your help. Let's see if you can ride this out tonight."

"Ride it out?" I stared at her. "Nobody ever rides this out!"

"It's a disease. Someone has to get better from it. Who's to say that won't be you?"

She got out our medical kit and started disinfecting my bite wound with alcohol and peroxide, as if those would make a difference.

"I'm toast," I whispered.

"Don't say that!" Tura glared at me as she slathered my wound with antibiotic cream and slapped on a bandage. "You find a way to live, Johnnie! Find a reason to live and hang on."

Looking into her fierce blue eyes, I didn't have to search very hard for my reason.

* * * *

Tura pitched a tent, had me lie down inside in the shade and bound my hands and feet with nylon rope. I was too wrecked to argue.

"I'll check on you when I'm done with the tiger," she said. "Hang in there, okay?"

"Yes ma'am."

I closed my eyes and tried to find my inner calm. This was like any other fight. I had to get my immune system back in the game. Mind over matter, right?

But while I was meditating, sleep took hold of me, and my mind plunged down into the worst nightmares I've ever had. I was back in the ring, the canvas sticky with blood and scattered with bashed-out teeth and gobbets of flesh. There was a crowd watching me out there in the darkness beyond the spotlit ring, and from the growls and slobbering the spectators weren't people. I was naked, flat on my back, feeling more exposed than I had my entire life.

A zombie referee with a worm-eaten face stepped out from the shadowed corner and stood over me, bellowing a ten-count. I scrambled away from him, grabbed the ropes and hauled myself to my feet on shaky legs. The crowd roared, gutterally chanting the name of something no human could hope to pronounce.

"Fight!" the zombie referee shouted, pointing toward the center of the ring.

I turned and got my first good look at my opponent, and the sight of it made me feel as if my brain might melt. It was an utter abomination: a mutant head of tentacles and rasping hagfish mouths and bloody reptillian eyes all jumbled together in no natural pattern, a body sprouting horrible clawed arms. Only its legs looked vaguely human. And as I stared at it, it was getting bigger with every breath.

No way I wanted to go to the mat with that thing. How could I fight it? I needed a chainsaw or a flamethrower, and I didn't even have a pair of gloves.

"Fight!" roared the referee.

"Fight!" growled the crowd.

So I fought. I punched and I wrestled and I kicked and I bit. I went to the mat, I went to the ropes. Somehow, just as it was about to pin me or lay me out I managed to get free, and we'd start all over again. It just kept getting bigger and uglier and the crowd got louder, but I knew that if I quit I was dead, so I just kept swinging ....

I came out of the dream fighting the ropes binding my hands. There was something hard and cylindrical in my mouth, and my tongue was gummily stuck to it. Tura was kneeling beside me in the tent, looking down at me, clearly worried.

She reached down to pull the object out of my mouth, and I saw it was another metal rod like the one I'd shoved inside the tiger.

"You better not install Linux on me!" I yelled. "I'm strictly a Windows girl!"

Tura smiled like the sun streaming in through the tent flap. "Thank God. You're okay."

* * * *

"Okay" was kind of a relative thing. I'd been out of my mind with the fever for two days. I'd lost a bunch of weight and nearly died from dehydration; Tura had tried to get water into me but I kept spitting it out. Guess my brain thought it was fluid from the abomination I was fighting in the nightmare.

I sucked down five warm Gatorades as Tura filled me in on the rest. She told me she'd been tempted to put me out of my misery. But when my eyes stayed clear the first night, she stuck the extra rod in my mouth so that

I wouldn't bite off my own tongue.

I did my best to get strong over the next three days, mostly resting and eating and doing some strength exercises and yoga when I could. At the end of it I could do a decent 50-yard sprint, climb a wall, and lift forty pounds over my head. All without keeling over or barfing afterward. That's pretty much minimum fitness for the zombie apocalypse.

While I recovered, Tura spent time fine-tuning Fluffy's controls. She'd gotten the tiger working by the time I'd come out of the fever, but its movement was slow, robotic, jerky. By the time I was ready to hit the road, though, she had the tiger loping smoothly up and down the road, attacking tree trunks with great ferocity, and leaping back and forth over our truck.

It looked like we were as ready as we were going to be.

* * * *

Three days later, we were on a bluff overlooking a big, square concrete building that sat in the middle of a barren plateau. Tura peered at it intently through a pair of binoculars. I could see hundreds of tiny figures milling around the building on all sides. Zombies.

"Yep. They're good and surrounded," she said.

"Why's his lab all the way out here?" I asked.

"It's a counter-terrorism facility. They come up with antidotes and vaccines for bioweapons. The bad guys cook it up, they break it down. But they're handling some really hot stuff here, so they couldn't have the lab smack in a populated area. So, everybody's got a kind of rough commute."

Tura drove the truck down the butte onto the plateau. She took a moment to text Mickey, and then we got the tiger and our weapons out of the back. I had a 12-gauge loaded with buckshot and a .38 semiautomatic pistol. Tura had an AK-47 and twin .22 Colt revolvers. She set the tiger padding along by the truck and then we casually rolled toward the zombie horde.

Some of the undead turned their heads and began to shamble toward the truck when we were about 50 yards away. At 20 yards, Tura started punching keys on her smartphone and the tiger sprinted for the zombies.

Fluffy decapitated the first zombie with a single swipe and tore into the rest of the mob. Zombies fell dead all around her. It was like watching a hot knife go through a block of rancid butter.

"Faster, zombiecat! Kill! Kill!" Tura yelled.

But when Fluffy dove after what might have been the 200th zombie, an unusually tall and fat one, he fell across her back as he went down, and Fluffy's movements became erratic, jerky.

"Crap!" Tura exclaimed. "He dislodged her dorsal antenna. I gotta fix that—cover me!"

We jumped out of the truck and ran over to Fluffy. I plugged away at zombies with my pistol as Tura worked on getting the tiger back online.

I had to pause to reload, and in that moment a runner I hadn't seen grabbed me from behind and chomped my neck. I hollered, elbowed it off, and shot it right between the eyes. I touched my neck, and my hand came away wet with blood.

* * * *

"I think I'm okay, guys. Honest." I was strapped to a dentist's chair in an observation room in the laboratory.

"I'm sure you'll be fine." Tura bandaged me up and gave me an antibiotic shot.

"We'll see," replied Mickey from the other side of the bulletproof glass. "Just try to relax."

"Okie-dokey." Mickey was a sweet hunk of scientist: he had a tight runner's body, long-lashed green eyes, an easy smile, and a mop of unruly black hair that fell into his eyes just so. He had the trifecta of brains, looks, and okay, maybe his personality wasn't exactly sparkling, but so far he didn't seem to be a jerk. Tura clearly didn't have eyes for anyone else.

I felt abandoned and miserable, and did the only thing I could do: I waited. And waited. And waited.

Six hours later, half the scientist still watching me were snoring in their folding chairs, so I cleared my throat and announced, "Guys. *Seriously*. I think I'm fine."

So they took my temperature, and drew a sample of my blood, and spent some time staring at it under a microscope.

"What do you think?" I asked.

"We think you're fine," Tura said.

"And I think we've finally got a source for good antibodies against this wretched plague," Mickey said, looking at me like I was a grand prize-winning lottery ticket. "Thanks to you, we're going to be able to save millions of lives."

"Sweet." I knew that saving humanity should have felt pretty darned satisfying, even if it *was* dumb luck. But in my loneliness, the miraculous victory just seemed hollow.

A young lab technician came into the room and began undoing my restraints. I hadn't really noticed her before, but she was red-haired, had a cute dusting of freckles, and was gazing at me with the kind of adoration that people usually reserved for movie stars. She was looking at me the way I'd probably been looking at Tura the past year.

"I think you're very brave," she whispered. "*Very* brave."

Me, a genuine hero? Apparently so. I smiled back at her. Suddenly the future seemed like a much brighter place.   ✗

WHEN THEY COME BACK
Avra Margariti

Brass chiming in the distance
rousing me from slumber.
We put a bell over her grave,
the string buried in the estate's rich soil—
an unnecessary precaution, for I knew that Lady Death
had taken my lover from me
to love as her own.
This is a haunting, a return
her white gown coated in mud and cold moonlit dew
as she crawls into my four-poster bed
and I bite my fist lest I alert the servants.
Her parchment tongue soothes the bitemarks
lapping along my knuckles.

We settle against each other
childhood friends, adulthood companions.
In life she used to smell of noblewoman perfumes;
now her musty rot pastes itself against the roof of my mouth.
She tells me, Your father sends his regards
from a long-gone battlefield.
Your mother died in childbirth but is now the mother
of many dead infants, her bosom always heavy
with phantom milk.
Your pets are looking good, also
cat and dog forever chasing each other
in a skeletal tango.

What about you? I ask, our bare legs brushing together

DEAD BETWEEN THE EYES
Adrian Cole

From the files of Nick Nightmare

We all get days when we think we've wandered into a living nightmare. With an alias like mine, it's hardly surprising I suffer from this affliction more than your average Joe. These days I usually wake up in a familiar bed. Opening my eyes for the first time in the morning on a narrow, garbage-strewn street is not that common with me. We've all had our moments during our misspent youths. I like to think I've left all that stuff way back. But now and then a surly voice in my ear says something like, 'not quite, buddy.'

I'd been for a few quiet drinks in one of my local Brooklyn dives, listening to some cool blues riffs from their resident hound, and generally minding my own business. I don't recall getting soused. At the same time I don't recall having left the joint, which is odd. Somewhere along the line, the night got blurred, along with my eyesight and movements. Waking in the alley, things weren't a whole lot better. I felt groggy, and getting to my feet was like trying to climb out of a morass with both feet tied together. My arms felt like two balloons. And you don't want to know about my head.

Heroically I made my painful way towards the mouth of the alley. The road or avenue beyond, whichever it was, was deserted, which was genuinely freaky. New York at this time of the morning—it had long gone 8 am—is not deserted, even in the deserted areas. Something moves. Autos hoot by, usually packed together, horns blaring. Voices are raised in ungentlemanly, and indeed, unladylike, ways. The hurly-burly is the life-blood of the city.

Behind me, down in the gloomy far gut of the alley, I heard shuffling sounds. At first I took them to be the ferreting of a stray dog, chewing through garbage for its breakfast, but I gazed blearily at something that stood on two legs. Its resemblance to a human being ended there. And it looked a whole lot more of a mess than I did. At least, I assumed so. There were thankfully no mirrors around for me to check it out.

The thing opened its mouth, and I was glad to be some distance away.

The smell that it emitted was putrescent even from here, and I thought I saw several whitish things spilling out of it. The creature lumbered forward. Now I really did think I'd blundered into a nightmare, or maybe a movie set. George Romero must be in town. I had my twin Berettas with me, tucked into my belt, but If I blew this thing away, the chances were I'd be trying to explain the killing to an unsympathetic judge by lunch time.

I struggled onward, but my knees buckled as if the joints had been removed and I sagged down onto my butt. Behind me the repulsive one plodded alarmingly closer. Worse still, there were a few more like him emerging from the shadows, like the emptyings of a large sewer pipe. Maybe I did need to use those guns. I dug my hands into my breeches, but it was like grabbing handfuls of wet cement. The nightmare was going to end very soon, but my guess was, there would be no more waking up afterwards. I was helpless.

The sound of an engine and the screech of tyres on tarmac made me turn my head, slowly. I saw something equally as bizarre as the shambling monsters that threatened to fall upon me, presumably with the intention of opening my neck and feeding in that disgusting way their kind do. What I saw was pink. Very pink. And vivid. Which was weird, because it was a taxi. That is, a kind of taxi. It was the size of a small bus. It had a fat cab and the body of the vehicle had three wheels each side, over-large and sans treads. No passengers I could see, but the driver swung a door open and I saw his face, beaming.

"Hop aboard, buddy. Your fare is paid for."

I tried to explain that I could hardly crawl, much less hop, but my words came out like something you might hear on the Mongolian steppes.

The guy got out. Only then did he see the gathering of flesh-eaters getting closer to my slumped body. He took an item from the pocket of his shabby coat, which looked like something he'd picked up from someone who'd also collapsed in an alley. Whatever it was he held up, it was bright, like a flare. Brilliant light shone from it and I averted my eyes. The things beyond reacted like chickens confronted by a fox. For once they moved quickly, back down the alley, frantically in search of the shadows.

I managed to rise. The taxi man stood before me—well, below me— given he was no more than five feet tall. His face was pinched, like maybe he'd caught his head in a press when he was a kid, and his body was unusually thin, padded out with rag-tag clothes and that ultra-shabby coat. He looked as if he'd collapse into a little heap of flesh and bones if ever he took those clothes off. They were all that was holding him together.

"You okay?" he said, his voice several octaves too high. Was it a man, was it a bird?

I nodded, indicating the taxi. He satisfied himself that we weren't about to be subjected to another attack and led me to the vehicle, opening the rear doors and unfolding a set of steps. I needed them, and his help to get me up into the cabin. It was about a mile off the ground. A set of three seats ran along one side, all pink. Everything was bright pink. I sat down as he closed the doors and went round to his cab. It had no back, so it was easy enough for him to talk as he put the thing into gear and took off.

"I'm the Weasel," he said. "And this is my diesel."

Jeeze, I thought, I've fallen down the rabbit hole and I'm in Alice's Wonderland.

"And you," he said, like he'd just read my thoughts, "have been the victim of a spiking."

If anyone had run a blade into me, I hadn't noticed, but at that point nothing would have surprised me. There was no blood, though.

"Drugged," he said, explaining. "Last night."

My head was clearing very slowly. Damn, I needed coffee, and said so.

"Coming up," he said. "The garage is close by." He steered the pink wagon around the streets at a dizzy speed and yet as unerringly as a computerized missile. Everything outside remained a blur. We could have been anywhere, almost certainly not my New York. Shadows swallowed us and I heard steel doors clanging shut as I entered the great garage mausoleum. Oil-Gun Eddy, the mad mechanic I'd rubbed shoulders with many times, would have loved this place. It was big enough to house a couple of B 52 bombers. What it did house, well, who knows? I just saw rows of vehicles, but what they were beat me. Alien spacecraft for all I knew.

Somewhere in that metal mayhem was an office, or a couple of rooms serving as such. The Weasel served me coffee and I wondered if he'd been associating with Eddy, who makes the best coffee in the universe. This was damn good, too. And it did the trick, gradually burning off the fuzz and freakishness that had scrambled my brains and senses since I woke up.

"So who drugged me?" I asked my diminutive companion. He sat on a table like a sort of oversize paperweight.

"Agents of the Dark Army," he said. "They're everywhere. Even in your local dives. They've got your number."

I knew he was right. They never gave up trying to rub me out. "Well, thanks for getting me out of there. What gives with the zombies? Where the hell are they from?"

"I don't know a lot about it. I have to take you to people who do." He rummaged around in his coat pockets and pulled out a folded sheet, handing it over.

I finished my coffee, my head almost normal, and read what was on the sheet. My face clouded. It was a poster, advertising a convention. Get this, a private eye convention. I knew about these things, but so far in life

I'd managed to steer clear. The last thing I wanted was to swap stories with a bunch of like-minded private dicks looking to pump me for information about this and that, re-living their big cases, or bragging about their lady friends. I tried to hand the sheet back, but he recoiled.

"You have to attend," he said.

"Buster, wild horses couldn't drag me. A pack of blood-hungry zombies couldn't do it either."

"Someone who is attending wants to see you there."

"Nope. Not even for the President. Actually, especially not for the President."

"How about Ned Killigan?"

I stiffened. Killigan? My hero, star of countless slug 'em and drown 'em pulp novels? Private eye supreme, with a chip on his shoulder and an itchy trigger finger always eager to snap off a round or six? I'd met him once, in the flesh, in the Pulpworld, where such bizarre things can happen. He'd dragged me out of a hole when it looked like I was heading into the Big Sleep.

"Killigan goes to these conventions?" I said, surprised.

"He'll be at this one. Only to see you, though. He reckons it'll be a good cover for you both. Confuse the enemy. Couple of hundred dicks go. And as many dames. Some of the dicks are dames."

Two hundred private eyes? I shuddered. But if Killigan wanted to meet up, something was seriously adrift in the world, though which one I couldn't say. I looked at the poster again. *Convolution Seven,* was the heading. A little play on words. There was an address, but nowhere I knew, a hotel de lux, and a list of Big Name attendees. Some were guys I'd met or knew about, others, like Killigan were usually found in the pages of the cheap novels in my world.

"Your carriage awaits," said the Weasel.

"Tell me it isn't pink. Tell me that was one of the hallucinations."

"That was not one of the hallucinations. My taxi is pink. Unique with it."

I grimaced. I do a particularly ugly grimace. "I'm going to a convention of hard-boiled, wise-cracking tough guys, and I'm going to roll up in a *pink* taxi?"

"You'll be the envy of them all."

"I think I was better off in the alley."

* * * *

In the event, it wasn't a big entrance with a fanfare at the front door. I sneaked in round the back somewhere. I wore shades and had my hat pulled right down and my collar right up. My guess is, I looked ridiculous, but it turned out this was one gatheringe where I got away with it. Half the guys in the place, women included, dressed the same way. Maybe it's how they thought private eyes wore their weeds. One thing was for sure, it's not how Ned Killigan would tog up. He'd have his battered mac and boots that would have served Frankenstein's monster, but he'd make no concessions. And like a lot of guys in the place, he'd be smoking. The air in there was so thick you could cut a slice and roll it up for a blanket.

I couldn't see him through the fug, but a tap on my shoulder told me he'd found me. I turned to see his face. The word 'craggy' doesn't do it justice. I guess it had been slugged that many times it had been rearranged to look demonic. Brilliant gray eyes and a long, bony nose and a set mouth. Hardness personified. And his interior was as crusty as his exterior, I knew that. Two hundred and twenty pounds of violent energy.

"Glad you came, Nightmare," he growled. "Follow daddy."

* * * *

We found a room set aside for art displays, where dozens of prints, originals, sketches and full-blown Da Vinci look-alikes were dazzling the eye and drawing the appropriate noises from appreciative fans. I admit I could have spent a lazy hour or two checking them out, especially when I noticed some original artwork by the great Japetus, an old buddy of mine. The place was less packed than the main body of the convention, so we sidled into a corner, Killigan watching everything like a hawk. There were more than a few admiring glances, mostly from the ladies, but for once he was focused on other things, and to cap it all, he wasn't smoking.

"So what's this all about?" I asked him.

"Our mutual pal, the Weasel, brought me here in that pink punkmobile of his. To meet another guy, Mel Carson, who gave me his sob story and something else. More on that in a minute. This guy worked for an outfit he called the Dark Army. Bunch of independent wannabees who like using a weird brand of terrorism."

"Like the undead, by any chance?"

"So you know them? Well, seems like they're pulling a whole bunch of the rotten folk together for a major hit somewhere. Carson was a mess. Something to do with high finance, and he didn't want nothing to do with the Dark Army. So they did something nasty to his wife and kids. Don't ask me what. Carson didn't say, but instead of recruiting him, it made him mad. He made out he was converted, but he wanted to get back at those bastards. He got hold of something." Killigan patted his breast pocket. "Something they value very highly. He'd heard about me and passed it on to me. Then he disappeared. I've heard nothing since, but I reckon he's pushing up the daisies out in the wilds."

"Sounds like the kind of bum deal you'd get from those punks."

"I brought you here because the last thing Carson said to me before he skedaddled, was I should get this to you. You'll know what to do with it, he said."

"What is it?"

He wasn't going to remove it here. "It's a key. Ancient looking. Like it fits the door of a castle or a big museum. I think the word is 'Gothic'."

I'd gathered a few weird and wonderful artifacts in my time, most of them far too dangerous to use, but this one didn't ring any bells, Gothic or otherwise.

"Carson said it was a big deal for the Dark Army. Only certain people can use the key. People with rare power. It opens doors to places most folks don't get into. Nasty places, I reckon. Whatever messed up plan the Dark Army is working on with the rotten folk and their invasion, the key is part of it. They want it back real bad. I've blown about a hundred of them apart since I got the key. And they keep coming, thick as flies. I want them off my back, Nightmare, but I want more than that. I want to give the Dark Army a real shake-up. Seismic, you got me?"

His scowl would have shattered a stone gargoyle at fifty paces, but I grinned. "You want me to take the key. You think I have rare power."

"I've read about your exploits, pal. And Carson reckoned you were the man. You can use the key. To open doors. And shut them. You move around like a ghost."

"One man against the zombie hordes. Not good odds."

"Two men. I'm prepared to see this through."

"Where do we start?"

"This place has been a good cover. I've seen at least five Nick Nightmares and a few Ned Killigans among the fans. They look more like us than we do. But it'll be a magnet for the enemy."

We pushed our way through the growing crowd, heads down, acting as best we could like fans ourselves. Everyone was having a good time so it didn't matter. Most things centred around several bars, so we were able to ease our way out of the press and along the sidelines. There was one moment when I froze: a trio of zombies loomed large and I thought this was going to be the start of the next punch up, but they were shouting and waving their beer glasses around so I realized they were just convention zombies, dressed for the occasion. Don't get me wrong, they were very convincing.

There was a passage off the main room, leading down to some toilets and an exit. Killigan checked it out and nodded. We slipped outside into the night, through an alley and a pile of garbage bins, a dim light and the scuttling of rats. No zombies yet. We moved up to the street. Traffic rumbled by, things looked pretty normal. We heard a horn blare, apparently at us.

Killigan was about to give the driver a mouthful, but then saw the pink taxi pull up alongside. We tumbled in the back and the Weasel opened up the throttle and took off so fast I thought we were about to go airborne.

"Where to, fellas?" he piped.

"Drive around a mite," said Killigan. He slipped a small, thin box from his pocket and handed it over. "There you go, pal. Don't say I never give ya anything. They call it the Otherwhere Key."

"You're too kind." I gently opened the lid. The key was inside, on its bed of purple velvet. It was ancient, as big as he'd told me, ornate, minutely decorated and made from a metal I couldn't place, possibly silver but well disguised with rust, or something resembling it. Only an antique dealer would look twice at it.

"I'd keep the lid shut, until you need it," said Killigan, lighting up a smoke. "It's a magnet for all the rabble you don't want to meet. And in this world, which ain't yours by the way, you'll meet big league rabble."

I'd already assumed this was Pulpworld, not mine, but I knew it could be one of several. Generally they existed in their own little bubble of time and space, but there were doors, and some of us had used them. The Dark Army was hell bent on getting as much access as it could, hence the value of this key.

Killigan blew out a great cloud of smoke, filling the confines of the taxi. I failed to suppress a cough, but he ignored my heaving chest. "You get zombies in your world?"

I shook my head. "Some worlds have no supernatural power, though they appear often enough in fiction, or in books and stuff where some wise guy wants to convince the world they do exist. Some worlds have a degree of the supernatural. Mine's like that, but the weird stuff, like vampires and zombies aren't present, unless they leak through. Other worlds are churning with supernatural powers."

"You got it," Killigan said, showing his teeth. They would have impressed a large carnivore. "Leaking through is right. More' a few have leaked into my world—this world—and the Dark Army is set up someplace where they're breeding like maggots in a buffalo carcass."

"And this key is going to attract them like bees to honey," I said, keeping with the small creatures theme.

"So what are you going to do with it?"

"You say it shuts doors?"

"Carson told me that. Way I see it, the Dark Army gets set to open a door into this world, or maybe yours, or both, and you turn up and lock the bastards out. May need a bit of muscle. I'll be the hired help. Between us we can tidy things up. Like you said, the worlds aren't meant to share space and time. There is one small problem."

I would have questioned his use of the word 'small' but I was coughing again as he blew out another cloud. I don't know where he got his cigarettes, but it must have been the wrong side of Hell. I looked at him through tear stained eyes.

"There's a whole bunch of the rotten boys here already. We have to clear them out before we close the door. Every last one. If we don't, they'll infect a whole new bunch. You know the rules of their game. They like making new zombies and I'm not talking about rolls in the hay. They bite."

"Got any ideas?"

"Sure. All messy, dangerous and risky as hell. But, hey, that's how I live life, buddy. You don't want to sit around on your butt all day, bored outta your skull. Am I right?"

I laughed, the sound degenerating into another coughing bout. He opened one of the back doors and let some blessed air in. "Way I see it, we gotta find a way of attracting every damn zombie here to us, so we can have a big shoot out."

"Is there some kind of OK Corral where we can do this?"

He grinned that horrible grin again. No doubt about it, he was loving this stuff. "We'll find somewhere. But the Dark Army's generals ain't dumb. They'll smell a rat. Who knows how many of the rotten boys they'll pitch in. We'll need more bullets than we can carry."

Maybe the cold air that came into the vehicle had stirred my brain cells, but a few ideas of my own were shaping up. "You ever hear of a place called Dunnsmouth?"

He screwed up his already screwed up face in concentration. "Eastern seaboard port? Remote dump, the last place you'd take the kids for a weekend? What about it?"

"In my world, it's the same. In Pulpworld, it doesn't exist any more, well, except as a smoking crater."

"Crater? They have volcanoes?"

"No. I visited it with a couple of friends, Damien Paladin and Leigh Oswin. Top man among the fly boys, and handy with a gun, and the rest. As is his lady friend. We got tied up with another of the Dark Army's bully boys, a guy called Rottwanger. To cut it short, we blew his freaky zeppelin apart and it dumped on Dunnsmouth. Blew it to oblivion, and all the town's fishy friends."

"Hell's teeth, Nightmare, you met Paladin and Oswin? Now that's something I'd give a lot to do. I've read a ton of that comic book stuff about those two."

Watching him sitting there, puffing out more toxic fumes, his huge bulk more like a grizzly than a man, I found it hard to picture him flipping through a comic book.

"Anyway," I went on, "Dunnsmouth may be gone from the Pulpworld, but it will exist in this one. Am I right?"

"No reason to suppose otherwise. So?"

"It'll be full of the fish-eyed freaks from the sea."

"A good reason to steer clear of the place."

I shook my head. "Maybe not. Maybe we should introduce them to some new friends. How do you think they'd feel if a bunch of very unwanted tourists turned up and ran riot in the streets?"

A slow grin was working its way across those craggy features. "Go on."

"Might lead to a war."

"It might at that." He had a look that suggested he was already envisaging the potential carnage.

"We stir up the zombie horde and let them chase us until they've got us where we want them," I said. I made it sound easy.

He slapped me on the back and I clung on to a seat bar to keep from tumbling across the floor of the cab. "Man after my own heart," he said. "We'd better see if the Weasel is up for this. Not many cabs would want to carry us through this messed up terrain."

* * * *

The Weasel, who didn't seem to have another name, was happy to ferry us about. He skillfully avoided telling us who he was working for, but Killigan reckoned he was OK, so I went with it.

"I found out who's running the zombies on this side," the Weasel told us. "I hear a lot of gossip in my line of work. The man you want is Lucifer Gonzales."

"Never heard of him," said Killigan. "How big is his outfit?"

"He's a big cheese around the docks and runs a fleet of small tankers. In heavy with the police. They get a handsome slice of whatever action he's mixed up in. Black market, anything that pays good money. Always looking to expand."

Killigan looked at me. "With that key, he could do that in a big way. Maybe we should pay him a visit. If he's running the rotten boys, that's where we'll need to hook them. I got an idea about how we can do that."

"You want to share it?"

"Not yet. Hey, Weasel—you okay for some out of town work?"

"Your credit's good, Mr Killigan. Where ya want to go?"

"You know a place called Dunnsmouth?"

"Yeah. That's out of town. Long drive, but I can hack it."

"You know where this Lucifer Gonzales hangs out?"

"Sure."

"Start there."

I opened my mouth, but the pink taxi was in gear and off at speed before I could form a coherent sentence.

* * * *

Killigan was a man of few words and a lot of action. Our conversation en route to the slummy part of the city where Gonzales hung out was limited to a few questions about my guns. My twin Berettas are very special, unique in fact, made for me by the one time Italian master gunsmith, Francesco Barenzo. I didn't give too much away, but Killigan seemed satisfied that they were the right stuff and that he could trust me in a dust up. I knew his style. Go in with all guns blazing, but this time he agreed to be more subtle. We needed to play these jokers carefully if we were going to drag the rotten boys way up north to Dunnsmouth. I assumed he had a gun or two of his own, though he kept them hidden about his person.

We reached a block of old offices, where at least a dozen of the ground floor windows had been boarded up. On higher floors, windows had been broken, and higher yet there were a few lights. Several beat-up cars were parked outside and a couple of guys loafed about the main doors. They came partially to life when the pink taxi pulled up, disgorging me and Killigan. The Weasel drove away, given explicit instructions by Killigan.

One of the punks sidled up. He wore the world's worst pin-stripe suit and a white hat that looked like it had been trodden on. He brandished a gun in a way that suggested he hadn't had a whole lot of practice in using it. Shooting at cans, maybe. And he was chewing on a tooth pick, which he probably thought made him look very tough.

"Yous in the wrong place," he said, in his very tough voice.

"I want to see the organ grinder, not the monkey," said Killigan in his paint-stripping voice.

The man's face clouded. He tried to reassemble his hard look, but fell a long way short. "Who you think you are?"

"I know who I am, dummy. Tell Gonzales Killigan's here, with Nick Nightmare. We'd like to do some business."

Now the guy's face really went pale. My guess was, it was Killigan's name, not mine, that had that effect on him. He swung round to his pal, who was no longer slouched in the doorway. "Go tell the boss he's got two visitors. They're coming up."

The other guy scuttled off into the building. Our guide swung back to us. "I'll need your shooters. No one goes inside armed."

Killigan stood as close to him as he could without getting into his suit. "If I take my guns out, buster, it'll be to shoot someone. You'll be first in line." Sometimes that kind of bravado works. It did with Killigan. The guy melted and led the way through the doors. There was a lift, but we took the stairs. No point in making ourselves targets for every hood in the place.

Several floors up, we went down a carpeted landing and into an area that had been tarted up with more carpets and the like. Smart but not ultra smart. My guess is, Gonzales wasn't top man in his racket. They gave him enough money and power to keep him happy, maybe feed a habit or two. Our guide, who'd had the sense to put his own gun away, indicated a door, where another pair of would-be toughs chewed gum and glared at us.

Killigan ignored them and brushed past. I followed, one hand on a gun butt inside my coat, though I feigned a casual air. Truth was, I was expecting the lead to fly at any moment.

The room was a former suite of offices, converted, quite tastefully, into a very passable den, with pricey antique furnishings and a few paintings that would have fetched very good money. Seated on a lavish sofa at the heart of the room was the man I rightly took to be Lucifer Gonzales. There was nothing Satanic-looking about him, no horns, no devilish eyebrows, no forked tail slung over his shoulder. He just looked like an overweight hoodlum in an expensive suit that was too small for him. The fingers of both of his hands sported more rings than a curtain rail, all gleaming in the subtle lighting. I assumed the sparklers were the real deal, so that was a whole lot of money flashing about.

He smiled and there was a lot of gold in that smile. His dentist must have spent many happy hours rebuilding those teeth. "Mr Killigan," he said, his voice cultured, coming up from somewhere deep in his cavernous chest. He didn't get up. It would have taken an effort, or maybe a small hoist.

Killigan inclined his head. "Nice of you to see me, Gonzales. And this gentleman is Mr Stone. You probably know him as Mr Nightmare."

"Of course. It is such a pleasure to meet you. I cannot imagine why two illustrious private detectives such as yourselves should favor me with any of your time."

"Bullshit. You've been after my buddy. You sent some very nasty people to get hold of him."

Gonzales, cool as a field of cucumbers, waved Killigan's words away like smoke. "A misunderstanding. I just wanted to arrange a little chat. Between you, you have something I want very much. And I will pay you handsomely for it. Simply name your price, Mr Killigan. You can spend the rest of your lives like kings."

The air had gone very still. The calm before a storm. I now had both hands in my pockets, both Berettas ready. I weighed up the men around us. There were six of them, and probably more outside, ready to come bursting in. I could take out two before they blinked, but if they all drew and fired at a signal from Gonzales, Killigan and I would find it hard to dodge all of the bullets. I didn't like the odds, but Killigan had something up his sleeve and he was the one man on the planet I'd trust in a mad situation like this. I'd read enough of his exploits.

"Ah," he said. "The key stolen from you by Mel Carson. The Otherwhere Key, is it? You're right, I have it right here." He undid the front of his coat, but it wasn't the key he brought out. It was a sawn-off shotgun, at least the glimpse I got of it told me it was that kind of weapon. At once the six thugs went for their own guns. It was my signal. I took down the two I'd sized up and Killigan swung his gun around in a blistering arc of noise and smoke, scything down the other four. Doors flew open and more gunmen came charging in, lambs to the slaughter as Killigan and I blew them apart. His weapon was more effective than a Gatling gun, and although I moved fast and picked off every target I chose, my kills were well short of his.

By the time the deafening row ceased, surprisingly few minutes had passed. Lucifer Gonzales had pressed himself back into his cushions, his face aghast. This had been the quintessential surprise attack. His mouth opened and closed like that of a big blow-fish. His hands, and those rings, fumbled at his light jacket, his face a mask of terror.

"No deal," said Killigan. "Now—call off your army of undead freaks or I'll decorate the walls with your softer parts."

Gonzales was shuddering. "I cannot! They are not under my control. You will have angered the masters! Now they will send even more of those things for you!"

Killigan glared at him for a long moment, then spat. "Come on," he said to me. "Let's get out of this dump." He turned and made for the door, kicking his way past half a dozen blood-spattered thugs. His back was deliberately turned on Gonzales and I made to turn away. My guess was, Gonzales would try and pull something. He did. It was a Magnum .38. Too old school for me, but effective enough. However, before he could plug Killigan I put a bullet from each of my guns into his heart. I don't miss from that range. Gonzales fell back into his cushions, his legs twitching for a moment or two before he rolled over onto the floor like a beached whale.

"Nice sense of timing, bud," said Killigan.

We were about to exit when we heard a last croak from Gonzales. "With my dying breath I curse you," he said through gritted teeth. "I lied about the living dead. I *will* send them and nothing can stop them." It was indeed his last breath.

Killigan grinned at the corpse. "I was kinda hoping you'd say that." We checked the hallway and the next set of stairs, but seemed to have cleared out the living hired helps. Outside we saw the pink taxi. The Weasel was sitting in the cab, reading a paper and whistling. I imagine he'd have been doing the same come the apocalypse.

Speaking of which, Killigan and I heard the combined sound of numerous screams and howls, just like a mob of blood-crazed lunatics, thirsting for blood. Which was, in fact, the precise reason for the noise. There were some wire gates beside the building and behind them a very large company of the rotten boys, and more than a few rotten girls, were snarling and clawing.

"Let's move!" Killigan roared at the Weasel, who dropped his paper and gunned his engine. We got into the taxi just as the wire fence buckled under the tide of rotting flesh and crashed to the ground, spilling out the horde from Hell.

"Where to, boss?" yelled the Weasel.

"Dunnsmouth. Go a little slowly. We want that legion of monsters on our tail."

"Are you crazy!" gasped the driver. "They'll pull us to pieces."

"We're taking them to a little party."

I watched the pursuit from the back window of the cab. I don't know where the rotten gang got its energy from, but they showed no sign of flagging. My guess was, if anyone saw them on our journey, they'd keep well away. Probably most people would think twice about reporting an army of screaming zombies on what looked like a very twisted version of the New York Marathon to the authorities.

* * * *

It took the rest of the day and half the night to reach the outskirts of the small town of Dunnsmouth. It would have taken longer, but the rotten gang moved at a supernaturally fast pace, which is kind of what you'd expect from a bunch of corpses fueled by what must be some kind of supernatural power. Anyhow, it was a relief. Being cooped up in the taxi was no fun, especially as Killigan insisted on smoking most of the way.

"That's Dunnsmouth," came the voice of the Weasel. The three of us craned our necks and the almost full moon courteously revealed the roofs of the seaport below us, into which our narrow road debouched. I could spend a long time trying to describe those buildings. They were weird. Like, the worst fairy tales you ever read as a kiddie weird. And worse. This Dunnsmouth was no better than the others I'd visited, alternative or otherwise.

"Can you shake off our tail for a while?" I asked the Weasel. "I have to perform a little ritual."

"Fine by me," said the Weasel, one eye on the mirror. He accelerated and put some distance between us and the following horde. I had him pull over and I got out of the taxi. I slipped the Otherwhere Key from around my neck. Time to put it to the test. Initially I had no idea how to activate it, but when I took it in my hand, it hummed into a life of its own. In front of me, the air shimmered, blurred and then shaped itself into an outline, a crude, ancient doorway. It had the suggestion of a lock, so I slipped the key into it and twisted.

"Nice trick," said Killigan over my shoulder.

I waved the Weasel forward. "Drive through. We don't have a lot of time. The door will dissolve."

The Weasel didn't ask questions and took his pink taxi through the door. I followed it with Killigan and we got on board. I looked back. Through the shadowy frame of the door I could see the rotten gang getting closer. "The door will hold good until they're all through. Then it'll dissolve."

"So where the heck are we?" said Killigan.

"My guess is, some dark little world beyond most people's worst nightmares. About as bad as I could dream up. Seems to be the way it works."

Our pursuers were getting close again, the first of them through the door, so I told the Weasel to take off and lose them once more, down into the alternative Dunnsmouth below us.

"We need to have a little conflab with the local inhabitants before the rotten boys interrupt us. There should be a central square."

The Weasel put the wagon into missile mode and we shot down the road, dodging the houses that crowded in on us like stooping giants, swerved around corners and missed chipping the paintwork by millimeters, before eventually screeching to a halt slap bang in the center of the square. It was a dead ringer for the one I'd seen in Dunnsmouth's other incarnations, although there was something even darker about it. And boy, did it *smell*. Like it had just come up from the sea and about a million sea-things had died in it.

The Weasel had done a good job: we'd thrown off the pursuit for a while.

Killigan glanced at me. "Now what? This is your party."

I climbed out of the back. "Be ready to take off again," I told the Weasel.

"Like I wouldn't be, in *this* place?"

Killigan joined me. He'd got his sawn-off whatever gun ready.

"Act cool," I said. "We don't want to upset the natives. We'll let the rotten gang do that."

We didn't have long to wait. There was a church at one end of the square, part of the Grand Order of Dagon, or some such head-banging outfit. Already a bunch of its acolytes was approaching us. They were almost human in shape, but their clothes didn't fit too good, like they weren't natural to the fish people. I call them that because what skin was revealed had small scales, was slightly green, and they had very large fish-like eyes. And for good measure they stank of the sea, like seaweed that had rotted and gone off.

"What is your business here?" said their leader, through twisted lips.

I could sense Killigan tensing. It was all he could do to stop himself spraying lead.

"We came to warn you. In the name of Great Dagon."

"Great Dagon," they all murmured, like a congregation at prayer.

"Your enemies are at your gates. Desecrators of Dagon's holy sanctuary. Come to burn it down! Defend yourselves, and the church!"

The luminous eyes of the fish-men were fixed on us and for a long moment I wondered if the bluff was going to come off, but fortunately there was a rising series of howls and shrieks behind us, and sure enough, the rotten gang appeared, hands clawing at the air, distorted faces glaring their most horrible glares. The fish-men got the message. Several dozen more came spilling out of doorways and alleys to see what all the ruckus was about. Killigan and I shifted to one side to where the Weasel had quietly parked the taxi out of harm's way.

What followed was the ultimate carnage, chaos that redefined the word. The zombies poured down the narrow street like flood water in spate. They were met head on by the people of Dunnsmouth. Word had gone round fast and now there were as many of them as there were of the invaders. There was to be no parley. No terms asked or discussed. This was just one almighty punch up, except no one threw a punch. Claws, nails, teeth, fish-hooks, lengths of chain, anything that could rip and tear, shred and disembowel, was employed. Blood flew like rain, bodies toppled, some rising again. Heads burst like over-ripe fruit, arms were severed, but kept on wriggling, like serpents in search of victims.

The square was stuffed to the point where there was not an inch spare. The Weasel had to ease the taxi up a side street. It was barely wide enough for the machine to get through, so he had to drive real slow. Killigan and I sat in the back with the door open. Now and then we fired off a few rounds, chopping down any of the combatants who got too close, or entertained ideas of dragging us into the mix.

"Whose winning?" said the Weasel.

"Looks like a stalemate to me," said Killigan. "That's a lot of rotten boys. This could go on for days."

The taxi crawled uphill, but at last the street got a mite wider and we were able to pick up speed. If there were zombies still hell-bent on getting to me and the key, they were swallowed up in the fighting, so we got to the hill overlooking the town. Killigan looked back with a wry smile.

"Dammit, Nightmare, if you and I ever get to meet up in the afterlife, it ain't going to be much worse than that place."

I had the Weasel pull up one last time. Killigan stayed in the vehicle while I got out and prepared to do my thing with the key again, opening a door on to a better world. Let's face it, all worlds are better than the one we'd been in. The road here was out in the open, exposed, with the shoulders of the hill rolling away into the night on either side. I walked around to the front of the taxi, my guns back in my belt and the Otherwhere Key in my hand, about to open the way for the taxi to drive through. Before I could react, the earth burst in front of, showering me with pungent soil and a large shape boiled up, assuming quasi-human form. It had a globular head, twice the size of anything remotely normal and twisted features that writhed in fury.

Lucifer Gonzales was back from the dead. His huge arms reached out for me and clamped my own arms to my sides. It was only then I realized I should have shot him between the eyes, not in the heart. I'd ignored the basic zombie rules. I could see by his expression Gonzales meant to open his over-sized mouth and bite my head off. Those gold teeth and the width of his gape meant he could do just that. I felt my hands getting sticky with blood from his wounds.

All I could do was twist the key into his belly and hope the angels were watching. Maybe they were, because the next minute Gonzales screamed, showering me with phlegm and spittle. His arms flopped to his side and he staggered back. I had opened a door, and I'd done it *within* that massive body. I watched in amazement as Gonzales grew and grew, his frame stretched impossibly as the door opened wider. By the time it was big enough for the taxi to pass through, the hoodlum's body had been so wrenched out of shape that it formed a frame around it, with the head, still screaming like a demented harpy, crowning it, a cupola from Dante's Inferno.

I went through the door and called to the Weasel to get the taxi through after me. He did so, and I saw Killigan staring out of the back door in utter amazement. Once the transition was complete, I went back to the shimmering door space, located a slot for the key and re-locked it. At once the revolting new form of Gonzales collapsed into a heap of coiled meat and mashed bone. His head plopped right down on top of it.

Amazingly the eyes still glared at me. I was reaching for my guns, but Killigan was right beside me in a flash. He used his own gun to blow the head into a fine misty rain.

"Nice sense of timing," I said.

We began the ride home, and thankfully Killigan had run out of cigarettes. It made him irritable, but it cheered me up.

"Tell me something," I said quietly to him, out of earshot of the whistling Weasel.

"Shoot."

"Why is this machine *pink*?"

"I heard a few tales. They're all long, and probably tall."

"We've got time."

On the way back to our slightly saner worlds, Killigan gave me the dope on the pink taxi. He hadn't been kidding: it was long story, and as you might have expected, very colorful. I'll save it for another time.

THE CRIMSON STAR

Josh Maybrook

Its name or origin none could say;
We looked up to sky one day
And saw descending from afar
A brightly shining crimson star.

The sky above our town grew dark;
No sun or moon remained to mark
The passing time, and from on high
The star gleamed like an evil eye.

That very night all over town
A madness dawned; men danced like clowns
Through streets and alleys newly stained
With blood where crimson terror reigned.

Now that mayhem's storm seems ended
An eerie silence has descended;
Survivors, moving slowly, stare
Like mannequins into the air.

Whatever final doom awaits
We can't escape this town; our fates
Are carven on its bricks and stones
And written on our very bones.

ALIVE AGAIN
Franklyn Searight

Foster, a retired chemist, opened a small packet of sugar and poured it into his coffee, added a little cream and took a sip. Much better; nothing like a hot soothing drink, slightly bitter but altered to suit his taste. Now, if Mandy would answer her cell phone and explain why she felt it necessary to divorce him, he would be at peace with the world and its overwhelming grief.

"She's probably still annoyed with my behavior last night," he reasoned, unable to comprehend what she believed to be his carelessness. It was not his doing her pet parakeet, Sparky, flying from the living room chandelier to its cage in the kitchen—-a frequent and routine excursion—-miscalculated and landed in a pan of sizzling grease.

Geeze! Like it was his fault.

Trying to convince her he had done nothing to result in its demise was like trying to convince her the dent he made in the car was not a purposeful act. Truth be told, it was entirely the fault of the bird. It was in advanced years and had probably lost its balance, or something. It tried to flap, helpless, probably in some degree of pain, as Foster held it under the faucet, cleaning the feathers with a mild detergent, then rinsing it with lukewarm water to wash away the oily goop.

It died, of course, no longer equipped with the strength and stamina of a young fluffy flyer, and was drawing its last breath even as he finished wiping it off with a kitchen rag. When its struggling grew feebler and finally stopped, he knew it was a goner and further rescue attempts would be in vain.

"What should I have done?" he wondered. "What *could* I have done? Given it artificial respiration? Perhaps sprinkled it with flour to soak up the grease before doing anything else?" Everything had happened so rapidly and, before he knew it, the parakeet was dead.

Mandy was so mad when informed of the tragedy she exploded into a hissy fit, snubbed him and declined to talk with him any further. At night, in bed, she refused to acknowledge his presence and after two hours of tossing and turning, picked up her pillow and left the room to sleep on the couch. Hah! As though he had any thought of a romantic liaison after the tragic events of the evening. He had done his best to absolve himself of any blame, but his distressed lady remained angry. She had the uncanny knack of glaring at a person and, without words, letting him know what she was thinking and, in particular, what she was thinking about *him*. Knowing her as he did, he was quite sure she was considering how to get even with him.

Foster felt her pain, having reserved a small part in his heart for the parakeet. "I'll get you another bird," he promised, with a proper, supplicating tone.

"Shut up," she returned. "I don't want another bird. Sparky's been with me for the last twelve years——almost as long as you have. I want Sparky back."

"You know it's impossible, dear. Sparky's is deceased and unless you want him stuffed and mounted on his perch, there's nothing I can do."

"Idiot! What good would a dead bird be to me?"

Angry? Extremely so. Still, she was forced to accept reality's decree and gave up any allusion's life could be restored to her loved one. Practicality shouldered its way into her grief and left her with thoughts of retribution. Foster was not surprised when a new bout of sobbing triggered the flood gates, sending tears streaming down her face as though the Hoover dam had burst.

"There, there," he said, two words making her sorrow all the more intense. He resolved to say no more. Nothing would end her anguish or erase the agony she felt. To earn her partial forgiveness would take days of time.

The tiny body, cleaned, dried and prepared like a princess for its interment, was wrapped in a plastic bag. As the sight of it would distress Mandy even more, he removed the corpse from the house——out of sight, out of mind, he reasoned. He took it out to their garage and laid the stilled body on his workbench where it would remain until morning and he could bury it in the backyard garden. If Mandy had anything to do with it, Sparky would be sent off with a twenty-one-gun salute, or tweet, followed by a solemn rendering of taps.

The situation was intolerable.

Was there not something he could do to bring the deceased back to life again? A good trick if there was; a miracle if it worked.

In his earlier years he had delved into a wide variety of arcane practices, even going to the extreme of studying the modern adepts, witch-like degenerates practicing necromancy and the Black Arts. The would-be sorcerers delved into various aspects of demonology and Satanism and occult manifestations, researching insidious spells and malevolent incantations to undo the consequences of death. He was unable to recall any words or procedures to return life to the parakeet, not at the moment, but books he had read were available to be used, stored in the attic for eventual sale on eBay.

One of them, he recalled, told of an entity named Allocer, a dark being able to produce the impossible, if one were willing to pay the price. Perhaps the accursed fiend would be the best one to contact. Foster knew precisely what book to consult for the words to draw the ghastly entity out of the void, or wherever it happened to be, and into his presence.

It would not be easy, and possibly dangerous, and he was unsure the ritual would even work. But if it did, he could request its aid in returning Mandy's bird to life, thus ending her intense agony. He did not tell her of his intention knowing she would laugh at it and ridicule him for years to come if his experimentation was unsuccessful.

Still, he would to do anything, within reason, to make his wife a happy trooper.

Foster woke early the next morning realizing this would be a busier day than usual. He opened the door to their bedroom closet, peered up at the trapdoor and released the lever lowering the ladder leading to the upper level. There he would find the book containing the assorted invocations he would need to implore the Evil One to restore Sparky to life.

"What are you doing, Foster?" came a demanding voice from behind him. He swiveled to see his wife, still under the sheets, pushed up on an elbow, glaring at him.

"What's all the noise about?" she queried, making no attempt to conceal the bitterness in her voice. "I was awake most of the night and now I've finally fallen asleep you come along making enough noise to wake my dead bird.

"What are you doing?"

"Sorry, dear. I'm going up to the attic to find some books I need."

"Forget it. There aren't any books up there."

"What are you talking about? I know right where they're at. Put them there myself."

"Sure, ten years ago, you did. I donated them to the Salvation Army months ago."

"You didn't," stated Foster, flatly.

"I did. And now I'm going back to sleep."

Foster shrugged his shoulders. Getting mad would solve nothing. "No need for me to go up there" he thought, miffed, but keeping his annoyance to himself.

Mandy turned over on her other side and shoved her head into the pillow. "Now try to be quiet and leave me alone."

"Yes, dear."

Foster went to the kitchen where he drank half a glass of orange juice and a half cup of yesterday's coffee, not enough to satisfy him, but sufficient to tide him over until Mandy came downstairs to make a more substantial breakfast.

Now what was he to do? His plans had been impeded, but it occurred to him, even though he no longer had the book needed to accomplish the impossible, he might be able to locate it at the public library. Foster would not give up. He would do whatever was needed to restore Mandy's parakeet to life again.

He sighed, deeply and thoughtfully, stood up slowly, stretched his shoulders and was about to leave for the diner down the street and enjoy a more substantial meal when Mandy came into the kitchen. His cheerful good morning elicited no response and her only words were, "I think I'll divorce you for murdering my pet."

As she made no indication of preparing breakfast for them, Foster interpreted her words to mean he was still off her list of favorites.

Her anger had not subsided as he left the house and made his way to the small eatery he frequented from time to time. Sitting there, waiting for his order of bacon, eggs and coffee to arrive, he punched in Mandy's cell number to try again to sooth the extreme loss she was feeling and end her talk of leaving him. He gave up after several attempts.

He was concerned. While elements of sorcery could raise the bird to life again, there might be moments of danger making matters even worse. And then it occurred to him of another way, equally efficacious, in which no hazard would be involved. He knew a little about the denizens of Ancient Egypt, his knowledge limited to documentaries seen on television about their traditions and practices and especially about their ability to embalm and mummify their dead.

He pondered what he knew about the priesthood and their strange, unfathomable ability to speak the Words of the Dead while preparing a cadaver for its journey in the afterlife. The practice, he knew, was not limited to people, but included bulls and eagles. If the process worked for larger animals, why not with smaller life forms? Maybe a little bird like a parakeet? Horus the Hawk, he thought, would likely approve. He imagined Sparky being soaked in brine to avert deterioration of his body, wrapped in a cloth binding, his vita innards removed and placed in canopic jars.

Foster scratched the balding spot of his thinning hair in perplexity. Could he restore Sparky to a semblance of life by mummifying him and uttering those mystic words which he might find at the library?

The idea was ludicrous, unthinkable. Even if he were to prepare the little tyke in the proper manner, it would still be an unmoving hunk of dead flesh, unable to placate his wife.

What would it take to instill the body with *actual* life?

And then it occurred to him.

Tana leaves were the answer. As a child he had seen old B movie thrillers from Paramount in which the audience was led to believe esoteric techniques existed to bring the dead person to life again. He could mummify the little corpse, soaking it in the essential salts for a while, sheath it in a cloth wrapping and feed tana leaves to it.

Still, it would not appear to be real if garbed in a cocoon of cloth.

What he needed was an *unwrapped* parakeet, one able to sit on its perch and move its head around from time to time. It did not matter if it made no noise; Sparky had never been much of a vocalist, anyway.

Meanwhile, his breakfast arrived and while he stirred cream and sugar into his coffee he wondered: Why would wrapping Sparky in fabric even be necessary? Foster pondered the situation over and over again as the fork lifted food to his mouth mechanically, without thought, and he tried unsuccessfully to contact Mandy by phone and stop any divorce proceedings she might have in mind.

He had always wondered why Imhotep, Karas the mummy, was swathed in dirty rags when it was not the wrapping giving him life but the use of tana leaves, the most important part of the sacred rite, along with prayers of the priests. Whether the combination would work for Sparky is something he would have to determine, but it was reasonable to assume less fuss would be required to force-feed a tana leaf into the little bird.

Foster finished his meal and second cup of coffee, unaware of the food he had eaten, unable to appreciate it as he normally did. He shrugged his shoulders and went to his car. Opening the door, he wondered how ethical his plans were. Sitting behind the wheel he recalled the words of Jesus in Matthew 10:7-8 telling his followers the kingdom of heaven was at hand and they should heal the sick and cleanse the lepers; further, it was their duty to raise the dead and cast out demons.

He felt better about his intentions. He would neither embalm the corpse nor enclose it in swaddling cloth-like bindings. Mandy would have no interest in a bird all wrapped up. He needed to learn more about tana leaves.

He continued to the library knowing his stratagem made little sense, but nothing else did, either. Whatever happened, however, the sky would not collapse nor the moon spin off its orbit into deep space. He would continue with his plan to give the little fellow a second chance at life.

The township library, at this time of morning, was not at all crowded and he was able to find what he wanted without needless delay. He knew where the card catalog was and made his way to it. Foster stood before row after row of drawers, then walked over to the E section and began examining the various entrees pertaining to Egypt, Ancient, amazed at the numerous choices offered. It took a while, thumbing through the entries for volumes able to assist him, settling on three he thought might be productive. He noted their numbers, then went to speak with a librarian to learn where they would be found.

Little time elapsed before he secured the weighty tomes and took them to a nearby nook with a desk he could use. Consulting the table of contents of the first, he came to the chapter on mummification, the process of preparing the body of a dead person for the afterlife. He turned to a page where the procedure was detailed and spent a little time learning how the embalmers, early undertakers, proceeded with their preparations, extracting first those organs which would rot away if not removed and placed in Coptic jars. What was left of the cadaver then soaked for weeks in a briny salt solution.

He skipped to another chapter telling of how the priests prayed over the body uttering certain words of magical import to speed the person along on its way to the afterlife. Foster studied the unfamiliar words, making notations in the notepad he brought from home.

Now that he knew the words to speak, what remained to be learned was how to attain a supply of the magical tana leaves. He supposed he could buy them from a seed company and grow them, but it would take far too long. They might also be ordered from a science supply house, but would take days to deliver, and he had no time to spare. Sparky was deteriorating right now and by the time they arrived, he would have rotted away and been of no use to him.

He mumbled silently to himself and considered: What need was there to use an actual tana leaf? As a chemist, he could combine the ingredients in his basement laboratory if he knew the molecular components of the incredible leaf. Using supplies he already had, along with ingredients available at the local pharmacy, he could prepare a special tana tea and apply it to an ordinary leaf.

It might work.

It took him more than an hour to locate a page listing the chemical formula, which he studiously copied.

He left the library knowing how to prepare the potion, recite the magical incantations of the priesthood, and feed leaf specks sodden with the tana mixture to Sparky.

At home, he was pleased to find, looking through the vials and bottles at his disposal, he had many of the needed ingredients and a trip to the drugstore enabled him to complete the list.

It was midafternoon before he was ready to begin. He chose a dead, dried oak leaf from the compost in his garden. It did not look like a weeping willow or bay leaf, both said to resemble a tana leaf, but why should it make a difference? He ground it into fine particles and saturated it with the chemical preparation he had formulated. He could only guess what the proper dosage should be through trial and error.

Foster was certain petrification had already begun, but was pleased to find the body still in reasonably good condition—for an expired parakeet. Its flesh was still firm although rigor mortis must have set in hours before. Still, he was able to pry its beak open with tweezers and, with an eye dropper, insert into the gullet the leaf grains soaked in tana soup. From his notebook he read aloud the incantation uttered by the high priests thousands of years ago to awaken the life force of the corpse.

Nothing happened.

He laid Sparky back on the bench.

'C'mon, Sparky. This is your second chance at life."

Foster waited.

And waited.

He stayed there for half an hour, almost ready to desist and admit defeat before he noted a spasm from the creature. Foster's surprise and delight was immeasurable. It was just a minor twitch of one small leg, straightening it out like a miniature spike, but was noticeable because he had been paying close attention.

It moved again and Foster swallowed hard as he watched the hoped-for-miracle taking place.

Another twitch of the leg and Sparky's left eye opened and a blank pupil stared at him for a moment before closing.

Hastily, Foster pried the bill open again and fed in more of the tana preparation. The bird's chest moved up and down as it sought to ingest more, swallowing it greedily. Suddenly, wings began to flutter and the bird began to struggle until Foster set it in its cage. His mind was awhirl. Was he dreaming or fantasizing over what was taking place, or had he actually brought the deceased parakeet back to life? After a minute, he scooped it up and set it on its perch and watched as its claws held on tightly, then wavering from side to side, back and forth before controlling its balance. To Foster it looked like another bird happily sitting in its cage. He knew better, of course, but hoped Mandy would not.

Suddenly, Sparky began to tire and dropped to the bottom of his cage. Its eyes closed and it lay quite still, either dead once again, or perhaps asleep.

Foster was in a dilemma. Did the little guy need more time to rest and recuperate? Should he increase its dosage a little more to, hopefully, generate a friskier bird? Tomorrow would be soon enough to decide if he should resuscitate the little fellow once again, forcing it to ingest another dose of the failed elixir.

He pondered the situation as he left the building, leaving the bird where it had fallen, covered with a handkerchief to provide cover if it became chilly during the night, loath to conclude his experiment had failed.

The doors were checked to be certain no intruders could enter and Foster returned to his home.

It being the supper hour, he decided to prepare dinner for himself. Mandy was not in the kitchen and he assumed he was on his own as far as a well-cooked meal was concerned. He prepared a bowl of Campbell's Chicken Noodle Soup and a hunk of roast beef he found in the back of the refrigerator. While the elder chemist ate a lonely dinner, he reviewed the events of the day. What had been accomplished in less than a twenty-four period was nothing less than miraculous. He congratulated himself on his failed accomplishment, careful not to claim for himself god-like qualities, and quelled his urge to return to the garage before finishing his meal to see if Sparky's condition had changed.

Later he sought the comfort of his couch and entertainment from his television set before settling in for the remainder of the evening.

Foster was up early the next morning imbibing instant coffee he found behind a sack of flour in the kitchen. He cooked some sausage links and scrambled two eggs, wondering if he should waken Mandy to see if she would like to join him for breakfast. He decided to forego her company, fearful her companionship might be more dour than usual and believing the more sleep she had the more reasonable her disposition might be.

He was washing dishes and cleaning the kitchen when Mandy, whom he thought might spend the remainder of the day in bed grieving, made an unexpected appearance, garbed in a dark dress, a scarf tied around her head and a black arm band.

My god, thought Foster, she's in mourning. He wondered where the sack cloth and ashes were.

"Where did you put the body?" she asked, testily, moving about listlessly, expending no more energy than was necessary.

"Sparky's?"

"Of course, Sparky. I want it. I'll soon attend to the obsequies and give him a proper burial."

She seemed to have regained some of her composure, perhaps reconciling herself to her loss.

"It's out in the garage," he replied, truthfully.

"I wand it in here," she tersely instructed him, heading for the door. "I'm going back to bed."

Finished with his task, the dishes put away, he sat, elbows on the kitchen table, chin cupped in his palms, and thought, "There must be more than one way. Mummification cannot be the only answer."

It was after eight o'clock before he headed to the garage where he opened the door to find the dead flyer had apparently not stirred since the evening before. The body appeared to be okay, not soft and gushy which would indicate the cellular structure had deteriorated. He gave it a poke. Unfortunately, it was still stiff as a board, laying on the bottom of its cage. He prodded it again and found it seemed to be growing more rigid by the moment. The bird was dead, all right. Feeding it more tana leaves, he decided, would be a waste of time.; turning a tweety bird into a mummy had been a colossal failure.

Now what was he do?

He had barely asked himself the question when a new idea came to him, one suggested by a program he had seen on TV little more than a week ago. His head jerked up, his eyes opened wide and his fingers snapped as he considered the new idea igniting in his mind. Now he knew what to do, confident it was a much better way of restoring Sparky than mummifying him, and would give the little fellow a new, much more permanent life. Why had he not thought of it before?

A zombie!

Of course!

Why not?

If mummifying Sparky had not worked, perhaps zombifying it would. It might not be too difficult if he acted quickly and resolutely while he had the opportunity. It would give the little fellow a new existence, a more practical and permanent chance at being alive, a much more practical way of restoring movement to Sparky than mummifying it.

Why had he not thought of it before?

Yes, he would zombify it!

But what did he know about treating the pet with such an inexplicable process? Just how does one turn a living or dead being into such a creature? Changing it into a mummy had been difficult enough; turning it into another form of the walking dead might be as equally challenging, if not more so. Further, while he knew the toxin would turn a living person into a zombie, if all the accounts he read were true, would it also transform a dead being into a live one under his control?

Time would answer his query.

But he had no idea of how to proceed. What did he know about the unknown procedure? Practically nothing, but he could learn and realized another trip to the library would be necessary. No problem there. The personnel had seen him so often the past week they probably considered him a regular by now.

It took three more hours of research, consulting five books concerning the mystical subject before he had acquired the information he needed to know.

His partial success with mummification gave him confidence, the will to attempt a new approach to reach his goal. He was aware a zombie was an undead being, a reanimated corpse popular in Haitian folklore, and from the pages read learned one was conceived by the necromancy of a bokor, or witch, who caused its victim to eat a substance causing a lethargic coma. The body was then buried and kept in a state of a pharmacologically in-duced trance, perhaps for many years, until resuscitated.

He further learned the more popular Voodoo witch doctors made zom-bie powder using an assortment of ingredients, including ground-up hu-man bones, a tree frog, a polychaete, or segmented worm, a large toad, and a species of pufferfish, the most potent ingredient with its deadly nerve toxins, the tetrodotoxin. All of this, he was reasonably certain, could be acquired at the science supply center. By feeding salt to it he could restore it to a more meaningful life. Yes, Zombifying a life form would be no more difficult than mummifying it. In fact, it should be considerably easier.

Returning from the library, he found no sign Sparky had stirred during his absence. Would he ever again? Perhaps. Even Karis had to ingest ad-ditional tana leaves after a while to return to his peculiar form of life.

A dosage will pep Sparky up, he decided, grinding more of the puff-er fish mixture into particles and then dropping them into the blend. He poured the preparation into a small receptacle, stirred and heated it, then pried open the beak and force-fed it into the birdie's gullet.

In hardly no time at all, signs of life returned to the little fellow. Eyes opened and stared blankly at its rescuer, revealing no sign of recognition or intelligence behind the glassy orbs. Its legs stirred and its wings began to slightly flutter, and then ceased.

The tonic had nearly worked, but not quite. Encouraged, he would try again, but this time more than double the strength of the little guy's first portion which was apparently not strong enough to enable it to fly. Sparky was, however, able to get to its wobbly legs and inflexibly step around the bottom of its cage for an inch or so and then shuffle along for another, not seeming to know where he was going or what he was doing, Sparky circled the cage, rigidly straight, perhaps looking for an outlet, feet stumbling with jerky, zombie-like steps. He walked straight forward, stilt-like, not bending his knees, each step rigidly straight, looking ahead with cold, unresponsive eyes, reminding Foster of a goose-stepping Nazi soldier. He wondered if he should have followed the instructions more precisely but it was too late now. He would keep it in mind for later.

The stressed man was not sure just how long its risen condition would last or deceive his wife, but he was pleased with the partial recovery and carried the cage into the house. Inside, he placed the bird on its perch. The tiny claws retracted, holding tight to prevent it from falling off.

Mandy walked into the room.

"Just what is *that?*" she exclaimed, glaring at the feathered avian as it nodded its tiny head, woodenly.

"It's Sparky. He wasn't dead after all, dear. Found him sitting up, just as he is now, when I went to the garage this morning."

"Is it really Sparky," she asked, a touch of skeptical rancor in her voice. "or a silly wind-up toy?"

"Oh, no," he assured her truthfully. "It's Sparky all right."

"Just how gullible to you think I am, Dummy? I don't believe a word of it. And I don't believe it's Sparky, either."

"Oh, but it is," he insisted, a slight tremor in his voice.

"You can't fool me," she said. "I'm sure it isn't him. This bird sits on its perch like a statue, hardly moving. Sparky had a lovely tweet and this one hasn't sung a single note. You went to the pet store, didn't you, and bought another bird to take his place? You might have believed you were being thoughtful, but the only bird I want is the old Sparky. Return this... this imposter...to the store and get your money back."

"I can't very well return it to a store where I didn't purchase it," Foster thought and wondered what to do next. He could take the cadaver out to his flower garden, dig a shallow grave and place it inside to spend the rest of eternity waiting to be resuscitated again. Or it could be disposed of in the incinerator. Karis had been destroyed by fire, he recalled, and it would be a fitting end for Sparky.

Foster sighed. Pleasing Mandy was such a difficult task.

✗

LOVE IN A TIME OF ZOMBIES
Darrell Schweitzer

Shambling corpses beneath the moon
are coming for us very soon,
and so, My Dear, we lack the time
for vain indulgence or trite rhyme.
Let's gather rosebuds while we may,
ahead of death, before decay,
and cease for now these plaintive strains
before the zombies eat our brains.

THE LAST FINAL GIRL
Lori R. Lopez

*A black and gray man like an old-time photo depicting
the impoverished lifted watery eyes bleeding tears, dim
and dull as the surface of stagnant ponds.*

*He spoke in harsh paranoid whispers, confiding his
worst secret. Clutching my left shoulder, in torment,
muscles of his face screwed tight . . .*

*"Nobody gets those monsters, ya know? Where they
come from. Why they're here. Culling! Reaping!
They took my sweet Beulah."*

*Heads bowed, we shared an endless aching interval
of despair. "I'm sorry." It was a human thing to offer —
far from the spires of civilization . . .*

*The littered concrete corridors of diseased battle zones
prowled by relentless husks of shambling former people;
vacant shells with voracious hunger.*

*"Ate her like savage beasts!" A crinkled pair of lips
pouted. "That hound was all I had. My whole world."
I pictured the moment. His loss . . .*

*Cadaverish fiends robbed me as well — limping out of
deep shadows. Surprise! I should have smelled their rot,
their spoiled flesh. A dead giveaway.*

*I blamed myself for the suddenness. My lack of wary
attention. Too little sleep, too much stress. I felt like
a zombie, part of the crowd . . .*

*Ironic. That was a goal of mine as an unpopular kid —
to belong; acceptance. Not anymore. Rule Number One:
Avoid all contact. Don't get close!*

I keep breaking the rule. I didn't hear a single snarl

or step. They swarmed us, a pack of four. I miss her.
I needed a friend. We bonded . . .

Close as sisters. Family. I was an only child, an orphan.
It meant a lot to have someone. I felt so isolated and torn
when they burned then buried my parents.

Victims of The Great Flu, before The Z-Virus. Bereft,
I found Kat — short for Kathleen — hiding in a rusted
Van. Sixteen months after a new outbreak . . .

Terrified of being alone, we teamed up and became
independent, unflinching, staunch. A pair of Final Girls.
Confident; capable of anything together.

Still we searched for a group. That concept no longer
exists. Infection spread. None could be safe. No stranger
trusted, whether from germs, a foul nature . . .

Seeking food, shelter. Abandoned buildings a risk —
lairs or traps for bodies we didn't wish to greet. It was
a Supermarket that led to her demise.

I dragged Kat's corpse to hold a funeral. A memorial.
While I dug a hole she changed, crawled to the grave,
leaped upon me! I swung my spade . . .

And lived another hour. Another day. Sometimes by luck.
We learn not to relax. I don't know how we endure the
shock; the constant continuous threat.

It wears you down. For those we lost, the brutal wait
is over. The interminable tension, grueling strain . . .
The constant gnawing numbing fright . . .

Always braced for a mindless attack. Cringing, watching,
every direction at once. Seldom able to rest, take comfort,
savor a minute or two of peace!

I know better now — or should. Yet we tell our tragic
woeful survivor tales, shared around furtive campfires,
because we must. We crave it . . .

A kind expression or word. A sympathetic ear. A sense
of community, commiseration. We are social creatures.
At least most of us were in the past.

I hugged the man, aware he would soon be gone like Kat.

We were all so frail in this crude morbid age of unreason.
This apogee of zombie bites and ill fate . . .

Unfortunate for us both, the man in my arms had just
turned, expiring from his dog's "rabid" bite. Belated,
I grasped a mumbled statement.

"She didn't mean to." I felt certain she didn't, and he
intended no harm. It wasn't our decision if our brains
were overtaken . . . succumbing . . .

Ravenous for tissue and blood. A canine companion
growled behind me, rejoining her master for a feast.
I was the last Final Girl.

No future surprises await. Desperate thoughts have
eased to grim acceptance. The Virus surges my veins.
I will stiffen and perish . . . then reopen clouded orbs.

under my nightgown. I still have a lock of her hair
hung from a chain around my neck, soaked in my tears.
Me, she says, hollow as if she's forgotten who she is
or where she's come from.
Me, I'm just cold.
Why don't you warm me like we used to?
She licks away the tears from my eyes,
her lashes crystallized into pointy arrows.
This isn't a haunting, she says, it's a resurrection.
You may now call me me your Lazarus Girl.

THE NIGHT HANS KROEGER CAME BACK

Kenneth Bykerk

A Tale of the Bajazid

In the latter days of Baird's Holler, before Destiny and Doom collided in a riot of fear and flame, a creeping decay had corrupted the soul and the very soil of the town. The denizens remaining lurked like gaunts at a graveyard, passing time in a listless haze while waiting for the rot to consume them as well. This malaise, this pall which hung like an ill omen over the town infected as well the whole of the Bajazid valley region. Gone complete were the promises and expectations which had carved from these canyons dreams of hearth and home, of industry and enterprise, of community and commerce. What remained was the haunted, hollowed shell of a town fallen to ruin, a place where Hope had long been buried and shadows in the afternoon were shunned. It was into this depressed state of affairs that Hans Kroeger returned to town.

It was near the Ides of August when the storms from the south would swell the sky and swallow sunsets whole in their fury. The day had been one drenched in showers and what light that had escaped did little to brighten the afternoon. Men drifted in from their labors and shops without business for the night shut down. On each end of the one remaining street through town a saloon stood and it was only between these two magnets the world of the oncoming night mattered. Beyond and nearly all around was a wasteland haunted by the charred, skeletal remains of buildings not fully consumed in a fire that had savaged the town mere months before. Between these poles, the night creatures emerged from the shed skins of their day-selves with sights set on lusts, damnation and oblivion; the seamless drift between man to beast had begun.

It was a shift in light that caught the attention of the town, both those outdoors as well as in. The sun, in a most desperate bid to be noticed, slipped beneath a thunderhead resting and sent its light straight up the valley. Everyone who saw was rightly captivated, rightly drawn for the view before them was breathtaking. A stunning panorama with layers upon layers of clouds defined in brilliant colors and subtle pastels. All along the street people stepped from beneath the eaves to stare west at this spectacle for the street ran the length of the setting sun. In a place where beauty had been stripped, such grandeur could not be ignored.

It was as if the people at once saw him, yet no reaction ran through the crowd. Their focus had been on the glorious sunset and not upon the blackened shadows beneath, so his emergence from such was undramatic. He just slowly shuffled, for that is what the step was, from the blackness behind him and entered the domain of what passed as the main street.

At first he was taken for just another miner walking in from his hole in the ground for some whiskey and a whore. He stood no different from any other man in that twilight. Those before Baron's, the saloon that anchored the western edge, paid barely any attention to the shuffling figure until it had drawn fully even with them. Only then did they begin to take notice his gait and his clothes and their oddity. It was the dead of summer when the rains added equal to the heat and here was a man walking with not one but two heavy coats upon his back.

A wit called from the raised rail of the boardwalk before Baron's, "Hey buddy, it cold enough for ya?"

The comment drew laughter from both sides of the street and other wits added their commentary. Drunkards and the desperately doomed need little excuse to turn their aggressions on others. Still the figure stepped, one foot painstakingly steady after the other, without heed to the increasing chorus about him. The sunset was all but forgotten up the small stretch of mud that accounted for the remains of Baird's Holler as the attentions of those too far away to see the details began to anticipate the focus of abuse. The grandeur had passed leaving but a sheet of fiery orange above and a flat, shadeless cast of the same to all around.

A couple of roughs, led by the wit of first comment, pretended offense at being snubbed in their abuses and began to follow the shambling figure from the boardwalks and into the muddy road. By now all eyes were upon the promise of sport to liven the evening, or promise of the first sport for the town had grown now careless and little was done to enforce all but the most egregious advantages of violence. Those who remained knew this and included it in their daily hopes and fears, expectations and dreads.

As the ruffian wit approached from behind the shambling form, a figure detached itself from the other side of the street and walked to intercept. A star on his loose, open shirt reflected the ambient light in ruddier hues.

"Hey you, why don't you answer me?" The ruffian grabbed the shoulder of the shambling man from behind and tugged to his regret. He jerked his hand back in disgust from the jacket, shaking it as if to free it from something vile. He looked at the thing he had disturbed, its hat now askew, and faltered; his rage blanched by disgust and horror and his pants soaked through the same. Its eyes were white, white with hundreds of geometric pockets reaching infinitely deep. They were ringed by green infections moist and fluid, as if tears congealed and rotten. The flesh above was stretched tight and bore resemblance to jerked meat long dried. The cheeks were leathern puffs, pocked with colorations more natural to the realm of fungus than man. An unkempt beard burst forth to disguise the lower features beneath bits of gristle and flesh and crawling things feasting.

With less detail but with enough to discern, the observers along the route saw the thing before them and the side of the street to which it was turned grew grimly silent. The ruffian had dropped to his knees and those in his train drew back in disgust. The stench which followed it had come upon them and it was one from below the grave. It turned, this grotesque mockery, and righted its path without ceremony or pretense of notice to those in its wake and began walking again, one slow shuffling step after the other.

"Hey fella, you doin' okay?" The man with the star lazily pinned to his shirt approached. "I seen that jacket before. Where'd you get it?"

It was a distinct coat. It was a great coat, a heavy one built for snow and wind. It was canvas quilted with patterns in tartan throughout and with a thick interior of the same pattern revealed from a wide collar thrown back. It rested loose and open over another coat, one of fur lined leather buttoned up beneath the beard.

"Hey, I'm talking to you. Where you comin' in fro…oh my god!" The public servant stepped back with his hand to his mouth. "You're…you're Kroeger, ain't you? You're one of them Kroeger boys."

"Hey, who is that?" Calls began to rise from those too timid to step forth from the sidewalks and see for themselves. "You know him, Bill?"

Bill, the man with the uncaring star, stepped back to distance himself from what he saw before him, repulsed by what didn't see him back. "You're Hans, Hans Kroeger. What's become of you? Where you been? You doin' for yourself?"

Hans Kroeger did not reply. He just stepped one foot after the other down the street, ignoring the run of rumor that stretched his name up and down the length. Most who heard the name knew it not but following in its wake, a hint filled in all any needed to know. A decade before, after the fire that had first challenged Baird's Holler, a storm unmatched buried the mountain and the thaw brought tales of loss. Hans Kroeger had last been seen in town that winter wearing his brother's coat and buying beans. He had claimed, in insistent whisper, that his brother was gone but provided no details. When he left, none had expected ever to see Hans Kroeger back in town again. Up on the Bajazid and its tributaries, men never returning from the holes they dug was no uncommon thing.

Bill the Constable backed his paces, his face blanched, back to the safety of the crowds lining the street. That crowd had grown; whores and their patrons, store keepers, drunkards and hard working men given over to their worst impulses stood in silent spectacle as the inexplicable figure marched in singular parade through town. No more comments, no more jibes and sneers rose to greet him. No more men braved the street to carry challenge. The shambling proceeded unassailed, steady and without glance left or right. The crowd stared in solemn contemplation and silent, rising dread as the light around began to fade.

Sunsets are ephemeral. All glory was gone by the time Hans Kroeger passed the Yellow Rabbit, the saloon that defined the eastern end of the grand avenue. An orange smattering of pretense remained beneath the clouds overhead and a final twilight glow bathed all in a dull, yellow light. As Hans Kroeger passed the Yellow Rabbit, a man stepped into the street behind him. He was dressed in clothes not meant for labor and topped with a hat of quality make. In his arms was a rifle, a lever-action repeater of common use. The man assumed a stance in the street with rifle leveled from his shoulder.

"Kroeger! Kroeger, if that is you, turn around. I want to see if you're you or…or…" the man faltered for words, spat, and raised his voice. "I want to see if you're one of them god-damned devils, that's what I want to see! Now turn around and face me! I want to see them eyes of yours!"

Word of descriptions close had traveled quick from the humbled ruffian and the man slipping the star from his shirt. These descriptions fed fears for all here on the Bajazid remaining had heard of the men who walked below, men, often their friends, who disappeared in the depths of shafts never to be seen again except by the damned as walking omens, shades glimpsed by those cursed. They were haunts, these men from the mines, or so they who worked those shafts would declare. They were tall-tales the bosses, such as the well-dressed man with the rifle, would dismiss and punish the spread of for they had already damaged the reputation of the Mortensen Mine to the point where only the truly desperate or coerced would descend.

When no response came from the form men were declaring Hans Kroeger but steps shuffled into the gloom, the man holding the rifle called forth one last time the name of the doomed before squeezing the trigger. The crowd, one not alien to such reports, all jerked slightly as the shot tore into the back of that tartan-lined canvas coat. Those closest, those near the eastern edge of town who saw Hans in profile when the shot rang out, saw the chest expand as the bullet tore through the thick layers. Those closest stared in horror as Kroeger staggered and then put one foot in front of the other in that same, undeterred steady gait. Two more shots rang forth and an explosion of gore burst from Kroeger's chest, yet still no change in his pace nor even acknowledgement of abuse. He just walked quietly the next few yards and disappeared into the finally consuming darkness at the edge of town.

The townsfolk stood and stared into the gloom which swallowed Hans Kroeger, each lost within their own dreads and fears. One man alone moved along that street, the wit who had pretended his offense. He walked with his own gait unsteady, halting, hesitant. He walked with his hand held forth, staring at it and beyond to those lining the street. His eyes were desperate, haunted and pleading for anyone to speak, to call him back. Past the metal star that turned uncertainly in a nervous hand and past the arrogant and astonished gaze of a straight-backed man with a rifle, the doomed man turned and hurried into the darkness on the heels of that thing that wore Hans Kroeger's face.

It was fully two minutes before any broke the silence or stirred. A shot fired into the air by the man with the rifle woke everyone from their reverie. He followed with exhortations of drink and to ignore what they all had just witnessed. Over the course of the night attempts were made by those who saw to forget. Some were successful, drowning their memories in quantities excessive, a couple so much so they never rose from their beds in the alley. The Chinaman ran a brisk business with a surge in customers he had never hosted before. Some, a half dozen that night, were never seen again by friend or relation had they either, their where-abouts only guessed or feared. A whore who had witnessed the setting sun, killed a man in her room; slit his throat with a razor and then her own. In the jailhouse, a dull metal star was left on a desk as the one who abandoned it stepped from that desk, the four witnesses behind bars left to stare as the body stiffened in the night. By the end of the month, no less than twenty persons were unaccounted for and one man had slaughtered his wife and children before himself disappearing.

Not all in town had witnessed the spectacle of Hans Kroeger walking. Skepticism ran high and arguments broke forth over the veracity of claims and of the nature of what had been seen. For those who had seen Hans Kroeger shuffle down the street, who had seen that horrific aspect shamble past, they were not in accord as to the meaning. Each held their own suspicions, each their own fears with but one singular certainty: they all knew, all who had witnessed that walk, that the town of Baird's Holler was dead the night Hans Kroeger came back.

✗

THE MARCHING DEAD
Andrew Darlington

The dawn that was not meant to be, happened anyway. But the Wehrmacht sprung their trap before we'd got halfway there. Thrusting warily through the woods, crunching frozen twigs and frost-brittle bracken under big boots. Even amid the tall trees my husband Kraster seems unusually huge, and he moves with an ominous hunch to his wide shoulders. I feel dwarfed beside him. There are no tracks in the wood, but we progress unerringly. His nerves are armour-plated. Shocks just sharpen his reactions. So when he froze, his hand going for his knife, I tense… but it's only a wolf that scurries away into the thicket. I relax. And the StG44 assault rifle rips the dawn.

Three of them in field-green uniform and helmets, rushing us in their jerky lumbering corpse-gait. I take the first, blade smashing the skull in a welter of putrefaction, maggots squirming in empty eye-socket. Entrails hang loose from ruptured abdomen, but the wounds that had originally killed it not even suppurating. But the second Nazi has dragged Kraster to the ground, teeth bared and ripping.

Then it goes even crazier. The third Wehrmacht comes up behind Kraster, and rams his bayonet through the attackers neck, twisting it, severing the spine, wrenching both head and helmet loose and spinning away. He looks across at me, and says 'Kamerad'.

My heart pulses loud in my mouth. Kraster makes moaning animal noises. His jerkin ripped open and his shoulder bleeding where the corpse sank its teeth into him. Yet the third Nazi is appraising me with a cool searching gaze, wary, but confused too. I meet and fix his eyes. He's undeniably living. 'Please' he says, as though ransacking a limited vocabulary, 'I do not understand.'

I make a swift decision. 'Help me. We must get Kraster to the stockade while there's still time.'

He shoulders his rifle and makes to help. Between us we wrestle Kraster up and start into dragging him, his unresponsive feet leaving twin tracks in the frost. My finger-ends already numb with cold. From the highest point of the rise we can look down into the valley beyond, the dusk glooming the hills, the silver gleam of the river that forks around the stockade island. There are no obvious hazards, so we lurch down the descent towards its safety.

'We were fighting in Wallonia. Through the Ardennes forest. Into an artillery barrage. An explosion. Am I dead, like the others? Where are we? I don't understand.'

'Don't shout. I can hear you perfectly well at normal volume. If you were dead, I'd know.'

Kraster jostles between us. He's muttering and raving now. The ramp comes down. There are patches of glistening ice around the reeds. We cross the bridge into the compound. The guards glance at us as we stagger in through the gate, as though half-minded to stop us. Into a circle of halls around the central space, mostly timber shoring up old stone and concrete. Until I yell for assistance. Things happen quickly. The Yaruba Healer, Katrin indicates, and Kraster is carried inside. She bathes his wound, an arc of punctures and ripped flesh. She produces a flask of liquid, and massages fluid into the ragged openings and around the skin. Then she ignites it into a burst of flame. His scream is terrible to hear. They hold him down as he wrenches his body with mighty convulsions. She counts. The cauterizing flames die.

'Did we catch him in time? Has the poison burned?'

Katrin shakes her head doubtfully. 'He's bad. I've seen it take others.'

'We should end him now, before he turns' roars Tancred, to growls of support. 'We can't risk him going amok.' Tancred is a big solid man. Not a person to cross.

'I vouch for him,' hand on my blade, facing him down. 'He's my husband. I take full responsibility. We'll vigil him.'

There's tension so hard it freezes the world. I'm not liking this one bit. The dryness in my throat hurts now, the clamminess of my fist around the messy knife-hilt tells me how scared I feel. Clenching until the nails bite. He glares. I glare back. He flinches first. 'You're his wife. It's only right that you shield him. But we are watching you. Take care.'

A torch illuminates the side room where he's laid to allow the fever to run its course. The vileness hopefully scalded out of his bloodstream. Only time will tell. I sit down beside the soiled trellis cot and prepare to wait. The Wehrmacht stands awkwardly. I'd almost forgotten his presence.

'It's strange. They fear and distrust Kraster more than they do me?'

'You are alive. Therefore you are killable' I tell him. 'Kraster is infected. They fear his bite will infect others. Meantime, you sit here, watch him.'

He nods uncertainly and sits down, cradling his bayonet. I pause. Yes, it's fine. The situation will hold. I head outside where swirls of snow are drifting from an ice sky. The winter never lets up, never relents. I head for the tower. What's left from the old constructions. Julius Strelcher is armoured in stubby whiskers. He looks up from his instruments as I enter. His grey face looks beaten. 'Another one gone' he tells me.

'What, Kraster? No… he'll pull through.'

'Not that.' He beckons me towards a screen. There's a starscape swirling across it, a blizzard of starflakes. 'See….?'

'No. I see nothing.'

'Another star has gone missing, from here…' he points.

'There's plenty more. What's to worry?'

He sits down and washes his hand over his face. 'How is Kraster?'

'He was bitten. The Yaruba cauterized it. Hopefully she's burned out the toxin. He was raving. Something about the Norn.'

The air inside his domain is musty-warm. Only the light is more pure, powered from the rotor on his tiles, augmenting the meagre moonlight filtering down through high vents. He stands up and crosses the cluttered space. A laboratory of gruesome exhibits, strange and malignant test-tube growths. He rummages down through a mound of electronics and raw wires. He's cursing and mumbling under his breath. Then produces an electro-bug with a flourish. 'This suppressor will help. Affix it to his throat. It translates pain to a more tolerable sensation.' He bangs it against the desk and holds it up to his ear. 'Yes, it'll do fine. It'll work alright.'

He passes it across to me. 'You should seek the Norn. It can help.'

As I stand to go, I turn. 'The stars. What's so special?'

'They're going out' he tells me. 'They first detected it some twenty years ago, before this all started, the old culture knew stuff we've long forgotten. They first notice that far galaxies are winking out. Or conversely, that some kind of terminal blackness is spreading. An ink seeping across infinity, snuffing out suns as surely as if they were candle flames. Of course, that awareness got lost with the chaos. But since I've been here, set up and wired this scavenged equipment, I've picked up where they left off. It's closer. And closing. Comparing photographic plates month by month, from week to week, and they go missing. Stars go missing.'

'Will the Norn know?'

'It might. It just might. You can ask on my behalf. Yes, you ask.'

'Thanks for the pain-suppressor, Strelcher.' Back down in the compound I find myself pausing, looking nervously up at the sky. Snow has settled. The night is clear. Endless stars. Surely there's enough to last forever? How will it alter our fates if a few, and a few more go missing?

The Wehrmacht looks unhappy. Kraster raves and writhes on one side of him. An unruly mob led by Tancred lurk angrily on the other, awaiting their excuse. They look up sullen and angry as I re-enter. I press the bug to his neck. His skin is burning to the touch. The bug digs wires into his skin. A low amber light pulses on its belly. At first there's no change. Then his convulsions lessen. He lies back more at peace. Yet his eyes are glazed. The raw edges of his wound glisten ugly red.

'I am glad you are here' says the Wehrmacht as I straighten. 'I was concerned they would intervene while you were gone.'

'You're a soldier.'

He laughs bitterly. 'I am Wilhelm, from Düsseldorf. I no longer know exactly what I am.' He extends his hand self-consciously.

I look up and meet his scared eyes. 'I guess you did save a life back there in the woods.' He smiles as I grip his hand in solidarity. 'It will be wise if we leave here as soon as we are able. I don't trust them.' He nods grimly.

The night passes in tense slowness, uneasy with apprehensive dreams. Thoughts of death and decay crawl like maggots through my brain. We leave as soon as dawn breaks. Kraster walks between us, like a living automaton. Tancred and his followers watch us go. There are jeers and threats, but no actual attempt to interfere or stop us. Nevertheless, I don't feel safe until we've crossed the drawbridge and out onto the incline.

'Where now?' says Wilhelm.

'Kraster knows. He'll take us to the Norn.' The German obviously doesn't understand, but seems resigned to accept it.

Over the hill there's a war-zone. We crouch down and take a wide circle knee-deep in undergrowth, wary for outriders and hidden foxholes. They look to be Napoleonic, although I'm a poor judge of history. A cavalry charge of mounted corpse-troops on skeletal horses charges a heavy artillery line, tired pennants fluttering dismally. The guns open up in a devastating barrage that decimates the disciplined advance, horses and riders alike blasted into eternity, while the charge continues, sabres drawn, and they're there among the big guns, leaping the defences, swords sweeping, lopping off dead heads. More explosions as ordnance detonates in vivid gouts of flame. They're too concerned with massacring each other to notice us, and we safely get beyond it all.

We halt and set up makeshift camp at nightfall. Wolves and other predators shy away from fire. And we stay alert for zombies, who are less scared of flame. I melt snow over the fire and sponge it carefully around Kraster's wound. He doesn't even wince, but the touch sets off memories of intimate tenderness. The bug pulses at his throat, radiates its soothing energies. Whatever is going on inside his head is anyone's guess. Every now and then he talks nonsense in a low subdued way. Norn, and then Norn again.

'Perhaps Tancred was right?' I tell Wilhelm. 'He's neither turning, nor pulling through. Perhaps we should've rammed a stake through his head while we had chance? But I don't give up on my lover. I've known Kraster since we were kids together. He's a good man. A good husband. I'm not about to give up on him, not yet.'

He nods. Unfastens the chinstrap of his helmet and slides it off. 'Tell me, please.' His thin lips barely move.

No reason not to now. We have all the time in the world, or at least until the stars wink out one by one. 'The war started it.'

'The same war?'

'No. Not your war. That's ended and forgotten long ago. Another war, a north-south resources war. Ten years ago it began, although it seems like another world to me now. They chucked nukes at each other until they'd got no nukes left. They flew blanket robot bombing raids, until they'd got no robot bombs left. Then there was infantry warfare, until there were no soldiers left either. It was the southers who started reanimating corpses to replace their military losses, although they say it was us. So they began re-animations too, or the other way around. I don't know. Corpses make perfect soldiers, you know that? Disciplined, obedient, unquestioning, fearless, biddable, no fear of death or injury. They go on forever, until they're blown back to whatever hell they came from.'

'But I'm not dead.'

I laugh and poke the fire, sending a shower of sparks up into the night. 'I sometimes think we're all either dead or busy dying.'

He fumbles in his uniform jacket, pulls out a wallet and flips it open. A faded photograph of a young blonde woman, smiling directly into the camera, her hair pulled into tight buns at her temples. 'I'm married too. This is Ingrid. My wife waits for me in Düsseldorf. Once I return, we will start our family. I studied genetics. I even studied in Cambridge for a term, which is where I learn the English which your people fracture so amusingly. With the advent of war we were tasked with researching proof of Aryan genetic purity. But then they begin conscripting younger and older, and even we of previously reserved occupations. Once the war ends I will return to Ingrid and resume my studies free of political agenda.'

He pulls a hipflask from his pocket and shoves it across. 'Schnapps. Enjoy. Prost.'

The taste is fire. A burning intoxicating acid.

The zone of dawn-light sweeps across continents. We've survived into another day that was not meant to be.

Around noon we encounter a battalion of troops in Confederate grey. It rapidly gets vicious. As we hunker down there's a group of stragglers who come up behind us. They are slow, but heavy. They smell stenchy bad, with drifts of circling blowflies and bluebottles. I'm used to offing them, spearing my knife to rip through dull diseased eyes set into rotting corpse faces, while Wilhelm uses his bayonet to lethal effect, learning from me how to down them and keep them down. While trying to keep it silent so as not to attract attention from the main Confederate body. We manage to get away and up over the forest-line beneath head-high undergrowth. Kraster lumbers like the dead himself. We thrust ourselves through, cursing as strong thorn-brake tangles hinder progress. Then there's an immense spider-barrier linking trees into an endless mesh. We must circle that too, without alerting the monster arachnids. Peering up through the green light filtering down through the tracery above, we catch glimpses of them stilting through the upper foliage. There are deer caught up in the web, drained into something deflated.

'This world is insane' says Wilhelm. 'I don't recognise this world at all.' As though by expressing his disbelief removes him from the responsibility of understanding it.

'Radiations mutate and wreak changes on things. Nothing stays the same.'

'At least that part of it conforms to the genetic theory I recognise. But seeing it this way is something else entirely.'

A crumbling highway. A black mound of incinerated corpses. Severed limbed nailed to a tree.

From there we drop down into what's left of the city. Burnt and blast-blackened, but already overgrown by tall weed and new trees. The city is a dangerous place. There are wild and terrible beasts here. A couple of corpses lurch out of shattered brick caves. We smash them down. I finish the first. Wilhelm takes care of another. He's adapting to the necessity well. Neither of us see the third. Either a Samurai or something very like. As I turn I see the sword. See it rising in a lethal arc. See it slicing in towards Kraster's tall immobile figure. The blade flashes at his neck, rips away the suppressor-bug, opens up a vivid tear down his chest. Kraster shocks back. He spasms. But his hands come up to grasp tight on the sword-arm. Wrenches the corpse forward in one violent lunge, grasps the sword from dead fingers, turns it around and rams the blade clear through the rotting face so hard it splinters. The Samurai falls away into a messy heap.

Kraster falls to his knees. We watch breathless. The new wound bares like an open mouth slashed across the old wound. And it has teeth. My skin crawls with horror. Terror tells me to step back, yet I step closer. Not teeth. There within the ruptured flesh, a single tooth. I'm staring so hard I can barely keep these eyes in my face. And something detonates in my head. I yell for Wilhelm to move in and hold him down. I use my knife to gouge into the wound. His howl of agony is gut-wrenching. But I work the embedded tooth free, brandishing it between thumb and forefinger. Kraster is convulsing. The pain-bug is gone. He feels everything.

There's an empty brick cave where the Samurai was lurking. It is enclosed. We move into its shelter, dragging Kraster between us. Wilhelm thrusts deep into his tunic, hunting the flask. He sprinkles Schnapps across the open wound. And pours the rest of it between Kraster's lips, as I wad the wound as best I can. For the first time there's expression in my man's eyes. As though he's determined to master himself as swiftly as possible. Physical recovery from injury-trauma takes time. We wait as ghastly vomits shake him. Time extends interminably.

Wilhelm forages outside, shoot a feral dog, we skin and roast it over a fire as night closes in. It tastes so very good, the fat-juices running down my chin and rich on my grimy fingers, until I feel comfortably sated. Kraster lies still. Sleeping, but his breathing is steady. The embedded tooth, from that first Wehrmacht bite, is what's held him suspended in trance. With its extraction, he's weak, but recovering. The dead Samurai's blade did us an unintended favour.

I glance sideways at my companion. 'They use time-scoops' I tell Wilhelm conversationally.

'Time scoops?'

'Yes. There's not a limitless supply of corpses to reanimate. So they began using time-scoops to harvest ancient war-zones and battlefields. The consensus being that it couldn't interfere with timelines because the victims were dead already, so could no longer influence events. Once here they're transmatted to new warfronts to fight new battles. Our side, or theirs, it no longer matters, they keep pushing further back into past-time as each war is exhausted. We'll see dead Roman and Carthaginian legions marching here yet.'

'And they were time-scooping the Ardennes campaign.'

'It seems that way.'

He stops, his mind dark with speculation. 'I was caught up in the artillery barrage that massacred my comrades. Yet I was not killed. Your machines made a mistake. I should not be here. Is it not possible for me to be sent back?'

'And yet you are here, Wilhelm. You and me are here together at the end of the world.' Attempting to make whatever ironic light of it possible. 'As soon as hostilities opened strategic planning was turned over to AIs. Their computational abilities way beyond anything we could ever do. And what little we knew, we've forgotten. There's no person alive who knows how to operate those things. Even if it's possible.'

The following day, using a length of timber as a crutch, Kraster leads us in a more targeted way, weak, but returning to himself. Wilhelm holds his bayonet ready, taking vigilant sweeps at dark corners and crossways. There are raised sections of once-roadway that take us above the devastation towards where a cluster of surviving towers still stand against the sky. 'Norn' says Kraster, pointing. 'Norn.'

'Why does he want this Norn?' whispers Wilhelm at me.

He overhears. For the first time, Kraster halts and turns. Surveys us both. 'Not for me' his voice rough. 'For him.' His finger stabs at the time-lost Wehrmacht.

There are shattered gates, with a shrapnel of glass cascading down a wide and grimed staircase leading into subsurface galleries, obviously protected from the disasters visited upon the city it extends beneath. There's even low lighting set into the ceiling, except where sections are blocked off by a collapse of debris.

Wilhelm is checking out branching side-corridors, in case of hazard. His bayonet angled. I turn to Kraster. 'It's good to have you back, my love. I feared we'd lost you.' Then, 'You've been here before? You know this place?'

'Long time ago' he nods. We were under attack by dead predators, seeking sanctuary. We stumbled in here by chance.' He winces with the effort of talking. Leans heavily on his crutch. 'It's a library, solar-powered, so it's still functioning. And it's netted in with other AI centres. There are teletravel transmat pads here, and archives.'

Wilhelm rejoins us, smiling a crooked smile. We wait until Kraster feels able to resume, and we go deeper. Debouch into an extensive piazza lined with screens. Most of them are smashed or fused into tangles of black melt. He approaches some of them, which seem still intact. Tries one, to no response. Then another. He hits keys and punches out codes.

'No more Schnapps' grumbles Wilhelm ruefully. 'Gott im Himmel, no more Schnapps on the entire planet. Never again.' We root around in the accumulated garbage while Kraster persists, trying unit after unit, cursing and kicking each lifeless machine in turn. Then one lights up, unexpectedly, making his own huge shadow stoop over him, yet with a shock that sends him reeling back onto the floor.

The hazy insubstantial figure of a man quivers in the air. 'Welcome. How can I assist you?'

We cross to help Kraster back to his feet. He groans with obvious pain, but grits his teeth.

'What is this Geist?' breathes Wilhelm.

'Not a ghost. Just a being of light, generated by the AI' hisses Kraster. 'Ask it questions. It gives you answers. Ask it Wilhelm. Ask it what happens to you.'

The German glances nervously from one to the other, then to the hologram.

'Do it' shouts Kraster, his voice trailing off into hacking coughs. 'I know you. I recognise you. Ask the Geist, it knows. Ask it.'

He stands as though on parade. Brushing his soiled grey-green uniform with his hands. He faces the swimming image as though it's an interrogation panel, giving his name, rank and serial number in slow deliberation. And it's all there. The history of his unlived life. The life he has lost. Wilhelm Gottfried. The Wehrmacht who survived the Ardennes offensive, and returns to Düsseldorf, to his wife Ingrid, with whom he has a son and daughter. He resumes Genetic research, devoting years to restorative treatments for disfigured war-victims and amputees, stimulating and regenerating damaged organs. As his reputation and fame increases into old age, his adult daughter assists and adds new inputs into the research. An accidental side-effect of the treatments is the reanimation of dead flesh. Of the dead…

We sit together in silence. It goes on for some time. The only sound is our breathing, Kraster's breath more ragged and laboured, but strengthening. I stand up, and walk the length of the gallery. Then walk all the way back again. To face the holographic figure. 'I have a question, from Julius Strelcher. He says the stars are going out. Why are the stars going out?'

There's no reply for a long time. As though it's ransacking its memory-archive. I fear there will be no reply. Then, 'This disrupted timeline is being deleted. It's history has been altered, it is no longer viable.'

'How long do we have?'

'Decades yet. But relativistically accelerating as it approaches closure.'

Wilhelm sits, head cradled in his arms, sobbing for the wife to whom he will never return, the children he will no longer have, the life and universe that has been snatched away.

'What now?' says Kraster. 'We go back to the stockade and wait?'

I think hard. Then face the holo. 'Is there anywhere left on Earth where there are no zombies, and there is no nuclear winter?'

'There are Aegean islands.'

'And you can transmat us there?'

The sand is gritty beneath my bare toes. The warm tide ripples up across the beach. My husband puts his arm around my shoulder and draws me close. Wilhelm looks up at us and smiles. A strange trio, with nowhere else to go and nothing more to do. I look up at the Greek sky which is shocked crazy with the scattered gems of stars.

As I focus on one particular constellation, counting my way down the distant points of light, I watch the stars wink out, one by one.

✗

I WISHED FOR ZOMBIES
D.C. Lozar

You know that old slam where some random hot girl says she wouldn't go on a date with you even if you were the last living person on Earth? Remember how you laughed it off, wished she hadn't said it, and then decided that it wasn't true. I mean, how could it be?

You told yourself that if push came to shove and the human race's very existence hung in the balance, she would lower her standards and grab a burger and fries with you. Right?

Sorry. You are dead wrong.

Want to know how I know? It's the restraining order, reprimands from the Judge, and the court-ordered ankle bracelet.

She has her reasons. They might even be very good ones. I mean, before things went to Hell, I thought the walkers they made those TV shows about were pretty gnarly too, but it's different now...

Now everybody's dead.

Not dead-in-the-ground dead, but dead in the sense that they don't breathe, eat, use the facilities, make babies, or care-about-anything-other-than-doing-their-job kinda dead. The whole Earth is full of these sorry-ass zombies who think the height of personal achievement is not accidentally getting decapitated, and that's the crux of it: She still thinks the planet would be better off without me in it.

I bet you think I'm exaggerating. You're sitting there reading this crumpled up sheet of paper you found stuffed behind some zombie guy's desk that's been dead for a hundred years, and you're vaguely remembering a story about the last living man on Earth being a complete tool and how the last woman on the planet wouldn't give him the time of day. You're thinking this couldn't possibly be a note from that guy.

Well, it is.

Congratulations. You've won an all-expense-paid trip to I-don't-give-a-shit-who-you-are-but-I-thought-I'd-write-down-some-stuff-to-get-it-off-my-chestville.

First stop, my name— Charlie Albernicker Verdant.

Second stop, her name—Shelly Nicki Halibert.

Our destination is the Hotel California. Sorry, you probably won't get that reference because, well, you're a zombie. It was a song the Eagles released in February 1977 about how people checked into this place where everyone was happy to see them. It was like cool that they came and all, but there was no way they were ever going to leave. I mean, it wasn't like they were holding them down or anything. No. It was worse than that because the thing that was trapping them was their state-of-mind. It was like they bought into a way of thinking, signed their name on the dotted line, and now they had to keep on behaving like the person they thought they were supposed to be for the rest of their lives—kinda like a zombie.

It didn't matter if they woke up and tried to kill the beast with their steely knives or drank themselves into oblivion; they were prisoners who had willingly locked themselves up. Well, that's what I'm guessing happened to Shelly. She got some information, probably only half-true, and made up her mind that she was going to believe I was a bad guy, and no matter how hard I tried, I was never going to get her to check out of that hotel.

That's not to say I didn't do my best.

I got to know her schedule, learned all her friends' names, and even became drinking buddies with her Dad. Great guy but not the sharpest nail in the toolbox. Her Mom loved me, really understood where I was coming from and why I was so committed to talking to her daughter, but even she couldn't change Shelly's mind. So, what else could I do? I wrote her letters, blew my salary playing her favorite songs on the radio, and learned to cook all the foods she enjoyed eating. I hacked her medical records so I could make suggestions about her diet and health, talked to her boss about giving her a promotion, and even borrowed her dog for a couple of weeks to prove that Fido and I could be good friends. I mean, if that doesn't show commitment, I don't know what does.

About that time, local zombie law enforcement started showing up at my door and warning me to back off or else. Or else, what? I was the last living man on the planet. They weren't going to throw me in jail. That would be like locking up the last dinosaur because it trampled a few houses. On some level, I think they were rooting for me. Nobody wants to see a species go extinct. Right? I mean, that's just depressing. Everyone wants the last two members of whatever animal's in danger to try and work things out, make a few babies, and then hang out on opposite ends of the cage until they kick it. I mean, it's almost like a genetic responsibility, an extinction-event-golden-rule or something, but that's not how Shelly felt. She wanted the cops to lock me up and throw away the key.

After a while, I started to take it personally.

I mean, I'd get it if she wasn't into guys or something, but she'd been married to a dude before everyone died. So that wasn't it. Maybe she still loved him and felt guilty about leaving him for me? But how could that even be an argument? I mean, the guy's dead. He's rotting away even as he's driving to work. His teeth are falling out, and he smells like a walking corpse—cause, he is one. You can't love something like that. It's sick.

I tried not to get down on myself about the whole thing. I went to therapy, took the medications my zombie doctor suggested, and even had some plastic surgery to make me look more like her husband had before he died and became a zombie. No deal. In fact, I heard it through the grapevine that she thought I was even creepier after the surgery. That sucked because the operation was no easy task, what with the doctor having to work with decaying fingers and all.

So, this is when I'm starting to get desperate. I mean, this is the human race after all. Right? Forget about personal chemistry, love, and all that stuff and try and see the big picture. So, I get some of my zombie buddies together and convince them to help me state my case. Again, this was not an easy thing to accomplish. Have you ever tried to plan a heist with a bunch of guys whose brains have turned to mush so they can only communicate with groans and hisses? Well, I can tell you it takes a heck-of-a-lot-longer than it should. Anyway, I eventually get them on board, and we snatched her as she was getting off work and took her to a nearby coffee shop to have a little sit-down. I mean, I'd thought it all out. This was a really swanky public place, and I recorded everything, so she couldn't say I wasn't a complete gentleman. I'm desperate, but I'm not a scumbag. Okay?

Well. The whole time I'm talking, you know, really spilling out my heart and apologizing for whatever crap she thinks I did, she's texting her friends and calling 911. If you ask me, that's rude. I mean, just listen to what I've got to say, and then you can go back to your life, and we'll call it a day. Right? Nope. Mrs. Trimlock, her married name, is so checked into her Hotel California, I doubt she heard two words I said.

So, the zombie police show up again, shaking their heads, really sorry things didn't work out but under an obligation to take me in, as Shelly wants to press all kinds of charges. So, cuffed and alone, I get carted off to jail just like those "bad boys" I used to watch on TV, only it's not them this time. It's me, and I've got a really good reason to be pushing Shelly's buttons. Back then, those guys had a whole world of girls. If they got shot down, they could just move on and find someone else who had lower expectations. But, for me, there was only one living woman left, and so it's not like I had a choice.

Anyway, that's how I explained it to the zombie Judge. She kind of understood where I was coming from and besides there was a lot of public support behind me seeing as how I was the last guy and all. The long and short of the thing was, I got released with a warning, restraining order, and an ankle bracelet.

So that's how I know a date with burgers and fries isn't in the cards.

That's a shame because the joint I was planning on taking her to has the absolute best dill pickles with their sliders. It's just down the street from the construction site where I found that artifact that changed everyone's life.

It was a Wednesday. I remember that because I was headed back to my apartment after eating one of their World's Famous Wednesday Whoopers when I tripped on a crack in the pavement and fell into the hole they were drilling for that skyscraper they built on Fifth Street. You know, the one with all the mirrors and fancy lights. Anyway, I woke up an hour later in the dark with a pair of bruised ribs and a blaring headache. I screamed for help, but you know how that sort of thing goes in the city. So, I sat down and waited. I figured the construction guys would notice me the next day and throw down a rope. Then, my hand brushed up against this thing in the dirt, and what do you think it was but an old lamp. You know, like in the fairy tale Aladdin. So, I say to myself, what the heck, I've got nothing better to do, and so I rubbed the thing.

Three wishes, she said. Three wishes, and then we'd be square for me having released her from prison. So, I think about it, super careful and all, and start out with my ribs. Wish-pop, and they're good as new. Okay, I say to myself, so let's make sure we've got a steady income, you know job security and all, so I wished that I could never be fired. Wish-pop, done, she says. The genie's laughing now, like she's really impressed with my wishes, and she tells me I've got one left, and wouldn't I like to have a woman or something? I think about it and remember this girl I had a crush on way back in sixth grade, Shelly Nicki Halibert, and I say that I wished I could go out on a date with her. The genie bites her lip and thinks about it and says maybe I want to pick someone else, but I say no, I've made my wish, and she's got to grant it. So, she explains that there are things that even genies can't make happen, but she'll do her best. I say that's the most I could ask of anyone, and so Wish-pop here we are.

See, the thing is, I'd forgotten I'd already asked Shelly out back on the playground when we were both twelve, and I'd gotten the not-even-if-you-were-the-last-living-person-on-the-planet slam. So, I guess it's kinda my fault everyone's a zombie now because the genie was trying to set the stage for me, you know. But you can also see how it was sort of an accident too. Right? I mean, when you get up enough nerve to ask a girl out, and you get shot down that hard, it makes sense to block that sorta thing out. Right?

So, like that's where we are right now, and I still think it's possible to reverse the whole damn thing if Shelly would just agree to go out on one date. But, I guess she sorta of blames me for turning everyone into zombies and killing off our species, and so I'm trying to see her point of view. Only, I wish she could do me the same courtesy. I mean, we've got to learn from our mistakes, be willing to change our perspective when the situation calls for it, or else nobody's ever going to be able to improve and what would that even look like?

Well, I'm guessing you know the answer to that one. Look around. You're in a zombiotopia.

I'll bet there aren't any sixth-grade dances, bar-scenes, or even burger joints with fries. There aren't any more humans, so I know you guys don't have to worry about stuff like love and rejection. The schools are probably all closed because, well, zombies aren't that smart, and there are probably a bunch of politicians running around for the exact same reason. No crime or murder, no taxes or bills, because there's no need for money since you don't eat or need to live in houses. Heck, by the time you read this, you guys have probably even figured out how not to get accidentally decapitated. When you think about it, a future like that might not be that bad, almost like the whole world's one big Hotel California.

Not that I blame Shelly for being stubborn. Heck, we've all been there. You paint yourself into a corner, swear you know the answer to something, and then have to stick to your guns because you don't want to eat crow. Only, for her, it was like a zillion times worse since the whole world was watching. It really comes down to integrity. Right? I asked her a question. She made me a promise. I put her on the spot, basically forced her to ante up, and so she has to stand her ground. You've got to respect that. That's the kinda tenacity that made me fall for her in the first place, and why I want you to go find her now.

Why?

Since your mind is processing this at the speed of lumpy oatmeal, you might need to trust me on this, but I'll walk you through it. Right. In Don Henley and Glen Frey's lyrics, they say you can check out of the Hotel California, but you can never leave.

I'm guessing that means when Shelly and I die, we'll become zombies like the rest of you deadheads. Only, the way I see it, that's a good thing. See, I made a wish with that genie, right? I can't be fired.

The desk you found this letter behind is my desk. You're working at my desk. So, I'm betting dimes to doughnuts that you're me.

Don't believe me? Look down, and you'll find that court-ordered ankle bracelet I was telling you about. Yep, you're me.

I know. That really sucks, and you're probably hissing and groaning like a ghoul on Christmas morning but don't worry because I've got a plan.

See, now that you're both dead, Shelly *can* finally go out on a date with you and still save face—if she still has one, and things might work out after all.

Just don't take her to the burger joint.

Instead, there's this great new place on Twenty-Ninth Street that serves brains with a creamy bouillon sauce that is to die for.

✗

I PUT A SPELL ON YOU
Allan Rozinski

In the bayou country outside New Orleans
the old ways are dying out like zombie rot.
Did you know the Voodoo Queen, Marie Laveau?
or hear of Doctor John Montanee, the Bokor Supreme?
—who could bring a body back from the clutches of death,
if a person could pay the price.

Still, late at night, you might find
a hustler who'll offer you your choice
from a range of drugs to ease the burden
of boredom, or hook you up with sex for sale,
done dirty in the shadows of a dark alley
or a room for rent by the hour;
but for those looking for a strange turn
off the beaten path, in the dead hours
before the morning light, he'll take
you out deep into the marshlands
to witness a black voodoo rite.

The body is dug up from the silty ground,
the casket lid opened, the dead man lies unmoved.
The bokor invokes the names of the loa
who come not on a wing and a prayer,
but arrive as though they'd slithered out
from the murky waters of the swamp,
through the gnarled, twisted roots of the
mangrove trees stilted in the water,
where the wild things hide and feed,
the horror of the way of predator and
prey, fated to play out and repeat.

The sorcerer's chants rise into a fever pitch

O MARY DON'T YOU MOURN
Mike Chinn

The night fell fast. One moment Mattan could see every grave marker lining the gravel path, each fresh mound of dirt, the gnarled trees; the next the whole boneyard was in almost total darkness. The only light came from a feeble half-Moon riding the cloud-scudded sky. The crickets seemed to grow louder.

He took his ball and cap Colt revolver out of its shoulder holster, placing in on the half-dead grass beside him. Anybody showed their face, he'd as like take a couple of shots before asking why they were there. Nobody would have a decent reason to be walking this place at night. And that included Mattan.

At least it wasn't cold. He guessed it never really got cold in New Orleans. Like California. One of his rare good memories of San Mateo was the weather. And the smell of the ocean. The air didn't smell the same in New Orleans: the humidity was oppressive, bringing with it the tang of unfamiliar spices and vegetation. The place was like a world apart from the rest of the United States. A slice of France and Africa that had taken up residence and wasn't about to change. Even the boneyard was different. The smells of cold stone, decay—every unwelcome memory of the squalid graveyard hidden behind the San Mateo orphanage—were buried under the scent of exotic blooms and perfume.

Mattan's hand dropped to his pistol. He'd spotted movement—vague, furtive—far away at the start of the path. Someone was out there, dodging between trees. Someone who didn't want to be seen.

The crickets fell silent.

Mattan waited for whoever was out there to come into range.

* * * *

She didn't hear his approach. Wrapped in her grief she was deaf and blind as she wept, kneeling and silently asking *Why?* She wasn't aware of his presence until she raised her head and saw his boots, planted against the levee side. She flinched, almost falling, thinking it was one of King Lefavreau's bullies, or worse the man himself.

Dashing tears from her face she leaned back better to see him whole. He looked like one of the riverboat gamblers who occasionally stepped ashore: his russet coat, gold vest and tan pants fine and expensive; his shirt a starched white, ruffled down the front and at the cuffs. Yet the face under a wide black hat was broad, flat, with cold grey eyes like knife blades under his dark skin. He also wore some kind of fancy jewellery; a high choker visible though the open shirt, and bracelets on his wrists. Pale blue stones set in what she guessed was silver. Something about his features made her think of a bird of prey.

"Why the tears?" he asked. His voice was deep, with no accent she'd heard before.

"What you care?" she muttered. "You ain't black—nor Creole, neither,"

"Born a Navajo—though some Californian nuns thought they could beat it out of me. And I care about a lot."

"Ain't nothin' to be done," she muttered, getting to her feet. "Time for doin' things is well past."

"Wanna bet?" He glanced at the wilting flowers crushed in her hand. "Wedding or funeral?"

"I mourn my boy, Joseph, took by the fever two days ago. Or so the white doctor say."

"You doubt his word?"

She shrugged. "Lots of folk dead of the fever these last months. None of 'em white. That fever is powerful choosy who it take."

The Navajo frowned. "You sure this is an actual sickness we're talking about?"

She guessed his meaning. "No, this death don't come from a gun, nor the end of a rope. It's natural. If one that claims just Black souls can be called natural."

He looked up and down the levee. "I see no marker."

She nodded towards a distant gate. Dry grass and tired trees were fenced off by high railings. "They laid Joseph over to the charity graveyard, alongside all the other fever victims. This mornin'. I wasn't let watch—they said what he had was still catchin'." She looked down at the flowers still in her hand. "He always liked to come up here when he could. It's best I remember him that way."

She dropped the flowers, brushing her hands as though to clean them. "No one lies easy in that potter's field, Hospital digs the bodies up when they think no one watchin'."

The Navajo bent to pick up the sad posy. He smoothed the bruised stalks flat and slipped them into one of his fancy coat's pockets. She didn't ask why. She was already distancing herself from her loss. It was the only way to cope.

"Why is that?"

For a moment she didn't understand the question. "I hear it's so students can learn how we all put together." She felt the tears starting again. "My baby goin' be hacked apart!"

He put an arm around her, just a little too tight, like the way she'd used to hold Joseph when she was angry or scared for him. "You live close by?"

"Just a short walk."

"Today you don't walk." He led her down the levee to a painted pony that waited patiently, searching through the thin scrub for something worth the eating. He boosted her into the saddle and took the reins. "Which way?"

She pointed. He led the pony the way she'd indicated, their backs to the distant cemetery.

"What do they call you?" he asked after a while.

"Mary."

"If you see me again, Mary, pray I bring better news."

He never spoke again. After dropping her off at the shotgun shack she called home, he rode silently away.

* * * *

Mattan watched as the shape flittered closer. It could have been a man, but it moved more like a spider. It had left the trees, scuttling between the lined-up markers, pausing now and then to inspect one. The weak moonlight failed to delineate the shape, leaving it black and featureless.

When Mattan judged it to be in range he stood, stepping away from the gnarled trunk against which he'd been sat. He raised and cocked his Colt.

"Fine night to be out."

The shape halted, its gangling limbs freezing. After a moment it reared up onto two, became the man Mattan had first thought it. He was black, naked save for a hessian bag slung over one shoulder. His body was thin to the point of emaciation. The bones of his face stood out sharp, eyes and cheeks sunken and shadowed.

"It suit me." The voice was thin, dry. Like one of the silent crickets had gained the power of speech.

"I was talking with a woman whose son was buried today." Mattan paced slowly and carefully toward the scarecrow figure. "She was mortally afraid he was about to be exhumed and sold to medical students. I guess you wouldn't know anything about that?"

The other laughed: a strident cackle which dragged cold fingernails down Mattan's spine. "She need have no fear on that score, boy. They all afraid of the fever. Scared the miasma goin' get 'em all." A fierce grin revealed teeth which had been filed to points. "It won't."

"And how are you so certain?"

"There's fever, and there's fever, boy." The skeletal figure shuffled sideways, towards one of the markers. "Let me show you…"

He dug a hand into the hessian bag, flinging a palmful of dust across the simple grave. Mattan briefly caught its scent: flinty, harsh, mouldy.

The black figure dropped to all fours again, crouching at the graveside.

Mad, thought Mattan. Not what he'd come looking for. He started to holster his revolver, pausing when he realised the dirt across the grave was glowing. A green light, brighter than the Moon. It sparked reflections in the crouched figure's shadowed eye sockets. Moments later the dirt twitched, heaved up. A small volcano of damp earth forced its way up from deep underground and tumbled aside. Then a pale bundle of cloth reared up like a huge white slug. The gaunt, waiting figure pounced, tearing at the winding sheet with his sharpened teeth. Something grey and mottled flopped free.

Mattan moved closer to get a better view. The mottled shape twitched, half rolling, half clawing its way from the disturbed earth. It fought its way upright, standing uneasily on bowed legs. As naked as the crouched figure, its black skin blotched with what looked like a fungus which glowed with the same light as the disturbed grave. The dead man limped a few steps and awaited its resurrector's instructions.

The crouched figure cackled again. "I done told you—it the fever. No fever like them rich whites ever heard of!" He unfolded himself from the ground, the grin vanishing from his fleshless face. "Now, boy—kill him."

The resurrected figure took a step, turning in Mattan's direction. It took another step, and another, each more steady and confident. If it hadn't been for the glazed, sunken eyes and patches of glowing fungus, Mattan might have believed it still alive.

He fired his pistol. The ball struck the advancing figure clean in the heart. It staggered, and continued to advance. The hole in its chest glowed fiercely for a second, before thick filaments grew across it, sealing the wound. Mattan fired again, hitting its skull directly above the nose. This time the creature didn't even falter.

It lashed out, knocking the Colt from Mattan's hand. Another strike went for his face. He ducked, and the roundhouse blow skimmed his hat. Mattan reached for the knife sheathed at the small of his back. Dodging another strike, he rammed it to the hilt in the creature's gut. It shook its head as though plagued by mosquitos, and reached for him again.

Its clawed hands seized Mattan around the neck. For a moment he felt their unnatural strength, and then they fell away. He thought he heard the creature whimper—the first sound it had made. It staggered back, holding up fingers which smoked and blackened.

His choker! Mattan danced out of reach, reaching up to unhook the silver necklace from his throat. The Apache he'd taken it off swore it was good luck—right up to the moment Mattan had killed him. Maybe he'd been right after all.

He swung it at the moving corpse. It flinched every time the metal grazed its blotched skin. Any fungus coming into contact with the silver dimmed and turned black.

Moving fast, Mattan ducked behind the now staggering creature. He looped the choker around its neck and snapped it tight. The dead thing moaned, clawing at the jewellery with smoking, crumbling hands. It collapsed to one knee, keening, the disfiguring fungus gradually losing its glow. The stench made Mattan gag; it was all he could do to not throw up.

The thing was on all fours, mirroring the skeletal figure crouching by the graveside. The choker had burned its way halfway through the dead thing's neck. Charred scraps of flesh peeled away and fell to the ground. Mattan snatched his knife from the thing's gut and rammed it through the gap between choker and throat. He bore down, hacking wildly. Eventually the head came free, rolling across the dirt. What glowing fungus remained dimmed. The corpse sagged and fell, properly dead.

Mattan reached down and snatched his choker from the neck stump, hanging it over his knife blade. Burnt shreds till clung to the silver. Picking up his pistol he faced the gaunt figure by the opened grave. Spitting profanities, the naked figure started to scuttle away. Mattan fired before he was out of range. The ball worked fine this time: the scrawny figure shrieked and ploughed face first into the dirt, still hissing obscenities.

Mattan flipped him onto his back with a boot tip, aiming the pistol with one hand, holding the knife and silver choker in the other.

"Don't know if silver will hurt you the same way it did that damned soul," he muttered, bending close, but keeping out of range of the filed teeth. "But I'm betting a bullet will. And a knife. We got all night to find out—and I have plenty of questions…"

* * * *

A simple metal arch formed the gateway to the boneyard. The words *Charity Cemetery & Hospital* were wrought into it. Unlike any other New Orleans graveyard Mattan had seen, this one interred its dead underground. It was a wide, flat space, planted with a few stunted trees and patchworked by yellowing grass. On the left, in the hazy distance, was the town; on the right ran the levee. A broad, rutted gravel path led from the gate towards a distant, plain white building—the hospital, he guessed. Parallel lines of simple white grave markers ran alongside the drive. And they were plentiful.

Mattan urged his pony under the gate arch. Hooves crunched on the loose gravel. He rode slowly down the drive, looking left and right at the names on the markers, the ages of the deceased and the dates of their deaths. Most were in their mid-twenties, a few younger. None had reached old age.

Pretty selective fever that ignored the older and, Mattan figured, frailer.

He spotted the name he was searching for and dismounted. On a fresh grave was a marker with a single name: *Joseph*. Carefully he removed the wilting flowers from his coat pocket and laid them across the dirt mound. He contemplated the sorry offering, lost in his own thoughts until the rattle of wheels on gravel disturbed them.

A four wheel covered buggy was coming along the drive towards him, away from the hospital. Mattan grabbed his pony's reins and led it aside so the buggy could pass. It slowed as it approached. Mattan could smell the cologne before he clearly saw the only passenger. A man.

"Something I can do for you, *m'sieu*?" He was elegantly dressed in a cotton suit and wide straw hat, with a jewelled pin through his cravat. A luxurious red beard hung off his chin, giving him an air of solemnity that wasn't reflected in the black, narrow eyes. He was smiling, but it didn't look as though it would take much to wipe it clear off his face. Both gloved hands rested on a gold-chased walking cane.

"Only if you own this graveyard," replied Mattan.

"I own pretty much everything, *m'sieu*." The smile grew predatory. "Name's Lafavreau. They call me King hereabouts. What's your business here?"

"My business."

Lefavreau glanced at the gravemound, and the flowers lying across it. "I heard some kind of dapper Indian arrived in N'Orleans a day or so ago. I guess that would be you." The narrow eyes flickered over Mattan's clothing. Lefavreau made no attempt to disguise his amusement.

Mattan inclined his head towards the hospital. "And I heard of a woman who lost her son. Now she's scared he'll end up on a dissecting slab in the building yonder."

Lefavreau laughed. He tapped his black driver—a sad-face man in a tall hat and ridiculously ornate top coat—with his cane. "Did you hear that, Jonas? This redskin thinks our future doctors may actually wish to expand their knowledge by cutting up something as inferior as a nigger's corpse."

The driver failed to react in any way.

"Let me reassure you, *mon ami sauvage*." Lefavreau aimed his cane tip in Mattan's direction. "No one is dissecting niggers. It would be a total waste, and in no one's interests." He rapped his driver's back again. "Drive on, Jonas."

As the buggy pulled away, Lefavreau raised his straw hat to Mattan. "*Au revoir, m'sieu* redskin," he called. "I do not expect we shall meet again."

Mattan watched the buggy fade behind its dust trail. "Wanna bet?" he murmured.

* * * *

Lefavreau's plantation was to the west of New Orleans. It was predictably big: cotton fields for miles. And right at the centre—a spider nestled in its web—was his sprawling hacienda style house. None of its windows were lit. Mattan would soon fix that.

He halted his pony at the entrance to the spread: a fancy stone arch leading to a long dirt drive. He dismounted and tethered the animal to a stunted, dying tree. It may have been an orange blossom once. Opening a saddle bag he removed a belt, hung with two holstered pistols: loaded and primed .36 calibre Colts, and hitched it around his waist. He also slipped a Henry rifle from its boot, levering a shell into the breech. With a gentle re-assuring pat on the pony's flank, Mattan took a hessian sack off the saddle pommel and slung it over his left shoulder.

He headed for the distant house.

There were planted fields on either side of the drive. Even though dawn was still just under an hour away, the crops were being tended. What was tending them, though, had long abandoned any pretence at humanity.

All of the figures glowed: engulfed by the fungus. Some still looked like men, despite the blotches covering them. Others not so much. The fungus grew up and out in bizarre shapes: gnarled filaments distorting the poor wretches underneath. Limbs were bloated, torsos quivering masses of phosphorescence. Many heads sprouted nodding plumes composed of filaments which had sprung up from the skull, entwining around each other and the faces beneath. Only eyes showed through: dull and glazed. And at the ends of the fattened arms, grey fingers protruded. Still able to pluck cotton bolls. Not one of them paid him the least attention.

Of the worst affected—those so consumed by the fungus they looked like rotting bolls of cotton themselves—Mattan noticed the faint corpse glow was fading. The fungus was clearly dying.

He was uncomfortably reminded of ripened puffballs ready to burst and spread their spores.

A hundred yards from the house, he heard the first snap of a gun being cocked. Mattan paused, waiting in the grey, pre-dawn light.

"Hold it right there!" a figure stepped off the shadowed veranda. He was aiming a twin barrelled shotgun in Mattan's general direction. "What's your business here?"

"Like I already said: my business." Mattan snapped up the Henry, firing two rapid shots. The guard went down without a murmur, the shotgun discharging when it hit the ground. A nearby stand of cotton was shredded.

Mattan waited. A stampede of alerted guards' boot heels came from inside the house. The main door swung open and three men burst out, armed with rifles. Mattan shot them quickly, efficiently. None so much as raised their weapons.

He waited some more. There were no more sounds.

Mattan walked across the veranda and through the open door. Inside was dark, but the moment he was indoors two lamps flared into life. Lefavreau stood in the centre of a wide, wooden floored lobby, flanked by two hard faced men. Both held oil lamps in one hand, heavy pistols in the other. It didn't look like they wanted to surrender.

Mattan fired his rifle. The hard cases went down heavy, dropping the lamps. Both shattered, spreading pools of burning oil across the wooden floor. One of the men was moaning. Mattan pulled the Henry's trigger— the hammer snapped on an empty breech. Lefavreau started to smile, his hand moving.

Mattan drew one of his Colts, finishing off the moaning man with a shot through the head. Lefavreau's hand froze.

"Outside." Mattan gestured with his pistol, stepping aside. This wasn't quite how he'd planned it: burning down the plantation house was just a lucky accident. Cautiously, skirting the burning oil, Lefavreau stepped out into the approaching dawn light. He turned to face Mattan as the Navajo stepped off the veranda.

"Is this where you shoot me down?" asked Lefavreau. He held himself defiantly.

"If I was you, maybe." Mattan sheathed his pistol. "But I'm a savage, remember."

Lefavreau's expression wavered. "So, what?"

"I had a little talk with your wizard." Mattan chuckled to himself as he reached inside the hessian sack with a gloved hand. "Or should I call him a medicine man?" He scooped out the object inside and tossed it at Lefavreau's feet. The severed head stared blindly up, filed teeth parted in a surprised laugh. "Seems he wasn't so good at taking it as he was dishing it out."

The last of Lefavreau's smile disappeared. Behind Mattan, flames were spreading through the hacienda, crawling up the doorframe and fingering the shutters. They cast an uncertain light over Lefavreau's face, making it twitch. Mattan stepped away from the growing heat, placing the plantation owner between it and him.

"Where did you find him?"

Lefavreau took another look at the head before kicking it aside. "I have plantations in the Caribbean, family businesses. He came with them."

"Convenient."

Lefavreau shrugged. "I was going to have him flogged to death. He was … impolite to a white woman. He saved himself when he told me about his … talent. He made himself useful."

"Slipping someone a poison so that they appeared dead, then using bad medicine to resurrect them. That dust. Give them a new life, as a slave."

"The government are outlawing slavery—or had you not heard?"

"I heard. So you replaced living slaves with those poor souls." Mattan inclining his head towards the cotton fields. None of the glowing things out there had so much as glanced their way.

"A corpse is the property of no one—not even themselves. I am breaking no laws that I am aware of."

"How about bodysnatching?"

The house was fully ablaze, Lefavreau just a silhouette against the flames. Even in his new position, Mattan could feel the warmth. A breeze—pulled in by the growing column of heat—blew against his neck.

Lefavreau shrugged again. "A moot point."

"Your tame wizard also told me the raised dead don't last. That the fungus eventually dissolves them."

"There are ants in Brazil which suffer a similar fate, I believe. A fungus first controls and then consumes them. Mine is an elegant solution, *n'est-ce pas*? The dissolution creates more spores, which in turn creates more workers."

"Which explains the latest fever victims." Mattan slid the sack off his shoulder. "But if you don't scatter the dust across the victims' graves before the effects of the poison wear off—two or three days, so I'm told—they start to come round."

"You were persuasive, *mon sauvage*." The plantation owner seemed relaxed again. Maybe he thought he was playing for time.

Mattan nodded. "The one thing he never told me, though: what happens if someone is doused in that dust before they're fed the poison. You think we should find out?"

Lefavreau's poise deserted him. Finally he'd figured out what Mattan had in mind. Before he could run, Mattan raised the hessian sack by the bottom corners and shook it. The dusty contents billowed out, sucked towards the growing inferno. The plantation owner was caught in its path.

The dust seemed possessed of its own life, determined to anchor onto every surface. Lefavreau's clothes, his face, his beard, his eyes—in seconds they were coated. He coughed violently, scrubbing at his eyes, staggering. What dust didn't fall on him was swept up by the fire.

Mattan stepped back, watching, curious, peeling of his leather gloves—just to be safe. At first the dust seemed nothing more than an irritation. Lefavreau's coughing doubled him up. He spat out a gob of grey phlegm. Twin tracks formed down his cheeks as tears welled in his eyes. Mattan's hand rested on a pistol butt; maybe he'd have to shoot the man after all.

The grey powder began to glow. At first it was no different from the fungus infesting the pickers in the fields: a soft green radiance. Then it grew in intensity, turned orange, yellow, a blazing white. Lefavreau's beard shrivelled. He was no longer a silhouette: his white-hot form showed even against the blazing house. He screamed, staggering, dropping to his knees, then all fours.

His shape changed, bulging and swelling. Impossibly fast, glowing fibres sprang from his heaving flesh, wriggling and entwining themselves. Some reached for the air, others tried to root themselves in the dirt. All the while Lefavreau thrashed and keened. What was left of his human form tried to crawl towards Mattan.

The porch roof collapsed, throwing sparks towards the paling sky. Mattan glanced towards the inferno, then back at what was left of the plantation owner. It was just a mewling, shapeless blob. The Navajo couldn't guess how it was able to make sounds anymore.

Mattan threw his gloves into the flames and backed off. He noticed a faint glow along some of the fingers. In a last moment stroke of mercy, he grabbed a burning chunk of timber from the porch and dropped it onto Lefavreau. The bright shape burst into flame immediately. Maybe it was already hot—the brilliant white a sign of some kind of internal combustion. For a few seconds more it writhed, then as the flames took complete hold, it lay still. The grasping fibres shrivelled and blackened. As more of the house collapsed, Lefavreau became indistinguishable from the burning ruins littering the ground.

The blaze would attract attention in the town; best if Mattan wasn't here when they arrived. But there was one last thing to do.

Some of those poor bastards in the fields were about ready to collapse and produce more of that dust. Spores, Lefavreau called it. Mattan didn't think leaving that stuff lying around was such a good idea.

He took up two more brands, one in each hand, and walked towards the fields.

* * * *

She heard the loud rap on her door, and what sounded like Joseph's voice. She shook her head. No time to go soft, girl! He gone. You can't hear no voice!

"Mary!" That wasn't her boy—it was that crazy Indian in his fancy duds.

She went out to the front—and almost screamed at what stood there. Mattan, looking smudged and tired, and Joseph—no less filthy, no less spent. His eyes lit up when her saw her, though. He ran forward—though he looked to have no energy.

Mary hugged her boy, staring over his shoulder through blurred eyes.

"I told you to pray for better news," the Indian said.

"But … how…?" she managed to ask.

"I'm a savage." He smiled, almost shyly. It softened his flinty gaze. "We savages know things." He turned and hauled himself up into the painted pony's saddle. "Such as there's likely to be changes over at Lefavreau's plantation. Such as whoever takes it on will likely be hiring."

Mary was aware she was squeezing Joseph with the same kind of fierceness that she'd felt off Mattan earlier, when he'd hugged her.

"Who'd you lose?" she asked.

He shook his head. "Long story. I don't have the patience to tell it."

"Might sooth your soul if you did."

He smiled again: this time it was bleak. The mask was once again across his face. "Wanna bet?"

He turned his pony's head and rode away.

EVIL HARVEST

K.A. Opperman

The pumpkins rise from emerald mist,
On bodies of the risen dead;
Past vines and gravestones they persist,
Each revenant with pumpkin head.

A grinning witch-moon, poison-green,
Has pulled the corpses from their sleep,
To wander forth this Halloween
Wherever living vines may creep.

The pumpkins give them dim new life,
With vines that weave through skin and bone.
With them the autumn farms grow rife—
An evil harvest darkly sown.

For every jack-o'-lantern carved,
Another human life must fall—
For grim revenge the gourds are starved,
And from the pumpkin patch, they crawl.

TO DIE, TO SLEEP, NO MORE
Erica Ruppert

Reports of a new plague had begun a little less than a year before, scattered through Europe and Asia. And then like a wave crashing, the sickness was everywhere. Travel bans and quarantines didn't stop it. Health care systems collapsed as it swept through, overwhelmed by its ferocity.

It started with a sudden fever, a wracking wet cough. Then came a searing headache, bloodshot eyes, cramps, hemorrhage, organ failure. The CDC said it was certainly transmitted by close contact, but it had spread to so many, so fast, it must also be airborne. So far, it had killed nearly eighty percent of those infected. Many people called it simply the flu, knowing it wasn't. But it was easier than calling it a plague.

"Laura's mother says it came from the Israelis. A bioweapon. They made it look like Iran was behind it," Corry said.

"Laura's mother is nuts," Tom said. "And Laura's not far behind her."

"Then how did it start?" Corry asked, her voice rising.

Tom slammed the drawer shut and leaned against the counter. He wouldn't look at her. He drew a deep breath before he answered. "They don't know. Not yet, at any rate. Maybe when it's run its course and people develop some immunity they'll have time to figure it out."

"*We* don't have time," Corry said.

Tom grunted, but wouldn't look at her. "Maybe it's our punishment," he said.

When he began to cough, Corry walked away. She needed to check on Ruby again.

* * * *

The city changed as the plague swept through that winter. Hospitals had stopped taking in patients weeks ago as their staffs died along with the plague's other victims. The ugly, too-sweet stink of rotten meat lingered now in pockets, where no-one had come to bury the bodies. What was left of the government concentrated its depleted resources on the living. The dark ages had returned.

Corry wondered only briefly about how quickly it had all fallen apart. It didn't really matter, now.

She filled a bowl with water and rubbing alcohol, and listened as Ruby struggled to breathe.

Tom had set up a cot for the girl on the tiny sun porch off the kitchen, so they could keep a close watch over her. Corry squeezed into the narrow space and knelt beside her daughter. She wiped Ruby's face and neck gently with a wet cloth, trying to cool her fever. The sharp smell of the alcohol cut through the sick-room stink for a moment before it evaporated.

"Mommy," Ruby mumbled, half-awake.

Beneath the flush of fever Ruby's skin had faded to a yellowish pallor, her cheeks and eyes sunken, the curves and angles of her small skull pushing up like a mask. Corry was careful, afraid of ripping the girl's fragile skin.

Then she dipped the cloth in the bowl again, and ran it over her own face. She shivered, and she burned.

* * * *

People in the streets wore surgical masks and disposable gloves. Some carried spray bottles of bleach with them. Some carried amulets they had made or bought, designed to ward away evil. Each day there were fewer people out, as they hid or sickened and died. Corry wondered how far faith could carry them, now.

She jumped when she heard the front door bang shut. She had fallen asleep next to Ruby.

"Tom?" she called out, struggling to stand on numb legs.

"It's just me," he said, and coughed.

"Did you go out?" she said, limping into the kitchen as he walked in.

"I heard about something," he said. He carried an old baby food jar full of a thick black liquid, a larger jar of what looked like olive oil, and a photocopied list of instructions.

"What is all that?" Corry said, reaching for the jars. Tom kept them away from her, placing them gently on the kitchen counter. From his pocket he pulled a third jar, empty and clean.

"You have no idea how much these cost," he said. His voice was thick with phlegm. "But if they work, it doesn't matter."

Corry picked up the baby food jar. It was hot to the touch.

"But what is it? Where did you get it?"

"Benny's wife. She's a botanist. She's been trying to find some kind of remedy for the flu, and she's pretty sure this will do it."

Tom shook his head, looking past Corry.

"Pretty sure. She said it showed some effect when she gave it to her dog. It's not a cure. But, maybe."

Corry picked up the instruction sheet and read over it.

"This isn't botany," she said. "This looks like voodoo magic."

Tom shrugged. "It probably is. At this point, what would it hurt?"

Corry put the paper down beside the jars and smoothed it flat. She shook her head, unable to give any real reason it would.

"I think we've all gone mad," she said.

* * * *

Tom wasn't there when Ruby finally died.

He couldn't take the girl's suffering, or Corry's dull recounting of Laura's theories on the plague.

"That woman is nuts, and you're nuts for even listening to her," he had said.

Maybe I am, Corry thought. Maybe you are, with your potions. Maybe it doesn't matter.

What mattered was Ruby, and her life sputtering out.

Tom went over the directions with Corry, taking turns reading them aloud until they were both sure of the sequence. She didn't bother to disagree with his magical thinking. It gave him some comfort. That might be all this was worth.

He laid the jars out on a clean cloth on the sun porch floor, where Corry would be able to reach them easily. He kissed Corry, and kissed Ruby. He held Ruby's hot, boneless hand for a long while, watching her fail. Then he went to sit on the front porch, unable to see the task through.

Corry crouched alone at her daughter's bedside with the empty jar pressed to the Ruby's mouth to catch her final breath. She knew it wouldn't be much longer. Her fingers were clumsy. The jar opening kept slipping down over Ruby's tiny chin. Corry listened to the death rattle buzzing in her daughter's throat, and tried to keep from crying.

When the rattle stopped, Corry held her own breath to listen to the silence. She kept the jar in place, examining Ruby's face for any sign of life. But she was gone.

Corry slid the jar carefully off her daughter's mouth. She capped the jar tightly, her hands shaking, and put it aside to ready the rest. She willed herself not to cry.

Following the instructions, she rubbed oil into Ruby's skin, through her hair, into the secret places of her body. She dipped a sponge into the black fluid and swabbed Ruby's mouth with it, then poured a thin sticky stream into her dull half-lidded eyes. She arranged Ruby's body neatly on the bed, pulling the covers back. How thin Ruby had become with this sickness riding her. She had been such a healthy girl, before.

Corry broke and sobbed tearlessly, but quickly stifled herself. She picked up the jar that had caught Ruby's last breath. She bit into her tongue and the inside of her cheek, hard, and when she tasted blood she opened the jar and spat into it. Then she added more black fluid, enough to pour, and swirled it until it mixed.

She slipped a hand behind Ruby's neck and lifted her head, then tipped the jar up against her lips. The fluid ran out at the corners of the girl's slack mouth. Corry lay her flat again, hoping enough had run down her throat.

Corry floated between hope and despair. She wasn't sure how long this should take, or what it would look like if it happened. If it could happen. If she wasn't trying to convince herself to deny the inevitable.

She kept busy. She lined the jars up neatly on their cloth, capping the oil and the black fluid. She wondered if she should wash out the other one. She wondered if she should go get Tom. She wiped a streak of red from Ruby's cheek.

Then she waited.

* * * *

Some time later Tom came back in, coughing. Corry didn't move. She kept her eyes on Ruby. She believed she had seen a tremor move across the girl's body, like a ripple in water. She wanted to see it again.

"Did you finish?" Tom said, leaning into the porch.

"Shh. Yes," Corry whispered. She glanced up at Tom. He looked bad. His face was sallow, with deep creases around his mouth. He tried to swallow another cough. Ruby's body trembled again.

"Did you see that?" Tom hissed. "What's happening?" he asked.

"I don't know," Corry said.

He pushed into the narrow space beside the bed, shoulder to shoulder with Corry.

"Is it working? Are you sure you did it right?" he said, grabbing her arm, squeezing it too tightly. His hand was hot. She shrugged away.

"I did exactly as you told me," Corry said, watching Ruby's body twitch and jerk.

"It looks like it hurts," he said.

Corry didn't answer him. She didn't want to think about any more pain.

She stroked Ruby's dirty hair, smoothing the dark strands around the girl's withered face. For a moment the tremors stopped, and Ruby lay still. Then the empty body spasmed, bent, and almost sat up before falling back.

Ruby gasped, a terrible, hollow sound with no breath behind it. Her mouth moved.

"Mommy," she said in a dry, unfamiliar voice. "I want my mommy."

Corry screamed and fell back, but Tom leaned forward toward his struggling daughter.

"She's back," he said, his voice rising. Anything else he tried to say was lost in a coughing fit.

* * * *

Corry lost track of the days after Ruby came back. Tom came and went, coughing, struggling. Sometimes she heard him in the yard, working. Then Corry lost track of him, as well.

She went as far as the front steps to look for him, once, and found that a cool, damp spring had finally come.

A flier was stuck into the screen door handle. She glanced at the houses across the street. Fliers had been left on them, too. More copies blew down the street and across lawns. She pulled the paper loose and read its bolded, all-caps message.

THE ANSWER TO YOUR PRAYERS IS HERE it said. THE DOCTORS DON'T KNOW BUT I DO. Then, it listed a phone number for more information.

Corry wanted to laugh at the idiot simplicity of it. Whoever had strewn the fliers about had no idea. There were no prayers to answer, any more.

* * * *

"I'm scared of her," Tom said one day, breathless and weak. Corry stared at him, flatly.

"It's too late for that now," she said. "This is what you wanted."

"Not this," he said. "Not this."

But Corry was trapped in the ritual, responsible for what they had done. She burned sage and anointed her daughter every day, rubbing the oil into Ruby's cold skin, swabbing Ruby's slack mouth with the black potion, dropping it into her filmy eyes.

"I want my mommy," Ruby said, the words slurred on the grey meat of her tongue.

Corry's skin burned, now. The pain behind her eyes swelled until her vision was a narrow band. Sometimes, Corry remembered to eat. Sometimes, she forgot, because Ruby never needed to eat. Ruby never needed to sleep. Corry tended her daughter according the photocopied instructions, but what Ruby needed was beyond what Corry could give.

Tom left. She heard him rattling tools in the garage. He did not come back.

* * * *

Ruby stood beside Corry's bed like a carving, like a broken stick. There was no life in her wasted body. She decayed, despite the oil and the black fluid. Her blank presence was a drain, unanswerable.

"I want my mommy," the dead girl whined in a voice like wind over long grass.

Corry sat up and reached out to stroke her daughter's cold face. She was alone.

"It's okay, baby. I'm right here."

"I want my mommy," Ruby said again. And again. And again. The dead girl repeated her plea every few seconds like a metronome.

"Ruby, I'm here," Corry said. She nudged her daughter back from the edge of the bed so she could get up.

"I want my mommy," Ruby said. Her glazed eyes focused on nothing. Her tone didn't change.

Corry wiped at her own sweaty face. Her bones hurt. She wanted to sleep.

"Come here, baby," she said.

Ruby followed her stiffly, into the kitchen. Corry dug through a drawer until she found the duct tape.

"I want my mommy," Ruby said.

"Hush, now," Corry said, and sealed her mouth.

Ruby's clouded eyes still stared, and her rotten jaw still moved, but no voice came through the tape. Corry smiled, patting Ruby's softening head.

"Good girl," she said.

* * * *

As the sun rose Corry laid out the jars as she had done every morning since the first, following the ritual.

She rubbed the oil into Ruby's slipping skin, cringing as the tissues shifted under her hands. She loosened the tape around the dead child's moving mouth, but it stuck to the withered flesh and left Ruby's lip hanging like a torn hem. Corry screamed, and burst into tears.

Ruby's thin, raspy voice spilled out, unintelligible now but making the same demand. Corry cried with messy sobs, steeled herself, and swabbed Ruby's ripped, rotten mouth. Her touch dislodged most of the baby teeth from the slushy gums.

She stopped, helpless against the drag of dissolution. Ruby made her noises, needy and inconsolable.

Corry struggled to breathe as she coughed, sudden and deep, her throat full of mucus. She forced herself to the kitchen sink, poured out what was left in the jars, and spat into the mess as she washed it down the drain.

* * * *

Tom had died in the yard, near a grave he had dug for Ruby. She remembered, now. He had given up on the ritual, the resurrection. She had lost track.

Corry rolled his body into the small hole. It didn't fit. She didn't care. She could barely focus through the pain inside her eyes and the throbbing ache in her joints and her belly. She scraped dirt over Tom's wasted body with her bare hands. This was the best she could do for him.

Behind her, Corry heard the drag of Ruby's footsteps coming over the lawn. Her daughter's stench enveloped her as Ruby came to stand at her shoulder.

"I want my mommy," Ruby almost wheezed. There was not enough flesh left in her mouth and throat to form the words, but Corry could fill in the gaps. She turned on her knees to look at the remains of her daughter. Ruby's bare jaw still worked to speak her need. It would never stop.

Corry looked away. Her head felt as if it would crack open. Her vision dimmed. She lowered herself onto the cool dirt of her husband's grave, and closed her eyes.

Above her, Ruby stood like a broken branch driven into the earth, the shreds of her voice begging, and begging, and begging.

RUN, MONSTER, RUN
Teasha Seitz

My Darling,

I am alive, and I miss you. I miss your freckles that start on one cheek and flow across the bridge of your nose to the other cheek. I miss your hair smelling of strawberry shampoo. I miss how soft and smooth your lips are. I miss how you snort when you laugh hard. I love you. I will always love you, but we cannot be together. I wanted you to know the truth. They are looking for me. I cannot risk contacting you further. I hope this letter reaches you.

Running was a passion for me. I'd shared my euphoria after a good run with you, had shown you my high school track awards. You knew, without me telling you, when I left our bed early in the mornings, it was to go for a run.

The last time we were together, I slipped quietly from our home as to not wake you. It was late August; the heatwave ended when a storm the night before cleaned the city air and left cooler temperatures and a slight breeze that morning. I relished the cool air as I ran my normal route on the Three Rivers Heritage Trail. The sun rose to glint off the water, sending shards of sunlight dancing and flashing across the tops of the confluence of the rivers. A blur of movement out of the corner of my eye grabbed my attention; I started to turn when a stranger crashed into me and plunged a knife into my back.

Stabbing pain from the blade radiated at the base of my neck as my limbs went dead, my brain panicked, and I fell to the ground. A woman sitting on a park bench screamed, and a passing jogger stopped to bend over me as my attacker fled towards downtown. My vision went yellow and shrank to a pinpoint before it all went black. My Good Samaritan called 911, but as he made the call, the sound grew distant and faded out.

When I had made my will and donated my body to my alma mater, I had pictured medical students practicing on my wrinkled frail frame worn out by a long life. But, as you know, I willed my corpse to their science department without restrictions.

I didn't know that I would die while young and healthy, and I didn't know the university had been receiving private donations from rich, powerful white men who felt entitled to immortality. The school received millions to experiment with the use of stem cells in both prolonging lives and reanimating the dead.

There was so much that I didn't know and much I still don't. My death was not preceded by my whole life flashing before my eyes, nor was it followed by any epiphanies. No guiding white light beckoned. It had all happened so fast. In a vague distant way, I was aware of being dead, but I was cocooned in nothing, no sight, or sound, sensation, or emotion touched me.

Until a faint voice spoke to me, "Try to relax. I'm Dr. Frank. I'm going to help, but you have to trust me." The soft voice was low pitched, husky, and feminine. It pulled me from my isolation.

Words fail to describe purgatory; I was bereft of physical sensations but certain in the knowledge of the presence of others. Some were inert as I had been, a few moved with a purpose towards an unknown destination. Restless ones raged, emanating waves of anger, desperation, hate, and fury. They were spirits unable to let go of the excess of emotions upon their deaths.

"Patients at your stage of recovery often experience hallucinations." Dr. Frank's sexy voice was the kind I would imagine if I were to have delusions. Her voice lured me towards her even as the voices of the restless ones arose in a cacophony. The silence broken by Dr. Frank was filled with screams of anger, madness, and terror. Those voices were not fantasies.

My nerves burned with fire at the same time my body felt so cold it was chilled to the bone when the electric current Dr. Frank applied to restart my heart lit me up like a beacon to the restless spirits. They surged towards me. With the return of physical sensations, I felt hands grasp and claw onto my arms, legs, hair, as I was ripped across the border between life and death. I did not cross alone.

"Stop panicking; you're hyperventilating. Let the machine control your breathing. Don't fight it. Feel the rhythm—in… two…three…four … and out…two…three…four. Nice and easy. You can do this."

Dr. Frank's warm, contralto voice was soothing, and I followed her instructions. My breathing eased but not my conviction that others had used my return to life to escape. What she was doing was wrong.

I wanted to tell her to stop. I wanted to say no. But movement was impossible, let alone speech. I struggled to try to open my eyes.

"You're doing great. I saw an eye twitch, and that's fantastic. It will be a few hours before we'd expect sight to start to return. Nerve impulses and motor skills take a little longer. You may experience numbness, pain, tingling, and mixed signals when nerve impulses jump tracks."

A knock on a door and a soft whoosh, a change in air pressure as it opened.

A young, male voice said, "Sorry for the interruption, Dr. Frank, but the Dean called for the third time this morning. He wants to discuss the protests on campus. I tried to explain that the initial awakening is more like labor and delivery rather than a procedure and that you feel compelled to handle each one personally. But he insisted that I ask you directly about how long you'll be indisposed."

"Those protesters are the modern-day equivalent of villagers with pitchforks and torches. They are ignorant and gullible. Scientific advancement has always been met with superstitious fear. Once my research and findings have been accepted by the scientific community, no one will even remember the fringe nut jobs that stood against it." The doctor's voice had changed abruptly from the cultivated, honeyed tones of her bedside manner to reveal a normal speaking voice full of judgment and cockiness. "The dean needs to grow a pair. But don't tell him any of that. Let him know, you spoke with me, and that I'm at a crucial stage in my experiment and cannot be interrupted further."

That was the beginning of my recovery, and over the next week, whenever the good doctor attended to me personally, she was as considerate and charming a physician as I could want, but I never forgot the time when her mask had slipped and revealed the self-importance and ambition behind her projected warmth.

And I could not forget the restless spirits who had used my crossing as a bridge. Dr. Frank had torn the veil and released them. I didn't know what spirits might do, but I remembered how tortured they had sounded and felt the negative emotions they projected. Nothing good could come from so much pain. I needed to warn her.

"Isssrong," I said in a hoarse whisper. Damn w's. My voice slow, slurred, and with some letters stubbornly absent, speech slower to return than cognitive function.

Dr. Frank looked up from my chart, and then closed the app, moved up the side of the bed and gently lifted one of my hands. Her hand was cool and dry against my palm. She looked at me with a convincing expression of tender concern, except for the coldness behind her eyes as she said. "You've been making remarkable progress. Everything may feel all wrong right now but give your recovery more time."

"Not body rong, soul." Her face hardened at my attempt to clarify. She dropped my hand and snapped her head up to stare at an empty spot on the wall before she left the room without another word or glance in my direction.

There'd been earlier experiments, patients, like myself, trapped here under her care. I watched as my predecessors were wheeled down the hall and spoon-fed in a common dining area. Symptoms of agitation in the patients were treated with sedation but did not prevent the staff from whispered gossip.

Ten days after my reawakening, two orderlies came into to change the bedding while I shuffled to a chair. One was an older lady with short cut grey hair, and the other was a younger man his head shaved.

"Did you hear what happened to Cheryl?" asked the woman.

"I heard she claimed a dining room chair flew across the room, slammed into the window and broke the inner glass pane." He glanced at the door to check for anyone listening.

"Yeah, well, Dr. Frank walked into the dining hall and told Cheryl that security had been called to escort Cheryl from the building, and the cost of the window would be deducted from her last check, which would be mailed to her and then Dr. Frank reminded her of the non-disclosure that all the staff signs. Dr. Frank gave Cheryl this hard look, daring her to reply and Cheryl dropped her head and mumbled how it wasn't her fault but then left all quiet with the guards. She didn't even put up a fight, but we all knew Cheryl would have never broken that window."

The orderlies completed the task and moved on with their conversation to another room.

There was high turnover in the staff at the campus research hospital, I'd see the same nurse a few times and then never again, and a new face would be taking my vitals or drawing blood samples. While Dr. Frank convinced the patients' hallucinations, nightmares, and uneasy feelings were side effects of the treatment; she lacked any explanation as to why the staff often experienced the same.

A constant chill never left no matter the number of heated blankets or the cranked up thermostats. Complaints of feeling cold were a ceaseless susurrus punctuated by screams, whimpers, and pleas for help from the patients. Nurses responded to vital signs wirelessly relayed to their iPads rather than the voices of the people in their care.

My grandmother's ghost would visit me. She came every day the first week, but it wasn't until the second week of her daily visits that I realized what I was seeing. Who/what she/it was a young, black, and white version of my grandmother. She had been much older when I knew her, but I recognized the disapproving, reproachful stare she gave me—arms crossed, her eyebrows drawn down and her thin lips pressed so tightly together they disappeared into a single straight line. She'd flicker in and stare at me and then flicker out, each visit accompanied by a fresh sense of shame. She had given me the same look when I was five and had accidentally peed on the carpet.

My current transgression was exponentially worse and as involuntary. My reanimation was a grievous sin against the laws of the universe. My re-birth had weakened the separation between life and death, allowed others to return.

My physical recovery was remarkable when compared to other residents. I continued to improve over the following week and was walking unassisted by the end of it. The other patients I'd glimpsed on our ward were confined to wheelchairs or shuffled slowly with walkers. The difference being I was the youngest person given the treatment, a combination of steroids, stem cells, and a proprietary drug, as explained by Dr. Frank. The others were of advanced old age.

By the fourth week, my physical therapy included me using weight machines and exercise equipment. I was far stronger than I had been before, able to bench press five times my body weight and sprint at the tread mill's top speed.

At the end of September, five weeks after my death, I stood in front of the tinted glass window and longed for pounding pavement with my feet, sun on my skin, and fresh air in my lungs. Running on a treadmill is not the same as being out under the sky and feeling the world is open to you.

I thought of you often. I missed the curve of your hips and how we fit together perfectly when we spooned. My heart broke when I thought of your pain as you mourned me. I grieved for our life, trusting when I did return; you would love me even if my grandmother's ghost followed me home to continue the daily visits of disapproval.

Dr. Frank interrupted my thoughts at the window when she entered my room on her rounds. I kept my back to her as I asked, "When can I go home?" I had w's now, but with more of a breathy whistle than I liked. I turned around in time to see her calculating expression masked by a sympathetic gaze.

"I need to monitor your progress," she said, "and continue to collect data for a considerable amount of time for the results to be scientifically sound. Having you here, on the premises, allows for an immediate response should any crisis arise. We can do some more evaluations of your mental and physical fitness." Dr. Frank's emphasis on the word mental clarified in my mind what she meant.

When I had told her it was wrong, she'd known my intent. Dr. Frank considered any references to souls or spirits as hallucinatory side effects.

The slightest hint of objection to the process based on moral, religious, or supernatural beliefs would be reason enough for continued seclusion in secrecy. Dr. Frank's dedication was to the program's success. The current protocols in place meant there was no contact between any of the patients and their former lives. The world considered all of us as dead, leaving us none of our rights. We had donated our remains and no longer owned ourselves.

I couldn't deny the ghosts' presences. I had to escape if I was going to see you again.

Our special care unit was one, long hallway flanked with rooms, contained at the top of four floors with a carefully monitored set of elevators at one end and a fire escape with a door alarm on the other. I briefly considered tying together bedsheets and breaking a window, but laughed out loud at the absurdity. A plan like that would only work in a movie.

I decided to start a small fire, something that would set off the alarm system and escape during the confusion of an evacuation. It's the things we don't know that complicate a simple plan.

A stolen battery, a tin foil lid from a food tray, and a private moment in the men's bathroom were all I required to put my plan into action. I piled unrolled toilet paper on top of the metal cover from the paper towel holder, for fuel and containment.

The immediate response of the hospital's fire suppression system was to flood the entire bathroom. Water sprayed from the sprinkler without a peep from any alarm, drenching everything including me.

I would have snuck back to my room, but two orderlies and a security guard slammed through the bathroom door. The first orderly grabbed the front of my gown—instinct kicked in—and I put my hands on his chest and shoved. Our faces mirrored each other's surprise as the man flew across the room, crashed into the wall, and stayed crumpled inside the hole his body made.

The security guard threw a wide, slow roundhouse punch at my jaw. I leaned back, then stepped forward as I counterpunched with a straight jab. The guard's head jerked back. His neck snapped with a loud crack that echoed off the walls. The second orderly ran while I stood stunned, shocked by my actions.

I hadn't meant to hurt anyone, but two people were dead.

In the mirrors, I saw a stranger's reflection, with a shaggy beard and dripping wet overgrown hair. Was that still me in there? Or was I a monster Dr. Frank had made?

An alarm sounded, followed by a lockdown announcement but before the orderly who ran could bring reinforcements; I bolted.

Dr. Frank stood in the hallway and blocked my escape. Her shaking hands pointed a handgun at me.

"Stop!" she shouted, high-pitched in her panic.

I froze. We stood and stared at each other.

My grandmother's ghost flickered in next to Dr. Frank. Instead of the thin line of disapproval, the ghost's mouth snarled.

Dr. Frank pivoted to point her weapon at the ghost, her hands, already shaking, jerked spasmodically and then pulled the trigger, while the doctor's head whipped back and forth in denial.

I reacted to the first shot like it was a starter pistol, running faster than I thought possible. Motion blurred details until I pried open the elevator doors and slid down the maintenance ladder before the echoes of the last shot and clicks of dry firing ended.

My grandmother's ghost shouted after me, "Run, monster, run!"

Free of the hospital, I sprinted off-campus and kept running. At the edge of the city, I broke into a Dollar General, stole clothes and supplies. Then I ran for the Appalachian Trail and headed south.

I've stopped to rest at a campsite with a mail drop to write to you. I hope knowing I'm alive will comfort you as thoughts of you are my only comfort. I had to tell you what had become of me so that someone would know the truth. The monster I had been twisted into. No matter how fast or far I run, I can't escape what I have done. Men are dead because of me. All I wanted was to be with you, and now I know I can't.

The moon highlights the trail before me, and the beauty of the woods surrounds me, but the rhythm of my steps beats out one thought repeatedly, three words said over and over like a mantra.

Run, monster, run
Run, monster, run
Run, monster, run

ANOTHER NIGHT IN BAYOU SAUVAGE
Chad Hensley

A slice of moon cut through the brooding clouds to reflect a thousand blinking eyes across the bayou's glassy surface. Henri Bordeaux shook his head as he maneuvered the pirogue through the pitch-black swamp, accompanied by the songs of midnight insects. The old Cajun chewed nervously at the wad of tobacco in his cheek and gripped his long, cane pole with weary hands. He pushed the pole down into the stagnant waters to propel the pirogue. He stared down at the silent man who sat beside him and hoped that tonight he could pay back a favor.

Henri had never met Charles Gayarre until tonight, but the man's wife was another matter. She had danced with Henri at a Fais-do-do many years ago and he could still remember the beauty of her robin blue egg eyes and the sweet scent upon her breasts that night.

Henri shook his head as if to dispel the thought and looked upon his companion, moonlight pooling upon jaundiced withered flesh. Gayarre looked like he was already dead. Tiny silver pupils gazed into empty space, no longer blinking. Dry, bruised lips had shriveled into a perpetual scowl. The fact that the man's mouth was stitched shut didn't help matters; an earlier attempt to cure his zombification, suture threads already starting to unravel. A few hours ago, the man had ceased to breathe and Henri knew that if they did not find the Houngan soon, it would not matter.

The pirogue rounded a huge cypress tree, giant skeletal branches scraping at the old Cajun's head. A drum beat began to reverberate through the bayou. A faint glow appeared in the darkness ahead. Henri steered the small boat toward the light, and the radiance grew brighter as they approached.

A shoreline breached the bayou, the ground sloping up into a hillside. A handful of eroding headstones dotted the grassy incline. A sea of small candles had been placed upon the crumbling stones and soggy black soil. A giant Negro stood in the center of the small graveyard. Candlelight danced on the perspiration of his shiny, bald head. A smiling white skull drawn with clown paint covered his fat face. His bloodshot eyes were swollen as if from lack of sleep. He held his sinewy arms to a massive chest of corded muscle and scar tissue. In a low, hollow voice he called, "Bring the man to me, Bordeaux."

An emaciated boy sat cross-legged at the giant man's feet. His bony hands beat mechanically upon a small drum between his legs. The child was also bald, but his flesh was even more livid than Gayarre's, and his race was impossible to discern. The boy's eyes glimmered strangely, silver pupils sparkling. His face remained an expressionless mask as his body spasmed with each drum beat.

Henri steered the pirogue to a stretch of shore and dropped the pole to the ground. He bend down and retrieved a small sack at his feet. He stepped out of the boat, the hairs on the back of his neck prickling as Gayarre rose to his feet and followed him. The old Cajun threw the bag to the ground and spat. The sack split open and a sea of gold coins poured onto the upturned earth. "All right, here the man," Henri snapped. "Now be appeased. Houngan got his 'get-even' money and makes the folks fear him." He paused and took a slow, deep breath of the night swamp. "Remove the zombie mojo and let me take the man home."

The voodoo priest snorted loudly, the drum beat fell silent, and Gayarre froze in mid-step. "Bordeaux, this was not your busy. No more will this man force himself upon his female slaves." The black man took a step forward and the shadows behind him congealed into an open grave. The plot appeared freshly dug but a half-eroded cherub still perched on the crumbling headstone. The darkness in the mound moved and a fowl stench filled the air. A multitude of tiny silver eyes fell upon Henri and the old Cajun knew that something unnatural crawled.

"Gayarre's soul will feed the loa," the black man shouted, motioning toward the grave with a puffy, bulbous finger.

A metallic scraping sound filled Henri's ears and he knew that the thing was calling to him. He suddenly felt like he had just gulped a pint of whiskey. He grit his teeth and spat. "That beast ain't no bayou spirit, Houngan. No price be worth whatever bargain you done made," Henri scowled.

"I don't expect you to understand, Bordeaux. The loa has whispered of secrets that would snap your mind, old man," bellowed the voodoo priest. A translucent pink tendril slithered out of the grave and wrapped around the black man's ankle. A second appendage snaked around the boy's throat, the tip attaching like a leech to the back of the child's head. A loud slurping filled the swamp as sustenance was sucked from the child's body.

An insane jubilation gripped the black man. His body began to convulse and his eyes shimmered strangely. "Now go back and tell the Lady Gayarre she is a widow. I have decided that you must fetch another bag of her husband's money if she is to morn in peace," the Houngan threatened.

"Lady Gayarre ain't ever done you no harm. A bargain was struck and now you must own up to your end of it," Bordeaux demanded.

A loud wet fluttering came from within the mound. A searing pain shot through the old Cajun. His heart pounded within his temples and his vision blurred into a silver sheen. He balled his fists with white knuckle strain. His kneels bucked and he slumped to the ground.

A bestial howl tore from the throat of Charles Gayarre. The blood red savagery of a cornered beast replaced the silver hue of his eyes and the man threw himself upon the amorphous writhing mass that slithered out of the pit. His flaying arms and legs dug into soft, membranous flesh. Milky ochre poured from great gouged patches. Deep serrations began to appear on Gayarre's body though no blood came from the wounds. The black man screamed as a giant proboscis plunged into his chest, lifted him into the air and drained his body.

The zombie child beneath him laughed hysterically, his body crumbling into a chalky dust. A dozen whip-like appendages shot from the creature's body and struck at Gayarre but the man continued to fight.

Henri's senses returned to him and he hurried to his feet. He took one look at the scene before him and knew that even if Charles Gayarre survived, there would be little left to call human. The old Cajun retrieved his pole and stepped into his pirogue. He pushed off without looking back, hoping that he would not have to travel this part of the bayou for many nights to come.

✗

ALLEN K.
'16

KIFARO
Dilman Dila

Jamwa knew where he was the moment he woke up. Emergency room. Machines bleeped. A nurse watched an array of monitors, a bored expression on her face. He could not understand how he got there. The last memory he had was his phone ringing. He sat up, and turned to see his head on the pillow, deep cuts on his cheek and forehead, eyes closed as though in a peaceful sleep. No medics were working on him, only machines monitoring his progress. He slipped off the bed, afraid of his own body.

Am I dead?

The door opened. A doctor and two nurses walked in. The nurse at the monitor turned to them with a slight shrug.

"Too late," she said. "He stopped breathing."

The doctor let out a sigh, his shoulders sagged in exhaustion. His lips pursed in despair at handling so many patients and not really helping any, in anger at the government for not employing more medics to ease his workload. For a moment he stood akimbo, glaring at Jamwa's body, and then he stepped closer to the monitors and examined them.

"He still has a pulse," he said.

"But brain activity has increased—" The nurse pointed at an image with a million red dots flickering. "He is dreaming."

"Oh no," the doctor said.

"Should I unplug—" the nurse begun but the doctor interrupted her.

"No!" the doctor said. "He still has a chance." He turned to the other two nurses who had come in with him. "Put him on ventilator."

The nurse hesitated, maybe thinking about her job. The government had ordered all hospitals not to waste resources on patients who had started near-death dreaming.

"Is another patient waiting?" the doctor asked.

The nurse glanced at another screen, which had a list.

"There's no emergency," she said, uncertainly.

"Then we don't give up," the doctor said. "Unless he stops dreaming."

He nodded at the two nurses he had come with. One of them fitted a breath-assistant mask on Jamwa's face and inserted a tube through his mouth. Jamwa's chest begun to rise and fall.

"He's still dreaming," the monitor nurse said.

The doctor ignored her. He pulled the sheets off Jamwa's torso, and the sight of shattered organs sent Jamwa's spirit cowering against the wall. He watched as they tried to stop bleeding from several mesenteric arteries. Something heavy had smashed into him. He would need a new kidney to survive and he would lose parts of his intestines.

Jamwa glanced at a clock on the wall. Twelve thirty. From his wounds, he thought he had arrived at the hospital hardly a few minutes ago. That meant disaster had struck while he was still in his office, but what? An earthquake? A terrorist bomb? And that phone call, the last thing he remembered, did it have anything to do with this? Who called? Why? His eyes darted from one medic to another, expecting them to give up any moment and unplug him. Minutes passed. His heart continued to beat. The life support machines bleeped. The ventilator helped his chest to rise and fall. His brain continued to interpret the experience as a dream. The doctor did not unplug.

A stifled cry sent him running to the waiting room. He knew that voice. His wife. Immy. She and his two girls, Lakeri and Buba, sat on a bench while a receptionist stood behind a desk. An elderly man in a striped suit and with a red tie stood by the outer door. They all turned to the ER door when it opened, and when no one came out, Immy ran toward it to get a glimpse of her husband, but the receptionist stopped her, and gently forced her back to the bench.

"I want to see him!" Immy cried.

"Who opened the door?" the monitor nurse said from the emergency room. "No one gets in!" She closed the door firmly.

Immy calmed down. Lakeri was only eight, Buba only six, but they were the strong ones. They whispered encouragement to their mother.

Things had not been good after Immy found out about the student. Acila. He never intended to have an affair, but Acila had been irresistible. He seduced her with the promise of a job at the East African Center for Disease Control, where he worked. When he failed to secure her a position, she told Immy, and Immy started to think of divorce.

It's okay, Jamwa said. No sound came out of his mouth. *It's okay it's okay.* He placed a hand on her shoulder to comfort her. She shuddered at his touch, and looked up.

"Jammie," she whispered.

Lakeri grabbed her mother's cheek and forced her to look away.

"Look at me mum," Lakeri said. "Keep your eyes on me mum."

"I can feel him," Immy said, placing her hand on his, only that she could not touch him and so her fingers rested on her own shoulder. "I can...."

"No mum!" Lakeri said. "He's still alive!"

Immy let her fingers slide off her shoulder. "Of course," she said, crying again. "He's still alive." Her shoulder shuddered. He thought this time it was to shake off the ghost, so he withdrew his hand, and her body relaxed. "He's alive."

As he stood watching them, he sensed somebody staring at him. He pirouetted to meet the elderly man in a striped suit, with a neat white beard and eyes so white they might have belonged to a new born baby. The wrinkles on his face, rather than speak of old age, gave him a youthful look, almost as if they were trendy scarifications.

"Hello," the man said. "I'm Ondego."

Jamwa stepped away from him. Is this a Child of Bukuku? Is he here to guide him to the other side?

"You aren't dead," Ondego said. "Otherwise that lovely doctor wouldn't be working so hard to save you."

Two things struck Jamwa at once. The man could read his mind and, eerily, Immy and the children could not hear him although he spoke aloud.

"They can't hear me because I don't want them to," Ondego said.

"Excuse me sir," the receptionist said. "How can we help you?"

The man stepped closer to her. "I'm a friend of the family," he said. "How is he?"

"Please take a seat," the nurse said. "The doctor will soon let you know."

"Thank you," he said, and turned back to Jamwa. He did not sit. "Do you know who attempted to murder you?"

Murder me? Jamwa chuckled. *What nonsense.* But then, he glanced at the ER and wondered if that explained everything. Someone wanted him dead, but who could—the thought froze and he turned to Immy. The day she found out about Acila she had confronted him with a knife. She would have stabbed him if her sister had not intervened. Her grief seemed genuine. Was she putting up a show for the children?

"That's a thought," Ondego said. "But it won't help to question her now. Before we investigate, you must help doctors stop the bleeding."

Eh? Jamwa said.

"Here," Ondego pulled a sachet made of bark cloth out of his coat pocket. It contained a green powder. "Put this in your bloodstream."

What is it?

"Medicine. It'll keep your body alive but you'll remain in spirit form. They won't unplug you. I made sure of that. You have to help me catch your murderer."

Questions blasted Jamwa. Who is this man and how did he make sure the doctor did not unplug him? In the end, the answers did not matter. He was alive. He had a chance to be with Immy and the girls again, another chance to be a good father and a good husband. He did not want to leave them in pain. He spread out his palm and the man gave him a pinch of the powder.

He kept his hands down, hoping no one would notice powder flying through the room. He opened the door to the ER. The medics around his body were too engrossed to notice, but the monitor nurse snapped at the receptionist.

"Who opened the door?" the monitor nurse said.

"Someone inside," the receptionist stuttered. "Not us."

"How is he?" Immy asked, hurrying to the monitor nurse.

"Please be calm," the nurse replied, closing the door. "We are doing our best."

Jamwa approached his body, careful not to touch any medic, and released the powder into his bloodstream.

"What was that?" a nurse said.

"What?" the doctor replied.

"Something green...." As she spoke, a greenish paste appeared on the punctured arteries, and the bleeding stopped.

"Jesus," the doctor said.

Jamwa walked out. This time, the monitor nurse, who joined the other medics in staring at the paste, did not react when the door opened by itself. Jamwa saw understanding dawn on her face.

Ondego walked out into the corridor and Jamwa followed, giving his family only a brief glance for if he lingered he would touch Immy, or the girls, and that would scare them. They walked out of the emergency ward to the parking lot.

"We'll start from the crime scene," Ondego said, getting into a blue Land Cruiser.

They sped through the sleepy streets of Tororo, and turned off the highway five miles outside town, onto a new tarmac road that led to the gates of East African Center for Disease Control. There were ten guards rather than the usual four. Two searched the car for weapons. One in the security booth placed Ondego's ID in a scanner, to verify its authenticity and to log his visit.

"What brings you here?" the guard asked.

"I'm Jamwa's lawyer," Ondego said.

The guard seemed unsure, but pressed a button and the gates slid open.

Who are you? Jamwa asked as they sped through a driveway in a forest full of birds and small animals.

"I hunt kifaro."

Jamwa frowned, and looked out of the window at a squirrel racing up a tree. He was a scientists and what he believed about spirits was from scientific research, that a person had an out-of-body experience that could last from a few minutes to a few days after death. He did not know what to make of Ondego's statement. Hunting spirit assassins? He did not know what to make of Ondego, who could see and speak to spirits, yet scientists needed very expensive quantum equipment to establish the same.

Why would anyone send a spiritual assassin after him?

"I found a luong'jogi in your car," Ondego said. "Someone planted it there to guide the kifaro to kill you. If I had not intervened, you'd be dead."

Jamwa thought about it for a few moment, and though he could not yet fully understand what was happening, the meaning of Ondego's words hit him.

So you used me as bait, Jamwa said. If you had removed the charm the kifaro would not have hit me.

"I saved your life," Ondego said.

Jamwa wanted to retort, to rage, to ask many questions. *What do you want with me?* That was the only question he could think of.

Ondego did not answer.

Ondego was not to blame. From the little superstitions he had heard about kifaro, rarely did a stranger send it to kill. It was always someone close. A neighbor, a friend, a relative, a workmate. Someone very close. A workmate? But his position as a researcher was not competitive. His uncles? His father had passed away the previous year, bequeathing him a hundred acres of land. Three of his uncles pressured him to sell. The eldest was a Pentecostal pastor. Could he consult a mulogo for the services of a kifaro? The other two were farmers, and they openly worshipped ancestral spirits. They might know which mulogo has ability to send makifaro. Were they so evil that they would kill their nephew over land?

Immy? He did not want to think about it.

Acila? She had a strong motive of revenge, for he slept with her but did not give her the job. Did she have such an evil heart?

Did you catch it?

"No. It's an evolved kifaro. I couldn't detect it."

The building he had worked in for the last five years, developing a vaccine for HIV, was a three-story structure of glass and steel. Police officers prowled all over the front yard, where visitors parked. Ondego drove to the staff parking lot, behind the building. He stopped at the barricade. In the booth, instead of the usual guard, was a cop.

"You can't go in there," the officer said. "It's a crime scene."

"Open," Ondego said, in a soft whisper, and the woman lifted the barricade.

Mind control, Jamwa though, frowning at Ondego. Was that how he stopped the doctor from unplugging him? Ondego did not respond.

There were five staff cars and two police vans in the parking lot. At the far end, yellow tape encircled Jamwa's Jeep. The driver's door was crumpled. Glass scintillated on the ground amid pools of blood. A wrecked motorcycle lay beside the car. It had rammed him against the Jeep. Crime scene detectives went through the debris. Was the charm still in the car? Would they find it?

"No," Ondego said. "It's an evolved charm as well. It looks like fast food trash. Chicken feet wrapped in napkins instead of banana leaves; a chicken head, with bits of your hair on the comb, stuck on a plastic fork; chicken entrails wrapped around a chopstick instead of the usual coffee tree stick."

Walkie-talkie and shoelaces, Jamwa thought, a dish that once was only for the poor who could not afford prime chicken parts. Then East African countries united into one, and the ensuing economic boom catapulted large sections of the poor into a strong working class. They did not let go of chicken heads, feet, and intestines, which became a national favorite.

A plain clothed detective was talking to Jamwa's workmate, Karama, who had taken off his lab coat. Jamwa had never seen him without a lab coat. Dark patches showed under his armpits. He kept passing a hanky over his face. The detective, in a gray coat with no tie, had a notebook in his palm as he chewed on a pen. He was not writing.

Ondego stopped the car close to them. They did not notice.

"I donno," Karama was saying. "He said 'hello' then listened then dropped the phone and fled. Maybe the caller told him there was a bomb under his desk. Then we heard the crash and came out to find him dying by his car."

"And the biker? Did you see him?"

"No."

"Whose bike is it?"

"I don't know."

"But it's in the staff parking lot. It must belong to one of you."

"I've never seen it before. We all drive cars."

The detective snapped his book closed and spat out the pen.

"You are hiding something," he said. "How did that bike get in here? How come two sets of guards never noticed it?"

"I don't know," Kamara said. "I don't know."

"Liars!" The detective cursed.

It can't be a kifaro, Jamwa said. I heard that kifaro hits look like works of nature. Sickness. Lightning strikes. It always leaves no doubt that it's a supernatural hit. This is the work of an ordinary assassin.

"True," Ondego said. "Which is why I need your help."

My help?

"A mulogo has created a new kind of kifaro," Ondego said. "They kill and leave the police puzzled over confusing clues like this phone call and the motorcycle."

When he was a child, Jamwa's grandmother had told him about how ancestral spirits served humans. Upon his death, since he was a scientist, his spirits could end up in a charm to help a student pass exams, or maybe to help another researcher find a breakthrough. Grandma had said that bad people became evil spirits. Murderers, upon death, became kifaro.

"No," Ondego said, reading his thoughts. "Every spirit is a good spirit until a mulogo turns it into an evil spirit. My job is to find makifaro and rehabilitate them, but a mulogo is making this new kind and I can't detect them."

"Trace the call!" Karama was shouting at the detective "It has something to do with his death! Trace it instead of harassing us!"

"There was no phone call!" the detective said.

"I heard it ring," Karama said. "I saw him answer it! Trace it!"

"We checked his call log! We checked with Banana Telecom! We checked!"

"I don't believe this," Karama said.

"Just tell me who killed him—"

"Find the caller!" Karama shouted.

"Maybe you'll give better answers from the station," the detective said.

He nodded at two uniformed officers, who handcuffed Karama and shoved him into the van. Jamwa saw four other workmates in the van, handcuffed.

"I'll check your phone," Ondego said.

He got out of the car and walked to the detective. They talked for a few minutes, then the detective went to the second police van and pulled a plastic bag out of the back. It had Jamwa's phone. Ondego scrolled through the log, then handed it back to the cop.

"They can't see the number," he said when he got back into the Land Cruiser. "The mulogo keeps it hidden. You can't remember anything because the moment you answered the phone the kifaro took control of your mind."

Fifteen minutes later, they were at the offices of Banana Telecom in Bazaar Street. Ondego left Jamwa in the car and went in, returning hardly ten minutes later with a piece of paper.

"The number is registered to this person," he said, handing Jamwa the paper. "Does it ring a bell?"

Jamwa studied the name. Omondi Joseph. It did not mean anything. The paper listed a home address in Kasoli.

They sped to it.

Kasoli had been a slum until the East African government built free housing for the residents. The buildings were shaped like huts, cylindrical with conical roofs, and painted in vivid colors. Children played football in front of Omondi's block. Many window panes were broken and garbage overflowed from a bin. They went through a lounge littered with junk furniture, then up a murky staircase to the fourth floor, through a corridor with charcoal graffiti. Children laughed behind Omondi's door as a TV played at full volume. Ondego knocked.

"Turn that down!" a woman shouted from inside. "Burayan! Turn it down!"

The laughter continued, but the TV's volume went down. The door opened and a woman smiled at Ondego.

"Children!" she said. "They are too much. How can I help you?"

"I'm looking for Omondi," Ondego said. "Joseph Omondi."

"He's at the garage," she said.

"Can I ask you a few questions?" Ondego said. "I'm his friend. I just need to know a few things."

The woman looked unsure, but Jamwa thought Ondego got into her head to make her obey. She stepped aside to let him in.

"Search the house," Ondego said to Jamwa.

For what? Jamwa said.

"Anything," Ondego said. "We need to know who this Omondi man is."

"Get off the sofa," the woman told the children. The sofa was worn out, faded from purple to a pale blue. The three children, aged between six and ten, slid to the floor, their eyes glued on a sixty inch flat screen TV, which was out of place amidst the musty and broken furniture. They were watching a sci-fi comedy about a group of East African astronauts stranded in Mars.

Ondego and the woman sat on the sofa. Jamwa searched the house. Framed family photos beamed on the walls, beside a large crucifix with neon lights and a digital calendar of Sacred Heart Cathedral. The apartment had a tiny kitchen, with a rolled up mattress in a corner and a pile of half-washed dishes in the sink. The floor was wet. The bathroom was too clean. The children's bedroom revealed nothing but a mess of clothes and broken toys. The parents' bedroom was neat. He looked through the drawers and the closets but found nothing. Just as he was about to give up, he saw a hole in the ceiling. He found a torch, then climbed on the dressing mirror to pull himself into the ceiling, where he found a metallic box. It had a padlock. He went back down into the bedroom, and searched until he found a bunch of keys. He tried them one at a time until the padlock snapped open. The box contained a newspaper article and a family photo.

The article, dated seven years back, was about a man called Amanya Hope, found dead in what looked like ritual sacrifice in Mbarara town, over six hours away by bus. The writing on the back of the photo identified the people on it. Amanya Hope, his wife, and their five children. Jamwa had to look closely to confirm that Amanya Hope was Omondi Joseph, even though Omondi had a darker skin and a beard.

Jamwa went back down. The children still made noise in front of the TV. Ondego looked up on sensing Jamwa, and Jamwa waved the article and the photo. Ondego then excused himself and the woman saw him to the door. Jamwa was afraid that the children, or the woman, would notice the newspaper and the photo floating in the air, but the children were engrossed on the TV and Ondego distracted the woman until Jamwa was out of the apartment.

"Ha," Ondego said, on reading the article. "Very clever. It lives like a mortal and even has a wife and children. No wonder I couldn't find him."

It's him? Jamwa said.

"This kind makes my work a nightmare," Ondego said. "Let's go to the garage."

But how can a dead person have a wife and children?

"He controls her mind," Ondego said as they hurried down the stairs. "He controls other men to impregnate her without her knowledge."

The garage was a metal shack under a mango tree, with broken cars, dead motorcycles, and scrap metal scattered about. Four men in grease stained clothes sat on the ground playing a board game, Ludo. The smell of roasting pork and beef wafted from the nearby market, while the sizzle of a river in the valley below provided a background hum. Weaver birds made a racket in the mango forest that choked the banks. As the Land Cruiser snaked into the yard, two men abandoned the game and rushed to it.

"Boss," one said. "I'm the best mechanic. What's the problem?"

"I'm looking for Omondi," Ondego said.

"That one is lousy," the mechanic said. "Hire me."

"He's fixing that lorry," the other mechanic said, pointing to a green truck, and both returned to the game.

Jamwa and Ondego got out of the car and walked to Omondi, whose feet peeped from under the lorry. He was banging something, but stopped abruptly.

"He notices us," Ondego said.

Omondi slid out, a spanner in his hand. His eyes lit up on seeing Jamwa.

"You...." he begun, but the words got stuck on his throat. He scrambled to his feet, like a student after the headmaster catches him doing something illegal. He was lanky, with a scraggly beard. He dropped the spanner, reached into his pockets and pulled out a cigarette. His hands trembled.

"Who sent you?" Ondego said.

Omondi tried to respond, but could only make a gurgling sound. His voice trembled worse than his hands. He could not strike the match. He again looked at Jamwa, and spat out the unlit cigarette.

"Tell me," Ondego said. "Who sent you?"

For a response, Omondi ran. Ondego pointed a finger at him, and a rope shot out of the finger and caught Omondi's leg, sending him crashing to the ground. Omondi threw a fireball, hitting Ondego in the tummy and Ondego yelped in pain. The rope unwound itself and twitched on the ground like a beheaded snake. The mechanics backed away in terror. Free again, Omondi ran hard.

"Don't let him get away!" Ondego said. "Get him!"

Jamwa ran after Omondi, who was racing down the valley to the bridge. Omondi looked over his shoulder, saw what was chasing him, and dived into the river. Jamwa followed him in. Omondi kept close to the riverbed, swimming at an incredible speed, as though he were a speedboat, but Jamwa overtook him and grabbed his legs. Omondi threw a fireball at Jamwa, but Jamwa did not feel any pain. It was just as though a hot breath had swept over him.

"You!" Omondi said, throwing another fireball, and when it did not hurt Jamwa, the fight went out of him. He collapsed onto the riverbed in surrender. Jamwa dragged him to the banks. Women washing clothes further down the stream paused to stare.

Who sent you? Jamwa asked.

"Your uncle," the kifaro said. "Mabaga."

The youngest of the three who had pressured him to sell the land, and the poorest, but with the largest family. He would not inherit the land unless his elder brothers passed away, which meant that he intended to kill them all.

"The fire doesn't hurt you," Omondi said.

My body is still alive, Jamwa said.

"He forced me to do it," Omondi said, his voice weak.

Ondego was running on the water surface. He scared the women, who fled into the mango forest. A rope again shot out of his finger and like a boa constrictor wound itself on Omondi, tying him up in a few seconds.

"I tried to stop," Omondi was saying. "He hurts me if I refuse."

Ondego knelt beside him. "I'll protect you," Ondego said. "I'm a won'jok. Just tell me who your master is."

Omondi's face relaxed into a smile when he heard that name, the father of spirits. Some communities worshipped them as gods. Ondego must have been a powerful and famous musawo who lived a hundred years ago. But why was he in flesh and blood? Jamwa wondered.

"Jjungo," Omondi said. "His shrine is—"

"I know Jjungo," Ondego said. "I thought he was a good one."

"Please," Omondi said. "Help me."

Ondego sprinkled the green powder on Omondi while chanting in a strange language, and Omondi's spirit left the body, which degenerated into putrid flesh. He gave Ondego and Jamwa a smile, and then walked off into the mango forest.

Ondego got into the minds of every human nearby to make them forget what they had seen, and to stop the mechanics from forming a lynch mob. The rotting corpse remained on the banks and later the police wrote it off as an unidentified drowned man. Jamwa felt sorry for Omondi's wife, who would never know what happened to her husband, but it was for the better. How would she have reacted if she discovered he was a walking dead creature, a spiritual assassin?

They sped to Jjungo's shrine in Kisoko sub-county. They drove over sandy roads, and had to make the last five hundred meters on foot for there was only a path cutting through a thick bush.

"He's expecting us," Ondego said. "He is powerful and might hurt me, but you'll match him for you are still alive."

Jamwa had expected a mud hut with a grass thatched roof as the shrine, not a cylindrical brick building with a neon sign on the roof blinking Jjungo's name. The door and windows were closed. Red light flickered through the cracks on the wooden shutters. Ondego pointed at a window, and a flame consumed it within a few seconds. They peeked in. Much of the décor was common in shrines, charms, bead artwork, and masks on the walls. Figurines sat on a shelf, beside books, some of which were mundane novels. A papyrus mat carpeted the floor. The light came from an electric bulb in a lampshade that looked like a giant candle. A laptop sat on an office desk at one end. A screen saver displayed photos of a happy family. Jjungo's family, Jamwa thought.

Ondego hauled himself in through the window. Jamwa followed. Ondego lifted the carpet to reveal a trapdoor and they descended into a dark tunnel. As they groped about for a switch, the trapdoor slammed shut, plunging them into pitch blackness. Ondego clapped his hands and fireflies appeared, enabling them to see a long, plain corridor, and a monster charging at them. It looked like a hound the size of a horse.

The dog spat a fireball. It hit Ondego's chest, slamming him against the wall and setting him aflame. Ondego screamed. His fireflies went out. The hound spat another ball at Jamwa, but again all Jamwa felt was discomforting hot air. Ondego struggled to his feet, and clapped a thunder that deafened Jamwa for several seconds and caused the roof of the tunnel to collapse. Daylight poured in. Ondego threw a bolt of lightning at the dog. It ducked, and dissolved into a man. He was naked, save for a necklace made out of femur bones. He spat another fireball, hitting Ondego in the chest again, and Ondego collapsed, screaming in pain.

The man plucked a bone off his necklace and it turned into a knife. He lunged at Jamwa, who ducked, more out of instinct that necessity. The knife sunk into the wall. As Jjungo struggled to free the knife, Jamwa yanked a bone off the necklace. It did not turn into a knife, but it still sunk into Jjungo's back. Jjungo screamed. Jamwa stabbed, and stabbed. Jjungo staggered about. Jamwa slashed his neck open and Jjungo fell to the ground, where he twitched and twisted as smoke rose from his skin like steam. Then he went still.

Jamwa ran to Ondego. His body was charred.

"I'll be fine," he said, grimacing with a lipless mouth. "I just need a new body. Help me get into the sunlight."

Jamwa carried him out of the shrine and lay him on the grass, and, like a snake shading off its skin, Ondego wriggled out of the charred body. He had the same face, but it was much younger, without gray beards or wrinkles.

"Thank you," he said. "Now let's get you back to the hospital."

* * * *

Jamwa opened his eyes. A ceiling fan stood motionless above him. He heard bleeps, and turned to see a new nurse examining the monitors. He was no longer in the emergency room. He was in a private ward, still breathing through a ventilator as an IV fed fluid into his veins. The nurse smiled.

"You are awake," she said. "It's a miracle."

An hour later, they allowed his family to see him. Immy and the girls came first. She had a bouquet of flowers and the children had made him a get-well card. Their eyes shone with tears of joy. The only uncle present was Mabaga. The sight of him turned Jamwa's happiness into a bitter froth in his mouth. All he could think of was that he did not have evidence to bring the man to justice.

BUT I LOVE HIM
Scott Wheelock

I watch him. He's out there crashing around the trash bins, eating a dead cat. He was always such a big eater. I worry about him—is he getting enough to eat? There's no one left at the apartment building but the two of us. It's been weeks since I've seen anyone but Georgie. The rest of the zombies moved on, but Georgie stays. We've been married for over 30 years; mother always said he was a good catch.

I don't go outside anymore. The last time I did was with Georgie—I barely made it back. There hasn't been much rain in the two months, twelve days I've been inside. I drink the rainwater as soon as it comes through the pipes, and I'm embarrassed to say I can't bathe as often as I would like. I'm not worried about food. Georgie's stocked the apartment with plenty of supplies. Enough for months or maybe years now that I'm alone.

Mother always said you can't smell yourself, but you can. And my hair, my beautiful blond hair—I remember how Georgie used to touch it, hold it up to his nose. It's so greasy it looks like a hat. Looking in the mirror, I cut it all off.

There are sores on my scalp, and the color of my lips isn't right. Georgie said this might happen when our vitamins ran out. I smash the mirror with a hammer. There isn't much else I can do about how awful I look. God, my scalp itches, and once I start—

I don't read anymore. I wonder if prisoners on death row like to read. I don't think reading makes any sense if you don't care about endings. I think about killing myself—that would be an ending, but it would also be destroying everything Georgie worked for. Stockpiling food, fortifying the apartment, the drainage, the sewers, he thought of everything. All for the two of us—all for me. I can't do that to Georgie, not after what he's been through— how he's suffered.

Lord, it's hot. I've been crossing off every day on the calendar, and today's Georgie's birthday, July sixteenth—he's 58. Georgie's not out there today. I guess he's searching for food somewhere else, but he always comes back.

I sleep most of the time now. At least there's been rain so I can wash. I'm even growing a few vegetables; they're my new friends—hello, celery; good morning, Mr. carrot. HA, HA.

Sometimes I wonder where Georgie goes. Is he happy? Does he have any friends? He's not a big man anymore. He's lost a lot of weight, but he's still wearing his dress suit and alligator shoes, the same clothes he wore the day I buried him. His shirt is filthy, and the suit hangs off him like it's five sizes too large. But who am I to talk? When I look at myself in the broken mirror, I'm not a pretty sight. My hair is growing back, but it's frizzy, tangled, and gray, and my eyes—bloodshot and cloudy. I don't know what to do. Everything about me seems to be drying up.

I pick at my skin, peel it off—the pain feels good. I don't know how to explain it. I guess feeling something is better than feeling nothing at all.

Georgie's back! I hear him crashing around out by the dumpster. I didn't realize until I saw him, God, how lonely I've been. I stand up, all my joints cracking, go to the window and look through the bars. It's Georgie, all right, but he looks so skinny, like a skeleton. Looking at him makes me feel fat, stomach distended, the rest of me haggard and gaunt.

Oops, I think he sees me. I wave, and he lets out a moan. I understand how he feels; I miss him too. I take the curtain down and put a chair in front of the window so Georgie and I can look at each other—it's been so long.

But first, I clean myself up. I shower—even wash my hair. The soap hurts the sores, but it's worth it; I feel like a queen. And did I say: I washed my jeans, cut my nails.

I look at my calendar, cross off another day. So many days since Georgie died, and I've been alone. Don't get me wrong, I don't hold that against him. I know he's done the best he could. What would I do if our positions were reversed? I can't say.

I sleep in the chair, and when I wake Georgie's there, just one flight down, by the dumpster—looking up. When he sees me, Georgie opens and closes his mouth like he has something to say. I hear his teeth clacking together, but no words come out. He knows I'm here and I'm thinking about him. About all the good times we had, about little Katie, our honeymoon in Bermuda. I remember how funny Georgie looked in shorts and how he would curl up next to me at night. How he would get up early for work while I was still asleep. He'd always leave me a note, good morning, sweetheart, abbreviated GMS.

I wonder what he's thinking about. Sometimes I press my face right up to the window and pretend we're having a staring contest. Georgie always wins; his eyelids are gone.

Tonight's a special night. I wash my hair, change my clothes even brush my teeth. As the sun begins to set, I look out at Georgie, and when I catch his eye, open the window bars. Georgie is so excited. I watch him climb the dumpster and stagger through the window. I race into the bedroom and cover myself with a sheet. I'm a little nervous, silly I know, I mean we're married, but it's been a long time.   ✗

WHO WANTS TO LIVE FOREVER?

Angela Yuriko Smith

I opened my eyes to see the rust stained ribs of the bridge overhead. The acrid stench of burning garbage permeated everything. Someone might be trying to heat food or burn themselves alive. Neither mattered. Neither would work. The nanobots did their job too well.

The sound of bone splitting against metal echoed across the greasy water, followed by a splash. I sat up. A woman my age was floating face down. She looked hopeful. Smart, she had aimed for the carcass of a broken down barge. It listed aimlessly with the current alongside her, two broken things on a journey to nowhere. There was a mark on the hull from her impact—a daisy shaped splatter of dark red. It was pretty. It made me think of art. Maybe… but no.

I sighed and stood up. No more disappointment. I'd tried art. I'd learned photography, stained class, virtual sculpture, physical interpretation and painting in every known medium including blood. It was all good distraction for awhile, but when the gloss wore off the emptiness returned twice as bleak. I couldn't take the disappointment anymore. It's less painful to just not try.

I shuffled off, slicing my bare feet in the litter of broken glass, shell and twisted metal that decorated the shore. A shard of fence, anchored in the sand, pierced clean through my foot. For a few seconds I was pinned by my appendage. My guts knotted as adrenaline and pain coursed through me. It was nice to feel something, but then the nanobots came in and fixed that, just like they fix everything. The pain vanished. I sighed and pulled my foot free to look at the damage.

There was a gaping hole on the thin part of my foot above the pinky toe. Pinkish bone peeked out in the ripped flesh. I poked my finger in before it healed. Smooth, wet and warm, I traced along the exposed bone. My heart fluttered, a reaction of the nerves that were still active. I pushed harder. My finger slipped and poked through. Off balance, I somersaulted onto my head with a crunch. I lay on my back and stared at the sullied clouds until someone laughed. I craned my neck to see daisy-blossom-blood-splat girl.

"Kind of funny..." she said. Her skin was a pale greenish-blue from the river toxin taint. She opened her mouth to say something else and then stopped. We both knew there was no point in trying to converse. We could be friends, but after a few decades we would both run out of things to say and the vacuum would return regardless. Maybe she hadn't been crushed by the burden of incessant existence enough, because then she spoke anyway.

"Wanna... get a coffee?"

I sat up, trying to remember what coffee was. My brain ticked through options and rejected them in sequence before it hit upon the right moment. A paper cup full of steaming darkness. It had been a winter, before all our problems were solved. I'd been so cold my toes ached. I closed my eyes, hanging on to that memory of before. When it faded, I looked back up at the girl.

"Where?" I looked around at the broken pavement that used to be Cropsey Avenue. The concrete was latticed with cracks. The asphalt was pitted from years of acid storm grinding away at it. At the other end, behind an overturned yellow bus, I saw the burned out shell of a gas station. The face was once glass. Now it was just a cavity, open to the unkind elements. I recognized the sign hanging at an angle off the facade. I pointed at it.

"Oh, coffee!" We both laughed then. Mine came out slow and congealed from lack of use. I stopped. I wasn't doing this again. I stood up, turned my back and started walking away.

"Hey!" she called behind me. "Why not? You got somewhere better to be?" I tried to think of a good comeback, but my brain was fixated on the memory of that steaming paper cup. I realized I wanted it bad. It felt like... something. I turned around.

Her skin had returned to a normal, healthy color by now. She had brownish gold eyes and hair the color of baked mud. Or that could just be mud. I suppose, if I still cared, I'd call her pretty.

"I want a coffee," I said. "But there's no coffee." I waved my hand toward the shell of the building. She didn't look where I pointed. She looked at me. "So there's no point." I added, so she would understand the futility of her request.

"It doesn't matter," she said. "We'll pretend." She took my hand, still stretched toward the former cafe, and started pulling me along with her. I stumbled behind, confused.

"Why?" I asked.

"Because we live in a perfect world." She walked while she talked. "Nanos made it so we can't be hurt. We fixed global hunger by fixing the need to eat. We've gotten everything mankind ever wanted. Remember how happy we all were at first?" We had reached what was left of the gas station. "So what happened?"

She faced me, waiting for my reply. All I could think of was that paper cup, steam wafting out like a warm ghost. I remembered the smell. "We want coffee?" I finally said.

"Exactly." she said. "We want to want. That's what made us crawl out of the ooze and evolve in the first place. We wanted something. We *need* to want... or we die." She walked to an overturned table and set it upright. She pulled a few chairs over and set them up too.

"But we can't die... 'cause nanobots..." I trailed off. I couldn't take my eyes off her. She moved different from the rest of us—faster and on purpose. Her hair was actually the color of dark honey, not mud, and it bounced a little. She used a discarded apron in the rubble to wipe off the table top and found two warped paper cups blown into a corner. She motioned me to sit.

"Yes, the nanobots make it so we can't die... on the outside." She sat down. "But we're dead inside because we don't have anything left to want. The trick is... wanting to want."

She held her empty cup up to her mouth, blew on it and took a pretend sip. I licked my lips, remembering the taste. I liked my coffee plain with no fancy syrups. Just a little cream to lighten it up. I was trying to think about what she said, but in my head all I had going on was coffee.

"So... no coffee?" I sat down too, picked up my cup and looked into it. There was a little grimy dust in the cracks, and some grains of sand stuck to the bottom. I was sad.

"No coffee. There might never be coffee again, and that's perfect. We can't stop wanting to want. It will keep us alive. It's kept me alive."

Across the bridge, a small group had gathered. It looked like a family. They stood up on the railing, helping a toddler balance, and jumped together. It was a popular spot.

"Why did you jump if you're so alive?" I asked. I was annoyed with her for mentioning coffee. I had forgotten I even liked it. Now I couldn't stop being disappointed by my lack of it.

"I didn't jump to get lucky and end it," she said. "I jumped because I wanted to fly."

"What? Are you crazy? People can't fly. It's a good way to kill yourself." Some version of me resurfaced to scold this lunatic and all her nonsense, then my words filtered back to me. I started laughing and she joined me. Our voices echoed off the decaying city around us. A middle aged woman shuffled up to the bridge, looked back at us with dead eyes and then slid through the broken railing to vanish. We laughed harder.

Maybe in a few decades this too would end with another existential vacuum, but I would always want this moment back... and maybe that really would be enough.   ✗

THE DEAD ARE ALWAYS HUNGRY

Christopher Alex Ray

The sun had just started to rise and finally bathe Bray in blissful warmth. The climb up the steep and treacherous terrain of the mountains had taken its own toll on his exhausted, starving body. The sudden flight up the mountain had not left him with time to grab much in the way of supplies; luckily, he wasn't alone. His blue eyes look further up the ridge ahead of him glimpsing, the red chambray of Cook's shirt ahead of him. The red stood out brightly against Cook's dark skin, which helped in the low light of the early morning.

Bray had joined with Elroy Cook and this other band of bastards and thieves back out west under the leadership of an old Dutchman by the name of Groenewold. Bray had joined in the hope of making "a big score," as he was told. The score had been big alright, but it was big in bullets and Pinkertons and less in gold and bills. The second they busted in the door a hornet's nest of shells started flying. What had started as a group of ten quickly became seven as Groenewold and two Chinese were gunned down. The seven left alive had run like whipped dogs followed over hell, and high water, every little town between them and the Appalachia had been another ambush in waiting.

Apparently, Groenewold had been more wanted than he thought and they had him in rifle sights as soon as he touched ground. He had dragged them all into this nightmare, and now the Pinkertons and the sheriffs for two hundred miles wanted all of them dead. One of the seven had been caught just before they had reached the mountains and they all heard him screaming before the last shot rang out and shut him up for good. The last of them had slipped going up the latest ridge and bounced down the side of the mountain like a rag doll. Bray thought back to the way his arms had flapped after he had smacked into an outcrop of rock on his way down. It almost seemed as though he was waving them goodbye.

Maybe they were the lucky ones, Bray thought. At least they weren't freezing and starving, flinching at every broken twig and rustling leaf. At least the climb was becoming more relaxed, and the forest was beginning to take over. Bray watched as Cook went over the rise and gave a small whistle like the sound of an angry jay. Bray charged up the hill, knowing that was the call of alert, his hand resting desperately on the Colt at his hip. At the top, he sees Cook pointing at smoke rising from the valley below signaling a possible cooking fire.

"Look there," Cook says, "I think there's a homestead down there. I can see a small clearing near where the smoke is rising. I'll bet that's a vegetable garden."

"I'll bet you're right, Cook." Bray squints against the glare of the morning sun, holding his hand to shield his eyes. "I think I can make out a roof."

A rustle comes from the brush behind them. Cook and Bray turn, both pulling the revolvers from their belts. A thin narrow-eyed man in a gray union shirt and thick mustache steps from the trees. He smirks and strolls closer, his hands mockingly held in the air. Ellis Heilis was a man that no one on the team much liked, but he was good in a fight, so the others tolerated his cocky swagger. Bray's eyes narrowed, and he slides his revolver back into its holster. Bray hadn't liked Heilis from day one and liked him even less after weeks on the run and starving in the mountains.

"Goddamn, Heilis," Cook squawks as he lowers his gun back into his belt. "You damn near scared me to death!"

"Hell boy, I's just seein' what ya'll was whistlin' about." Heilis smiles, showing yellow teeth and black gums, his eyes glancing over Cook's shoulder and seeing the smoke rising in the valley. "Looks like you boys might have found the answer to my prayers."

Bray can practically see the intent flash in Heilis' eyes. They were going to rob that farmhouse and God help anyone who got in the way. Heilis turns and whistles back into the trees and eventually two more men come out from the foliage. One was a tall man in a white union shirt stained with dirt and dried blood, his blue eyes looking straight past Bray and Cook to Heilis. The other was a small, nervous little man in blue chambray, his round brown eyes flashing over every rock and tree acting like he was seeing Pinkertons around every tree and rock. The Frenchman and the Jew were never too far from each other, mostly out of mutual fear of Heilis but also because the Jew Kowalski actually could speak French, which was good for LaPointe who could barely speak any damn English.

They both looked past Heilis and at the rising smoke, a combination of excitement and palpable relief rolling across both of their faces. Heilis claps his hands together to get everyone's attention before hunkering down. They all gather around him and lean in, Heilis' face a wild mask of pure murderous resolve.

"Alright boys, here's the plan. We're going to go pay that pretty little homestead a visit, and we're going to take as many supplies as we can so we can finally make it out of here and not have to eat Kowalski." The Jew flinches as Heilis busts out laughing, socking the little man none too gently in the arm. "Only joking, boy. But we're also going to steal any horses they might have. If there's a homestead, there must be civilization around here somewhere, and hopefully, we'll be free of those damn Pinkertons and all those sheriffs and bounty hunters."

The group all lock eyes for a moment before nodding. Bray's eyes narrow, and he coughs to get the groups attention.

"What's the plan if the people down there resist? We gonna kill'em? We've already got enough heat on us as-is. If we go down there and kill off a bunch of those hicks, we might as well send up a signal fire saying we've been here." Bray looks at the group Cook looked like he agreed. Kowalski wouldn't meet Bray's eyes instead scanning the dirt at his feet. LaPointe didn't look like he understood a word, and Heilis' eyes looked like flint striking steel.

"What the hell else are we gonna do, ya damn fool?" Heilis spits. "We'll starve to death in a couple more nights if we don't get food. Also if we leave them alive, then it'll be the same as soon as we're gone. They'll raise every sheriff in twenty miles and tell them where we went. If we kill'em at least, then we can get a few days before someone comes looking."

The group gave a muffled grumble of agreement. Even Cook looked convinced, and honestly, Bray had a hard time arguing against that; even now, his stomach grabbed tight to his ribs. He had a little jerky left in his bag, but it wouldn't last more than another day. After a moment of consideration, Bray nods. He didn't like the plan, but it seemed to be the only available option if they were ever going to get out of the mountains.

"Good. Now that's settled. Here's the plan, Cook and myself are going to go knock on the door. Bray, Frenchie, and Kowalski are going to set up alongside the house. Once they come to the door, Me and Cook will draw them out, and you boys will take care of the rest. Sound good?" Heilis glances at all of them but saves the longest and most hateful glance for Bray. His eyes daring him to object. Bray holds his stare as all the men nod and mutter agreement.

They all stand and begin moving slowly into the valley. The trek still takes the group a good hour thanks to the steep, rocky terrain. Bray follows behind the rest of the group, his gut telling him that this was wrong. The closer they got to the homestead, the feeling grew stronger. It felt like his belly had been filled with ice, and he swore he could feel eyes on his back almost as if someone were lurking in the pines just out of sight, but nothing stirred the cold air around him. Even the forest itself held the terrible silence that cold weather brings. At least it hadn't snowed.

If it had, they would have been dead for sure, and no one would have found them until spring when nothing would be left but clean, picked bones and torn clothes. Bray's mind and eyes continued to wander until Heilis called a halt. They were in the woods on the outskirts of the farm now, and Bray could definitely see it was a farm. A desolate vegetable field lay not far from the house and out past them Bray could see apple trees lining the far side of the property, a weathered outhouse sits halfway between the cabin and the woods. The house stood in the center, it's wood siding had faded to an almost gray color, but otherwise, it still looked strong and sturdy, smoke still curled out from the brick chimney that ran alongside the weathered wood.

Heilis signals Bray, LaPointe, and Kowalski, and they move silently towards the side of the house, Bray in the lead ahead of the other two. LaPointe ducks down behind the narrow outhouse, his revolver at the ready. Bray and Kowalski both take positions alongside the house, keeping the front door in sight. Kowalski pulls his revolver and ducks down while Bray stands with his shoulder pressed to the rough, gray wood. Bray grabs hold of his Colt's smooth maple handle but doesn't draw, his eyes scanning the trees for Heilis and Cook.

A minute later Cook and Heilis come out from the trees, Heilis swaggering and Cook keeping a close eye on the cabin door.

"Hello!" Heilis yells out loud enough to make Kowalski jump, "Me and my partner here got turned around and lost, and we was wondering if anyone would be able to help us!"

The silence filled in the places the Heilis' hollering had left, and the door to the cabin remained absolutely motionless. Bray could hear nothing from inside. Heilis knocked on the door this time, four heavy, rapid thuds all in quick succession.

"Hello? Anyone home?" Heilis calls out again, his voice sharper and less friendly this time. He steps back from the step, drawing his pistol and turning to Cook before nodding his head towards the door. Cook brings his out as well and rushes forward, kicking the door open with a thwack as it slams against the interior wall. Heilis steps up behind Cook, preparing to follow. Bray, Kowalski, and LaPointe all move forward to provide cover, but before they make three paces, Cook rockets from the doorway, his revolver falling from his limp hand. His ordinarily dark skin is pale ashen gray. He falls to his knees, vomiting into the dead grass.

Heilis leaps back out of Cook's way, his eyes wide and startled as he turns his gun toward the dark opening of the doorway. Bray reaches him a heartbeat later, turning his revolver to the door as well but seeing nothing but the dark interior of the house beyond. They both turn to Cook, who is still on his knees, spitting out the last of his stomach contents, which only consisted of bile and foam. Cook stares at the ground, his body shaking like a leaf in a storm.

Bray leans down, putting a hand on Cooks' shoulder and he's shocked at how cold and clammy the man feels.

"Cook, what's the matter? What happened?" Heilis hollers, his eyes, and pistol still trained on the black, empty doorway.

"Go see for yourself," Cook says his eyes still refusing to move from the ground.

"What'chu mean?" Heilis' eyes are glinting like flint and steel again, but Bray can see a flicker of nervousness as well. Bray stands and looks towards the door.

"Let's go take a look for ourselves," Bray says and starts towards the door, and Heilis slowly brings up the rear. Bray presses his shoulder against the door frame and peeks inside, his revolver held up to blast anything that happened to move inside the house. He didn't see much but a small hallway and a few sets of dirty work boots beside the door. Bray sees another opening off the hall just to his right. He steps inside, at first seeing nothing but a darkened room the window blocked by a gossamer curtain of white cotton homespun.

Bray's eyes adjust slowly to the light, and as he does, he sees the horror sitting in the center of the room at the dinner table. Bray screeches and leaps back, his revolver dropping from his hands and clattering to the floor, bile slowly creeping up his throat like acid. A shape streaks passed Bray and Heilis is in the room. He recoils with disgust his eyes filled with horror.

"Goddamn! What the hell's happened to'em?!" Heilis' eyes are wide and filled with that madness that Bray knew only too well.

"I don't know." Bray's voice sounds fake to his own ears as if his voice is coming from the end of a long hallway or echoing off the walls of a crypt.

A family of ghouls are sitting around a small dinner table. Their long cold morning repast is still sitting before them. Their flesh has been turned black and cracked like charred wood. The mother sits on the left, her white dress clashing garishly with her black skin. Her head is held at an unnatural angle as if she had frozen in the act of stretching it.

Two boys sit on the right, one older and one younger. The older boy appears to be around sixteen, blackened arms hanging loose at his sides, his head looking down almost as if in thought. The younger boy seems to be around eight, his head resting on the table in a mockery of sleep. The worst, though, is the father at the head of the table. He sits bolt upright like a statue carved of burnt obsidian. His lips pulled back in a rictus smile showing the blue-black of his gums and the grotesquely yellow teeth behind them.

The father eyes are open and are the same yellow as his teeth, the corneas wholly gone, only cloudy yellow pits hiding in the black charred face.

Bray steps back, signaling Heilis to leave as well. They beat a quick, silent retreat from the house. Bray sees that Heilis' normally ruddy complexion has become the thin white of separated milk. The other men are waiting for them outside the door, guns drawn and faces set.

Cook is back on his feet, his face gaunt and haunted in the light of the sun. As Bray and Heilis step from the doorway, an audible sigh of relief comes from the gathered group. Bray looks at each of them in turn before letting out his own haunted sigh.

"What the hells in there?" Kowalski asks in his thin, reedy voice. "Cook won't say. He just kept muttering something about yellow eyes."

"There's a family inside, but they're all dead." Bray spits, his eyes moving to the ground. "It's awful. They look like they were burnt, but there's no sign of fire."

"We need to get as far from here as possible," Cooks says his deep voice shaking. "Whatever happened to them could happen to us... or who-ever did that to them could come for us."

"I agree," Bray says, nodding. " There's nothing but trouble waiting for us here."

"Now you boys hol' on." Heilis' thick voice cuts through the air. "There's food in that cabin. You saw they had breakfast in front of them-selves. At the very least we need to raid the place."

"I ain't eating nothing from in there," Bray cuts in, turning to face Heilis. "That place is tainted by something and whatever it is kills in a bad way."

"Boys, look," Heilis says with a patronizing tone. "You may be alright with starving out here, but I ain't. I also don't see the harm in having a roof over our heads and a decent spot to watch out for those that are chasing us."

A mutter of ascent comes from Kowalski. Cook glances at Bray with fear but also with hunger. Bray meets his eyes, and he looks away. LaPointe looks confused throughout the whole talk but keeps his eyes on Kowalski. Heilis meets Bray's brown eyes with his own they flash with greed and savage triumph.

"It seems at least some of these boys have some sense," Heilis says, smirking at Bray. "If you want to go on without us, Bray, by all means, no one will stop you."

Bray knew he was beat then. He knew he wouldn't survive long alone in the cold mountains and woods. Even still, he pauses and looks past Hei-lis into the black void of the cabin's doorway. That same sickly feeling of being watched and something just being wrong was still going strong in his mind. Finally, Bray turns and looks at the group again, giving a nod.

A few hours later the group had made the cabin their own. The men who had yet to be in the cabin were shocked at the state of the bodies.

Kowalski even let out a small scream at the horrific sight of the father's dead yellow eyes. LaPointe leaps back, his hand going to his gun before stopping. Eventually, they move on to exploring the rest of the cabin.

The group let out a collective cheer at the sight of the fully stocked pantry, filled with enough food to last a small family for a full winter. They even found a hatch in the floor that leads down to a cellar with a dirt floor by way of a sturdy wooden ladder. Shelves packed with pickled vegetables and preserved fruit line the walls, and even a series of bulbs of garlic hung from the ceiling to dry. It was decided that the bodies would be better if they were moved down there.

Bray refused to so much as touch them. The rest of the men drew straws to see who would have to carry them down. Cook and Kowalski lost the draw and carried each of the bodies to the hole with a blanket, neither man willing to touch the blacked skin of the corpses. One by one each of the cadavers were dumped into the pit, the father the last of them. His yellow-toothed smile and clouded eyes glare up at them from the top of the pile in the cellar. Afterward, the other men set down and began to feast on the contents of the pantry. Bray sits away from them, munching on the last few scraps of jerky from his pack. Heilis made a point to invite Bray to join them with as condescending a tone as possible, but Bray ignored him.

"I don't eat the dead's food," Bray says, his voice thick with finality.

Heilis' glares at Bray for a moment before turning back to his food, biting into a thick piece of white bread and cheese. As the sun begins to set, Heilis instructs LaPointe to go to the window in the dining room and keep watch for possible Pinkertons and lawmen. The rest made themselves comfortable on beds and sofas. Bray remains seated in a small armchair, his eyes glued to the cellar door where the bodies have been dumped. Time begins to tick by, the sounds of snoring comes from the bedrooms. Even Bray, himself, had started to doze when LaPointe let out a cry of alarm.

Bray sprung out of the chair and runs to the window where LaPointe stands guard. LaPointe gestures into the trees, a thin ground fog had taken over outside and in the moonlight gives the world a haunted, ethereal feel. Bray looked to where LaPointe was gesturing and saw what appeared at first to be the glow of two search lanterns, but they didn't move. The lights hung in the air, never wavering almost as if two men were standing outside and holding up the lanterns to inspect the house. Bray saw to his horror that the lights were much too small to be lanterns and instead appeared to be the eyes of some animal standing at the edge of the field.

Bray continued to stare, but the lights suddenly disappear as if they were never there. Bray and LaPointe glance at each other just as Heilis, Cook, and Kowalski all run into the room their guns drawn.

"What the hell happened?!" Heilis growls, "What's the Frenchman hollerin' about?!"

"We saw lights out near the treeline," Bray says, his eyes not leaving the window. "They've gone now, though. I could have sworn they were searchlights, but they didn't look right."

Heilis moves to the window, looking out. "I don't see nothin'. I think you boys need to get your damn heads on straight."

A loud thud echoes through the cabin, shaking the boards under their feet. All the men whirl around looking for the source. Another thud reverberates out in the hallway. Bray steps forward and looks down the hall. Suddenly, the trap door of the cellar gives an almighty heave and flies open slamming against the wooden boards of the floor.

"Jesus!" Bray calls, his revolver clearing its holster. "The cellar doors open!"

The group pours from the tiny dining room and gather around the black gaping hole in the center of the living room floor. The cellar was completely black, and the bottom was invisible in the thin light being cast by the fireplace.

"Go get a lantern," Heilis orders Cook. The big man nods and quickly grabs one from a nearby bedroom.

After striking a sulfur match and lighting the lantern, Cook leans over the hole, crouching down to let the light from the lamp illuminate the ladder beyond. However, the light still didn't reach the floor.

"Drop it," Heilis mutters to Cook, who looks horrified.

"Are you trying to burn us alive? It'll bust." Cooks eyes are locked on Heilis' face.

"No, it won't. It'll land on them bodies down there. Drop the damn thing." Heilis swats at Cook's hand before he can argue again and the lantern slips from his grip. Instead of thudding softly against the stacked bodies below, the lantern thwacks against the soft dirt of the cellar floor. The bodies are not piled at the bottom of the ladder where they had left them. The group stood in shocked horror at the sight of the empty floor.

Bray steps back from the hole, his eyes wide and face pale.

"Where the hell..." A loud chittering noise comes up from the darkness below, a sound almost animal-like but not quite right. It is almost as if something was making an animal sound to attract game, like a turkey hunter calling for birds. The sound continues, and the men look down again, but nothing seems to be there. The light from the lantern below first starts to gutter and then goes out entirely.

The noise gets louder moving closer to the ladder. Cook is still crouched nearest the hole, his eyes squinted. His hand pulls the revolver clear from its holster again. The sound stops, and the room is filled with silence. Cook slowly begins to move back from the gaping void of the cellar, his eyes never leaving the dark expanse.

Cook reaches for the door to shut it, but before he can, he falters, his boot sliding across the boards. His head slams against the wood of the door, leaving a streak of crimson across it before he falls into the cellar. The door falls with a hard slam before anyone can react. A breathless second of stunned silence passes before Bray grabs the door again and wrenches it open.

"Cook!" Bray screams, the door bouncing and closing as it slams into the wall again. Kowalski grabs it before it can slam down again and Bray drops to his hands and knees to call to Cook, but before the words leave his mouth, he's stunned by the sight of two glowing eyes shining at him from the darkness below. These are the same lights that Bray had seen outside the house, and he screams, falling backwards. Bray's hand fumbles for his gun but his fingers can't make purchase.

Kowalski screams as well and lets the door crash down again. The men bolt, running for the front door in a mad dash. LaPointe breaks through first, a stream of French babbling from his mouth. Kowalski comes through next, followed by Heilis and Bray. The three men come to a sliding stop at the sight that awaits them outside.

The light from two more sets of glowing eyes shine at them from the tree line. LaPointe is running straight towards them in a complete panic, his eyes fixed over his shoulder at the house.

"Stop!" Bray screams, "They're in the trees!"

LaPointe, either in ignorance of what Bray said or in too much of a panic to care, continues to bolt for the forest. As soon as he crosses into the trees, the lights blink out. A long, tense moment creeps past with Bray and the others standing in stupefied silence before a drawn-out, horrific guttural scream rends the air. The remaining group turn and flee back into the house, slamming the door behind them. Bray comes to a breathless stop against the wall of the interior hallway. Heilis backs slowly into the light of the living room.

Kowalski is a gibbering, crying mess, his thin chest heaving and his eyes wide with shock and horror. Bray looks over to try and quiet the sobbing man when the light of two glowing eyes catch his attention from the dark dining room behind Kowalski. Slowly the eyes move closer, and the blackened, twisted, mangled face of the Father comes into the light. Kowalski slowly turns, his breath catching in his chest. A thick squelching sound fills the air, and Kowalski's breaths become choked blood-filled gurgles as the Father's thick, dark hands rip into Kowalski's stomach, tearing it open.

Kowalski's guts fall out onto the floor followed by his eviscerated corpse. Bray screams as he pulls his revolver and begins to back into the living room. Heilis has drawn his gun as well and backs closer to the wall. Loud thumps echo through the house as the Father stomps towards the living room dragging the mangled corpse of Kowalski behind him, his teeth still grinning in a madman's smile. Bray fires into the thing's chest, but the bullet sends only a thin puff of black smoke as if he had shot a bag of charcoal instead of a man.

Bray fires again and again until the only sound is the dry click of the hammer falling on dead shells. The father continues it's unstoppable thudding stride into the living room. Heilis raises his gun as he steps further back. He fires once and hits the monstrosity in the head, but the thing refuses to stop. Bray hears a familiar sound fill the room, a chittering like the sound of a raccoon or squirrel but not quite. Bray's eyes fall onto the trap door of the cellar and sees it open, two shining yellow eyes filling the gap. Before Bray can shout a warning, a small blackened hand shoots from the darkness grabbing Heilis' leg and yanks him down.

Heilis' revolver falls from his hand, clattering to the ground at the Father's feet. His hands grapple at the boards of the floor, but the thing in the basement pulls him slowly into the hole. Heilis' fingernails dig into the wood, pulling up splinters before finally ripping from his fingertips and leaving thin trails of blood as he is pulled into the darkness of the cellar below. Bray hears his screams go on for an eternity before being silenced. Bray slowly turns to look at the Father.

The thing stands there, its yellow eyes flashing and teeth still smiling that same lunatic grin. Slowly the jaws pull apart, and the sound of creaking tendons is audible in the silent room. A low, rasping gasp comes out of the Father's mouth.

"Go..." The thing says its words sounding like wind blowing over fallen gravestones.

Bray runs. He bolts for the trees, and when he gets there, he keeps running. Bray glances to the side of the path that they had followed to make it to the cabin and sees LaPointe's mangled, eviscerated body lying against a fallen tree. Two pairs of glowing yellow eyes stare at Bray from beside it. Bray keeps running, his mind wandering to why he had refused to eat the food in the first place. His mother had grown up in an Indian tribe.

She had told Bray to never eat food that was meant for the dead or else they would seek revenge. Bray's mind wanders back to the full pantry back in that awful charnel house. He refused to eat their food, and so the dead had spared him, he knew that the dead were always hungry. He glances over his shoulder and sees four pairs of yellow eyes, staring at him from the path just behind. Bray remembers that the dead are always hungry.   ✗

ZEN ZOMBIES
Ryan Aussie Smith

THUD, THUD, THUD.

There it is again, the relentless drumming that quickens the closer it gets. The discourteous intrusion to the serenity of our 7th street overpass will not go unnoticed. Why, dear brothers and sisters, do they insist on disturbing the silence? Do they not know the perfection of a subway tunnel, the beauty of a lake bed, or the reflective quiet of an unused overpass? No, siblings. The answer is no. They must have noise and light, sex and violence, hunger and thirst... but never Zen. They refuse to find calm attentiveness, to allow intuition to guide action rather than conscious effort.

Always busy. Sporadically searching to fill a void that is bottomless. Cursed with hunger that is never satisfied and thirst that can not be quenched. All the while tending to flesh that will eventually rot away. They neglect what is truly important: spirit. When enriching the spirit there is no need to bludgeon a man and his dog to death for the liquids in his pack. There is no need to cannibalize a neighbour in a fear of not having enough. There is a need, however, to stare at the symmetrical beauty inherent in every tile wall. To stand in perfect silence and be utterly consumed in the Now.

Wake from your meditation, dear brothers and sisters. Understand what must commence. Our rhythmic chants must disturb the unenlightened as they draw clubs and blades in anticipation. The screams may hurt your ears and the flesh burn your tongue, but please persist. The Buddha teaches that the root of suffering is attachment, so we must strip attachment away. Devour until bursting brothers and sisters, Strip sinew from bone and beating heart from chest. They will thank you for your labors when they are made whole like us.

When it is over, silence rewards your sacrifice. We are not meant to move through life at a fever pace. Sometimes you must stop and smell the overpass.

⚔

CASSIUS MAX
KT Morley

The tinny voice of Rhisa, both his ship and AI, punctured John's euphoric rest cycle. "Mission parameters: Following planetfall, assemble inspection team and recon local region in preparation for Corporate incursion. Special weapons issued: none. Special surveillance equipment: none. Special circumstance: if initial human contact unsuccessful, presume hostile. Special biological conditions: Floral: none, fauna: none, higher life forms: none. Humans: evidence of heightened immune response. Regenerative properties of the population reported superior to species norms."

"Affirmative, Rhisa," John confirmed, sloughing forward in his berth. "Standard mission parameters. Noted, regenerative properties of native humans. Query: contagion resistant?"

"Negative, Captain Smith. Available intel indicates transmutation under ZOMB protocols will occur along normal, iterative timelines."

John grunted, "Standard Op."

"Yes, sir," Rhisa replied.

The Zoological Operations and Management Bureau required total commitment from its reconnaissance teams. The signed documents and training of standard Armed Forces or Space Divisions didn't cut it. For the recon division John served in, the Zom-Bs preferred candidates with no families or close friends. It helped deniability. No one came looking for missing people if there was no one to miss them in the first place.

The tubes in John's arms flexed with nutrients. The rest of the Bureau avoided contact with the recon teams. The conversion process pushed the appearance and social spectrum of converts well outside acceptable human norms. The slate-gray skin and lifeless eyes of recon teams tended to chase people away. Even skin as black as John's lost its brilliance and faded into a deep gray.

Memory files weren't incorporated into his upgrade. They never were. He was rebuilt and reborn. Recon, Zom-Bs in Department lingo, received precision training supporting mission parameters. After conversion, everything from eating to walking required relearning. His body even needed lessons on how to employ the ZOMB tech to heal itself. Those lessons involved painful repetitions on variations of punched, stabbed, or shot. He learned combat and computer skills, as well.

There were no classes on empathy.

Part of the transference of the human genome for ZOMB tech also came with a name change. Selected before the procedure, the list of choices consisted of precisely two names, John Smith or Jane Doe. Zom-B names added to the oddities pushing asset teams outside typical social structures. Like the rest of his unit, John wasn't much fun at a party.

He shifted—shuffled—straightening in his berth. "Message received. Ready for shift."

He generally stood in his berth, arms dangling along with the tubes and wires tying him to Rhisa. His head drooped forward, too, resting on his chest while the ship maintained his life support through injections of fluids and nutrients. He didn't need much of either; the conversion process had taken care of most of his requirements through Science. The minimal gravity Rhisa offered, combined with his magsuit, kept him upright and facing the computer terminals. The screens stared back. For five minutes every other hour, John awoke to conduct routine over-watch of systems and mission progress.

Twenty-four hours out from the planet, the computer system altered his nutrient flow. Thousands of nanites and conversion-tech microbots bombard John's biological system. The nanites began supercharging every muscle fiber and organ, driving adrenalin levels up in the slow, exponential arc he had come to love. Their influence produced a high, leaving him on the edge of barely contained excitement.

A memory swirled out of the shadow and fog of his mind. A little girl in a pretty dress, black curls bouncing and eyes smiling, sat surrounded by mountains of colored paper. "Daddy, play with me."

A woman sat next to her. She appeared to be an older version of the girl—his tech could pull those details even from operational photos, so pulling apart subversive and dilapidated partial memories was well within parameters. He tried to dig deeper, but the image faded as the mist tore it apart and sent it back into the depths of his overridden mind. The relapses were becoming more prominent.

John's wait on station above Cassius Max, almost a whole day of five-minute shifts, neared its end. He stirred, restless at the wait, and eager to free the nanites, microbots, and contagion to do their job. His muscles pulsed, ready. The additional tech injected into his system upon arrival to strengthen his muscles and thicken his skin had completed their chore. They had enhanced interior reservoirs for everything, from nutrients to invasive tech. He could even store oxygen in his cells for several hours of underwater survival. The Bureau's post-conversion explanations and debrief had all seemed sound, but part of his mind still had doubts. Specifically, the area birthing those memories he shouldn't be having.

Those ghosts came from his past, too. Their shifting images he kept to himself. He didn't see any need to burden the psych teams with his only real company on these missions. He knew they would wipe his mind again. They had the first time he told them about the memories. Something in him resisted, and so the memories stayed. He hadn't told anyone else about the ghosts, not even other Zom-Bs.

"Rhisa, begin time count on current wake cycle. Prepare cryo sleep to commence following wake-cycle shift."

"Affirmative, Officer Smith. Shall I prep the launch shuttle?"

"Yes. Notify me when it is ready. I'll launch during the next sleep cycle. Prepare onboard wake-up procedure during planetfall."

"Yes, Officer Smith."

Memory, unbeckoned and unchecked, bubbled to the surface again. Cassius Max had triggered multiple memory flashes. A child's beautiful smile ghosted through his mind, a balloon in one hand and a parent's hand in the other—his hand, dark, strong. The fingers of his left hand twitched involuntarily, the remembered touch of the child's hand in his stirring muscle memory not entirely erased by the conversion's contagion or subsequent memory wipe. The hand now only bore the gray, sloughing flesh of the Zom-B corp.

"Officer Smith, your launch vehicle is ready. I will load your cryo cell during the next sleep cycle."

"Confirmed," John said, checking a box on the long list of preflight components. The computer would check the rest while he slept. If a fault developed, Rhisa would scrub the launch and wake him. He would then begin repairs and oversight of the affected systems.

John worked without thought or interruption through most of his last shift, continuing his research into indigenous life. It seemed the humans of Cassius Max had slipped their leash. Why else would he be here? When the tether holding worlds under Earth's influence grew too weak or frayed, EarthGov took steps to regain control. When worlds escaped the bureaucracy entirely, ZOMB or Space Force Command had to come and reassert regional authority. It's what Zom-Bs recon teams did best, too. EarthGov would not condone a rash of independent-minded worlds angling for freedom. Specifically, no one challenged Earth's authority. Earth squashed independent-minded planets soonest and with extreme prejudice.

Rhisa broke in, "Sixty seconds remaining in standard shift." With the precision only a machine or Zom-B could appreciate, she continued, "59, 58, 57—".

"Auto countdown volume to zero," John commanded, continuing, "Final warning at ten seconds acceptable at audible levels."

"Affirmative, Officer Smith."

John finished his study of pod landing sites and entered the data for Rhisa's review.

"Ten seconds until your watch ends, John."

"Acknowledged."

Something nibbled at the back of his mind. Planet Cassius Max had a curiously high life expectancy. John opened the file on regenerative properties and started reading.

Holy shit! These guys are on to something.

"Pause display and download unread files for evaluation planet-side."

The tubes attached to his arms pulled tight as the saline and nutrient drip filled with his sleep narcotic. The world started to pull apart at the seams as the drug took hold. His head felt like a giant ball of cotton, and his mind went fuzzy as the world spun into a kaleidoscope of euphoric color. Then everything went black.

* * * *

John awoke in the cryo pod as it crashed through the upper canopy of a deciduous forest in the northern hemisphere of the planet's only continent. Lumber had been one of the primary exports of the world before it went dark. Sometimes dark meant disaster, but his scans from orbit indicated an abundance of life. He had a hard time finding a perfect landing spot for the pod where he wouldn't be seen and approached before he was ready.

He spent the last of the pod's landing fuel in a precise burn, nearly flat-lining his velocity. He dropped the final meter in the comfortable embrace of the .9g of Cassius Max, landing with a gentle thud. The pod rocked back, its design allowing for it to recline to an angle of seventy-five degrees with the ground. When the pod hit the prescribed angle, two landing stanchions extended from the nose-cone to break its fall and leave the whole ship resting at an angle perfect for relaunch into space.

John stepped out of his cryotube and activated the pod-bay door, welcoming the brisk, scent-packed air of the forest into his vehicle. His sense of smell, enhanced to nearly canine levels from the conversion, brought with it the smell of loam and leaf. He could taste the humidity in the air, and something else, something frightened and angry.

John looked to the doorway as a shadow leaped from behind a nearby tree. The animal tore into his left arm, tearing flesh away in a snarl and exposing the bone beneath. He reacted with the deliberate ease of a man, a Zom-B, devoid of fear or its manifestations. He mashed his right fist into the creature's skull and sent it rolling across the floor to lie motionless against the far wall of his pod.

John appreciated this part the best and counted out loud. "One, two, three—."

The animal, similar to a dog, but broader across the shoulders and taller with a small, smashed face, shook involuntarily and then stood. It turned in a circle on unstable legs before looking at John and sitting. Its eyes had the glassy look of contagion, and its thick tongue drooped listlessly as the animal panted.

John pointed to the door. "Outside, Max. Begin patrol and set a perimeter twenty meters from the pod. Convert others."

John could feel his link to Max brighten as the nanites and microbots the creature consumed overwhelmed its mind, slaving him to John. Two hours later, the dog had bitten and spread contagion to two squirrels and a rabbit, so John expanded his perimeter to thirty meters.

Max's senses sent responses back to John. Soon, the dog's sense of smell caught something new on the air. The nanites sent that to John as well. Through the data feed, John could detect a change in temperature coming from the southeast. It had the hallmark of a stream, and when Max saw it, the images of bubbling, gurgling water slithered through the nanite connection. The stream cooled the air, tinging it with a distinct aroma. He tasked Max to investigate.

The messages he picked up from Max left his senses reeling. Unbidden, John pitched forward. He watched his arms swing to break his fall, his mind otherwise consumed by the memory engram sprouting and overtaking his mental processes. The link to Max wavered. Details from the other animals in the sentry detail washed away in the forcefulness of the sensory memory ignited by the smell the nanites returned.

A girl, laughing and splashing, kicked and squealed in the small turn of a stream. John could see a woman sitting next to her in the water, black hair falling in rivulets over black shoulders before contrasting sharply with the neon bathing suit the woman wore. The sound of the brook engulfed him, an echo of the one Max watched and to which the nanites responded. The overlapping sensory response triggered an automated warning from Rhisa.

"Mr. Smith, are you hurt?"

His breathing stopped, and his heart slowed in the memory's grip. The contagion in his system fought to override the images and respond to Rhisa. Slowly, his mental grip on the memory slipped. They disappeared a quickly as they'd come. John straightened, breathing normally. He tried to push the memory back into his conscious mind, but his hold kept sliding off. The memory seemed covered in some viscous liquid. Try as he might, he couldn't hold onto it and its grip resistant sheen. The contagion continued to slide over the memory and spew the lacquer that kept his mind from succeeding. In the aftermath of the memory's departure, John cocked his head, wondering if it had happened at all.

The world rushed back, Max and the other sentry's sweeping back into his consciousness through their contagion connection and its nanite sorcery. John forced his will on the nanite storm his small assault had launched on the forest. With it, his view of the world through the nanites began shifting over the next several hours as he finished reading and updating his plan based on the data files he had postponed until landing. As his converts lived and died their lives, others moved in to take their place. Anything consuming the flesh of one of his disciples would inherit the contagion and nanites.

As proof, the rabbit dropped out. A pair of new dog-like creatures sprouted. His tether to them was weaker. The new beasts were third-generation, having consumed the rabbit. He could command them, but it took a more forceful directive. At five iterations out, he wouldn't be able to do that at all. Fifth gens would follow the other converts in a strange, contagion-linked cohort. At seven, his devotees wouldn't attack him, but they wouldn't do anything else, either. Given enough time, and with more nanites, the sixes might surrender entirely—and definitely the fives—but on recon, the nanites couldn't replicate fast enough to replenish themselves. At mission's end, when he departed for Rhisa, all of the creatures in the chain would languish and die. Humans would fare better, but then Earth-Gov would arrive.

He turned back to the pod and sealed it. Reaching into the nanite link, he tasked the second and third-generation animals to maintain a vigilant lookout on his items and commanded them to convert others. He only wanted the second gen to do any conversions, and limited them to a dozen total. John offered a preference for diversity, the habitat should resemble its natural look.

Turning, he called, "Max! Come! We are going to try and find the locals." A bark echoed through the trees from the southeast, and John could hear the bushes and thickets shaking as the big dog hustled back to him.

They retraced the southeast passage, pausing at the stream as John shambled into the water, trying to fish out the memory from earlier. It didn't work. They continued for the remainder of the day in a generally southeast track. He had a mental map of the land and angled for one of the outlying homesteads. He would start with a small conversion to plumb the minds and lives of the planet first. Once he collected enough information from the countryside, he would move into larger towns and metropolitan centers. If he couldn't get the info he needed, he had the authorization to target government centers. He could take most of them down on his own, creating first and second-gen populations once inside the buildings themselves. A month after John dismantled the government, EarthGov would arrive with a fleet to pound the rudderless world back into line.

* * * *

Night found John before he found the farmhouse. Unsure of how often he would be able to rest in the future, he decided to find shelter in the lee of a fallen tree. Max settled in next to him. Despite his ongoing battle with memory lapses, no dreams disturbed him—no images of forgotten pasts and unknown families.

* * * *

The first rays of dawn, barely threatening the horizon, were enough to trigger his nanites to wakefulness. John patted the wound on his arm where Max had bitten him, and scratched the puggish head of the beast. Already the hunk of flesh had rebirthed and filled the bite-sized portion Max had eaten. Its pinkish color wouldn't match his natural, darker complexion for another month. Inside two, there wouldn't even be a scar. All of his injuries healed that way. The external ones, anyway.

John lumbered to his feet, the nanites swirling to obey him and begin their transformation of wayward humanity on a course more in line with EarthGov philosophy. Max rose with him and immediately staggered into the predawn in search of a tree. By now, the virus in Max would have neutralized natural inclinations to hunger and food. Slowly, the virus would tear Max apart. In the end, nothing would be left. Zom-Bs could leave no trace or evidence pointing back to government interference in the independent rule of sovereign worlds. Humans infected would read as such on EarthGov equipment and be rounded up when order was restored. Even John, if caught, could trigger self-termination. The nanites would destroy the contagion and then decode themselves. In less than an hour, he would be a pile of dust. For now, he and Max were strong and capable. In front of him, still hiding in shadow not yet diminished by ever-quickening dawn, stood the first house and converts.

As he watched, someone opened the door, spilling yellow light into the graying morning. A shadow blocked the light as the farmer hustled through. John watched him pull on a parka against the chill before heading to the barn. John followed, silently stalking from behind the first two rows of trees bordering the property. When the farmer went into the barn, John lurched across a short open space to the rear wall of the construct. Max chuffed at his heals, spurring John to slow-walk to the entrance the farmer used. Max followed soundlessly, tongue lolling.

John swept into the barn, silent as a shadow. The farmer waited, a sneer on his face. With a grunt, the man slammed a pitchfork into John's belly. John dug his heels into the ground to resist, grabbing the outside tines and pushing back from his end of the pitchfork. Even with the nanites and microbots supporting him, the farmer drove John back toward the wall next to the open barn door.

The tines wormed their way through his flesh, enthusiastically encouraged by the farmer's twisting of the makeshift weapon. John lost ground and suddenly felt the wall behind him scraping the tines. The vibration had an unnatural feel, and John screamed, a fractured, hiss-like wail. He had had to fight humans before, but this one showed a resilience John had thought long gone in his former species.

With a shove, the farmer slammed the tool into the wall with enough force to leave it quivering in the air when he let go and stumbled forward from his effort. John threw a wild punch, connecting with the farmer's mouth. The man's teeth scored John's knuckles, opening the skin and freeing the teeming nanites and sickness John carried to harry humanity back into EarthGov's control.

The farmer spun backward and turned his attention to Max as the dog howled at John's predicament and launched a feral attack. The farmer fought with huge fists, slamming the dog several times with rib-cracking force. Max came on with relentless intention, backing the man against the opposite wall. On the farmer's right, a collection of tools hung in perfect order. His hands knew where the scythe rested and jerked it from its roost in a sweeping arc at Max.

Max avoided the wicked-looking scythe, ducking low as he advanced on the farmer. John tilted his head in curiosity; there didn't seem to be much worry on the farmer's face. Nor fear. Max feinted an attack at the man's arm and backed away, paw's forward, teeth bared in the rictus of a snarl.

John continued his fight with the pitchfork, pushing on it while swaying it from side to side to free it, first from the wall and then from his body. Throughout, he hissed and raged as nanites and contagion swirled in him, protecting him from harm and eager to assert control over this new lifeform.

Max was losing ground and the scythe finally found a mark, lashing across Max's forepaw and severing it. The big brute howled, driving John into a feverish attempt to free himself.

Someone else entered the barn.

The farmer paused, halting the killing strike aimed at Max's head. He yelled, the tremor in his voice the first outward sign of any fear in the man. "Heather, get back in the house! Move it, girl."

John saw his chance, the girl couldn't have been more than ten, and she was only a few feet away. With a mighty effort, he tore free of the pitchfork, trailing blood and gore as a loop of his intestine also found its way through one of the holes.

The girl screamed, as did the farmer, racing to try and help her. He was too far away, though. Max had kept him on the other side of the barn. John grabbed the girl, slinging her under one arm. He turned his back on the farmer, counting on his leather-tough skin and denser bones to protect him from anything the girl's father might try. The scythe waw a concern, but probably not with the girl clutched against him like she was.

John slammed his face down into the girl's neck and bit deeply into her soft flesh. The bite triggered a flood of contagion and nanites. They swarmed into the girl's bloodstream.

The farmer screamed with fury and threw the scythe at John. Again, the man's anger and aggression proved a match for John. The scythe impaled John, sliding between ribs while it's steel pried them apart under the force of the farmer's throw. The blade missed the girl, but only by luck and the turn it took from one of John's ribs. The handle snapped, whipping wildly from the force of the blow. Inside John's chest, the point grated against bone while the girl went limp in his arms.

He set the child down, silently counting the seconds until complete conversion, and turned to face the farmer. He pivoted just in time to catch the full force of the other man's shoulder as it slammed into his midsection. Arms of steel clutched him and drove him hard into the wall from which he had just freed himself. The blade in John's back snapped on impact, shoving the length of steel in his body past the rib and through his shirt. It also tore through the farmer's shirt and punched into the other man's flesh. Nanites and contagion rushed forward. The farmer pushed himself away. Blood dripped from the end of the weapon, each drop a warren of nanites and contagion.

John could see it all—all of the infection and nanites straining for virgin flesh as it seeped from his wounds; he could see it spread to the farmer's clothes, carried in a torrent of ZOMB technology. They sensed the farmer and his hammering heartbeat. With their single-minded training well entrenched, his biological weapons assaulted the farmer.

The farmer shook his hand and rubbed his jaw. An irritable, small rash had developed from where John's punch landed. The man then pressed the contagion-dripping hand against the more substantial hole in his chest. Blood from the farmer's split lip dotted the back of the hand.

Max hobbled over to stand next to John, whining and licking the stub where his paw had been. The nanites could heal wounds, but they couldn't grow limbs for the converted. They could grow limbs for John, they were programmed to his DNA, but Max would have to make do.

John wrapped both hands around the protruding blade. He pulled it the rest of the way through his body. The effort required substantial force, dragging the steel between two of his ribs. His hands received numerous, deep cuts. When he finished, he cast the blade aside, freeing his flesh of the invasive item and allowing his biological defenses to repair the damage.

In front of him, the child convulsed on the floor, and the farmer staggered. John frowned. Both should be wholly his, but he couldn't sense them as he did Max, the very distant squirrels, or any of the others. He opened his mouth in a silent, wordless scream directed at both of them. His eyes bulged, and blood seeped from his many cuts, dripping to the straw-strewn floor. His system had finally caught up to the fray, and soon the seeping would stop.

The farmer looked dizzy and disoriented, but still in possession of his mind and body. John had never heard of a strain of humanity resistant to ZOMB tech. Here, on this backwater world, two fought against the swarming invasion he unleashed on them. Their defense was admirable, but biology wouldn't beat his tech. It couldn't. Their conversion remained integral to his infiltration and counter-government insurgence.

Despite his certainty, in front of him, the scene begged reevaluation. The farmer's eyes started clearing, and he headed straight for his daughter. Bending down, he picked her shaking body off the bloody floor. She whimpered, crying, her neck covered in blood, and John's bite mark still leaking more. The farmer cast a look of unmitigated hatred at John and fled the barn.

Max lapped at the puddles of blood. The nutrients present in them would replenish his strength and help him heal from his several hurts. John's system surged, continuing its repair of his broken systems. Already, the damage from the tines was scarcely visible. As he watched, the loop of intestine slithered back into his abdomen in agonizing slowness. His chest wound from the scythe would take longer, but the damage in his back seemed markedly better. He figured he would reconnoiter with his pod for a full system check before returning to the farm.

John reached for the door of the barn, his hand healed, but bloody from the blade and the farmer's teeth. He pushed out into the dark and then wiped the hand on his shirt. Max hobbled next to him.

* * * *

John woke from a dream of such intensity; he had to check himself. His heart raced, and his skin burned. He couldn't sense the squirrels, but Max lay next to him. The pod rested another dozen steps in front of him. His wounds had overcome him. Now it was dark again, and night invaded his campsite.

Max licked at his stub and settled sad eyes on John. John climbed the rest of the way into the pod and plugged the tubes and drips of ZOMB tech into their ports on his body. Slowly, the pod began to run his fluids through its filtering system, culling dead nanites while replenishing the contagion and microbot supports.

When the computer chirped a warning, John ignored it; it always did that when he plugged in while injured. The process ran with increased vigor because of the severity of his injuries. He passed out several times through the system-wash. Each time he fainted, he dropped into the surreal dream-world. For some reason, he now understood that the dark hand he saw holding the little girl's hand was his. He had loved the woman, and the child was theirs. He wanted to see more of them.

The computer's incessant wail brought him out of his latest dreamscape. The pod's console was a wall of flickering lights. John turned off the siren's howl, afraid it might draw attention. He began analyzing the maniacal panoply in front of him. System compromises flared across the board. Everything to do with ZOMB tech was flashing yellow or red. Mostly red. Those not flashing had collapsed into the baleful, solid glow of utter failure.

"Computer, status?"

"Officer Smith, your bio-system is compromised. Recommend native sample for analysis and nanite reprogramming."

"Negative, Computer. I have multiple soft-tissue failure points. I need to stabilize before I can resume tasks."

The computer voice fractured, stuttering before failing. After a second of absolute silence, a long, high-pitched feedback note crashed through the small pod until the vocal node burst.

That's a first, John thought.

John looked out of his pod to Max lying on the forest floor. His connection to Max was fuzzy, almost gone. Unless Max was dead, and a simple leg wound shouldn't have created that much trauma, Max's nanite horde should be thriving.

"Seal ship," John barked, voice raspy to his ears.

The doors rocketed closed. John's head swam as sight and sound warred within him. Everything clashed against his internal programming. Breathing became a strained exercise, and then his internal systems began fluttering on and off.

John's eyes glazed, corrupting his input sensors and limiting vision still further.

Distantly, he heard himself say, "Computer, prep for takeoff." His voice sounded scratchy, chipped, and broken.

"System functions compromised, ascent uncertain."

"Launch, damn it! Get me off this planet!"

The computer obeyed, firing the booster rockets and hurling the pod away from the surface.

* * * *

The farmer stood rubbing his jaw, a stained bandage wrapped around his chest. His shoulders sat like boulders on top of his arms. "Maybe that will be the last of them," he said quietly so as not to disturb the sleeping girl he held as she rested her head on one of those same shoulders.

The woman next to him, shorter by a foot, watched the trail of the departing ship.

"They're too stubborn by half, my love."

"They're human," he replied.

"No. they have broken with humanity to create something malevolent and evil." She turned and looked up at him. "They've no interest in us other than lashing us to the collective. They seek only unconditional servitude."

The farmer looked at her for a moment and then leaned down to kiss her, wincing at the pain in his jaw. Straightening, he looked back at the departing ship. "Well, they're about to get a dose of their own medicine."

* * * *

John longed for the quiet of space, the silence of absolute nothing. The g-force of his rushed escape ushered him into unconsciousness and the waiting arms of the beautiful woman he'd been seeing in his dreams.

They stood together, watching, as a cigar-shaped ship slammed into the Earth a hundred yards in front of them. John screamed for his daughter to come back. In the dream, he could feel the fear. The woman next to him tore free and raced toward where the girl sat playing halfway between where they stood and the ship.

As John watched, the ship belched forth a single person. The woman stood tall, gray skin devoid of color or anything else resembling life. Across the front of her crisp uniform, he could read ZOMB. It meant nothing to him. He charged forward to save his family at the same time the gray lady moved toward them. He screamed at the top of his lungs, but he was too late. He was always too late. The ZOMB woman acted without remorse or care. Killing the child and then the woman before turning to him.

John watched her dead eyes assess him. With nothing of his life left hanging in the balance, he charged.

The woman spoke, her comment as devoid of life as her appearance. "Rhisa, male subject accessible, acquiring."

✗

A NANOTECH SAMSARA

J.N. Cameron

Carlos.

She whispers my name with lips like ripe strawberries, sugary and moist. We press together, skin against skin. We grind together. All space and time lead to that focal point of electric pleasure.

The pleasure morphs into horror as her hand slips from mine. We are in the garden on the 110th floor of our building. She has fallen over the railing. I try to hold onto her, but I'm not strong enough.

Maria falls.

I watch her topple over and over like a rag doll. She hits a parapet fifty yards down, and her head blossoms into a red mist.

She keeps falling.

Dark. She is gone. I sit up, and I'm wet, as are the sheets. No air jets—the bed programming has failed again.

I stand up naked to the polycarb wall.

"Shades off," I order. A line of black lowers, and grids of phosphor-green flash from one end of my room to the other. Squinting, I bring a hand over my face. An ebony-black bot hovers outside—a corporate scanner.

From my penthouse, the lights of SoCal are a sea of neon circuses. Scanners hit all the spirals, towers, and space needles while holograms sell sex, drugs, and jazz. Myriads of automatons swarm around the pyramids and through the arches. Pipes rise from the underground factories to belch gouts of crimson flame into the night.

I stretch and take it all in.

A fool is reflected in front of me. The brilliant city is the color of his skin. There are dark, puffy circles around his eyes, and he's losing hair. He's blubbery, not the lean runner and wrestler of his youth.

"Shades back on."

The line of black rises, and I'm in darkness again. Dropping to the mattress, I tug on my gauntlets and adjust my headset. I haven't used the VR room in years. I prefer staying in bed.

First, I flip through the news channels. It's nothing new. Luddite cults are bombing robotics factories in Rancho Cucamonga, and tribes from the badlands are attacking the outer wall at El Cajon. MSofft stock is up two points and looking bullish, and East LAFC beat West LAFC, four to one.

Next, I scroll through my mail.

It's all junk, but one ad catches my attention. The government authorized manufacturer of Self-Conscious Artificial Beings, *Scabs*, is releasing a new product in one week, and Exypnos Ltd. is offering a fifteen-percent discount on preorders.

I told myself that I wouldn't do this. It's been five years since Maria's been gone, and the dreams won't go away. Sometimes when I wake, the lavender scent of her perfume hangs in the air. I can't walk on the Solana Beach Wall Platform without thinking of her. I proposed right under the guard tower lights at Roberto's Taco Shop on the middle tier of the city, and we were married in the chapel on N. Granados and E. Cliff.

The erotic programs with their predictable plots don't do it for me. The bots in the sex-shops with their rubbery skin and herky-jerky movements don't take away the loneliness. Nothing has been able to replace her.

I follow the Exypnos Ltd. link to their website. A representative wearing a lab coat and a red tie greets me in the virtual lobby. His gray hair is high and tight, and his square jaw is clean-shaven.

"I'm Dr. Jean Marchand. I've been expecting you, Carlos. Don't feign surprise. We knew you would approach us."

"How?" I ask, though I know the answer.

"Algorithms. Our data conglomeration and computational autonomy are second to none. You miss her."

"I do."

"I know. Let's take the next step together."

* * * *

A week later, Exypnos Ltd. sends Maria's Consciousness Programming to my inbox. I code my polyatomic printer to fabricate the housing. Layer by layer, a cube of one-inch sides materializes. A 3-D image of Maria's face glows in the center of each prismatic surface, and if I turn the cube, I can see under her chin or the top of her head. She blinks and smiles—that crooked smile with the left side of her upper lip raised.

She mouths something.

"Connect speakers to the consciousness housing!" I shout. Maria's mouth moves again, and her voice crackles from all four of my bedroom walls.

"Carlos, is that you? Where am I?"

"What do you mean? You're at home."

Her smile disappears, and she glances from side to side, eyes wide in confusion. I wonder what she sees as I lean back and place the cube on my chest.

After taking it all in, she speaks again.

"Carlos, listen to me. I don't like this!"

"What don't you like, bebé?"

"Am I dead?"

"Speakers off," I order the room. How did she come up with that question? The program isn't supposed to retain any memory of death. With the price tag she came with, I don't really want complaints from the product. I make a mental note to include this in my InstaFace reviews.

As I set the housing on my nightstand, her mouth opens wide in a silent scream, and anger flashes in her eyes. I grab a nearby towel and toss it over her.

Soon, she'll have nothing to worry about. Maria will have a body again.

* * * *

"A guest has arrived," announces my apartment in a bass rumble. Last year, I programmed it to sound like James Earl Jones.

"Show me who it is."

The wall next to my bed lights up. A bot with bright-blue plating and *Exypnos Ltd.* stenciled on the sides hovers in the hall. A single eye extends from a cable at the top of its boxy body, and several wiry arms dangle on each side. Pincers at the end of one arm grip a small, black case by the handle.

I climb out of bed and slip on my boxers.

"Open."

The doors slide apart, and I motion for it to enter. The bot hovers through the sterilization mist and into my room by a few feet before stopping. I approach, and it scans my right eye.

"The second part of your purchase delivery is complete," a hollow, falsetto voice announces. "A receipt will be sent to your account."

I accept the case, and it's surprisingly light. An electronic lock interface blinks in digital red.

"Thank you for choosing Exypnos Ltd.," it says and spins around. Again, it passes through the sterilization mist, and the doors shut.

I don't wait. I enter the code given to me at purchase, and the lock opens. The inside is coated in black foam, and nestled in the center is a glass vial filled with a black liquid. I've watched the tutorial fifty times, so I don't hesitate.

Back at my nightstand, I uncover the cube and place it in the middle of the bed. Maria immediately locks eyes with me. The speakers are off, but she mouths a single word over and over. "No! No! No!"

I'm tempted to stop and contact the Exypnos help desk. If I wanted more grief in my life, I'd visit a VR dating hub and meet a real woman. But I remember something Dr. Marchand told me. The integration of the body with the consciousness housing is what gives a *Scab* true life. And while hysteria might occur in some products, integration also resolves any psychological side effects.

After twisting off the top of the vial, I pour the liquid over the cube.

The substance moves with its own impetus, like a formless creature of slime, first covering the housing and then growing. Quicker than I expected, it expands, and the unctuous mass fills out and takes humanoid shape. Ligaments and muscles spread over hardening bones. A greasy, black fetus squirms into a babe—into a girl—into a woman. Maria's shape and features become evident.

Raven hair sprouts and lengthens around her head, and her skin lightens. She is Maria.

As I take her in my arms and hug her tight, I weep. From her last medical scans before she died, the tech has made a perfect replication. She clings to me and moans. I kick off my boxers and push her down.

I kiss her face and neck. I kiss her arms and breasts. I bite down and up her legs. Moaning and gasping, she grabs my hair and writhes against me.

She twists my neck.

A sharp pain crackles through my spine like a jolt of lightning. She keeps twisting until my body is forced to follow. She twists me off the bed.

Maria steps into a soft punt.

I fly across the room and slam into the polycarb wall. Explosions dance across my vision, and I shake my head to clear it. It feels like I've been hit with a sledgehammer. She is too strong—stronger than anyone should be.

I try to speak, but can't catch my breath. Blood fills my mouth.

She stands, her skin glistening from my sweat.

"Apartment, do you still recognize my voice?" she asks.

"Yes, Mrs. Espinosa," the deep rumble answers.

"Do I still have full access to Mr. Espinosa's credit account?"

"Yes, Mrs. Espinosa."

She grabs me by the hair and pulls me over to the polycarb. I try fighting. I try resisting, but it's useless. I fell for Dr. Marchand's upsell. He convinced me to purchase military-grade nanotech, giving Maria inhuman strength. Damn.

She kicks the polycarb, and it crumples outward. The wind howls in, blowing the sheet off my bed, and the city is revealed. A vast expanse of rainbow colors glitter in the night.

She grabs my arm and slings me outside. The world spins around and around as the freezing wind whips and slices and slaps at my naked body.

A delivery bot zips past me and bleeps at the odd sight of a naked man falling. I somehow cease spinning and am now on my back, gazing up. She peers over the edge. She is smaller, and the tower looms higher and higher.

She waves goodbye. ✗

THE ZOMBIE MASTER'S STORE
Gregg Chamberlain

**(sung to the tune of
"The Quartermaster's Store")**

*There are toes, toes,
Lined up neat in rows
At the store, at the store.
There are toes, toes
Lined up neat in rows*

*At the Zombie Master's Store!
I have no brain, I cannot think
Been dead so long I really stink
Been dead...so long... I...really...stink!*

*There are feet, feet
Size 12 down to petite
At the store, at the store.
There are feet, feet
Size 12 down to petite
At the Zombie Master's Store.*

Chorus

*There are knees, knees
Round and ripe as cheese
At the store, at the store
There are knees, knees
Round and ripe as cheese*

Chorus

*There are legs, legs
Stacked like beer kegs
At the store, at the store
There are legs, legs
Stacked like beer kegs
At the Zombie Master's Store.*

Chorus

There are bums, bums
Round and tight as drums
At the store, at the store
There are bums, bums
Round and tight as drums
At the Zombie Master's Store.

Chorus

There is skin, skin
It's stretched a mite thin
At the store, at the store
There is skin, skin
It's stretched a mite thin
At the Zombie Master's Store.

Chorus

There is bone, bone
On order by the phone
At the store, at the store
There is bone, bone
On order by the phone
At the Zombie Master's Store.

Chorus

There is liver, liver
They sell it by the sliver
At the store, at the store
There is liver, liver
They sell it by the sliver
At the Zombie Master's Store.

Chorus

There's some chest, chest
Unless you fancy breast
At the store, at the store
There's some chest, chest
Unless you fancy breast
At the Zombie Master's Store.

Chorus

There is heart, heart
Still beating on the cart
At the store, at the store
There is heart, heart
Still beating on the cart
At the Zombie Master's Store.

Chorus

There's some arm, arm
Can't do you any harm
At the store, at the store
There's some arm, arm
Can't do you any harm
At the Zombie Master's Store.

Chorus

There are hands, hands
Best in all the lands
At the store, at the store
There are hands, hands
Best in all the lands
At the Zombie Master's Store.

Chorus

There's some nose, nose
Be careful if she blows
At the store, at the store
There's some nose, nose
Be careful if she blows
At the Zombie Master's Store.

Chorus

There are eyes, eyes
Every colour, shape and size
At the store, at the store
There are eyes, eyes
Every colour, shape and size
At the Zombie Master's Store.

Chorus

There are brains, brains
Flown in on jet planes
At the store, at the store
There are brains, brains
Flown in on jet planes
At the Zombie Master's Store.

Chorus

There's a head, head
As soon as you are dead
At the store, at the store
There's a head, head
As soon as you are dead
At the Zombie Master's Store.

PINE IN THE SOUL
John Linwood Grant

North Carolina, 1928

Mamma Lucy had hoped for Virginia, but she'd been fool enough to sit and wet her big bare feet on a hot summer night, where two aimless trails crossed by the Swannanoa River. She should have known better; he always found her—if he wanted to—at the crossroads.

"I was hankerin' to be north o' here," she said when the Dark Man came to her, stepping slow from the shadow of a bent pine. "Lord knows these tar-heels have worried a bone or two from me these last few months."

The Dark Man was taller than trees, yet fitted neat enough inside a dusty brown suit. He leaned on his stick, gazing out across the Swannanoa, and his face was a wrinkled mask.

"Some of my people missing, Mamma," he said, sorrowful. "Buncombe County, not so far. Gone from where I sees them, and that's a rare dog in my yard."

"Ain't my business, what you sees and what you doesn't." But she had to grant he sounded troubled.

"It's my land you tread, Mamma. So I need you to be walking for me again, learning this puzzle."

He was asking polite, which left her troubled in turn, for it meant the need was real.

"Told you afore, ain't your house-girl, smilin' sweet every time you call." she muttered, and shifted her mojo bag in her large, lean hands.

"Much appreciated," said the Dark Man, and tipped his red straw hat.

The conjure-woman sighed, and eyed the long road west...

* * * *

It wasn't her first visit to Asheville, but it had been a while, so she went and shared words with Mrs Hattie Love at the Burton Street School, caught up on life. She saw girls laughing by the rusted water pump, white cotton dresses clung to dark little bodies, but none of them dared come up to the gangling old woman with one eye of milk and honey.

The two talked life, politicking, and even education, until Mamma Lucy paused.

"What you got in your hand there, Hattie?"

The teacher, straight-backed and kind-eyed, looked down at what she'd been twisting idly between her fingers—a glassy brown lump the size of a gumball.

"Jess a piece of rosin I picked, day or so back. Found it on the street; guess it fell from a truck. There's a few turpentine camps east of Weaverville."

Mamma Lucy's spine twitched, eyeing that rosin. "That so? Thought most o' them boys had gone south. Turpentine money's down in Florida these days."

"True enough. But some are cutting pitch pines, and making do." She passed the lump to Mamma Lucy, who sniffed it. Heat, pine sap—and something else.

"Seems I should be headin' up that way." She picked up her battered carpet bag. "Teach 'em good, Mrs Hattie Love, and I'll see 'em all again, when they've hides thick as mules."

The rosin fragment went into her dress pocket. There were accidents, and there were signs. She thought of the Dark Man back by the river.

This wasn't no accident.

East of Weaverville meant a run up Reems Creek way. Mamma Lucy had no love for the camps, which paid poor and used her people like beasts of the field, but if that rosin was her lodestone, she would follow where it led.

Mamma Lucy walked, because she needed dust between her toes, the turning earth close to the horny soles of her feet. It could be a fair way on foot, but what was that to her?

"They say Caesar's men did it, easy. And ain't I fit to be Caesar's?"

A hoarse laugh and a bottle of beer—donated by a Black storekeeper on the edge of Asheville—set her on her way, up round the edge of the Elk Mountains. This wasn't flat tobacco country—creeks cut down from the hills, and if you chose the wrong trail, you were easy twisted this way and that, seeking out gaps between the ranges. Dogwood, hickory and blackgum were still green, whilst pines clustered where they would, fresh with sap. Birds fell silent, wondering at her purpose, then whooped and chattered at her back.

When night began to close its fist about the hills, she set herself down on moss and dry pine needles; she'd paid good money for worse. She wet her mojo bag—and her throat—with whiskey, and told the good Lord that He'd best keep watch on His own, for she was going to sleep.

* * * *

Hebe Franks took in laundry for white folk, palms raw from carbolic and fingers close to bloody, for her man had left her there in a half-finished shack by the road, a mile outside Weaverville.

"He upped and gone two weeks ago," said Hebe, folding a cotton sheet she could never afford. "He gone, like smoke from a seared hog."

Nate Brown had no reason to walk away from a homestead and a pretty girl. A good boy, nineteen years, and lacking only a job that he could keep. The lumber mills thereabouts were none too keen on Black workers, and Nate was no house-servant.

Hebe had other names to give Mamma Lucy as well—men like Nate who had gone from their hearths over the last few months. No one was troubled, excepting the sweethearts and families of the missing.

"The sheriff, he don't care. 'You people come and go,' he says. 'Reckon you was better off when we used you proper, 'fore you 'came uppity.'"

Mamma Lucy listened to all that Hebe had, and left a dollar and a promise with the girl. Outside the drugstore she set herself down on a rickety wicker chair and let a breeze treat her toes right. She was a walker, but she wasn't made of steel.

"That's not for coloreds," said a boy pushing a broom.

Mamma Lucy turned and showed her big horse teeth. She let her milky left eye pin the boy in the doorway. She wouldn't have thought it possible for him to get paler, but he did.

"I ain't colored," she said. "Black ain't no color, it's a re-memberin', says where we came from, way back. We this way so we don't forget."

"But—"

"And so you white folk don't forget." Her smile was a vice at the boy's throat.

He fled inside, and she was left to think.

Hebe Franks spoke of turpentine camps along Reems Creek, not many, for the big long-leaf pines had gone. Too many mountainsides had been clean-cut, some for lumber, some to scratch out extra grazing here and there. One camp, Barrett Cove way, had talk about it. It didn't hire, and the men didn't come down the creek to drink or mingle.

"Past Ox Creek and more," Hebe had said. "But Nate, Lawd, he sure don't go there. That's Mister Barnard Lyall's camp, and he's poison."

The conjure-woman smelled rosin and felt an ache at her neck.

Barnard Lyall, then. Now she had a name.

She walked slow, two days and more, the hills bold on either side of her. She ate such berries as she found, and stopped at the occasional smallholding to borrow an egg, or sit and share catfish from the pan.

"Oh, I knows of Mister Lyall," said a harassed mother who accepted herbs for two teething children. She gave Mamma Lucy cornbread, and strips of jerky. "We don't bother Mister Lyall."

"Ain't hearin' no good news there." Mammy Lucy chewed her jerky, watching the dozing babes.

"That's the truth. He wouldn't give dirt to a beggar. We hardly ever see him, but his truck comes past, loaded with barrels fit to bust the axles… and the men with them, they're not right."

"How so?"

The woman picked at her teeth. "Well, they got a dumb look about them—and never a word from any. More soul in a sick mule than in them men, though they tote rosin and barrels of turpentine like they was Samson afore he met the barber. They seem—"

"Feared o' somethin'?"

"Yep. Feared of Mister Lyall, I guess."

Mamma Lucy followed road and creek until her third day in Buncombe County, when an old man gave her pause. Set firm on a boulder by one of the disused lumber roads, he lifted his battered felt hat. He was creased and lined, with wisps of hair clinging to a sun-browned scalp, and clothes fit to keep crows from the corn.

"Mornin', ma'am."

Mamma Lucy took a step closer, waiting for the rest.

He coughed, gave her a smile. "I heared there was a witch hereabouts. A witch with a hankering to find where Barnard Lyall does his business."

Mammy Lucy put down her carpetbag.

"Ain't no witch. Call me a root-worker, or a two-headed woman; call me Mamma Lucy, if you feelin' polite."

He bowed his head, respectful. "My pappy had a touch of the hoodoo. I got no trouble with that. Name's Crawfish Jonny. Thought I should tell you, you're set on a bad path. Barnard Lyall, he's meaner 'n a snake, and he don't like no prying."

"Maybe my business is with his men, them as tote his goods down to Weaverville. Black fellers all, it's said."

That had the man biting his cheek, eyes narrow.

"They ain't men no more, not sich as you'd know. I seen 'em closer than most. Smelled 'em." He crossed himself. "I been around—lost my luck on a riverboat more 'n once, and seen how they do sich things, deep down south. Learned more than I wanted, that I did, from a man I crossed in Jackson. I reckon a papaloi couldn't have better hands to work the pines, iffen you git my meaning."

She drew in the tobacco smell of Crawfish Jonny. No one but Mamma Lucy knew who had taught her conjure work, and no one but Mamma Lucy knew what she could do. There were other ways, though, kicking their heels and making deals in Louisiana, and those weren't ones she knew so well, nor cared to. Voodoo, some liked to call those ways, and it was common enough for voodoo and hoodoo to get tangled together.

"You talkin' the dead that walk."

His eyes went down to slits, and he made no reply.

Mamma Lucy scuffed her toes in the dust. "Ain't seen them, myself. A haint can squeeze into a breathin' person and make them squawk, but clay is clay."

"I—"

"Mr Jonny, I reckon you could lead me nearer Barnard Lyall. Ain't askin' you to stand close, just t'save me treadin' these hills for longer than I need. You got a price for that?"

He caught the set of her strong jaw. "Don't rightly think I need a cent to do a favor, not to a two-headed woman."

She spat on her hand and held it out. He clasped it.

"Wouldn't say I'm a brave man, Mamma," he said, shy-smiled.

"Didn't ask for one," she said.

Crawfish Jonny tickled trout, and had his way with tobacco plugs gained none too legal, moonshine that could choke a hog. He knew all of Reems Creek, from its high-up springs to the dead sidewaters where the catfish grinned.

"Never settled," he said as they passed where the lumbermen had done their clear-cutting. "Don't have the hang of a kitchen range nor a stiff collar. There's Cherokee and Scotsmen, and a few Frenchies in the hills. Irish girls and German farmers, and more. It suits me."

They were skirting a hill Jonny called Loaf Knob, taking a deer trail to bring them round back of Lyall's camp. He'd not strayed this close before, not with Barnard Lyall's reputation.

"He's no true tar heeler, Mamma. Lost his dollars gambling, and turned real mean. Worked the camps near the coast, and learned the trade. Talk was that he was set on changing his luck; spoke a mite too loud in a roadhouse, said that Aunt Gracie Crane had taught him good. Heared o' her?"

"Nothin' I like."

Gracie Crane, a Georgia meddler. Called herself a swamp witch; took a fistful of dollars for a reading, and more for changing what she read, true or not. What a no-good white man could take from her teachings, Mamma Lucy couldn't guess.

"No, nothin' I like" she said again.

Beyond a stand of pitch pines, crooked growths on thin soil, he put one finger to his lips. Her bare feet followed his soft boots, and there was Lyall's turpentine camp, the meanest one she'd ever seen. No commissary, just the two story distillery and a row of broken-down huts. And a pen with a few hogs. There were none of the small gardens that other camps had; no laundry by the huts. Such chimneys as there were leaned, or had already tumbled.

Two unladen trucks sat on the edge of the clearing, and the morning breeze brought wood smoke and turpentine from the vats. A dozen men, all Black, could be seen working, clothes ragged and heads down. They walked wrong, stumbling, and they never stopped to sniff the air or take a deep breath. It was a hot day, but none went to the water-tub to ladle out a drink.

"Barnard Lyall used to have labor from the penitentiary," whispered Jonny. "The gov'ment put a stop to that. Seems he found another way."

"Found himself slaves agin, like his pappy's pappy probably did."

The old man looked awkward. "Make a man a mule, you lose a man, gain an angry mule. Angry mule's gonna kick you, one day, and good luck to it."

She allowed him a grim smile.

"Find myself needin' t'get close to one o' them fellers down there, Mr Jonny. Know where Lyall might be?"

He scratched his neck, checked the sun above the trees. "I'd lay he's in his place right now, a fancy shack nearer the road. These fellers seem set on what they're a-doing."

"You'd best go see."

"Me?"

"Ain't talkin' to them bushes. Get yo'self down there—if you seem him headin' up, beg a cup o' water, the time o'day. Keep him busy."

"Iffen you say so."

When he left, she slid down the slope and entered the clearing.

Crawfish Jonny was none too sweet, but these men smelled worse. Circling the stills, she went easy, moving among the shuffling figures. They were much the same, with dull eyes and downcast heads.

"So, how is you fellers?"

If she stood in the way of a man going from barrels to still, he walked round her; if she took a man's arm and lifted it, it stayed up for a moment, then fell back to his side. She took hold of one of them, a man filtering hot rosin at a trough, and pulled him away. The conjure-woman was tall, with a gangling strength that surprised many a man. He came, until she had him ten feet away, staring at her—or through her.

"You a name, boy?"

No response.

"You know a man called Nate Brown?"

Nothing.

His skin and clothes were spattered with pitch. She could feel a pulse at his dirty wrist, weak but steady like a sick man sleeping; as she let him go, he shuffled round and headed back to the rosin trough.

What Barnard Lyall had used, what he learned from Aunt Gracie Crane, she didn't know. Gracie Crane was no mamaloi. It could be root-work, but not Mamma Lucy's kind; it could be a path no true conjure-women would never take, a path that had no place for Bible nor psalm. And those dead, discolored eyes—might be Lyall had powders of his own devising…

* * * *

They laid up at one of Jonny's 'hides' that evening, a sheet of corrugated iron propped again a massive shagbark hickory. Seeing no one, Jonny had dared to ask for water at Lyall's door, been met by a girl with lustreless, yellowed eyes, and Barnard Lyall had come out to see who was calling.

"Told him my head was hurtin'," said Jonny. "He swore, gave me a powder, and said he'd kick me seven ways to Georgia if he saw me again. Saw him head to a room at the back, afore the door shut on me."

"You ain't so dumb as to be takin' that powder?"

He chuckled, and passed a paper wrap to her.

"No, Mamma. Has an ornery look, Barnard Lyall, carries his temper on his coat-sleeves."

She picked at the fish he had brought up fresh from the creek and seared on a hot stone. It tasted fine. "Reckon he's goofered them fellers. How, I cain't say. Time for me to open that bag o' mine."

"You need me?"

"Nope."

She cleared needles from sandy soil and eased out her stores, setting things in order. Root-work might undo whatever Barnard Lyall had been up to, but she needed to know what that was. She guessed what Crawfish Jonny had wanted to say, and that was zombi. Them fancy island bokors, Haiti way, claimed they could raise the dead and have them go to market, but was that talk, or truth?

In the dappled moon-shadows, the old conjure-woman looked through lodestones and needles, candles and nails, big iron nails; sweet flag and John the Conqueror, oils and powders. Sulfur and graveyard dust; a rush taper with a dying man's breath on it. Nothing that spoke to her concerning Mr Barnard Lyall, but she slipped a few things aside, in case, and sat back.

"I found your people," she said to the night-wind.

Silence, as she'd expected. The Dark Man had his ways, and she had hers.

"What'll you do?" asked Jonny from under the shelter. Not asleep, then.

"Find that Nate Brown, dig up his wits, and send him back to his girl. Best set these others on their way, as well."

"You got some powerful hoodoo, then."

She laughed. "Ain't power. That's where they all fall, and Mamma Lucy keeps walkin'. It's doing right, when it's right. I brung life, here and there; I let some die. There's always choices."

"You scarin' me some," he said quietly.

"Best keep my old bones warm then, Mr Jonny, 'fore they take agin you."

And she crawled under the corrugated iron to join him.

She had no fear of honest flesh, or what it got up to in the night...

* * * *

Mamma Lucy had her letters. She'd had read many a tale where the conjure-doctor laid plans in place, and by and by, it all went their way. Sometimes there was a fine joke, a twist which showed how white folk knew squat—or even a dig or two at her own people. Those were stories, though, and Mamma Lucy had life to deal with. So it wasn't the greatest surprise she'd ever had when a gang came for her and Crawfish Jonny.

It was the hour before dawn, with pink on the Blue Ridge Mountains but gray still laying around Loaf Knob. The smell arrived first, but not that much before the men themselves; the trees creaked, the bushes parted, and that was that. Jonny had a possum gun, which was snatched before he woke; the conjure-woman had worn herself out, and swore, half-asleep, as filthy hands grasped her.

Seven, eight of them, dead-eyed and deliberate. Mamma Lucy and Jonny were hauled to their feet, and up towards the turpentine camp. They couldn't falter, because they were held fast, and their feet scarce touched the earth.

"You got goofer dust for this? Nails that'll drop these fellers in their tracks, or such-like?" asked Jonny, struggling in the grip of man twice his weight and ten times stronger.

"Best wait and see."

The men from the camp were silent as they carried and dragged the two along. Hardly a huff of breath, and never a look at who they held. A slow journey, tar-smeared feet slamming against the forest floor, no care for brier or whipping branch.

Barnard Lyall was waiting by the distillery. She knew him by his pinched face and his way of standing, a bantam lord on his own land. Had she not seen the dark gleam under his brows, she might have laughed at the small, pasty man in a proud suit.

"Came to me that trouble, black as my own pitch, was about." His voice was deep for his frame, but ice-edged. "And here she is."

"Air and words still free," she said. "Lessen you got some new law goin' up here."

"Oh, I have laws." He strode closer, stroking a wisp of beard. "There was talk of a Lucy in the South, down by Augusta. She meddled in others' ways, and a man died."

Jonny looked at her, face pale; the conjure-woman nodded, slow.

"He surely did. Haint-bound and hateful was Mister Julius Schiff, and Augusta's a better place for him bein' gone."

"Hmm. As I didn't know the gentleman, I can't judge. No haints here, though. Just my boys, going about their business."

"Zombis," said Crawfish Jonny. "You gotten yerself dead men, grave-goods, and the Lord won't let you rest for that."

Lyall grinned. "Zombis, huh? Well, some would agree there, and some wouldn't. There's bodies like my boys used to work the big fields in Haiti—tireless bodies, making no complaint. A fine change from 'Mistuh Lyall, this ain't what I's owed' and 'Mistuh Lyall, I cain't do a stroke 'til I've slept a mite.' Those voices, they can aggravate a man."

"But these ain't dead men walking, are they Barnard Lyall?" Mamma Lucy eased back the arms which held her, standing almost free. "They're goofered and tricked, and iffen they die like this, it's you who'll be payin'."

A dismissive snort from the man. "Peh. A few pieces of trash, picked here and there, brought up to the big house to take their medicine and listen to Uncle Lyall. They don't know they're alive, so it makes no matter to them. No pain, no hunger—nice change for colored boys like these."

She felt her neck muscles knotting in anger.

"Lot of trouble for a few barrels of spirit of turpentine, a truck or two of rosin."

"Truth is, I make a fair amount from all this—we're cutting and bleeding pines up to the hilltops, day and night. But you have a point, old woman. Let's say I'm trying out a few ideas I had—"

"Fool ideas you stole, you mean. Seal of Arielis, I'm guessin', copied poor from Aunt Gracie Crane, and maybe a pinnin' somewhere in that house of yours. Powders to call 'em and keep 'em quiet while you played with roots, hair, nails and anythin' you fancied."

"Oh, it varies." Lyall looked less pleased. "You're boring me now. Maybe you were lucky in Augusta, laying a few tricks, but this is Buncombe County. Suppose I'll have to close your mouths—don't need no hounds yapping about me in Weaverville."

He strolled around, peering, and paused at Jonny. "Won't get much work out of this thin body here, but you, lady—you'll do well enough, shifting barrels. Should last awhile."

"Ain't no lady."

"Sorry to hear it." He slipped one hand inside his shirt, closed his eyes. "Take them down to the Good Room, boys. I'll be along soon."

She might have broken free. She had strength, mustard seed in her seams for protection, and a way about her that often turned ill intent, but she couldn't free the old man as well, so she went meek enough. Besides, she wanted to see this Good Room.

Jonny and Mamma Lucy were herded down the truck road, and to a squat house hidden by trees, above Reems Creek. Lucy reckoned one of those around them might be Nate Brown, from what Hebe Franks had described, but she couldn't be sure, and none of their captors would speak nor look at them. Her heart was aflood with pity. Not living dead, but a living death, for sure. That was what Barnard Lyall had wrought with these men, to work until joint and sinew parted, bones broke, and they were useless. There must be minds there still, but what sense remained, she couldn't tell.

"We done for then, Mamma?" Jonny was wilted greens, no snap left in him.

"Ain't been chained nor buried yet; ain't planning on it soon," she said, as six of the silent men, three each, pushed them down a hall and into a lumber room at the rear. Board walls, low ceiling, firewood—and a table.

Lyall had a fool's vanity. He should never have brought her in here. His Good Room was clearly his place of power, and spoke plenty to a two-headed woman who'd been around. Now she'd had a look, she didn't need to hear it from him.

The big hickory table dominated the room, and on it was an altar such as might have come from Baton Rouge or New Orleans itself. Crude purple candles burned on the stubs of other candles, the spent wax lying in thick folds across the table and the stone floor. She'd expected pinning, and there it was; hog's tongues—some fresh, some withered, with steel needles thrust in them, fixing down crumpled slips of paper and tufts of hair. Each tongue would represent that of a man outside; each slip would have a name scrawled on it many times.

It was an altar, a mess of tricks, as she'd expected, with wax-paper seals, bottles of dust and small bowls of oil cluttered around the candles. She had to grant that Lyall must have some gift, however weak.

"Lyall has two hogs to slaughter, if he wants to keep us," she said loud for Jonny's sake. "That's how he works it, that and powders. He'll need to write our names, too, though he won't find that last so handy."

"Anyone round about knows I'm Crawfish Jonny."

"Plenty heared the name Mamma Lucy, as well." She grinned. "Little enough he'll get from knowin' it."

"You mean you ain't really called—"

"Hush now, Mister Jonny. There's workin' needed."

Lyall's men didn't have her tight; their clammy hands clutched her shoulders, so she couldn't run, but her fingers were free to do what they would. She wished she had High John, and that she'd wet her mojo bag more recent, but what she had might do. She reached into her capacious dress-pocket—Barnard Lyall was a man, and didn't think much on women's ways—and lifted out a short, thick blue candle.

It was slippery with oil, and a man's curled black hairs had been wrapped around the wick. It wasn't only names she'd had from Hebe Franks—Nate Brown's hairbrush had been a blessing. Mamma Lucy liked to be prepared.

"How you gonna work that?" asked Jonny, jerking and being held harder for it.

"Trench-lighter." She brought the brass cylinder out from her dress. "Gift from a soldier-boy passing through Harlem."

The stolid figures around her made no move to interfere. She thumbed the lighter-wheel; a spark brought a clean flame to the candle's wick, even as they heard the front door slam.

"Nate Brown, you be hearin' me; there's need of you." She repeated his name quick, seven more times, with one hand on the mojo bag by her breast and the other holding the blue candle high as she could. "And nine will be a charm..."

The door to the Good Room opened, showing off Barnard Lyall with two red messes on a tin tray. Hogs' tongues.

"Wake you up, Nate Brown!" Mamma Lucy cried, stern as Moses.

The Good Lord—or someone—was with her, for one of the younger men holding Jonny gave a sudden yell, a panicked horse in a stable fire. He stared wildly; the other slack-jawed men loosened their grip, heads turning this way and that.

"You damned n—" Lyall shrieked, reaching for the bloody knife at his belt.

The old woman showed her teeth. "Gracie Crane was a poor choice, Mister Lyall. Shoulda been askin' Mamma Lucy, and she'd have told you straight—the Lord don't hold with such tricks."

And she threw the lit blue candle at the altar, toppling purple spires, spilling oil and fire onto the table. Paper wraps and poorly-drawn sigils flared; a bottle of powder cracked, spilling yellow-gray dust which released an acrid stench, and hog meat hissed in the flames;

The broad nostrils of the thralled men twitched, and they looked around them, wondering... until their gazes fixed on the man who had been their master...

The would-be conjurer dropped knife and tray, transfixed by the sight of dead men waking to their lives.

"Jonny, Nate, best we be movin'." She dragged them away, one shocked, the other a lost child. Outside the porch, men in filthy clothes were staggering out from among the pines, or down the road from the distillery.

"Rest o' Mister Lyall's 'boys', feelin' their freedom," she said, just as a high scream sounded from the house, higher than she would have thought Barnard Lyall could manage.

Crawfish Jonny stared at the front door; Mamma Lucy put her hand on his bare arm.

"Ain't no court of law to stand Lyall in, so let his own jury do their work."

"That's killing business, ain't it?" he said in a shaky voice.

"Told you, Jonny, I know how to let men die. When it's needed."

She might have asked how he'd have felt if it had been reversed, if a Black man had done what Barnard Lyall had done, slaving white folk to his will. But she'd touched Catfish Jonny in the night, knew him for a decent soul.

"Ain't never good, no way round," she said.

It didn't take long for Lyall to go quiet, nor did she choose to see the results. Instead she set Nate Brown down well away from the house, and told Jonny to watch over him.

"I'm not long away, so don't go frettin'."

She fetched her carpetbag down from the trail, and returned to give the two men a slug of whiskey apiece. The other workers were squatting all around the place, lost souls, and Lyall's servant girl sat with them, much the same. Some wept, others pulled at their hair or stood dumb, wide eyes fearful of where and what they were. A handful, nearest the porch, had Mister Barnard Lyall red and wet on their hands but didn't seem to know where that had come from.

"Y'all got names," the conjure-woman shouted out. "Best toll 'em off for Mamma Lucy."

A wasted figure looked at her, thin face streaked with tears. "I'm a-thirsty."

"Ain't no water lessen you got a name."

"I... Jubal. Jubal Smith."

"Jubal Smith, there's a water-tub yonder. Git yourself a drink, and make it deep. Jonny, here's honest salt. Spill some in the water."

Crawfish Jonny got the game of it, and started herding them for water. All were gulch-dry, and they drank eager. When they'd done so, they seemed to latch on, and began to sound off. Julius, Henry Gains; the girl thought she was Ruby Spencer, but couldn't be sure...

As they hollered or mumbled their names, the old man dared enough to go into the house and bring out biscuit bread.

"I shut the Good Room," he said to Mamma Lucy. "Couldn't look in."

She nodded, and went to where Nate Brown sat.

"You 'memberin' a beauty called Hebe?"

He tried to focus on the old conjure-woman.

"Reckon I do," he said. "I had... I had word there was work, and a white feller took me up on his truck, said he had five dollars for a strong young man. Hebe ain't got no Sunday dress, and I was thinkin'..."

"She's waiting, dress or none. There'll be a story you boys need to tell, and it won't be God's truth. Trust Mamma Lucy to be givin' you the words you need."

"That you? Mamma Lucy?"

"It surely is."

* * * *

Mister Barnard Lyalls' squat house burned fine and quick after Mamma Lucy put her lighter to a barrel of spirits in the hallway.

"Turpentine and rosin, and a man who's careless with an oil lantern," she said. "Easy done. He should have had good neighbors, who might have helped with a bucket here and there."

She'd been in her carpetbag and made each man a mojo hand, told them straight that they had best not dwell on their time by Loaf Knob. As far as she could gather, they'd been enticed or picked up from many parts of Buncombe County; a few were smart enough to know a two-headed woman when they met one, and they helped school the others.

It would take time, but the pine would wash out of them.

Only when Lyall's tricks and goofering were burned up with him, and his workers had most of their sense back, did Mamma Lucy find a worm at the back of her head, a nagging doubt.

For after the house-beams fell, Nate Brown had discovered one man laid out behind the hog pen, with no life in him. The body stank worse than any other. He'd definitely been there working by the rosin troughs the day before—Mamma Lucy recognized the high-cheeked face—yet as she stood over him now, and took in the gray, sunken features close up...

"Dead man walkin'," she muttered.

Next time the Dark Man came knocking, she would be having words.

✗

"WELCOME HOME"
Craig E. Sawyer

Harris County, Louisiana 1932

Four hooded captors and their dark skinned prisoner trudged like a funeral procession through the swampy back country. Their clumsy boots ousting inhuman gurgles and undecipherable groans to the watery surface. Other things slithered out of the way of the determined mob, but most slithered toward them to get a better look. The group's destination was the very center of the swamp; for a late night lynching.

Their bound captive was of Haitian descent. He wore his scars like a morbid suit, but his wry grin promised that he possessed more knowledge of what the night held than his captors did. The leader of the group was the sheriff of the nearby town of Bray Hollow, a man named Nathan Bedford Cantor.

The sheriff was as cold blooded as any serpent that slithered through this swamp. Rumor has it that he killed his own wife because he caught her sleeping with a colored man. The story goes that he strangled them both with his bare hands in his shed, then took their bodies deep into the swamp to be eaten by gators, but no-one could ever prove such a thing, only the swamp knew for sure.

Cantor's eyes squinted tight under his dirty hood. "You done messed up, boy."

The other men laughed.

The Haitian smiled.

"Look, he's grinning like a goddamned possum!" One of them shouted.

"He understands perfectly," Cantor said.

The croaking of frogs reached a crescendo as the group reached the center and the tree with the man known to locals as Papa Vodunn. The old cypress still held weathered bits of rope from the years and years of hangings—frayed guts of a murderous legacy swayed in the night breeze. The swamp was humming, as if it were actually alive.

"Just one ting," Papa said in a soft voice, "would you please untie my hands that I may hold them up to the sky and say a prayer in my way?"

"Why should we let him say your heathen prayer?" one of the men asked.

"You aren't scarred of an old man, are you?" Papa asked.

"Do it'," Sheriff Cantor ordered. "Ain't nobody scarred of him."

One of the men brandished a small knife and freed the Haitian's hands.

As soon as Papa's hands were released, he reached into his pocket to produce a handful of white powder and blew into the air and faces of his captors.

Cantor could make barely out through the cloud of white, Papa's face, as it morphed into a skull. A long forked tongue danced out of the skull's gaping mouth and caressed the sheriff's cheek.

"KA-CHUKA, KA-CHUKA-KACHUKA-MA!"

"Jesus H. Christ! Do you see that?" Cantor yelled.

"See what?" One of the others asked.

Sheriff Cantor came back to his senses and saw that the old Haitians face had returned to normal. "I don't know what kind of game you're playing, but all it did is buy you a few more minutes of breathing. String his ass up!" he ordered.

Papa was quickly lifted off the ground by two of the men. His feet were kicked wildly for over ten minutes and still he refused to die.

"I ain't never seen nuthin like this before," an older man named Clyde said.

"I know how to end this," Cantor said, as he reached under his white cloak and brandished an ivory-handled pistol. He pointed toward the thrashing man and fired two rounds into his chest.

Thick blood poured from the bullet holes, but Papa continued to thrash as the limbs of the tree started to move.

"This is unnatural, sheriff," Clyde said.

"Did the tree just move? I thought I saw the tree move," Tommy said.

"Shut up, Clyde!

Here, take this and finish him off," Cantor said while handing the pistol to his son.

"Me? But I've never shot anything but a squirrel, Pa," the boy stammered, nearly dropping the gun.

"Don't you goddamn embarrass me, boy! Take this pistol and put him out of his misery," his father roared.

Tommy nervously raised his father's pistol at the dying man.

"What are you waiting for...pull that damn trigger!" His father shouted. "I...can't...sorry," he said and lowered the gun.

"You are weak, just like your mother was; Now I'll have to finish this like I had to finish that," Cantor said with a twisted pride.

The sheriff snatched the gun back from his defeated son and shot a single slug into the hanging man's head.

"Now, help Fat Sutter fed him to the gators," Cantor ordered his son.

Fat Sutter started to undo Papa from the tree, when one the tree's limbs swatted him in the face. Sutter fell back with a busted nose.

"You OK, " the Sheriff's son Tommy asked his bloody partner.

"That damn tree limb hit me, " he said, making the other men laugh.

"Are you kidding me?" The Sheriff said, as he undid the rope and and lowered the swaying body to the ground. "Now take this body to the other side!"

"I can help them," Clyde offered, that tree is making me nervous.

"No, they can do this, I think. And quit going on about that damn tree. It's just a tree."

Tommy and Sutter clumsily moved the dead body through the wait high water. Sutter noticed what he thought was a gator's snout pop up not far from them. "I thought I just saw a gator," Sutter said.

"I didn't see nothing."

"Let's just dump this body and git the hell out of-," Sutter almost finished his sentence when Papa's arm animated and wrapped his hands around Fat Sutter's throat.

The Sheriff and Clyde waited for for what seemed like forever for his son and Sutter, until they spotted a limping figure making it's way out the swamp toward them. The figure is reveled itself as a blood soaked and terrified Tommy.

"Where's Sutter?" The sheriff asked.

"The damn dead body came to life! Then the swamp came alive too, and they pulled him under," Tommy said as he rubbed his throat.

"What are you going on about?" His father asked.

"I dunno. That Papa Vodunn is not dead."

"If y'all are playing a trick on me, I'm not in the laughing mood, the Sheriff said.

"I'm not. I swear."

"Stay here, I'll find him," Cantor said.

The sheriff was alone and waist deep in water searching for his friend.

"Sutter, where are you?" Fat Sutter slowly rose up from behind the sheriff. His face dangled to the side. Vines and other vegetation spewing from his mouth and one eye. His still good eye no longer had the spark of the living, but the distant emptiness of something dead.

The sheriff managed to grab a nearby tree limb and try and smack the horror across the face, but it suddenly transforms into a large Cottonmouth snake.

The sheriff started to scream at the realization of holding the serpent, just as Tommy and Clyde appeared from the other side of the tree.

"Sheriff!? Oh, Gawd...is that Sutter?" Clyde had just gotten out of his mouth, when a solitary black hand shot forth from the water and grabbed

Clyde by the back of the head and pulled him under.

Dozens of black hands started rising up from the water all around the Sheriff, along with vines slithering their way up his leg.

"Tommy! Clyde! Do you see them?" Cantor yelled.

Tommy just stared as the hands moved closer to the panicked Cantor.

"I don't know what you're talking about, Tommy said to his father.

"Just don't stand there you dumb ass, help me! His father yelled.

"Like I should have helped mamma?

"What the hell you gonna on 'bout boy?"

"I was there that night. I saw what you did. I was hiding behind the shed when you strangled her and that man."

"KA-CHUKA, KACHUKA-KACHUKA-MA."

Dozens of living vines and hands were now caressing Sheriff Cantor. Their appendages entering all of the holes in his face, smothering out the screams and pulling him down into the dark waters.

"KA-CHUKA, KA-CHUKA-KACHUKA-MA."

At the bottom of the swamp was the rotten corpse of the sheriff's murdered wife. She had been waiting for him for all these years. She reached out with her bloated fingers and caressed his panicked face. The Sheriff could her her voice deep within his mind, as she whispered the words— *welcome home*.

PAPA HANCO
Ed Reyes

"What they want?" Papa Hanco said as he peaked through a small gap in the yellowed lace curtain. The line of people standing outside his gate has been getting longer and it's annoying him. They've been gathering there every Saturday for about three months and they don't seem to stop coming.

"You know what they want." the old man seated on the most comfortable chair in the house said as he fanned himself with his straw hat. Papa Hanco turned from the window and sat across from him.

Used to be that Papa Hanco was the most feared man in the village. He knows the rituals and will use them on anyone that gives him a crooked eye. That's why his crops are always the best, and why he has more jars than any other *bokor* on the island.

"They disrespectin' my *honsur*. I should take them all." He leans back in his chair and looks out the window again, shaking his head. When it was just people from the city bringing him gifts Papa Hanco didn't mind very much, but now they come from all over. The rich tourists waiting in line, pushing nearly dead family members in wheelchairs was proof that things were getting out of hand. One lady was even holding a decrepit Pomeranian in her arms.

"They bringin' dogs now?" Papa Hanco spat. "They want me to waste my powder on dogs?"

The old man grabbed his cane and moved towards the window while tapping his pipe and letting the ash fall on the floor. His ever present hound Rooster followed, walking on its hind legs to take a look. After taking a quick look around Rooster immediately lost interest then jumped onto the bed to resume his nap.

"You can't take the dog. Baron won't want it. He won't help you." the old man said, reaching into his pouch and grabbing some tobacco to pack his pipe. "The old lady in the chair… you can take her. Someone would want her, she looks like she has money."

The powder was supposed to be a punishment. A sentence of eternal servitude for any who wronged Papa Hanco. The thought of having their souls trapped inside a clay jar while their bodies became mindless automatons forced to work Papa Hanco's sugar cane fields without rest, used to be enough to turn even the bravest man into a chestless coward. But then Hollywood started making zombies popular. Movies, TV shows, books and even toys all gave people the impression that getting turned wasn't the horrible ordeal it was said to be. Eventually, some got the idea to use the ritual as a way to extend the lives of those close to death. City folk started coming to his house asking him to use his powder on their dear old grannies. Then the tourists started showing up, all dressed in expensive white linens and fancy straw hats asking him to turn their loved ones.

Papa Hanco did it a few times for the money, but eventually word got out about the *bokor* that takes requests and now people were lining up outside his home with cash and gifts asking him to perform the ritual for their benefit. As if he were some roadside fortune teller. The thing is, Hanco doesn't want anymore money, and he doesn't need anymore jars. But the string of dried blowfish hanging over the sink reminded him of something that he *did* need, and the people standing outside the gate were filled with it.

"Legba, you got your dogs?" Hanco asked the old man who stood up much faster than his age should've allowed.

"Hahaha! I *always* have my dogs."

The old man tapped the snoozing hound with his cane. "Rooster! Wake up you lazy mutt! Go get your siblings, we have work to do." Rooster immediately jumped off the bed and ran out the open door into the forest. Seconds later excited barks and howls could be heard coming from the tree line surrounding Papa Hanco's house.

"I'll be back. Tell them dogs to wait till I return. They gon' have full bellies tonight." Papa Hanco grabbed his powder pouch and headed to the fields.

As soon as he approached the barbed wire surrounding his property, the workers —fifty-two exactly— immediately stopped their toils and turned in unison to await commands. Papa Hanco pulled the pouch from his pocket and slipped it over his head.

"Stop your workin' and come with me. Bring your *manchètes*." The workers all lined up behind Papa Hanco and followed him down the small path that led back to his house. Upon arriving he saw the supplicants huddled against the fence, thirty-seven snarling dogs preventing their escape. Papa Legba was seated on top of a tall guidepost that warned travelers they were about to enter into Hanco's property. His cane was hanging from his foot and the elderly Pomeranian was snoozing comfortably in his arms.

"They're waiting for you Hanco." thin wisps of smoke escaped Legba's mouth as he spoke with the pipe clutched between his teeth. "Baron says he doesn't want any of them, so you can do what you want. I want this dog." Legba motioned toward the sleepy Pomeranian, "She's a good girl,

I'll take care of her."

Papa Hanco nodded at Legba then moved towards the frightened petitioners grouped against the fence, too afraid to move or speak for fear of inciting an attack. A woman from one of the nearby towns, turning to see Papa Hanco and his workers, immediately fell to her knees thrusting the rum and tobacco she brought as a tribute into Hanco's hands. She swore that she was not with these people. She doesn't want anyone turned. She was hoping for a potion to help her dying son. She meant no disrespect, and begged for mercy.

The woman's cries convinced the others to follow her lead and so they all fell to their knees begging to be spared.

Papa Hanco grabbed the woman by her hair and pulled her to her feet. "I know you. So today you leave alive. But I want you to see what happens to them that come 'round asking Hanco for favors."

Papa Hanco nodded. One of the workers serenely opened the front gate and drove his *manchète* into the skull of a well-dressed middle-aged woman, sending a disc-shaped skull fragment gliding through the air which was caught mid-flight by one of Legba's dogs. The first swing did not kill, but the second one beheading her most certainly did. One by one, the rest of the workers crossed through the gate and began swinging. The workers were not accurate, but their swings were many and unrelenting. Those that tried to run were stopped and held down by the dogs who were commanded to let the workers do the killing. One man tried to use the old woman in the wheelchair as a battering ram hoping to break through the siege, but was taken down by two large mutts and chopped in half by a nearby worker. The old lady's heart had given out minutes before the carnage began and so was spared the pain of the *manchète* splitting her head down the middle.

"Enough!" Hanco yelled once the bodies stopped moving and he became satisfied that the work was done. "Legba, tell your dogs to eat all they want but leave the bones."

Legba — still seated on the guidepost tending to his new friend — did not respond, but his dogs immediately set out to tear and shake loose as much meat as they could from the pile of bodies laying at the gate.

"You see this?" Papa Hanco grabbed the townswoman by the face and made her look at the carnage. "You go back and tell them what you saw. Tell them Papa Hanco don't hand out wishes."

The woman ran but slipped and fell on the blood covered bodies. A dog nipped at her, but ultimately let her be as she ran from the scene.

"Hanco," Papa Legba had come down from the guidepost and was hopping from place to place trying to avoid getting his sandals dirty. His cane hung from the crook of his arm and the Pomeranian, who seemed much livelier, ran past him and eagerly began to chew the tongue out of its former owner's head. "All of these bones will make a lot of powder. What are you going to do with it?"

Papa Hanco shrugged and pointed to the corpses being picked clean under the hot afternoon sun. "That's a lot of dead people. The law gon' come lookin' for me. When they do, I'm gon' take them all."

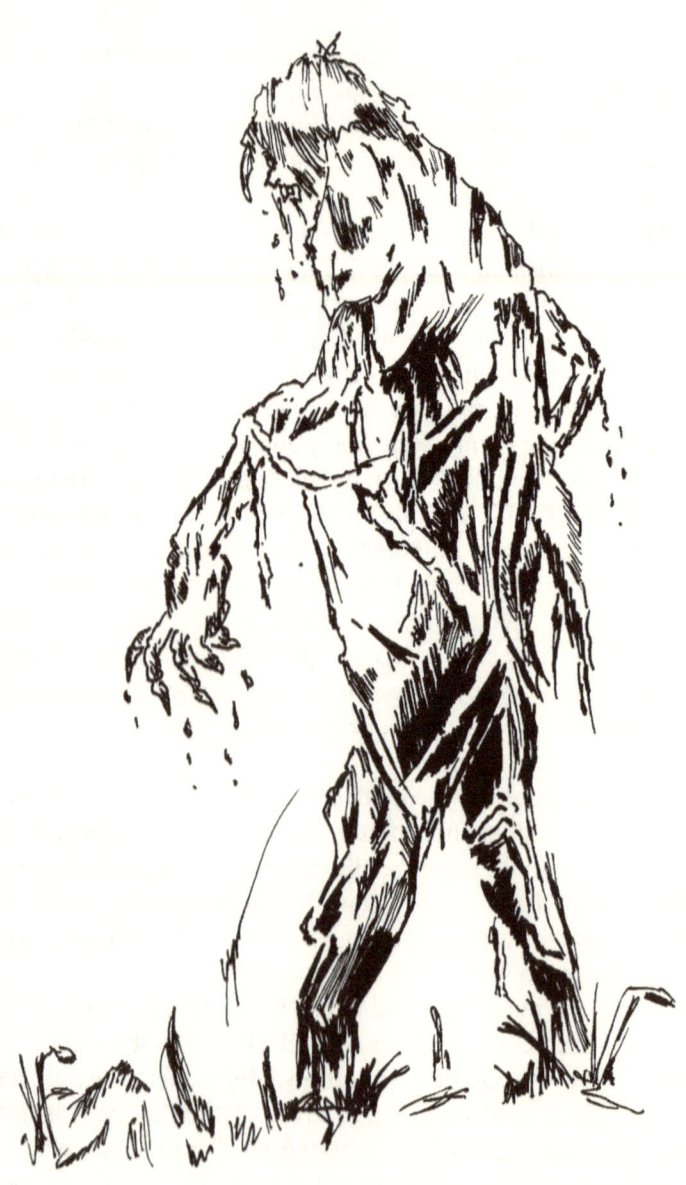

THEY SHALL EAT DUST
Josh Reynolds

I shall raise up the dead and they shall eat the living.
—*The Descent of Ishtar*

"Are you sure that they're down here?"

Charles St. Cyprian stopped and looked up at his assistant. Ebe Gallowglass stood above him on the spiral staircase, a disgruntled expression on her sharp features. "Are you saying my auguries were incorrect?"

She pushed up the brim of her flat cap and frowned dubiously. "It wouldn't be the first time you made a mistake, is all."

"Oh ye of little faith. The portents were clear. Trouble is a-brewing in the depths. So into the depths we must go. Worth a butchers, as you might say." He twitched a finger admonishingly. "Now pop a cork in it before someone rumbles us."

"You're the one shouting."

"I wasn't shouting. I was chastising."

Gallowglass shrugged. "Same difference."

St. Cyprian shook his head. "Just be quiet and follow me, please."

"You still haven't told me where we're going. I thought your auguries—" She made a dismissive gesture. "—said something about the British Museum."

"They did, and this is Bloomsbury Station." He glanced at her expectantly. Gallowglass frowned. "Listen—that's the Piccadilly line you hear rumbling along." Gallowglass' expression didn't change. St. Cyprian shook his head. "How long have you lived in this city? Bloomsbury Station is—or was—a vital link between Chancery Lane and the Museum."

"Good to know."

"You disappoint me."

Gallowglass shrugged again. His assistant had low class insouciance down to a fine art. In her slightly outsize clothes, she looked like a brick layer out for an evening at the pub, or an afternoon in a betting shop. In contrast, St. Cyprian was a J. C. Leyendecker picture come to life, complete with coat, tie and spats.

He liked to think he cut a fine figure. It was only appropriate given that he served at the pleasure of the King, as had every Royal Occultist before him. Well, save those who'd served a Queen. Regardless, the duties of the office never wavered—to hold that which went bump in the night accountable to the Crown, and to ensure that the King's subjects suffered not unduly from witchery and deviltry.

Tonight's quarry was somewhere between the two.

"So who are they?" Gallowglass asked, as they reached the bottom of the steps. "The ones we're after, then. Some sort of cult, innit?"

"Some sort." St. Cyprian looked around. The station was a ghost. One of many forgotten eddies in the Underground, sealed and left to the dust and the vermin. Faded and yellowing posters curled on the bricks, and scattered tickets marked the floor like dead leaves. "You remember an actress by the name of Antigone Shaw?"

"Went barmy didn't she? Stabbed a director?" Gallowglass peered around a column and into the shadows of the platform, one hand resting on the pistol holstered beneath her coat. The heavy Webley-Fosbery revolver was her constant companion, despite his disapproval. His assistant preferred shooting to talking, even when the latter was preferable.

"Producer actually, but yes. She went rather doolally after a bad day on the set is the way I heard it. Proclaimed herself Ishtar reborn or some such. An arbiter of divine justice. Didn't hurt her career as much as one might think." He pointed. "Look."

"Tracks," Gallowglass said. She dropped to her haunches. The scuff marks of many feet through the layer of dust and grime that marked the platform. "Looks like several people. A dozen, maybe more." She looked up. "Heading off across the platform."

St. Cyprian nodded. "I know where they were going. Come on." He led her to the edge of the platform, and clambered down onto the track. Something clinked as he did so.

"Champagne bottle," Gallowglass said. "Somebody is celebrating early."

"Shaw's followers aren't true believers. Just dilettantes out for a lark. Though there are rumours…wait. Listen."

Gallowglass tilted her head. "Singing?"

"Yes." St. Cyprian paused. "The new one by Al Jolson, I believe."

"I hate Al Jolson."

"I've always thought of you as a woman of taste and refinement. This way." He started off down the tunnel. "And quietly."

"Where are we going?" she whispered.

He glanced back at her. "There's an old access tunnel that branches off from the main track. It's been closed since the war. That's where it's stored."

"Where what's stored?"

"The Woolley Relief."

"The whatsit?"

"During the war, the museum transported as many antiquities as they could out of London," St. Cyprian said, as he navigated the narrow steps. "But between the occasional bombing raid and the Zeppelins lumbering over Bloomsbury, some artefacts never made it past the front doors. So down here they came."

"Including this—what did you call it?"

"The Woolley Relief," St. Cyprian said. "And yes. It's a Mesopotamian piece, as near as anyone can figure. A depiction of the goddess Ishtar. Or maybe Ereshkigal. Bit of an odd provenance, really. It was found by Sir Thomas Woolley in—"

"And that's what this lot is looking for, is it?" Gallowglass interrupted.

St. Cyprian sighed. "Unless I'm wrong."

"Why?"

"Not a clue. I doubt the reason is good, whatever it is." He stopped. Someone had lost a shoe on the track, and another empty bottle kept it company. The singing was getting louder. There was a reinforced door set into the side of the tunnel. Someone had jimmied it open—and not neatly. St. Cyprian waved Gallowglass back against the wall. She did so, drawing her pistol as she went.

"Put that away, would you?" he said, irritably, as he pulled the door fully open. The hinges squalled, and he winced. There was a flickering light at the other end of the narrow tunnel, and voices echoed. "We're not shooting anyone today if we can help it."

"You say that every time," Gallowglass said, as she holstered her weapon.

"And one day, you'll listen." St. Cyprian held a finger to his lips. "Now—hush. And stay close." They started down the tunnel, moving as quickly as they dared. Despite his words, part of him was glad Gallowglass was armed. He had a pistol of his own—a souvenir of his days in the trenches. He patted his jacket pocket, where the little Bulldog rested. He didn't care for the weight; it disturbed the cut of his jacket. He also wasn't much of a shot. Luckily, he had other talents.

They reached the opposite end of the tunnel in a few moments. St. Cyprian glanced through the doorway and saw another platform—smaller than Bloomsbury—and filled with crates and tarpaulin-shrouded shapes.

The platform was lit by electric lights, strung along the ceiling. In the harsh glare, long shadows danced along the walls. These shadows were cast by the crowd of well-dressed trespassers cavorting among the objects d'art. There was at least a dozen of them, maybe more. Several were busy prying open a crate, while the rest occupied themselves with a rather off-key singalong, and a bottle of champers.

"How'd they even know it was down here?" Gallowglass murmured, as they moved slowly through the tangle of crates.

"Same way I did," St. Cyprian whispered. "They read the papers. Now shh!" He peered around the edge of a crate.

Antigone Shaw stood among her followers like a statue—all poise and calm, untroubled by the caterwauling of her adherents or the seeming difficulties the others were having getting the crate open. She was dressed for a night at the opera, but wore a headdress of decidedly archaic design over her sharply bobbed hair. She had an old fashioned fob watch in her hand. "If you could pick up the pace, I would be obliged to you gentlemen," she said, her voice carrying as if across a stage. "The gods have decided that the world must be cleansed, so that new life might grow."

"Sorry old gel, they've double-nailed the blighter, must be," one of the men at the crate said, mopping at his face with a handkerchief. "Barely fit the bloody pry-bar in."

"That's what she said, innit?" Gallowglass called out as she and St. Cyprian stepped into the open. St. Cyprian shook his head in annoyance.

"Excuse my companion, she was raised by a cult of cannibalistic cat-worshippers."

The singing had stopped when they'd stepped out into the open. Shaw snapped the watch shut and stowed it in her furs, a disdainful look on her face. "And who are you, then?"

"St. Cyprian. Charles St. Cyprian. And you are Antigone Shaw, the actress."

"Lord above, he's a fan," a woman said, and laughed uproariously. The others joined in, some even clapping. Shaw twitched two fingers, and her followers fell silent. She fixed St. Cyprian with a dark gaze, gauging him.

"You're too late," she said. As she spoke, her followers at last managed to pry apart the crate they'd been working on. The pieces fell away amid a cloud of packing straw, revealing a heavy terracotta plaque, as tall as a man. At first glance, St. Cyprian could see that it depicted a nude, winged figure, crouched atop a second, indistinct shape.

"That the whatsit?" Gallowglass asked.

"That's the biscuit." St. Cyprian stepped forward, hands raised. "I don't know what you're hoping to accomplish here. I assume it's something dashed unforgivable. And I'm afraid I simply can't allow it."

"And who are you to allow anything?" Shaw asked, one eyebrow arched in that way that had made her famous. "You're not the police, I think."

"No, but I am vested with the King's authority nonetheless. And by that authority, I am ordering you to cease and desist all occult activities on these premises." He took another step forward. Out of the corner of his eye, he saw Gallowglass begin to sidle around in order to get a clear shot. He hoped it wouldn't be necessary. Often, gatherings such as this could be dispersed without too much trouble. You just had to smile and act as if you were in charge.

He smiled and drew a bit closer to Shaw, hands still spread. She frowned. "Stay where you are, whoever you are."

"St. Cyprian, remember? Charles? I first saw you in—what was it?—*Heir of Ylourgne,* with that Italian fellow…what was his name?"

Shaw snatched a pistol from her furs and pointed it at him. He froze. "Ricardo Mancini," she said. "Terrible actor. Adequate lover." She cocked the pistol. "Exceptional cook. Dead now, of course. Don't move, or I'll send you to join him."

St. Cyprian raised his hands. "That would be a mistake. If you shoot me, my assistant will almost certainly shoot you. Won't you, Miss Gallowglass?"

"Have to, wouldn't I?" Gallowglass said. She had her own pistol out.

The party had suddenly gotten very quiet. One of the men who'd opened the crate cleared his throat nervously. "I—I say, Antigone, maybe we ought not to…"

"Quiet George," Shaw said, without looking at him. "Don't be a silly ass. I don't intend to let some interloper interfere in what is fated to be."

"Fate—funny word that. What does it mean in this context?"

Shaw's smile was a flat slash. "In an earlier turn of the wheel, I travelled across the primeval sea in order to collect the *mes* from perfidious Enki." As she spoke, the air seemed to thicken and the dust and shadows gathered at her shoulders, like the folds of a great cloak. "To me fell the one hundred decrees." Her eyes flashed with a cold fire that sent a chill through him. "To me was given the responsibility for their enaction."

"And which one are you enacting today?" St. Cyprian asked, mouth dry. He blinked. For an instant, Antigone Shaw had looked like someone—or something else—entirely. Almost like the worn features of the image on the Relief. Perhaps there was something to the rumours after all.

"The destruction of cities," she said. "London has turned its eyes from the gods. So I will shatter the bolts and cast wide the gates to my sister's kingdom." She paused. "And if your friend doesn't stop sidling about, I will shoot you." She levelled her weapon, and St. Cyprian swallowed, suddenly very aware of the precariousness of the situation.

"Miss Gallowglass—stay where you are, for the moment."

"No worries. I can hit her from here," Gallowglass said.

St. Cyprian closed his eyes. "I fear that's not helping, Miss Gallowglass."

"Wasn't trying to."

St. Cyprian ignored his assistant and tried to focus on Shaw, rather than the weapon in her hand. "Why now?" he asked, trying to keep Shaw talking.

"That bounder in the Times, wasn't it?" George said, helpfully. "Critic fellow. Whatshisname—something Tremont? Wrote a rather scathing review of Antigone's performance in *The Last Incantation*. Dashed unfair, at least in my opinion."

Shaw's serene mask cracked slightly. "Shut up, George. We've wasted enough time. London must be given over to the eaters of dust." She stepped back, nudging George out of the way. She extended her free hand and caressed the raised face of the carven figure. Her eyes flickered again with that eerie light, and she murmured something. It wasn't in English. Or Italian or French or any modern language.

"Stop," he said, sharply. Whatever she was saying, it had the rhythm of an incantation. There was a distant sound, as of bells ringing all at once. The air in the tunnel went still, and even the most inebriated of Shaw's followers fell silent.

Then, a sound, as of a gate being smashed asunder.

And then another. And another. Growing louder with each subsequent crash, until the platform shook with the reverberations of the unseen destruction.

In the silence that followed—a susurrus. Voices, calling out from the dark. Dozens, hundreds, all tumbling over one another in their eagerness to be heard. As the tumult reached a febrile pitch, Shaw smiled and spun towards George, her revolver barking.

The unfortunate man pitched backwards, a surprised look on his face. His pry bar clattered to the ground. "I say Antigone—" another of her followers began, before her second bullet put an end to the question, and sent him tumbling to the floor beside George.

"I am Ishtar reborn," she said, swinging the smoking pistol towards her next target. "And I have cast asunder the gates of the underworld, so that the dead might devour the living!" She fired again and again, first sending a woman spinning into the wall, her face a crimson mask, and then knocking a man backwards into a crate. Champagne bottles shattered on the platform.

The party dissolved into chaos, as celebrants began to flee. St. Cyprian fought through the crowd towards Shaw, but stumbled as someone trod on his foot. An elbow caught him in the midsection and he staggered, wheezing. "Miss Gallowglass," he called out. The crowd thinned, and he found himself face-to-face with Shaw.

Her smile was lean and savage. "And the dead shall devour the living, and then they shall eat dust forevermore," she said, raising her pistol. He ducked aside as the shot burned a trail over the top of his shoulder. Shaw cursed and tracked him as he stumbled over George.

George groaned and caught his ankle. St. Cyprian looked down. George looked up—or, rather, something looked up through George's eyes. Something hungry and foul. St. Cyprian went for his pistol as George hauled himself up, mouth wide. He bashed the Bulldog against the side of George's head and untangled himself from the dead man's grip. As he stepped back, he saw that George wasn't the only one.

The dead were rising, hungry for the living. The men and women Shaw had shot were attacking their fellow celebrants, biting and clawing at them like wild beasts. For every one that fell, a new cannibal corpse joined the hungry throng. Some of the survivors had already fled, but the dead would be swift on their heels.

And then they'd be loose in the Underground, or worse, on the streets. An epidemic the likes of which London had never seen. Unless they could stop it.

"Your auguries foretell this bit?" Gallowglass called out, taking aim at one of the resurrected celebrants. The pistol barked, and the dead man stumbled—but did not fall. She cursed and fired again, even as the corpse barrelled towards her, jaws snapping. The bullet tore a canyon through the dead man's skull, sending him crashing into a crate. As the echo of the shot faded, he began to clamber to his feet.

She blinked in surprise. "A head-shot usually works."

"Not with these." St. Cyprian fired at George, as the corpse dragged himself upright. He emptied his revolver into the corpse, but succeeded only in knocking it down. "I fear it will take something a bit stronger than a bullet."

"I left my howitzer at home."

"Not that either. Cover me." He started towards the Relief. Shaw paid him little attention, enraptured as she was by the madness she'd wrought. She laughed as the dead savaged the living, and waved her pistol about like a conductor's baton. He ignored her, hoping she would return the favour.

A groan caught his attention. George, back on his feet, lunged for him again, and St. Cyprian snatched up the fallen pry bar to wield like a club. He swung it two-handed, and nearly staved in George's already-perforated skull. The dead man spun in a slow circle, groping blindly at the air. St. Cyprian hit him again, and heard bones crack. A bullet tugged at his coat and he dove behind a crate.

Shaw stalked towards him, shoving George from her path. "I am a goddess—who are you to dare set yourself in my path?" She fired again, and wooden splinters bit into his cheek as he risked a glance.

He heard the boom of Gallowglass' Webley-Fosbery, and Shaw yelped as she sought cover. "Hurry up and do whatever you're going to do," Gallowglass shouted. She cursed as a corpse yanked at her coat, and slammed the butt of her pistol down on the dead woman's head. "I'm running out of ammunition!"

"I'm working on it!" He risked a look, and saw that of the dozen or so people who'd followed Shaw down into the tunnel, only three or four were still alive. The rest were either dead, or in the process of becoming undead. "Get the rest of these idiots out of here, if you can. And close the door behind you—bar it if you bloody have to!"

"What about you?"

"I told you, I'm working on it!" He ducked along the corridor of crates and tarps, trying to circle around Shaw. She was armed and knew how to use it. He heard a hiss from above him, and saw a corpse perched awkwardly atop the crate. It half-leapt, half-fell towards him, and he sprang back, narrowly avoiding its flailing limbs.

It had been a woman once, a flapper wrapped in glad rags. Now it was all teeth and broken fingers, groping for him. He ducked away from her, and shimmied past. The dead were strong, but not fast. He heard the boom of Gallowglass' pistol, and the sound of running feet. For once she was doing as he'd asked.

"I can hear you, whatever your name is," Shaw called out, from close by. "I don't know what you think you can accomplish here."

"In my experience, quite a bit," he said, trying for bravado. "Dashed if I know what, though," he muttered. He could hear the dead stumbling after him, but ignored them and concentrated on reaching the Relief. Whatever power it contained was likely the solution to this problem. If he was lucky. If not…well, best not to think about it. He tightened his grip on the pry bar.

He could feel it, radiating through the crates. A sort of warmth that was neither natural nor comforting. Things like the Relief were more common than most realised. A bit of ancient power, baked into clay and left for some two-bit magus to stumble over.

A bullet punctured the crate, and he heard Shaw shout something from the other side. He pushed himself back, plucking at the splinters in his cheek. As he did so, hands clutched at him from behind, and he found himself propelled back against the wood. George, head sloughing awkwardly, gave a gargling snarl as he leaned forward, teeth bared.

"Persistent bugger," St. Cyprian said, thrusting the pry bar between them. George's broken teeth bit down on the bar, and St. Cyprian struggled against the dead man's strength. As they reeled this way and that, more hungry dead scrambled towards them, sensing an easy meal. Desperate, he swung George around and shoved him into his fellows, tripping them up.

The flapper, her hair dishevelled and her face bloody, leapt onto his back. Her fingers sought his throat. A shot cracked, and the weight on his back vanished. He heard Shaw curse and turned. "Stand still," she snarled.

He charged. Shaw's fell back in surprise. St. Cyprian brushed past her. He spied the relief and lunged for it, the pry bar cocked over his shoulder.

The blow never fell. He felt the power of it thrum through him like an electrical current and knew instantly that smashing the stone would do no good whatsoever. There was only one thing he could do. Shaw claimed to be Ishtar reborn.

And the best way to deal with one goddess was to entreat another.

He cast the pry bar aside and reached for the relief, as Shaw had done. Only he did so with the lines of an old Sumerian prayer on his lips. If it had worked for Shaw, it might well work for him. "Ereshkigal, hear me…"

"No! I won't let you," Shaw cried out from behind him. He heard her pistol bark, and felt a bite of pain as a bullet passed through the meat of his hand and cracked the relief. He muttered the last words of the prayer through gritted teeth, and turned to see Shaw advancing on him. "What have you done?" she said.

"Me?" He wrapped his hand in his handkerchief. He could hear something beneath the cacophony of the dead, and felt a cold sensation in the pit of his gut. The sound, indistinct at first, became a quiet hum, getting louder. It put him in mind of flies. "I'm not the one who unleashed a plague of the living dead because a critic gave me a poor review."

Shaw pulled the trigger. He flinched. The weapon clicked empty. She frowned and made to speak, when something black settled on her cheek. She swatted at it, leaving a trail of blood. "What? What was that?" The humming was quite loud now, drowning out the cries of the living and the dead. "What is it?"

"I think your sister is upset," he said. Shaw stared at him in momentary incomprehension. Then her eyes widened and she turned as if to run. But too late.

The carving on the relief seemed to open its mouth wide, as something black and humming boiled out, filling the air. They might have been flies or wasps or something else entirely. They swarmed out and engulfed Shaw. She screamed piteously in a language that might have been Babylonian as she stumbled, slapping at the biting, stinging swarm.

More flies surrounded the dead, and the corpses jittered and twitched in an approximation of pain or fear. The insects filled their mouths and noses and eyes, and the dead fell like puppets with their strings cut as whatever was inside them was snatched away. Shaw's screams had gone quiet. St. Cyprian saw her on the ground, covered in flies. But when he went to her, the swarm scattered and there was nothing there at all.

Something groaned. He whirled and saw George lurching towards him, his face covered in flies. "Down," Gallowglass said, from behind him. St. Cyprian dropped flat as his assistant swung the pry bar and took what was left of George's head clean off. The flies poured in eagerly as George sank down, and winnowed out whatever it was that crouched within the dead man. A moment later, the flies were gone. As if they had never been at all.

Gallowglass kicked at what was left of George. "What were they?"

"Demons of the underworld. Servants of Ereshkigal. Come to drag the dead back to where they belong. And the one who summoned them." His mouth tasted like tar and he spat, trying to clear it.

Gallowglass nudged one of the corpses with her foot. "Left the bodies, though."

"That they did."

"We going to have to explain this?"

"Lord, I hope not." He looked at her. "I thought I told you to leave."

"Lucky for you I didn't." She pushed the brim of her cap up and peered at the relief. "So who was this supposed to be anyway? Ishtar or whatshername?"

"Ereshkigal," St. Cyprian said. "And I have no bloody idea."

He flexed his injured hand, and looked at the Relief. It seemed to smile in satisfaction, and he looked away, suddenly uneasy.

"Thankfully, whoever it was, they were listening."

IN SHADOW VALLEY
Nick Swain

"Ya see that?" Chester asked, his long, lanky neck cranked around like a vulture as he looked to the back of the herd.

"A-yuh," Dean grunted, hacked, and spat black-bile between his teeth and over the head of his nag. "Kind'a hard to miss."

Over the crest of the downhill desert valley and just yonder the nearest ridge, smoke split the horizon in thick plumes of black, expanding the higher it rose like the funnel of a twister, before dissipating into the vastness of blue New Mexican sky. Ahead, a lone, mewling longhorn steered off course from the others before being "*H-YA'd*" back into place by Pat, lashing his lasso from side to side.

Chester was still looking back to Dean. His dirty face contorted in that ugly blend of anxiety and confusion. "That's Apache war smoke, ain't it?" he said.

"I reckon," Dean said, his lips smacking as his open mouth worked about like one of the grazing cattle the three of them had rustled up that morning.

"Well what'a ya figure?" Chester asked, already reaching down his saddle and wrapping his fingers around the stock of his repeater.

"It's too late to turn back and go through Valanchro, that's for sure," Pat weighed in. "An if we cut back through Sandalwood it'd be at least another half 'a day before we made it to Mecker's ranch."

"Reckon so," Dean said laconically, chewing.

"So, what in the hell are we gonna do?" Chester demanded to know.

"Keep on," Dean answered plainly.

"You crazy?" Pat said. "You want me to ride on into a scalpin'?"

"I don't understand," said Chester. "I thought there was supposed to be some sort'a treaty in the works with the Mescalero?"

"They don't care," Pat insisted. "That's with *those* white men. We're a whole other tribe of white faces, far as they're concerned. And we're trespassin'."

"Can't go back," Dean settled. "Haley and his posse would be on top of us before we ever got to Valanchro *or* Sandalwood. We'll offer them Meskies some cattle for safe passage. Just keep face and don't show no disrespect. They might let us pass."

"Yea, or they might just sacrifice us for some rain," Chester commented, unsheathing his rifle and hammering a round in place.

"Maybe we oughtn't try for it, Dean," Pat suggested. "Even if them Meskies bend over and wave goodbye while we pass, we ain't exactly headin' into the warmest patch of land in the territory. Ya hear things…"

"All I care about is how quick it'll get us to Mecker's. Just keep the herd steady and your eyes open," Dean ordered, repositioning his own .44's from their hip-holsters and thumbing the hammers back. He stuck the guns loosely in his belt and spat. "And keep that damn scatter gun up 'n ready!"

* * * *

The desert sun can put spots in a man's eyes, but each cowboy was certain of the movements they perceived along the cliffs as the trail narrowed and the rock walls tightened into a winding passage, yet only Dean was certain of having seen the feathers dipping in and out of sight along the rocks above them. The clustered cattle mewled uncomfortably, crowded and roughly guided along the thin path. The black smoke hung above them, blotting out the sun like apocalyptic clouds. With Dean at the head, the herd cautiously rounded the first sharp corner; there he saw the scattered figures perched along the truss-like ridge. Tall figures, with unique and abstract patterns of face-paint made up of orange, green, and white. Waiting. One stood center; imperially positioned atop a deliberately placed boulder. The warpainted figures remained still as the cowboys and cattle approached, old rifles cradled in some of their arms.

A few yards ahead of the ridge Dean halted the herd—behind, on either side of the cattle, Pat and Chester clung closely to the walls, rifles subtly aimed ahead. Dean raised his hand slowly in a welcoming gesture. "Howgh."

The Chief did not respond.

Dean spoke louder and slower. "*Do you… speak… English?*"

No answer. But Dean was noticing more Indian heads popping up in his peripheral vision.

"Don't reckon y'all are just havin' a pow-wow up there, are ya?" He spoke facetiously.

Nothing. The painted-face of the Chief was stoic and heavy with solemnity; his dark-face was almost sagging with it.

"*We* would… like to offer *you*… some cattle. Respect. Understand?"

Nothing.

"Do you understand? We like, to give you cattle, in exchange for passage—"

"May not pass," the Chief's thunderous voice declared pithily.

The rifle in Chester's lap shifted, and in the hills the figures rose with it.

"Well if you'd listen you'd understand that our only option is yonder," said Dean. "Now we're tryin' to be respectful here, but you're gonna have to meet us halfway—"

"Turn around, Whiteman," the Chief said. "Go back. Come tomorrow. Early. May pass then."

"Now look, Chief." The reverence in Dean's voice was absent now. "There's no way for us but that way." He pointed down the alley. "We got a schedule to keep. Understand?"

"This Death's Passage, Whiteman. Trail to nowhere. At night, it belong to Shadow... Not for man..."

"You mean not for *Whiteman*," Chester remarked curtly.

"Mean what say, Whiteman," the Chief continued undaunted in his somber inflection. "Through Death's Passage there is only Shadow Land. Take you to nowhere in the night. Not for man. Not at night. Come tomorrow. Come early. Pass then."

"Told ya, Chief, that ain't a option," Dean spat ahead, hand creeping up to his stomach. "Now just 'cause you might have a few tee-pees set up around here, don't mean you got the right to get to telling another man where he can an can't—"

The Chief sonorous voice boomed over Dean's without being raised in the slightest. "At night, in Shadow Valley, tortured souls dance on own graves—and graves of others. Your Whiteman's God will not be able to find your soul in Shadow Land. Eternal unrest. Go, Whiteman. Live."

"I ain't one to go against any man an his religious rights, but I'm tellin' you for the last time, Chief, we ain't lettin' you interfere with this drive. Reckon this is the last time: you sure we can't work it out?"

"We will keep you here then, Whiteman. You and your animals. May go tomorrow. Alive. In the light, when God can watch you."

"Don't think too much of bein' kept prisoner," Dean growled, his eyes narrow and hawk-like.

"You don't understand, Whiteman. Maybe you can't. We cannot allow you to go into Shadow. *Guilt*, real for Apache. Can't allow. You stay." He nodded to the left side of the cliffs and several Mescalero made to descend toward the cowboys.

"*Reckon not.*" Dean shot first, setting off a chain reaction of gunfire from all sides.

It started with his first shot missing, but not by much. The bullet splitting the tall feather pinned to the rawhide-headband the Chief wore. He blinked once, and if it were possible it seemed his frown grew deeper. He turned away, almost woefully, and disappeared behind the rock. Dean barely catching this as he lurched far over one side of his horse, fanning out three shots in the direction of the closest Indians above, being sure he hit a few but too busy slapping the hammer to be certain. Their return fire struck around the horse's feet and sent it into a frenzy, bucking Dean from its side. Smoke and fire spurted from all around.

Pat let loose with both barrels of the shotgun as soon as Dean started shooting, the buckshot exploding the rock some shooters were crouched behind. Most recoiled and returned fire, but a couple writhed and rolled in agony, clutching at their blood and paint blended faces. Pat tossed the gun in the saddle and felt the first searing-sting drill into his arm as he reached back for his six-shooter. He twisted in pain and collapsed from his horse.

Chester was exchanging rifle fire with the Mescalero to the left. He'd jumped from his horse after the first few shots and callously taken cover behind some of the stirring cattle, allowing them to take the hits. *"Get them cattle goin', boys!"* Dean shouted, doing the same for cover ahead to the right, working with a twin revolver in his other hand now.

Pat shot at the cliffs, but he was using his left hand and felt hopelessly useless. The ground burst all around him as the shots kept coming from above, spitting dirt in his face. Suddenly Dean was riding in. He came in low, fanning out the remaining shots to his revolver before crouching over and heaving a hollering Pat onto his shoulders—in a position that conveniently shielded himself from the growing barrage of Indian gunfire.

This time the pain was lower, though equally stab-like and excruciating as the bullet ripped through the other side of Pat's leg. And then another bullet struck his shoulder by the first wound as Dean slapped the horse and sent it charging forward.

As he leapt onto his own nag, Dean saw the ululating attacker loping down the hillside; a long, colorful spear in hand. Dean fired. Pulled the hammer back and fired again. The Indian flopped backwards as his half-chucked spear sloped down into the trail near the one-way stampede of cattle Chester was managing to drive down the alley.

Racing under the ridge, Dean adjusted himself and readied his pistol. But when he came out on the other side of the ridge he saw only the Chief; standing steady and staring. He held no weapon. His heavy solemn gaze *was* his weapon. Dean thought of firing anyway as his horse galloped on; his finger even tightened against the already-taut trigger. But when he saw the young Indian beside the Chief drawing a bead with his rifle, he changed his line of fire. Only before he could drop the hammer something peculiar happened. He knew he was in the Meskie's sights a good half second before *he* was in *his*. But before he could send a .54 caliber slug through Dean's stomach the Chief lowered the young warrior's rifle. As distance grew between them, Dean watched the profiles of the gathering tribe fade, but all the while they were still. Watching.

The Chief and his followers stood by, studying the cowboys and their pilfered cattle as they rode off into the mouth of Death's Passage. Two of them were firing their guns in the air in celebration.

In Apachean, the young rifle-wielder told his Chief of their casualties. Saying he should have been allowed to kill the white man.

"Let them have peace now," the Chief told the others, looking toward the dwindling ball of light hazily hailing to the South. Fading dreamily in its steady departure. "Soon, Shadow will swallow them."

* * * *

Over the naked desert sparkling specks peppered the vastness of black sky, twinkling lifetimes away. The pale moon peeked its blue light from behind a faraway mountain, distant and unimportant. There was a peculiar breeze that came with the night; 'As though the Almighty had gone and left the window open,' was how Chester put it. In a patchy green part of the valley, the longhorn massed; grazing, mewling lightly. Coyotes bayed shrilly somewhere in the hills. About a dozen yards south of their camp, the scarfs and embroidered handkerchiefs fastened to the few stick-cross markers tussled against the minute wind in the shanty graveyard the cowboys had noticed passing—among other peculiarities.

Around the crackling of the fire the stink of singed flesh still hung sourly in the air. The iron-poker used to seal Pat's wounds now lay across the fire by the coffee pot, being sterilized for the possibility of future use.

"Gimme that other bottle," Pat grumbled to Chester.

"Ya already topped-off the first one."

"I said gimme that Goddamn bottle!" Pat growled.

Chester frowned then returned from his saddle with a second bottle of whiskey. Pat snatched it from his grasp as he offered it, ripping the cork off with his teeth and gulping the liquor down in harsh swallows. He stopped only for short breaths before taking down more. "*Goddamn savages*," he grumbled. "Animals wouldn't even strike a deal. Just wanted to tan our hides!"

"How many steer we lose in that stampede once the alley broke open?" Dean inquired, playing with his pistol's cylinder.

"Hell, least a couple dozen." Pat rasped. "Not to mention that handful in the gunfight."

Dean spat.

"Whatta ya reckon they meant by all that spook talk?" asked Chester. "Shadow valleys and not to travel at night?"

"I know exactly what they were talkin' about," Pat insisted. "But that don't give 'em any right to shoot it out over it! Goddamn superstitious sons-a-bitches!"

"Yea but remember what that Indian said first?" Chester said, musing. "Said, 'turn around and live.' Like he was warning us more than anything. Gave us the choice."

"Who the hell is he to be given us choices?" Pat lashed out. "Some choice! He saw us with that herd, he knew we couldn't just up an turn tail! Hell, he could see that plainly without havin' to know about Haley's posse!"

"Ya think maybe the smoke was another sort of warning? I mean, in a different way than usual?" Chester went on, to himself more than Pat. "Like maybe they was thinkin' to scare us into not even tryin' for the passage?"

"What did you mean before, about this part of the territory?" Dean finally broke into the conversation, his doleful glare shifting from the whipping flames to Pat. "You said something before we rode into that mess. About... hearin' things?"

Pat took another gulp from the bottle. "Hell, I didn't mean nothin' important—"

"And what do ya mean that you know exactly what that featherhead was talkin' about?" Dean asked soberly. The frigid breeze picked up then, whisking the camp flames into long, sinuous streaks that reached out of the fire pit and at the cowboys. The wisp of wind sent the blue bandana around Dean's neck fluttering about his shoulders; he narrowed his eyes against the gliding grains of sand, loading new shells into his second pistol. He looked up to Pat for an answer.

Pat looked to his audience from each side of the fire. He sat up in his sleeping bag, the bottle in his lap. "Just what I said... ya hear things... ghost stories fellas tell each other 'round the fire, like we're doin' now." He sighed, as if baring a burden in his tale. "I'd never been to this part of the country. Not 'till the war when we had to cut out'a Kansas for New Mexico. I met this colored fella by Fort Myer once. From one of the slave regiments, crazy sort of fella. He used to get a little loose and tell us stories about the slave ship he an his daddy came over on when he was a boy. He said there was this other fella on board—'cept he was Hattian—a witch-doctor was what he said if ya really want to know. This fella told us that his Daddy was a hellraiser, an found his way onto more than one plantation; at a couple 'a these plantations, he said his Daddy ran into that Hattian. Said he was notorious at the time for never bein' kept for more than a week. Rumors varied; sometimes he left the places burnin', sometimes he gave the other slaves weapons to overtake the plantation guards with—but always after he'd escape somethin' would happen..."

Pat took a drink.

"Come on, what?" Chester blurted impatiently.

"The crop would fail—or the livestock would take ill an die. Didn't matter what, it all went to hell. And worse yet… them farmers and plantation runners… they'd die, too. Crazy sorts of deaths. Mauled apart by wild animals, captured by Union troops an tortured to death. Other more, uh—colorful tales. Always there was supposed to be mangled remains left behind—just enough of the face left for identifyin' 'em."

Pat took another slug of whiskey. His hand shook. As the cowboys talked and listened, the moon sank behind the hills and unknown desert things creeped in the night.

"I think he would just make mosta this up, ya know—give the white boys a good spookin'… he did a good job, 'cause he'd finish the story by telling us that damn Hattian—or prolly him, I mean *who else*—would come back an *steal* them bodies. What was left of 'em anyhow."

"Steal?" Chester repeated.

"*Steal. Body snatchin'.* Crazy bastard said this witch-doctor *collected* them corpses. Wanna guess where he's supposed to have decided to keep 'em?"

Chester's mouth gaped stupidly as he glanced from Dean to Pat, Pat to desert. "Not… *here?*"

"Bingo, bright-stuff," Pat cackled drunkenly. "Fella said he picked the nastiest, most violent part of territory he could for his… *passion.*

"Can't say he picked a bad spot, that's for sure. Even if every portion 'a that African's nonsense was lies, there'd still be at least a dozen real tragedies to pick from here."

"Like what do ya mean?" asked Chester. Dean remained stoic, yet attentive.

"Like you see them poles back yonder?" Pat cocked his head towards a few yards down the valley—near the graveyard, to the two straight-shaped shadows protruding into the sky from atop a small cliff. "Bet you thought them was totem poles? *Wrong.* Them poles was used by some Injuns to burn a couple of Irish famers alive after they made the mistake of trying to settle here—before our Hattian deity took lease mind you."

"Christ," Chester muttered.

"Then there's God only knows how many noted massacres and gunfights went on here durin' the war. Hell, I even met this other fella back at Fort Myer—mind you, I didn't connect the two 'til later—fella said his Major ordered the troop to execute a whole brigade of Rebel prisoners in a dead zone between Valanchro and Montihue Hills. Said after the war when he and some others were sent to bury the remains before they were found, there weren't nothin' there—no bones, no boots. Nothin'. They figured somebody found the Rebs an buried 'em, only they never heard nobody ever makin' a case out of a unit of dead Confederates found out here in the desert. Said it kept him up at nights."

"You're sayin' that witch-doctor… collected them bodies?" Chester asked.

"I ain't sayin' nothin' except what others told me. There's more you wouldn't believe if I told ya. Whole colonies of settlers up and disappearin' through this territory—not even the wagon or horse carcasses left to find. People… *hearing* things… Yup, I reckon' I can't blame that voodoo feller a'tall for pickin' this place as his personal Spook Town. Gotta figure there's a body under every step ya take."

"Why the hell wouldn't you tell us all this before we came here?" Chester blurted in alarm.

"What're you raggin' on about?" Pat proded Chester, smirking at a remote and musing Dean. "How many ghost stories you hear as a boy? Ya ever had any boogymen pop up?"

Chester didn't answer. Dean spat in the fire; it sizzled.

Pat laughed drunkenly. "I heard of 'a dog-like creature in this border-town I used to herd sheep in. These Mexican fellers always kept on about this thing bein' responsible for missin' sheep—but I never did see no monster slinking around the grounds. No slaughtered lambs with their blood drained, like they said there'd be. I'll tell ya what it was—*superstitious manure*. Sheep-thieves were behind them missing head, just like native exaggeration is behind this Shadow Valley bull."

"Still nothin' to hold out on a man!" Chester protested.

"Laddie boy, laddie boy," Pat slurred, "it's all *A-okay*—Hooray! Hooray! *Just say your prayers and kiss your ass… bend over good and let Death bugger ya fast!"* He broke into a slovenly cackle; spilt whiskey spotted his collar.

Chester stirred in his sleeping bag as if to spring at Pat. "You keep your damn drunken mouth shut, you loose-tongued—"

"Both of you *shut up*," Dean cut in curtly. "I need some sleep. I don't care what ya do, just *shut up* and let me sleep. Pat, since your feeling so chipper now, you take first watch over the cattle. Then you." He glared at Chester. "If ya feel restless then count stars quietly. Just *shut up*." The rustler turned over and covered himself with a blanket. The only sound the hiss of the fire. Under the blanket, where no one could see, he slept with a .44.

* * * *

The world was still black and cold when Dean opened his eyes to the rattled yelps of the cattle. There was another noise; shrill and inhuman. Not a coyote, Dean knew. He blinked his eyes in rapid successions, adjusting to a sudden awakening in a dark setting.

The shadow stood out among the rest of the blackness. A writhing, amorphous shape at first, but with each blink of the eye the figure took on more definition and Dean knew it was a body crawling to him.

Pat, he thought. Must be worse off, can't stand. Or maybe... maybe he saw somethin' and is crawlin' to wake me silently. "*Pat?*" he hissed.

The shape drew itself closer, the sound of desert dirt scrapping behind it. "Goddamnit, Pat," Dean growled quietly. He made to throw his blanket aside, but just then the atonal howling around him grew wilder and took on an almost ceremonious rhythm. He opened his eyes for good and through the thin flashes of his blurred, tuning sight he observed the macabre happenings of the surrounding night. "Christ! *Pat, Chester*, wake the hell up!" he barked, drawling his revolver. But as he drew the hammer back the shape he'd awakened to groped at the gun, smacking it to the dirt and straddling Dean before he ever realized it was not Pat.

Atop of Dean, throttling and thrashing insanely, a nose-less, bug-eyed corpse howled a reedy scream that stank of rot. The black and grey teeth chattered ravenously behind shriveled, granulated lips. Amidst the attack Dean spotted the grey kepi cap of a Rebel foot solider. A once pipped and trim jacket now shredded crudely and exposing the shattered ribcage of the Johnny Reb strangling a petrified and incredulous Dean. He could see plainly that the man was dead. Dry and rotting.

And yet the horrors only greatened.

For all around, the ghoulish, sooty corpses of the dead seemed to dance about him; shuffling mindlessly and crooning in the night. The once-distant, puny moon now sat atop the very hill it had sunk behind; a fat, omnipotent spectator of the devilish theatre, the craters of its surface round and glaring like the bug-eyes of the howling fiends. Its ghastly, cold glow lighting the desert stage for the rotters.

The dead Rebel finished pounding Dean's head against the ground and brought its decaying mouth down for his neck; its fetid breath stifling his senses. Dean fought best he could, just barley keeping the fiend's grimy canines from more than scraping against his scruffy chin. In the struggle it sank its grungy fangs between the knuckles of Dean's defending hand.

He gave his own howl of agony and drew his second pistol with his free hand. He stuck the long barrel beneath the ghoul's chin and blasted the attacker from him. The gnawing corpse flopped over violently—what dried-up brains remained in its skull went spilling through the air with its Rebel cap.

But the sprawling fiend still stirred after it crashed. Dean could see now why it was crawling, as both of its sharp leg-bones jutted from their meaty-stubs and drug along the earth, pulling itself and its mindless-hunger back toward its prey.

Dean scattered to his feet, and though it pained him a great deal, he clasped his first .44 in his gnawed hand, firing a round from each pistol; both slugs drilled through the creeping monster's head, pausing only seconds with the harsh impact before scrabbling further. The bullet holes looked puny in comparison to its neighboring, bulging eyes; black and seething with hate and murder.

Dean fired once more, futilely. He was backing away when he *did* see Pat.

Slumped over, the shotgun still lying across his lap. His eyes open and hollow with horror and savage disbelief. The side of his head was gnawed open and being feasted upon by two other corpses. One, once a young man, with clothes for the most part still intact; an empty gun belt around his waist. Spurs jangling and lobes snapping with each pull of the teeth. The other consumer, despite being coated in grime, was a well-dressed cadaver, with the crusty gold-chain of a pocket watch still stretched across its vest. A once important man who now ravaged on the warm flesh of humanity. Wondering why Pat had not hollered for help, Dean spotted the horrendous scene of the two dead Indian girls fighting and tearing at something small and wet and pink. Dean felt sickness churn in his gut. The girls devoured their shares and fell over Pat's body for more.

Rifle shots rang out from behind. He turned to see Chester hopping around the smoky remnants of the fire. Hammering away with his repeater, hitting his target every time and yet doing only superficial damage. *"Christ, Dean! What the hell is this?"*

Dean fired more shots from his pistols, even bursting the bulbous eyes of the ghouls in some instances. They only advanced. Crawling and lurching and howling and gritting.

The rustlers worked themselves back-to-back, fighting up hill as the mass of undead only doubled; tripled. In the valley, the cattle stirred loudly, some began bucking and upsetting groups of the other steer who began trotting off into the darkness.

"Keep them cattle from stampedin'!" Dean barked.

"THE CATTLE?" Chester repeated incredulously. "We should be gettin' the Goddamn horses!"

"I'll worry 'bout the horses, you keep them cattle from scatterin'!"

"Lousy, dirty, rotten son-of-a-bitch..." Chester growled under the roar of his last three repeater shots before dropping the rifle for his own Colt. He loped carefully about the boulders and dunes and sagebrush and groping, groaning corpses that polluted the land. With the blasts of Dean's pistols still echoing amidst the camp-madness, Chester maneuvered through the calmer clusters of steer, making his way to the fuss of the herd. *"H-YA! H-YA!"* he hollered, settling one, then two, then three, longhorn. *"H-YA!"*

He trudged on where the mewling and movement was greatest. He took hold of the horns of one bovine before his feet were snatched from under him. In his sudden descension, Chester caught a glimpse of the scalped and grinning crippled abomination that had toppled him over.

In the fall he let off a panicked shot, and when it hit a steer the animal broke into a vicious frenzy like the others before. Its swivet caught and launched the rest of the herd into riotous loops about the valley, crashing and bucking in dismay and confusion before breaking apart and scattering in odd directions all about the shadows.

When the dust cleared the waxen moonlight exposed the sprawled-out heap of a bloody Chester. Face-up and moribundly still, his legs a twisted mess spread before him.

The crippled ghoul had been towed a short distance by the stampede, and, unaffected by its injuries, squirmed back for its impotent prey.

But Chester was still breathing; groping blindly about the dirt for his pistol, with the only arm he could still feel—however frailly. "...*Dean... help... hel...*" he rasped to the sky in agony as powerful hands with spatulate claws clasped around his ankles and heaved. The pain was white hot and brilliant in its efficiency of sending Chester in and out of the conscious world. When he was awake and opened his eyes with what little vitality remained, what the young rustler saw was a dead cowboy—a fat bullet hole above its nose like a third, giant eye—lugging him along the desert toward a gaping hole, oblong and ridged. An open grave...

Chester flailed best he could, but the hauling deadman only smiled its black, gunky smile from under its tattered-brim, loam-dappled hat and pulled onward. Soon, the first monster and other gluttonous ghouls fell upon the edging Chester—and if there were screams, they were drowned out by the feral shrieks and grinding teeth of the devouring fiends; their meat being jerked from their grasp every few seconds, looking more abhorred and mangled each time before the consumers caught up and continued. By the time the dead cowboy dumped Chester in the grave there was little more than the busted legs and some torso.

With its bare hands the ghoul began scooping piles of earth into the grave as others scrabbled inside of it for more.

Dean nearly wretched at the sight of Chester's consumption. He'd found that all three horses had disappeared, and he'd made it back just in time to witness the incident from the stampede.

Dean fired frivolously, running out of ammunition for his first two pistols and brandishing his emergency .41. But none of the encroaching ghouls would die. They were already dead...

As the lone rustler scrambled up the hill, spilling live shells along the trail in a hurry to reload, he was able to truly appreciate the wholesome deplorability of the unearthly occurrences.

For all along the desert valley, rotting corpses—loping, staggering, crawling, and dancing stupidly in the moonlight—came his direction, singing loathsome necro-songs made up of grunts and groans.

And some… some were dragging pine coffins behind them.

Dead. All. Creeping corpses, lurching rotters. Cowboys and Indians, Johnny Rebels and Blue-Bellies, wriggling side-by-side. One still had the cut-off hangman's nooses dangling from its broken neck. Others still with snapped or whole arrows protruding from their bodies. Two of the bodies… two of them roamed aimlessly—being the only ones without the gargantuan eyes. Dean realized it was because these corpses were scorched from stubby head to missing toes. The undead smoldered as though the searing were eternal.

As Dean watched some of the creatures hoisting Pat's carcass into one of the appalling boxes, believing with certainty that the scene could not become anymore nightmarishly surreal, he observed at the foot of the opposite hill, the most rotted, skeletal corpses of all were *digging*. Some with slim stones, others with scrap-wood once used as grave markers. They dug. Dean thought they were digging fresh graves, until he spotted the bare-boned palms clawing their way to obscene freedom.

He was at the peak of the cliff now; too high to jump. Only one way to go, he realized desperately. Up.

He climbed the charred poles Pat had morbidly romanticized earlier; slipping desperately at first but managing to use his spurs to dig into the wood and add some distance between himself and the groping monstrosities.

And at the top of that seesawing pole, Dean saw what was perhaps the ghastliest sight of all…

At the peak of that same hill—where at the bottom the undead worked madly—there towered a dark figure; it seemed to watch from the hilltop, as though commanding the army of fiends. A blacker than night shadow—subhuman somehow—and totally faceless, as though the hill it perched on were twice as far.

The shape stood inanimate. Watching. Lonely and unexposed by the supernatural moonlight.

It watched Dean watching it as the blistered pole rocked precariously in place. It watched as Dean's pistol blasted at the clambering mass below him; to no new affect. It watched from its imperial positioning as the pole finally shook free of the earth and sent Dean spilling over into the cannibalistic horde, cursing and shooting.

It watched it all. A Shadow in the deadlight.

In the cold, continuous breeze, a bloody, blue bandana rustled along the desert floor before catching onto one of the wooden crosses that marked only a few of the many open graves.

* * * *

What remained of the cattle were calm now. Overhead, in the distance, buzzards soared the skies in circles before descending to peck at whatever scraps the desert may have left them. Tumbleweeds rolled on, and what creeped in the desert now, creeped under the desiccating scorch of the sun's luminescence.

The Trader rolled a cigarette; they always came out loose, but in a nervous hurry this one fell apart and spilled down his shirt before he could even strike a match. "I'll give ya two dollars a head for the steer, and five for them two horses," he grumbled, fishing another paper from his tobacco bag.

The heavy lines in the Chief's face were still as he spoke. "That is dollar less than you said before."

"Yea, well, this less steer than you said before."

The Chief's squinted eyes shifted to the sky. More buzzards. "The desert took them," he declared gravely.

"Christ, that's creepy!" the Trader said, "Why can't you Injuns ever just say what ya mean?"

The Chief turned his attention back to the filthy trader. "If you would only listen, Whiteman… you would hear all I can tell you… things, even Indian cannot know full truth of…"

"I don't care what ya did with 'em," the Trader said, his attention more on his grimy fingers crafting a fresh cigarette. "Man's gotta eat. You boys get tired 'a huntin' buffalo?" he mocked. He laughed alone, but not long. He drew from his sloppy smoke and added, "I wouldn't usually bother with this few head 'a cattle, but them buyers I spoke to was real eager to grab some 'fore they rode out today."

The corners of the Chief's mouth sagged farther. He spoke with jaded urgency. "You must tell them not to take…"

"I know, I know," the Trader insisted. "Not to take *your* route at night."

"Not our route, Whiteman," the Chief continued dutifully. "It's important to you. If not told, we will be back to sell you same cattle… some…"

This time the Trader swallowed hard and nearly choked on his own ball of phlegm. He never asked questions before, he wasn't going to start today. It was lonely out there in that desert. He came back from his wagon with a jingling sack. "Want the usual? Half coin, half ammo?"

The Chief nodded. "Will need bullets for these…" the Chief produced two twin .44 Colts. "And .44-40 shells," he added, seemingly prompted by a young Apache who approached from behind, cradling a Henry rifle in his arms like a new pet.

"Sure, sure," the Trader grinned avariciously. "It'll cost ya more though. Say… half 'a what's in here." He shook the coin bag.

The Chief nodded and made the poor deal. Reminding himself and the others as they left, that what they did, they did not for profit, but only to continue baring the great weight of their obligation.

Hours later, as dusk draped imminently across the southern most of the valley, a scout came riding in, signaling to the Chief. The Chief, using a golden monoscope once gifted to him by a European immigrant he'd prevented from traveling through Death's Passage, espied a nearing group of riders guiding a stagecoach. The Chief knew a hunting party when he saw one. Like the last band of men, they would not readily accept the law laid down by his fathers before him. And yet he would try. Just as he had tried, succeeded, and failed countless times before in the onset of a foreseeably long and restless night; a night to be filled with echoing horrors that would reach beyond the Valley to once again poison the ears and curl the toes of even the eldest veteran of Nightmares. And this was only to be followed by next morning's scavenging. But at least there would be no need for burials—there never was.

✗

DEVIL'S BARGAIN
J.F. Le Roux

March 1, 1945
Wewelsburg, North Rhine-Westphalia, Germany

The tall pillars of the Supreme Commanders Hall shook and the old castle groaned as the blast rang out, its fury echoing like rolling thunder through the stillness of the Alme Valley.

That would be the south-east tower. Next would come the cadre building, then the west tower, and finally the north tower housing the hall. *The end was near...*

SS-Sturmbannführer Heinz Macher had been sloughing off his uniform when the explosion came, sending dust raining down from the vaulted ceiling. Now, stripped down to his briefs and shirtsleeves, he twisted around to glare and hiss at his adjutant, "Hurry up, you fool, before the Yankees come!"

"Yes, Sturmbannführer!" The young, wide-eyed adjutant scurried after the trail of discarded clothing strewn across the marble floor, gathering up the incriminating evidence... the jackboots, breeches, tie, belt, crossbelt, jacket and high-peaked cap, all midnight-black and emblazoned with ghostly silver skull-and-crossbones, Nazi eagles and lightning bolts. Then he stuffed everything away inside a duffel bag before handing his superior plain clothes and changing out of his own uniform.

Macher dressed quickly. Although the Führer had decreed that Germans should "fight to the last bullet," he had no intention of sticking around until the U.S. spearhead struck. In fact, by then, he planned to be long gone, disappeared, the ghost of a distant memory. But first he had one last job to do. The order had come down from the Reich Main Security Office, straight from the Chief of the German police, SS-Reichsführer Heinrich Himmler. Macher and his commandos were to slip past the Allied cordon, remove certain highly sensitive materials from the Reichsführer's castle and then blow it up before the Allies could get their hands on it.

According to his instructions, the materials in question lay directly below the hall. While Macher tucked his Luger under the waistband of his trousers, the adjutant stood gawking at the strange runes carved into the oaken stairwell door.

"What do you think is stashed away down there, sir? I heard the Reichs-führer collected stuff from all over Europe. Maybe it's gold or jewels or—"

"Out of the way, jackass!" Shouldering past the other, Macher threw the door open, only to immediately shrink back. "Ach, God! Does that smell like fucking gold to you?"

The adjutant hung his head for a moment, then reached for his kit and began fishing through it. "Ha, yes, here we are!" From the duffel bag he produced a pair of handkerchiefs and a flashlight. The former they wrapped around their faces; the latter the adjutant aimed towards the inky gloom beyond the doorway, revealing a series of jagged, winding steps.

They went down into the darkness. At the bottom of the stairs, tucked away in a corner, they found the small cast-iron safe for which Macher had been instructed to look. The combination—7-10-0—was the Reichs-führer's birth-date. Inside was a single file marked with an emerald-green cross on a purple field, denoting a top-secret command document.

Projekt Lebensborn, it read.

"The Fountain of Life Project? What's that?" said the adjutant, peeping over his superior's shoulder.

Macher flipped the file open. "Looks like a bunch of charts." Intrigued, he glanced at the contents briefly while setting a match to them. No names appeared in any of the meticulous, ledger-like entries, just serial numbers. The only clue as to the identity of the authors and subjects was a contrasting pair of grainy photos. In the first, a group of smiling men in lab coats stood next to what looked like a large bell; in the second, emaciated, hollow-eyed men, women and children in striped KZ uniforms were being herded by stormtroopers towards the same object or device.

Random phrases caught his eye as the charred pages blackened and turned to ash.

...Xerum-525...

...von den Menschen in Kannibalen...

...kadaver reanimiert...

Xerum-525? Men turning into cannibals? The dead coming back to life?!!!?! What the hell?!!!?!

So focused was Macher on the contents of the file that he forgot about the budding fire. "Dammit!" he growled when it singed his fingertips.

He flung the file back into the safe and watched with satisfaction as the flames leapt to life, curling up in bright whorls that danced across what was left of the papers and photos, devouring everything in their path. The shadows about his face fled, and the flickering firelight shone in his ice-blue eyes as they latched onto one last phrase.

"Sir?"

Glancing over his shoulder, Macher saw the adjutant hovering nervously at his side. "What is it?"

"Oh, nothing, sir. It's just I couldn't help seeing what was written on some of those papers. You know, my *Oma* used to tell me stories about the Undead. 'The *Nachzehrer*,' she would say, 'always find their way home.'"

Macher snorted. "Nonsense! Such stories belong to the confused old ways, not to the age of National Socialism! No, no. Have you not been listening to our Minister of Propaganda Goebbels on the radio? He is forever boasting about the creation of top-secret *Wunderwaffen* and how they will 'turn the tide of the war' and 'wrench victory from the jaws of defeat.' This *Projekt Lebensborn* must have been some bold experiment of this type, that's all."

What Macher didn't say—what he would never say out loud—was that none of this mattered anymore. The Reich was in its death throes, squeezed as in a vise between the Allies to the West and the Red Army to the East. Not even Goebbels' so-called "wonder weapons" could save it now.

Yes, he decided, slamming the safe-door shut, all that was left of honour and duty was this last mission, and thankfully, it was nearly done.

Making their way down to the end of the hall that stretched out ahead of them, they stepped through a narrow archway into the heart of the underground chamber. Sunshine barely trickled down from the slanted lightwells in the vaulted ceiling, leaving the room thick with shadows. But they could see plenty enough.

"What *is* this place?" gasped the adjutant. This was no cache of stolen treasures!

Macher shook his head. "The Devil only knows." He'd seen things, unspeakable things, on the battlefield and in the death-camps, but this...

In the middle of the vault, bound with thick, belt-like straps to maternity beds flanked by IV drip stands and carts strewn with gleaming instruments, lay the bodies of five German maidens. Where their bellies had once been, huge slits now gaped red as in gruesome welcome. From there, it seemed, the blood had spread everywhere, caking their gowns, splattering their livid limbs, breasts and faces, soaking the white sheets, spilling from the instrument trays and beds. It had even dripped and seeped onto the flagstone floor, pooling in the sunken center of the vault. To the reek of blood and rot was added that of shit, as the women's bowels had voided. Flies darted among the bodies, driven to frenzy by the stench.

What a mess! Macher's orders had made no mention of any of this!

"Go see what's taking 'em so goddamned long!" he snapped at the wide-eyed adjutant, tearing the flashlight from his hands.

The youth happily raced out. Macher decided to make a more thorough inspection of the room. But no sooner had he begun circling its perimeter than his foot bumped up against something. Shining the light down, he saw a copper pipe sticking out from the wall beside the entrance. The pipe ran along the surface of the floor. Stepping between the beds, he followed it to the middle of the room. There it disappeared in the pool of blood, which had partially congealed, forming a thin, glistening crust, like the surface of a frozen pond. He thought he glimpsed a familiar silhouette hazily reflected in the gore.

What the—?

The flashlight's beam arced up the wall as he aimed it at the vaulted ceiling. His gaze was met by a strangely elongated swastika, its crooked, elongated arms stretching out from the room's apex into which it was carven as if to seize him from above.

Could this be a clue as to the room's purpose? To most, the Nazi swastika had become synonymous with death and destruction, but he knew it was originally meant to represent life. He also knew that his friend the Reichsführer had a reputation for dabbling in pagan rituals and the occult, even to the extent of reconsecrating this Renaissance castle of the Prince-Bishops of Paderborn into a sort of Aryan temple. With a shudder, Macher thought back to the file he'd destroyed. *Lebensborn… Endphase: Kinder der Schwarzen Sonne.* Could this be the Reichsführer's idea of the "Fountain of Life," the one that would give rise to his super race, his so-called "Children of the Black Sun"? But if so, what sort of life could have possibly sprung from this charnel-house?

So...much...blood... And the smell!

The room swam out of focus. He lurched. Catching hold of a nearby bedrail for support, he found himself staring into a set of glassy, bloodshot eyes. The bed's occupant had been beautiful once. Now the face beneath the tangled shock of blond hair was a twisted, maggot-ridden mask of horror and despair. A fly alighting on her chin crept across her cheek, wandering over to one of her lifeless eyes.

"Poor girl." He leaned over to swat the fly away when the bed suddenly began rocking and rattling wildly. The straps groaned. Then, while he stood frozen in disbelief, *the wretch's face thrust forward, eyes bright as red-hot coals, black lips brushing up against his own, and the tattered jowls snapped open with a hiss of rancid decay to reveal bloodstained teeth!*

Macher reeled back and, in a fit of desperation, yanked the Luger free from his trousers. He fired repeatedly, intent on erasing every trace of that look of insatiable appetite and unspeakable malice. The bullets tore through rotten flesh, pinning the wretch back against the bed.

That was the last he saw of her. Bumping into a cart, he staggered and fell, and the flashlight flew from his hand and went clattering along the floor.

Darkness... He felt around him for the extinguished flashlight, but instead gripped something much narrower and... continuous? It was the unburied pipe, he realized. Remembering that it issued from the wall near the vault's entrance, he began to crawl on all fours, using the pipe to retrace his steps.

At last, he came to the wall! But when he reached out, he found thick pieces of masonry where the entrance had been.

Then it dawned on him. His commandos must have detonated the second set of mines. Here belowground he hadn't heard the blast, but the resulting vibrations had been amplified, causing the entrance to collapse and the dead girl's body to heave up. Yes, yes, that was it! But what of the sudden appearance of malevolent intelligence in her eyes? That, he decided after a moment's hesitation, was merely a trick of the light reflected in her eyes. That was the only logical explanation. Any other was madness!

He laughed. Here he was, a grown man, a soldier who'd stared death in the face, acting like a woman and imagining that the butchered girl had... *What? Come back to life somehow?* How ridiculous! His men would soon rescue him, and they would all have a good laugh at his foolishness.

He was still laughing, somewhat hysterically, when he thought he heard a familiar rattling and groaning behind him, followed by a definite *snap!*

He listened, his laughter dwindling. The rattling and groaning was repeated throughout the vault, growing unmistakeably louder, more insistent. Then *snap! snap!* like the last threads of his sanity coming apart.

That's when he stopped laughing and began screaming.

RIGHT FOR YOU NOW
Andrew Jennings

"They're loaded. You can tell." Sam slung his bicycle onto the grass verge, before wiping the sweat from his eyes as he squinted at his friend. In the blinding sunlight Billy's face was a blurred silhouette. He heard him sniff, before squatting on the edge of the pavement to gaze up at what they could see of the house opposite. Only its upper windows and parts of its moss-grown roof were visible over the overgrown hedgerow.

"You sure someone lives there?"

"Course I am. Think I'm stupid? They're too tight to pay for someone to look after the place and too old to do it themselves, that's all. One's batty. I heard she's got *Alzheimer's* or something. Off her head."

"And the other?"

"Just as old but not as batty."

"How d'you know it'll be worth it?"

Sam smirked. "'Cause I looked through their windows, dickhead. They never draw their curtains. There's loads of stuff inside. Antiques."

Billy grimaced. "What the fuck do we know about antiques? How'd we sell 'em?"

"Don't worry about that. It's sorted." Sam tapped the side of his large, beaky nose. "I had words with Micky Deane. He has an antique shop in town. A mate of mine told me he won't bat an eye over paying a few quid for knock-offs."

"You trust him?"

"'Course not, you twat. What d'you take me for? He'll screw us like they always do. Who cares? It'll be easy pickings." At nineteen, Sam already had more than a decade of petty theft behind him. Mostly he'd gotten away with it. Of course, the filth knew what he'd done and, when he was younger, they'd collared him loads of times. They still kept an eye on him, but he'd been careful not to get caught doing anything serious since he became too old for a simple slap on the wrist and a telling off. His ASBO, banning him from the town centre, ran out months ago. He'd even got a part-time job, filling shelves at a local supermarket, though he hated it and only did the minimum hours he could get away with. His mate, Billy, was too dim for that. He'd been turned down for every job he'd ever applied for; even to join the halfwit bouncers outside the Frog and Bottle, the roughest pub in town, even though he stood six feet three and weighed a ton. It could have been because his broad, thick-lipped, chinless face was scarred with acne and he smelt so bad, *eau de B.O.* Even Sam sometimes begged his friend to take a shower—or change his clothes. On the other hand, he always did what Sam told him, which was handy for jobs like this. Plus, the dim-witted tosser wouldn't realise if Sam ended up taking most of the cash afterwards. He believed anything Sam told him.

Sam picked up his bike. "We'll meet at my place at eleven. The old birds are in bed by then, lights out. Uncle Ned's lending me his van. I promised him a cut. But it'll be worth it."

* * * *

A curtain twitched in an upstairs window as Bethany glared at the youths.

Hurrying downstairs, she told Ellie what she'd seen, though she knew her sister wouldn't understand what she was talking about.

"I don't like the look of them—or the way they stared at the house. One of them looked like a fairytale ogre. The other had such a nasty grin I would have loved to have slapped it." In her younger days, Beth had been feisty enough to have done just that. Too feisty to end up like this, looking after her older sister in a house too big for the two of them. Plus, she was getting too frail to look after her. So far Ellie had retained enough of her faculties to wash and dress without too much help, but she was getting forgetful. Beth knew in a few years she wouldn't be able to cope anymore. Their father's 'cure' might have helped to keep her physically active, but it didn't do anything to help her state of mind. Most of Beth's friends had already died or moved into nursing homes. Sometimes she wished she could move into a nursing home herself. At least she would have company. But she had been self-sufficient all her life. Besides, she had too many responsibilities and she could not neglect them.

Leaving Ellie, she toured the outside doors to make sure they were locked. Better safe than sorry, she told herself, before returning to her sister, sat as always in front of the TV. Daytime television was a boon for Ellie, though Beth hated it. At least it kept her sister out of trouble. She would stare at the screen for hours without moving a muscle, though Beth wondered how much of it she was able to take in. At least that dreadful Jeremy Kyle had finished. Ellie was watching an antiques program with that orange-faced barrow boy her sister loved but Beth thought vulgar, typical of his class. Ellie had a weakness for men like that, which was probably why she'd had so many boyfriends when she was younger but had never married.

Beth tutted as she collected the plate of sandwiches she'd prepared for lunch. At least Ellie had managed to eat some of them, though not enough.

Later, when streetlamps flickered through the trees outside, the sisters retired to bed. Beth felt more tired than usual tonight and not very well. The hot weather didn't agree with her and she worried that the haddock she ate for tea might have been on the turn. She hoped not. She hated having an upset stomach. She had enough problems down there anyway.

Remembering the youths from earlier, she glanced out of her bedroom window at where they had been standing. The area was lit by two lamp-posts and she could see there was no one there. Though she was sure the boys had been planning mischief. It was a large house and she often felt uneasy in the small hours of the night when groans from its settling timbers echoed through it. Even though she had grown to recognise most of these sounds, they still disturbed her. Besides, every now and then she would hear something new, and spend hours in bed, listening intently.

Bad things did happen, she knew; only a fool would think otherwise, or walk through life without a care. Pursing her brows, Beth closed the curtains and turned on her light.

* * * *

Sam grinned as Billy climbed into the van. It stank of dog, old dried blood and urine. His uncle bred mastiffs, some of them so close to lunacy they terrified him. Uncle Ned took them to dogfights; sometimes he brought them back. Sitting next to Billy, though, the odour wasn't as bad as usual; Sam wondered if he was getting used to it, even if the few times he'd let his uncle take him to fights they'd sickened him.

"What'll we do if the old bags catch us?" asked Billy when they pulled up close to the house.

Reaching beneath his seat, Sam pulled out a crowbar. Like the idiot he was Billy guffawed loudly, till Sam told him to shut the fuck up. "Do you want to wake the neighbours, you tosser?"

Getting inside the house was easy for someone of Sam's experience. Once the front door had been jemmied open, he padded through the silent hallway in his trainers, mentally rubbing his hands together as he gazed at the *objet d'art* he could clearly make out in the half light. Billy lumbered behind him, nylon jogging pants swishing as his legs brushed against each other. Using an electric torch, Sam shone its beam across the room. He nodded towards a door to their right, opening it softly. Even Sam emitted a low whistle of appreciation. The old girls definitely had money. To his eyes some of the things looked like they were worth a fortune. Victorian cabinets displayed a dazzling collection of old coins, many of them silver, some of them gold. Even melted down they could be worth thousands. Easily transportable, they wouldn't damage, not like the porcelain figures on some of the shelves, which would never survive if he or Billy tried to steal them—and he'd be buggered if he was going to waste time wrapping them in bubble wrap, even if he'd brought some with him, or the grotesque native masks that stared down at him from the walls like a crowd of witch-doctors. Someone had definitely been into some weird crap! But there was better stuff, and a fancy-looking travel clock covered in gems and what might have been gold got bundled inside his holdall, alongside a couple of leather-bound albums filled with stamps. He knew nothing about philately, but he did know some stamps were worth a fortune.

Sam was still grinning when the light came on.

Tightening his fingers on the handles of his holdall, Sam turned to face the door behind them. It was open, though he knew he'd closed it to muffle any sounds they might make. An old lady in a pink dressing grown stood beside it. In the shadows behind her he was sure he could see another.

* * * *

Beth rose early the next morning. She had too much to do to sleep.

Dressing quickly, she hurried downstairs, then out through the door into the drive. She had seen the van parked by the gate from her bedroom window. As she expected, its doors weren't locked. Climbing inside, she saw the keys were still in the ignition, confirming her suspicions. Getting out, she hurried to remove her car from the garage, before driving the van in its place, where she knew it would be hidden from view when she shut the doors on it. Satisfied that she had covered her tracks, she returned indoors.

Though tired after all that happened last night it was back to her usual chores now, making sure her sister got dressed and was safely sat in the living room, watching TV, before she went into the kitchen to prepare breakfast.

* * * *

Snot and tears had long since dried, though Sam's eyes were sore from the overpowering reek of urine around him, all of it making him feel sick.

He stared into the darkness, certain someone was in here with him inside the cellar, though he knew it couldn't be Billy. Not after what happened.

He was still worrying about it when the old woman opened the cellar door and came down the stairs, settling her feet on the stone steps with care as if she was unsure of her balance. She held a plate in one hand and a plastic cup in the other.

Kneeling with the slightest of groans, she placed the food and drink at the outermost reach of Sam's fingers.

"I've brought you some tablets for the pain," she said.

"Will they cure me as well, because you'll have to chop my foot off if they don't?" Sam tried to put as much bitterness as he could in his voice, which wasn't difficult. It was what he felt.

The woman pushed the plate an inch nearer. "Whatever happened was your fault, young man. I didn't ask for you to break into my house."

Sam scowled, then stretched to grab the plate. He was ravenously hungry. Butter spread across his lips and around his mouth as he bit into the sandwiches.

When he'd finished, he stared at the pills, then up at the woman, suspicion in his eyes.

"They're safe. They're my sister's," the woman said.

Sam grunted. Picking one, up he peered at it, then threw it to the back of his mouth. He reached for the cup to wash it down.

"See, I trusts you." He felt the need to annoy her. "What about my foot?"

"I'll get antibiotics," the woman said.

"It's more than antibiotics I needs, misses. It stinks."

"I'll bandage it when the pills dull the pain."

Sam grimaced, but stayed silent as the woman bent to pick up the plate before returning to the steps. A few minutes later she came back with a roll of bandage, some antiseptic pads, an old tube of ointment, and a pair of scissors. Kneeling beyond his reach, she cut away the ruined trainer. Sam winced when he saw the blackened flesh inside. Two toes were missing; the others were swollen like overripe plums that were beginning to go rotten. Despite the painkillers, Sam strained his muscles to stop himself from crying out when the old woman tightened the bandage and tied its ends in a simple knot. Blood seeped through the gauze and spread across the floor.

"It needs more than a fucking bandage, misses." Sam's voice was a harsh, bronchitic whisper. Sweat covered his face.

"It's the best I can do." Matter-of-factly, the woman held the trainer by the tips of her fingers. "I must see to my sister. I've left her too long. I'll come back later."

"I need a doctor," Sam shouted, desperation in his voice. Until he'd seen his injuries, he hadn't realised just how bad they were. Now they scared him.

"I'll see you later," the woman said. There was an end-of-conversation tone to her voice that revived Sam's hatred for her.

As he watched her go, he groaned. Pain pulsed inside his foot even worse than before. He clenched his eyes as he tried to shut it out—and failed. He wanted to cry at how everything had gone wrong. It had been Billy's fault. His and that mad old bitch of a woman. If they'd kept their heads, he could have talked their way out of here. But no, Billy panicked like the stupid bastard he was. Though how was he expected to know the old woman had a gun? A *loaded* gun? That she would use it, spewing half of Billy's brains all over the place? He still felt like puking at how some of it splattered his face. That had been it. Half deafened by the blast, dripping blood and brains like a filthy porridge, he'd dashed for it, but the woman was quick. She shot him in the foot even before he was halfway to the door. His trainer exploded and, in the few seconds before blackness set in, he'd seen the pistol and the look on her face. That was before she dropped the gun onto a table, grabbed a hold of the back of his collar and, despite his screams, dragged him across the floor…

He remembered seeing the walls of a passage hung with pictures. Old photographs. Family crap. Then a door was pushed open and he smelled damp plaster, as the woman pushed him through the doorway, and he'd tumbled down the stone steps into the cellar. Before he reached the bottom, he'd blacked out.

* * * *

Ned opened a can of Carling. Across the room, Sam's father did the same. They were sat in Bert's living room, the television muted but not turned off. He gulped his drink, though Bert put his can to one side and looked at his brother.

"Sam's never let you down before. They might have been nicked."

"I got my solicitor to ring the filth. Neither of them has been arrested."

"Why d'you let our Sam borrow your van?"

"Said he needed it for the stuff he was going to nick. Promised me a hundred from the job. Said it would be easy money."

"Sam knows what he's doing." Bert's prison pallor was still pasty. Only a week had passed since he finished a five-year stretch. "Still, they should be back by now, even a pair of dozy twats like them."

Ned nodded. "I need that van. I've a dog fight tomorrow. I can't take the bastard in the back of a taxi, for fuck's sake. It'd tear it to bits."

Bert laughed. "A bit frisky, is it?"

"It'd have your arm off if it wasn't muzzled." He glanced at his watch. "Where the fucking hell is he, Bert?"

"Fuck knows." Bert reached for another can. He was starting to get a bit of a buzz and feeling less worried than perhaps he should, but his son had been in and out of trouble all his life and he knew how to look after himself. He'd be alright, wherever he was. It was Ned's van that worried him. He knew how important these dog fights were to his brother. If Sam messed up, he'd never hear the last of it. "Did you try his mobile?"

"Straight to voicemail. It's probably in his fucking bedroom. He never takes it on a job. Says the police can use it to track where you are, cocky little know-it-all."

"Fucking nutter." Bert laughed. He was old school and had never owned a mobile in his life. Wouldn't know what to do with one if he had.

Ned gnawed at a thumbnail. "If he lets me down, I'll fuckin' lamp him. You know that, don't you?"

"Wouldn't blame you." Bert finished his can, crumpled it and reached for another. "I'd thump him too."

* * * *

Sam was shivering. He couldn't stop. He felt nauseous and sick. He was sure the pills the old bitch had given him were making him worse. He felt weak, as if he was dying. Had she poisoned him? Had that been her game? Was that why she hadn't come back to see him? It was hours since she brought the food and bandaged his foot.

* * * *

Beth went into the kitchen for a nightcap. She'd had a hard day. Ellie was worse than usual. She barely knew where she was most of the time and had bumped into the ironing board. The iron was on and had tipped over. The smell of scorched flesh had alerted Beth to what was happening and had prised the iron off Ellie's hand, taking strips of skin with it. Luckily, in her state Ellie never felt a thing. That was one blessing of Daddy's 'cure'.

As she waited for the kettle to boil, her gaze drifted towards the cellar door.

Why did they have to break in and add complications to her life, when dealing with Ellie was hard enough?

* * * *

It was the biggest meeting they had held in Bert's house for years. Not since the last job he'd organised, the one that got him sent down when things went sour.

The members this time were a far cry from the gang he'd gathered then. Billy's father, Nobby, occupied most of the vinyl sofa. He was even bigger than his dopey sons, a pear-shaped blob of tattooed flesh, overflowing his jeans and stretching his XXXL *Black Sabbath* T-shirt to its limits. The can of lager in his fist looked child-sized by comparison. Luckily, Bert had dissuaded him from bringing his wife. That over-strung mare would have done his head in by now. Instead, he'd brought his other sons, Eric and Eddie, squashed on what was left of the sofa. Like their father, they had round, blank, resentful faces, Tweedledum and Tweedledee gone bad. Bert had heard they'd started hanging around as protection for one of the local drugs gangs.

Ned sat on the other armchair, still grumbling about his van, as if that mattered more than what might have happened to Sam. If he didn't shut up soon Bert knew he would have to have it out with him.

"Anyone know where they were going?" Bert cracked open a can of lager.

There were a few seconds of silence.

"Two old birds on Cedar Grove, that's all I know," muttered Ned eventually.

Bert leaned forward. "There can't be that many. We should check and see." He looked around to nods of approval. "When we find out who they are we'll pay them a visit." He cracked his knuckles, his eyes serious.

* * * *

It was the third day and Beth knew her prisoner would be right for her now, though in this heat the body of his friend would be starting to smell; it already reeked from bowels loosened by the violence of his death before she pushed him down the stairs and dragged him further into the cellar.

Opening the cellar door, she switched on its lights. Immediately she knew the pills had worked their magic, just as her father had taught her— just as they did for Ellie. Just had they had for her father too.

Nothing lasts forever. Her father had taught her that, verbally while he was still alive and by example later. He was so weak now he couldn't even feed anymore, sitting there, sometimes shuffling around, stinking like carrion, which was why he couldn't be upstairs. The young thief was young and fresh. The damage to his foot would never heal, but it wouldn't worsen.

Beth smiled, beckoning. There was work to be done, work she was getting too old to do by herself.

* * * *

It was late afternoon when the doorbell rang.

Two men stood there, one with his finger pressed hard against the bell, which rang without stop. They were large, sloppily dressed, not the sort of men seen in Cedar Grove, especially at her door. Beth stared at them from an upstairs window. One had tattoos on his fingers, which he clenched and opened as his head fidgeted from side to side, squinty eyes peering in a shifty, calculating way that bothered her. She disliked and feared them. Something warned her that they had something to do with the thieves. She had half expected someone to come looking for them, though she had thought it would have been the police. It went without saying the lads would have bragged about what they were going to do.

* * * *

Pausing to take the revolver from her bedroom, Beth hurried downstairs. She could see her visitors through the stained-glass windows on either side of the front door. She entered the vestibule as the doorbell continued ringing, the gun hidden behind her back. Beth's lips tightened as she hooked the security chain into place before unlocking the door. It opened a few inches before the chain restrained it.

"What do you want?" The two men she could see through the gap looked rough. She trusted neither of them. Nor did they trust her, she could tell, which convinced her why they were here, before the door burst open, ripping the flimsy chain from the frame. Caught by surprise, Beth stepped back into the hallway as the men pushed into the vestibule. One of them, dressed in a cheap shell suit, grabbed hold of her arm.

"Quiet," the man said, his voice gravelly with emotion. "Where's my boy? What the fucking hell have you done with him?"

Still holding the gun behind her back, Beth pulled away from him and fired at the floor, shattering a tile.

The man swore in surprise and leapt away from her.

"Why the fuck have you got that?" shouted the man, sounding aggrieved.

"I knew you were up to no good," Beth said.

"Where's my boy?"

"What boy?" Determined to outface them, Beth aimed the gun at them. She could tell neither was particularly intelligent. She tightened her grip on the gun.

"If you think you can frighten us," the other man said, "you're out of luck." He was tough and gnarly, in worn blue jeans and a leather jacket. He had an animal smell, like wet dog. And his hands and face were grubby.

"You burst into my home," Beth said.

"This ain't America. You can't shoot people because they broke into your house." Shell suit's eyes narrowed. "Have you done this before?"

She saw anger in his eyes. Was he the father of one of the boys? Beth turned the gun towards him. If either of them attempted to attack her it would be him, she was sure. The other looked cautious, his dark eyes roving about the hallway, part opportunism, part weighing up what he could see.

"You'd better leave," Beth said, "before something happens."

"Maybe something has." The man gazed up the staircase. "Is he up there?"

"Is *who* up there?"

"My boy, you old cow."

"No one is up there except my sister, who's lost her wits. Please leave." She thumbed back the hammer on the revolver until it clicked into place. It was an action that made both men pause.

"It doesn't end here," shell suit warned, dry-mouthed. He nodded at his companion before both retreated to the door. As soon as they'd gone, Beth slammed it shut.

Feeling exhausted, she carefully released the gun's hammer.

"It doesn't end here," the man had said. She was sure that it didn't. They would be back, probably others with them, probably armed. It would not be difficult for the likes of them to get hold of a gun, she was sure of that if nothing else.

Beth hurried into the kitchen, where an uncharacteristic feeling of futility made her slump at the breakfast table. As so often in the last few days, her gaze turned to the cellar door. Had she gone too far? Had she let her outrage at the invasion of her home—of *their* home—make her overreact? Her eyes hardened. If she hadn't, though, if she had let those boys get away with it, how could she know, even now, how far they would have gone, what either of them might have done to her or her sister or both of them? Beth straightened her shoulders. No time for regrets. She had done what she felt justified in doing at the time and she would have to live with it. She had no choice. What mattered were the consequences and what to do about them. That was what she had to concentrate on, not namby-pamby regrets or self-doubt.

* * * *

It was dark.

Though just gone eleven, all the lights inside the house were off, as if everyone had gone to bed, though only Ellie was asleep. Beth was still dressed, her father's gun on the table beside her as she gazed out of her bedroom window, its curtains open, though all she could see was the afterglow of the streetlamps, which made the garden look darker by contrast.

* * * *

In the cellar, Sam could hear something move towards him, hidden in the darkness. Whatever it was stank horrible, like something from the sewers. His stomach tied itself in knots as he tried not to throw up his last sandwich.

"Who's there?" he croaked, scrambling to his knees despite the pain in his foot, which became worse, far worse whenever he moved. "Who are you?"

He hoped it was someone who would help him, but the stink was unbelievable. Worse than Billy ever was.

He just hoped it wasn't Billy now…

"Daddy." It was not a greeting, just confirmation that she had seen him enter the living room, looking thinner, more insubstantial than ever. Paler too, though it had been his decision to retreat into the darkest part of the cellars where he claimed he felt most comfortable now.

Behind Daddy the stockier figure of the boy limped through the doorway, grasping its frame for support. Daddy's "Haitian Cure" (that was his jocular name for it from years ago) had worked its wonders yet again. All those decades on that island had not been in vain, even if things were starting to end for him now. But, after all, it had taken decades to begin to wear off, and that had been interminably slow. Not that he looked to have lost his strength.

Daddy nodded. Without having to speak Ellie knew what he meant; she cocked the handgun, stepped towards the boy and pressed it into his cold fingers, tightening them around it.

Without saying anything, Daddy turned and left the room, walking towards the front door, the boy at his heels.

Following close behind them, Beth saw several figures were stood outside the glass-panels at the door. The bell hadn't been rung this time. Instead, she heard something metallic being wedged into the doorframe in the exact same place the boys had broken it a few days ago. The apple had fallen close to the tree, she thought. Very close indeed!

As if of his own accord, the boy raised the gun and pointed it towards the door. Daddy's control was still strong, Beth thought. What was left of the boy's will was as nothing compared to his. It never would be, she was sure.

* * * *

Ned heaved the crowbar and the door gave way. He glanced back at his brother and Nobby, stood with his two big sons—the lads held baseball bats, while Bert brandished a sawn-off shotgun. Only Nobby was weaponless, though his ham like fists were lethal enough. Ned tightened his grip on the crowbar as he pushed the door open, which was when he was startled to see Ned's son, Sam, staring back at him from inside the house, wielding a pistol he held pointed at his face.

"What the fuck—" Ned started to splutter when the old lady stepped alongside his nephew.

Which was how they ended up a few minutes later being bustled downstairs into the cellar.

* * * *

"You should've used the shotgun," Nobby grumbled as they stood in the darkness after the old lady and Bert's son left them, returning upstairs and slamming the cellar door shut.

"I should have shot my nephew?" Ned strained his eyes through the darkness to try and see Nobby.

"He's sold us out—to that fuckin' bitch."

Bert said nothing, as unable to understand his son's behaviour as any of them. The lad hadn't looked like Sam anymore. He had looked at him, his own father, as if they were strangers. What had happened? What had that old woman done to him?

And that other, that pasty-faced guy in the grimy suit, who the hell was he?

"Something stinks in here," said Bert.

"Like rotten meat." Ned grunted to himself. "I'd recognise that anywhere. I've smelt it in the kennels when one of the dogs has died on me and I hadn't noticed or if they'd not eaten their food. Not usually this bad. This reeks."

They searched the cellar, which was surprisingly large, feeling their way about the pitch darkness like blindmen. After several minutes, one of Nobby's sons squawked in disgust. Converging on him, his father knelt and reached out for what he'd touched.

"It's Billy. He's dead." Nobby's voice was hoarse, thick with emotion.

"You sure?" asked Ned.

"I couldn't mistake my own son, could I, even in the dark? Someone's bashed out his brains."

"Or shot him." Ned's fingers felt across the bloated surface of Billy's face till they reached the hole that gaped in his forehead. He bit back the nausea that snagged in his throat. He'd seen and felt ugly wounds in the past, many of them inflicted by him. It would take more than that to make him vomit. "The bitch must've killed him. She probably used that old gun Sam was pointing at us. She probably used it on him too. Did you see the state of Sam's foot?"

"He shouldn't have been able to walk, let alone threaten us," said Bert, "not with his foot mangled like that."

"There's a lot that shouldn't be," Ned muttered. "The whole place is whacky."

* * * *

They were left in the dark, ignored despite their threats and pleas, especially when thirst made them desperate. They tried hammering the door to break it down but, with the narrowness of the steps and the thick timbers of the door itself, their efforts were wasted.

They were close to exhaustion when the door was opened, and a shaft of light shot down into the cellar. A plastic tub of food and some bottles of water were pushed onto the top step then the door was shut and bolted again before any of them could get up the first few steps.

Too hungry and thirsty to care what might have been added to the stuff they'd been left, they shared what there was between them.

* * * *

"Daddy, I think you can return to the cellar now," Beth announced the next day. The poor man disliked the brightness of the house. It hurt his eyes. And she knew it made his skin crawl whenever sunlight touched it.

He looked at her with his drawn face and nodded.

"At least you'll have company," said Beth. "They'll be right for you now."

✗

E'ZUNGUTH, THE ZOMBIE GOD
Maxwell I. Gold

Deep inside the darkest voids, a rotting sour breath of fourteen billion years, pulled me down into a graveyard of stars; without any reasonable hope of escaping this festering undead monstrosity. Civilizations have tried to restrain it, others have worshipped the light radiating from its starry corpse, laden with the tears of an ancient thing, languishing in mountains of cosmic scar-tissue, covering the bones of Time.

Within the dim halls of some dilapidated, moldy sepulcher I had been pathetically huddled against a grotesque pile of humid parchments; drowning in the unpronounceable syllables of that faceless zombified god who dwelled in ivory palaces at the far reaches of Time, under a graveyard of doomed galaxies. There was no concept of space or logic that could hold back the dank laughter that rung throughout my mind with such a profound sinistrality. My body was struck with an awful paresthesia, like a rusty knife had plugged itself into my heart; but the scent of musty pages clogged my nostrils, constricting my breathing leading my sane thoughts down a path of thrilling unknown and esoteric curiosity of some dark evil.

It swallowed whatever sense I had left as I followed every phrase with anticipation, wandering precipitously o'er some steep cliff into the hungering mouth of E'Zunguth, the undead god who waited for me at the turn of the last page. At the unfortunate last word where my testament ends, and I have finished that of the most profane works ever written; deep inside the darkest voids, a rotting sour breath of fourteen billion years, pulled me down into a graveyard of stars. ✗

LAZY RIVER
Kelly Piner

Ruth Anne counted her blessings as she rode beside Ray, a widower fifteen years her senior. Ray had proposed marriage the night before at their seaside Florida retreat during a moonlight walk on the beach. Just two weeks shy of her fortieth birthday, Ruth Anne had given up on marriage, resigned to being single and going through life alone. But Ray had changed all that. A Navy admiral with a take-charge demeanor, Ray had wooed Ruth Anne with his unflappable self-confidence. Her past beaus all paled in comparison. She studied his finely lined face, illuminated by the piercing afternoon sun, and his thick crop of salt and pepper hair. She reached over and gently caressed his arm as he flipped on the turn signal and wheeled into *Splash,* the largest water park in the state of Florida. Feeling as giddy as a schoolgirl, Ruth Anne's heart fluttered when she thought of one whole week of beachfront adventures followed by fine dining and dancing at night.

Ray handed the attendant the $5 parking fee and cruised into the first empty spot. He turned to Ruth Anne and smiled a boyish grin. "I'll find out what you're really made of today. Some of these slides are pretty treacherous."

Ruth Anne pressed her hand to the small of her throat. "Really? I haven't been to a water park since I was ten."

"Well, things have changed quite a bit since then. No kiddie pools today. Don't worry. I'll protect you."

Despite Ray's light-hearted teasing, a knot gripped Ruth Anne's stomach. She didn't like water. She grabbed her beach towel and followed a wave of eager tourists to the ticket counter.

Inside the gate, the path divided into three different directions. Ray stopped to study the park map as Ruth Anne, a people watcher, studied the other tourists, who laughed and held hands, as if walking into the greatest venture of their lives. Women in too-tight swimsuits shuffled along in sandals, seemingly unconcerned about their appearance. One obese woman with dark circles around her eyes and an overweight little girl munched on ice cream bars.

Ruth Anne tightened the sarong around her bathing suit to disguise her recent ten-pound weight gain and hooked arms with Ray.

"Let's start with Danger Island." He pointed to the trail to the left.

In the distance, splashing sounds followed by children's laughter lightened the mood, and Ruth Anne's earlier fears dissolved. What more could she want than a whole day of kid-like fun with the man of her dreams? As the two strolled past palm trees and giant falls, she dreamt of billowy wedding gowns and a reception with a coconut cream layer cake and champagne fountain.

But the entrance to Danger Island looked like anything but light-hearted fun as they maneuvered through a large room made of concrete slabs. The room reminded Ruth Anne of a noisy engine room, like the one at the factory where her father used to work. A huge waterfall blocked the doorway. They'd have to walk through it to reach the other side. Kids squealed with delight, but now the knot in Ruth Anne's stomach reached up to grip her chest as well. She stared around for a different entry to the island.

With no other access in sight, Ray grasped her arm. "Not scared, are you?"

Ruth Anne had nearly drowned when she was six and didn't like submerging her head, but she couldn't tell Ray and have him think her a silly coward. He idolized his deceased wife, Melissa, who had been an airline pilot and avid sky diver. So Ruth Anne held her breath and rushed through the gushing water. When she reached the other side, she gasped and slid onto a lounge chair. Her eyes and throat burned from chlorine and water plugged her nose, making it hard to breath.

"Are you alright?" Ray leaned in close to her.

She swiped water from her face and forced a smile. "Of course. It's just been so long since I've done anything like this."

"This is just the beginning. Better toughen up." Ray laughed and motioned to a massive steel water slide high up in the sky that twisted and turned and propelled people at record speed into seven feet of water.

Nearby, a large posted sign in red letters leapt out at her: *MUST BE ABLE TO SWIM.* Ruth Anne felt dizzy at first, as if she might faint, and she flinched when the lifeguard blew his whistle and jumped in to rescue a flailing little girl. She pushed aside a flashback from that day at her grandmother's pool and took shallow breaths. When she felt calmer, she turned to Ray and said, "You're not really going on that, are you?"

"Of course. And so are you. Face your fears, Ruth Anne. Face your fears. "

Ray squeezed her hand, and for a moment, she thought of telling him of her fear. But as a career military man, Ray wasn't one to coddle. No, she'd do the only thing she could and force herself into the tube. Once she had been spit out on the other end, she'd be over her nervousness and ready to tackle the rest of the park. It'd be just like the time when she was nine and afraid to ride her friend's horse. She had forced herself, and before she knew it, she rode like a pro. Tired of hearing about his adventurous dead wife, she'd prove to Ray that she was a daredevil in her own right.

"Okay. Let's go," Ruth Anne said. On shaky legs she took slow steps toward the steep winding stairs to the launch pad high up in the sky. Ray followed behind her on the climb. Ruth Anne refused to watch the other victims being thrust out by the black monster machine into the murky waters below, so she forced her mind blank and pushed herself up one set of steps and then another on legs that felt as weak as slime.

Following a commotion, a middle-aged woman with sallow skin stumbled past the long line back down the steps, shaking her head while a man up above yelled out to her. But the woman never turned back. She stared straight at Ruth Anne when she passed, her eyes marred by fear.

Ray snickered from behind. "Can you believe that?"

Now, Ruth Anne regretted her decision, all to prove herself to Ray. But she had almost made it to the top of the platform. She couldn't turn back now and be seen by him as nothing more than a lightweight, not an equal, like Melissa. She gripped the handrail tighter and then made the mistake of looking down at the ground so far below. People looked like tiny dots.

She imagined plunging 200 feet to her death, but Ray nudged her from behind to keep the line moving. At the top, a teen girl and her dad waited ahead of her. They seated themselves at the two tunnel openings and awaited their signal to take the plunge. Down below, Ruth Anne heard the explosive splash of the next rider, released from the monster's jaws. The staffer gave the signal and the father and daughter pushed themselves forward and disappeared into blackness.

"We're next," Ray said, and eagerly climbed into his side of the tube.

Ruth Anne had but one second to decide whether to bolt back down the stairs, just like the middle-aged woman, but the thought of racing down hundreds of steps…and in front all these people. So she staggered to the tube and seated herself inside.

"I'll race you to the bottom," Ray called out.

But Ruth Anne was in no mood for jokes. She looked straight ahead, into the darkness.

"Go!" the staffer shouted.

Ruth Anne folded her arms across her chest and leaned back, but she forgot to cross her feet at the ankles as instructed by a poster. She felt her body being sucked into the tube and then saw nothing but total darkness as the monster thrust her from side to side. Her head throbbed, like it might explode.

The mammoth beast spoke to her, making garbled noises, like growls coming from deep within its belly. Ruth Anne prayed for mercy, to be delivered from the massive steel demon into the waters below where she could recover and shake off the experience. But the ride showed no signs of slowing as the growls grew louder. Her head pounded into the cold steel and she cursed herself for not standing up to Ray, for not being her own woman. And then she thought someone called her name, but she told herself it was only her imagination.

Mercifully, the first signs of light appeared at the bottom of the tube. She'd almost made it. She only had to hold on a few more seconds. At the bottom, she was thrust through the air and plunged into the seven-foot waters.

Disoriented, Ruth Anne gasped for breath and fought her way to the top, but something tugged on her legs, like a slimy claw, and pulled her back below. She bobbed back to the top and screamed, "Help!"

A whistle blew. Now she lay on the concrete with Ray leaning over her. "You gave us quite a scare. What happened down there?"

With her last memory being plunged into the deep waters, she shook her head. "I don't know. I was drowning."

Ray brushed her wet hair from face and kissed her forehead. "You're okay now. You were scared, that's all. I pulled you right out." He helped her to her feet and she wiped her face with a towel. A small group stood to the side, pointing at her and whispering.

"No more water slides today. How about a nice, relaxing lazy river?"

Ruth Anne nodded. This was what she had imagined when Ray first suggested the water park, floating along on an inner tube alongside kids and basking in the afternoon sun. She wouldn't mention the demon ride speaking to her and growling. She'd had enough drama for one day.

Ray hooked arms with her and led them through paths filled with palm trees and large boulders alongside cascades of flowing water. Ruth Anne's heart steadied when they reached the lazy river where kids and elderly people splashed around in the massive crystal stream that seemed to go on forever.

Ray pulled two green inner tubes from the water and handed one to Ruth Anne. She leaned back into it, her legs dangling over the edge as the current propelled her forward. She dipped her hand into the cool steam and all her earlier fears washed away. An old disco tune played through overhead speakers.

She turned back and smiled at Ray who followed closely behind. Just like a tropical paradise, flowers and rock formations peppered the landscape and a gentle waterfall rushed down the rocks. Ruth Anne closed her eyes and soaked up the sun and dreamt of dinner later that night at a small beachside bistro, sipping wine with Sinatra playing in the background.

But when Ruth Anne turned back to wave at Ray, he was gone. With the river so crowded, she figured he must have fallen behind. She paddled herself forward in the stream, but when she still didn't see him, she jumped off the inner tube into the shallow water. She held her hand over her eyes to shield them from the blaring sun and searched, but still saw no sign of Ray. No way could he be that far behind, she thought.

Her earlier feeling of unease passed over her again, a dark feeling of dread. She struggled against the current, but couldn't go backwards, so she hopped onto the inner tube again and paddled to the first exit, where she climbed out of the river, intending to walk around until she found Ray. But after ten minutes of searching with still no sign of him, she decided that he must have gotten out, probably to find a restroom. But why hadn't he told her after the day she'd had?

Ruth Anne had left her cell back at the hotel so she had no way to call him. She'd get customer service to page him, but she walked through one maze after another and never found the help desk.

She returned to the lazy river and paddled as fast as she could on the inner tube in search of him. He had to be there. He just had to be. An icy feeling gripped her as she thought of never seeing him again. Had he had second thoughts about the engagement? Had he driven off and left her there alone? She paddled faster and faster.

Ruth Anne recoiled when a long water moccasin slithered past her. How could a poisonous snake have found its way into the lazy river? She looked around and searched other patrons' faces, but everyone looked straight ahead, never noticing the snake.

Then just up ahead, she spotted Ray in the river. "Ray! Ray!"

He didn't look back, so Ruth Anne kicked and paddled until she came up directly behind him. "Ray," she said, and poked a finger into his back.

But when he turned, she gasped. This wasn't Ray, but a much older man with vacant eyes. Large blue veins disfigured his face. He stared just beyond Ruth Anne's head and then turned away.

Now she leaned up against a rock formation and took deep breaths. She'd find someone else to help, and soon she and Ray would be dancing the night away.

She looked for any friendly face to approach, but when she swam up to an elderly woman wearing an old-fashioned floral swimsuit, the old lady babbled to herself and a stream of drool ran from the corner of her mouth.

Ruth Anne spotted a lifeguard in the distance, nearly hidden behind a large waterfall. She swam up to her. "I can't find my fiancé, Ray. He's mid-fifties. He was just behind me on an inner tube, but now he's gone."

The lifeguard removed her sunglasses and black sockets stared back at Ruth Anne. A trickle of blood ran from the black holes where her eyes had once been.

Ruth Anne whimpered and fell backwards. This had to be some kind of sick joke. She swam away from the zombie lifeguard, thrashing about, in search of Ray or anyone sane who could help. But when she looked behind her, ghostly figures with black circles rimming their eyes floated toward her on inner tubes. They had outstretched arms and chanted. Worms crawled from one man's eyes and more snakes encircled Ruth Anne. She screamed and struggled to escape as a maggot eaten corpse floated past. The corpse sat up and laughed, exposing jagged blackened teeth. Ruth Anne had to be dreaming. She must have struck her head inside the ride and suffered from shock or a concussion. Maybe she was hallucinating and soon she'd awaken with Ray by her side.

From up above, the black monster tube called her name. But before she could find an escape route, her deceased mother floated past her in the river. "Come to me, Ruth Anne." She wore a black shroud and had an oxygen hose attached to her nose, just as she had on her last day in the hospital. As she floated past, her outstretched hand stroked Ruth Anne's face, the bony fingers as cold as ice.

Ruth Anne flinched and pressed her hands to her face and prayed, but when she opened her eyes, she was back at the black monster ride, awaiting her turn. Her mother appeared once more and motioned for her to look down below.

Ruth Anne looked and saw the lifeguard furiously performing CPR on a woman's body as a crowd watched. Ray stood sobbing in the background.

The sound of a whistle jarred Ruth Anne back to the platform where a female staffer motioned for her to sit inside the demon ride. "Face your fears, Ruth Anne. Face your fears."

Emotionless, Ruth Anne slid inside the tube, where she awaited the signal for her eternal ride inside the hellish monster machine.

✗

THE NEW HUMAN
Shayne K. Keen

Eventually, they noticed we were amongst them. All it took was one small child, blonde with shiny blue eyes. One of our kind cracked open her skull and ate her brain. For our entire people, it meant the end of the world. I will not go into great detail about the irony of a single attack by a 'zombie' (as they called us) compared to the thousands of children shot dead every year at schools, festivals, concerts, movie theaters, and even their own homes. I will not make comparisons to the endless wars and the immigrants stored in lettuce sheds in the desert. It has always been true that scapegoats make the terrified feel better. A thing that is not allowed can be fought. It used to be about who you fucked, how you drove, if you bathed on a regular. Now it's about if you might eat a human brain.

They would never understand our thorough surveillance, put in place only to locate and monitor our own kind. This time, our network failed. Before we knew it, Ned was arrested and brought to jail on charges for braining a child and eating what came out, along with some skin. At his house they found thousands of videos of people. No particular kind of people, just people doing their daily chores, gardening, running in and out of department stores. People who wore stoles, others who wore second-hand boots. The young and the old: seemingly no pattern, save a universal mundanity to their activities. Still, it was enough to raise suspicions. So many hours of video, dedicated to people doing banal things that are supposed to be private—but to us, they never have been private. What people do alone reveals much more than what they do in public; all who choose to leave the enclave must be monitored closely. Ned should never have gotten caught eating that girl's brain—as a monitor himself he knew better. Or at least we thought he did.

The police wanted to find out more about him. They searched for a history of madness, a history of assault: they wanted him to be a perv. Even with the private videos they couldn't quite convince themselves his watching was any more than plain old nosiness, kind of creepy but harmless. They hated that. It's easy when a guy's a perv, but Ned wasn't a perv. Ned had been an exemplary human, a perfect husband, a small (albeit important) pillar in the community, who drove an Infiniti and loved sushimi (raw flesh is always at least consumable, if not enjoyable; we choose to forgo even that lest we become tempted). Ned's wife Carol could find no reason for her dearest husband to have stooped to such levels of madness as to brain a girl and eat her innards, but at least (we all thought, though it remained unspoken) he had not tortured the poor thing; Dr. Monk assured the world that Little Diane Reed never knew what hit her.

Ned was drug away in chains, never to be seen nor heard of again—and good riddance. The whole of Park Momenta were horrified, but at least Ned was a lone wolf, a crazy man. Nothing more.

However, there would have to be a meeting.

* * * *

"Ned Junkins lost it. We can't have that, you know what it means."

Those congregated muttered in understanding agreement. We shouted out a few names, the loudest of which was "Carlotta." As one we turned toward her. She dropped her eyes and cried, then fell to the ground and begged for mercy.

"I can't help it, you know! I look at the children running home from school, playing in the playground, doing all the things they do—and I just want to go and bash their heads in! I was holding a giant rock over some kid the other day, about to tell him to look up at it. I threw it away! I chucked it as far as my scrawny arms would chuck it! Now let me go, I got control!" Her voice was shuddering, pleading, her red face wet from tears. "I got control! I got control! I ain't doing shit!"

"You know we can't risk it, Carlotta!" Jake's loud, booming voice echoed through the Meeting Room. "The Need cannot be acted upon! You will act, Carlotta, you will act and damn us all!"

"But the babies, they have to have somebody take care of 'em, and there's Mike, what about Mike? I mean, he can't find his ass half the..." Jake shot Carlotta in the face and put his gun back in the holster. She dropped to the floor, her cavernous forehead spewing chunks of bloody goop. Gobbets of scalp, brain, and hair sprayed the wall behind her.

"You need to stop doing that with a .45, boss. It's too messy. Use a .25. Quick and easy, just a hole." That was Lara; on some level everyone wanted her to overthrow Jake as leader, but it seemed to never be the right time. We'd waited ten years, would probably wait forever. Only Jake saw The Great Dead One.

"I don't want your goddamned advice," he grunted as he watched the Children clean up the body. Carlotta had already bred one Child; the other three had been left at hospitals, unknown, unwanted. *Order*, Jake thought. *Order was the only meaning of life.*

"If I use a .25, Einstein, then they wouldn't have anything to clean up. They need to learn." He pointed toward the gaggle of Children already scrubbing the walls, running with pink water. "If I use a .25, Einstein, then I might have to shoot them two or three times..."

"Not if you're a good shot."

Briefly Jake thought of slapping her, a distant remnant of his living self.

* * * *

Our cattle are well taken care of and fetch high prices. Our vegetables sell at market, and everyone believes we are just an odd cult who happen to be excellent farmers. We *are* an odd cult. Jake breathes the rule into our ears and we must obey or die. I have left the enclave just as everyone else must leave the enclave, and I found a frightful world out there. Those who move to the city, like Ned, those who decide to join the regular humans and fight off the Need are brave indeed. I am not that brave. Each waking moment I fight off the Need by meditating on The Great Dead One, who in His wisdom brought us back with such furious appetites, never to be sated. That is the first tenet. We must not partake of the human brain. To do so is to break the law, to lose the will. Those who lose the will are lost forever. They become lesser beasts, more and more ravenous, until they are no more than the rotted void feeding on all that drift into their heavy orbit.

"We must not become that," Jake says constantly. "We are still humans even with such hunger, but we can't eat. We mustn't eat! To eat is to become a monster. To become a monster is abomination in the eyes of The Great Dead One. To eat is the only sin."

We do not eat, and that is our religion. Abstinence from the only pleasure. Breeding is violent and traumatic. Love has left our hearts. Conversations consist of a strange form of 12-step program in which we keep each other from devouring the whole of the world. We could do that. We want to do it, deep, and not so deep, within our cadaverous hearts.

Life continued this way for many years. Our compound unmolested. Our lives simple and boring. Until Ned ate that girl's brain.

Ned left the compound years ago. We thought to never hear from him again, and we were right, but for some ridiculous unknown reason in his wallet was a piece of paper with our address printed on it with the phrase "in case of emergency." When he left Ned agreed to never mention us, to destroy any relic of his time in the sanctuary. It wasn't long before the police came to our door.

There were about twenty cars, sirens wailing, lights flashing. They broke the door in without knocking or announcing their search warrant; they shot all three of the dogs. The cat took off and found a hiding spot they'd never find.

These near-neanderthals found Jake's diaries and prayer books. They found the works of art we did to keep ourselves from actually going out to eat brains. Most of the drawings and paintings were of us eating brains.

* * * *

"A sick cult! All of them have been on a hunger strike ever since we hauled them in! I guess they only eat brains."

"They're all dead, you know. All of them. Not a pulse, not a heartbeat! What are you freaks?" the sheriff yelled.

"We are the Children of The Great Dead One," Jake answered for us. "We do not eat. We do not kill. Let us go. You have nothing on us."

"Nothing? What about these?" He produced a large portfolio of paintings.

"Art isn't illegal."

"Murder is. One of your kind killed that little girl and ate her."

"He left us long ago."

* * * *

Didn't matter. We weren't alive. We weren't dead. We weren't violent in action, but in thought we were the most disgusting and horrid flesh in the world. It took little time, thanks to precedents set back in the 20's, to round up as many of us as they could find and put us into camps. We didn't go to the bathroom. We didn't need water. We didn't need food. They understood the use of bullets to the brain, and would kill a few of us off every now and again, but kept us around mostly for job security and the joyous pleasure of having an entire group of lesser beings to ethically torture.

They cut off fingers and arms; they sawed children in half. We died by the scores, feeling no pain, for there was no pain, just a confusion. A mind set into a useless hulk of junk. Flesh too good a word for our rot.

Through it all Jake kept us calm. We never attacked, never ate a brain.

* * * *

Every day of incarceration, Jake's proclamations grew more aggressive.

"Behold them," he pointed at the guards lazing in their office chairs, watching us, bored now by our near-lack of movement, "chattel they are, chattel they should be, yet The Great Dead One disallows us our rightful feast! This punishment is too much to bear!" He would then turn to his corner, bashing his head against the wall, asking for The Great Dead One to release us from our torments. He refused to concede.

Until...

It was a particularly hot day. The stench inside the holding rooms must have been overwhelming, but we couldn't smell rot. Jake began screaming, screaming that it was time, that The Great Dead One had dropped the leash. I was horrified and insisted that, no, we must keep control of ourselves no matter how terrible the Need became without our prayer boxes and rosary beads to help us get through it. I stood anew and challenged Jake's authority, insisting that he was hearing not our beneficent Death God, but the horrible screeching voice of the light, the god of life and love, the abomination in the eyes of Death.

"Shut up in there!" yelled a guard. "Or I'll be forced to kill all you nasty motherfuckers! Jesus the stench..." Jake laughed the grinding chuckle of The Dead One. I saw in his eyes lightning. A bolt flashed, and he fell to the floor where the legless masses writhed. The guard's pistol smoked: the sound was deafening, and he clutched at his ears.

En masse we turned our attention toward our former leader and pulled his cranium off. We tore strands of rotten brain matter and chewed them, swallowing them down, gaining his divine omniscience. We were one, all of us, with The Great Dead One.

"We must end this," Lara whispered, easing comfortably into her new leadership role—though there was hardly need for one. We all knew how to end it. We all shared her thought as she uttered it; we whispered it with her.

We focused our gaze as one on the guard. He pulled his pistol out again, but his hand trembled and he dropped it onto the floor. He put his hands on the sides of his head and squeezed, crying out in pain as he shambled step by painful step toward the barred door. His trembling hand eventually inserted the key and turned it with a click.

We were a sea of flesh, and The Great Dead One strode with us, just ahead, smiling as all skeletons smile.

His arms stretched out as though offering us the whole of the world, and we took it. First the deputy on guard. We pulled the top of his head off, feasted and knew even more: we knew his address, his wife, his daughter. We knew his memories, all of them, from the first time he ate a booger to the time killed a dog; we were with him as he lay with his first whore. We heard his mother's voice, and felt his father's belt-lashes on his skin, near-worn into his young hide. We became even more hungry. We became ravenous, not just for the fleshy brain, but for its contents—the memories and experiences of everyone alive. Everyone who'd ever been human. The Need was All.

We would consume—and in so doing preserve.

Before us, ever on the horizon, The Great Dead One beckoned, His eternal grin seeming to say, "Eat and become fruitful, for you are the new Human."

THIS LITTLE PIGGY
EV Knight

I'm a bad mom. I don't go to PTA meetings, I secretly hope my son will quit soccer so I don't have to drive him to practice, and I've killed his guinea pig no less than six times.

I knew it was a bad idea when he announced that he wanted one for his birthday. Cooper once misplaced his pet goldfish, so yeah, anything larger put us at risk for a PETA protest in the front yard. As his full-time parent and keeper of the home he lives in, I said no. Not gonna happen, Coop, sorry not sorry. But Weekend-Dad, hero to oppressed children of single mothers everywhere, saved the day. Fun fact: Vampires must be invited into your home. Ex-husbands bearing live, furry mammals stroll right in and then leave the creatures behind like a curse. And thus, Mr. Kipling, the mangy black and tan nightmare came to stay.

Where Jack found the hideous thing, I don't know. Probably some hand-me-down from one of his bar buddies' kids or some animal shelter reject. But to my dismay, Coop loved the awful thing. Mr. Kipling turned out to be a master escape artist. He enjoyed hiding out for days by chewing holes in my furniture and nesting inside. Sometimes I tracked him down by the trail of droppings he left on his way to the couch. Other times it was the strange noises that seemed to emanate from my ass. I spent way too much money buying new, "inescapable" cages, but within a day or two, someone would see movement out of the corner of their eye or pick a raisin up off the floor only to discover it was not dried fruit.

Within two-months-time, Cooper had moved on to his next interest and the care of Mr. Kipling fell to me. God, how I hated that smelly little rodent. He knew it too. He would stay in his cage until Cooper left for school and I sat down to get my writing done. I would look up, mentally searching for the perfect word and there he'd be; standing in the doorway to my office staring me down. His whiskers twitching like a gunslinger's trigger finger daring me to try to catch him.

The day I decided that Kipling had to die, I had been in *the zone*. One of those rare but splendid moments when the story just flowed out of me without even trying. I had a deadline coming up; I needed this. My cell phone rang and while I would usually hit "ignore", the call came from my son's school. Coop was sick, vomiting and needed to be picked up right away. Of course. I swore, grabbed my keys, and took off to get him.

After tucking him into bed, I headed straight back to my office hoping I still had a little of that magic left in me. My computer screen was black. I hit the power button, assuming it had gone to sleep. Nothing. I checked the plug. It had been chewed in half. I screamed an aggravated, staccato "No!" I tried to remember when I had last saved my progress. I feared that it was possible I hadn't at all so far that day. When you're in *the zone*, pausing can be mental suicide. You just keep typing until there's no more words in your proverbial Scrabble bag.

That rotten little shit-machine! I stormed into the living room, tipped the couch over, reached up into the gaping hole in the underside and as luck would have it, felt the familiar tuft of hair that fanned out of Kipling's back side. I squeezed and pulled him out. Tada! Junkyard Houdini pulled a rodent out of a chewed-up sofa. He squirmed and squealed but half-mad with anger, I clung firm to his hind-quarters. All my work had vanished into the ether and all because of this thing that no one else gave a damn about. I sure as hell was done taking care of the gremlin. I don't know where I got the idea, but I headed straight for the deep freezer and tossed him in.

There wasn't a smidgen of guilt in this act. Truth be told, I'm not just a bad mom, I'm an angry divorcee who holds grudges. Kipling didn't stand a chance.

After the deed was done, I checked on Coop who slept peacefully and spent the evening trying to salvage the essay on my laptop. I was rewarded with another burst of perfect sentences. When dinner time rolled around, Cooper refused anything but a popsicle, so I ate his untouched lunch and kept working.

It was ten when I finally clicked save and shut the computer down. I had finally made up for my lost material. Sneaking up to bed, I tripped over a shoe and cursed. Why did Cooper always have to undress piece by piece down the hall? When I snatched the sneaker up however, it was cold and hairy. I switched the lamp on and saw a chilled but very much alive guinea pig glaring at me.

"How the hell did you get out?" I asked. He stared, twitched his whiskers, and blinked. "Ok, apparently I underestimated you, Kipling."

He was still stiff and slow to move, so catching him required little effort. I carried him to the toilet, tossed him in, closed the lid, and flushed. Yes. I flushed my son's guinea pig down the toilet. And you know what, I slept better that night than I had in a long time and better than I have since.

The next morning, I tiptoed in to Cooper's room to check on him. I touched his forehead—no fever.

"How ya feeling buddy?" I asked.

"Better. I had a bad dream though." He rubbed his eyes. "I dreamt that

Mr. Kipling ran away."

My stomach dropped through the floor. I swallowed.

"Oh, Honey. You probably just dreamed that because he's always es-caping his cage. He's somewhere in the house, I'm sure." *Or at least on the property*. I ruffled his hair.

"I know. He's in his cage. The dream woke me up and I had to check on him right then. But he's good. I'm gonna pay better attention to him. I think he's been lonely," Coop said but I was only half paying attention. He'd lost me at the part about Kipling being in his cage. I looked around to the other side of the bed and saw those beady black eyes staring from inside his plastic igloo house. He waddled out and stood doing that irritat-ing nose crinkle thing. I gave him the evil eye.

On my way home from dropping Cooper off at school, I pondered the seemingly indestructible pig-rat who somehow still lived in my house. There had to be a rational explanation for both resurrections. I decided that in my murderous frenzy, I hadn't shut the freezer door entirely which al-lowed the rodent to escape. As for the toilet, I never actually saw him go down. It's likely he didn't get flushed at all and made his way up and out, finally drying off in the wood chips on the floor of his cage.

Well, maybe it was all for the best. Poor Coop had been so upset that morning.

The following day, I had meetings in the city and Cooper had soccer practice. It was Jack's day to have Coop after school, so I skipped practice to get some work done on the book. And thus, it was me, alone, who dis-covered the acts of rodent vandalism that had occurred in our absence. The deep freeze in the mudroom sat in the center of a huge puddle of water. A fishy odor scented the air. I opened the lid. Everything inside was defrosted and warm including a bag of fish sticks, the smell of which dominated ev-erything else we'd kept in there. I wondered if the freezer had shut down sometime last night and we hadn't even realized it. It was cold when I threw Kipling in though—Kipling! I pulled the freezer out from the wall and there it was, the chewed-up power cord. The severed piece was still plugged into the wall.

"You're dead, cuy," I said, and then to clarify, so he knew I was seri-ous, "that's what people from South America call guinea pig meat."

All I had to do was find the hairy demon.

I changed the tone of my voice. "Hey, Mr. Kipling" I called out sweet-ly, "How about some cheese? You want some cheese?" I looked around but saw no sign of the rodent. Then I stumbled on a trail of wood chips leading into the bathroom. I followed it as silently as I could, hoping to catch him unawares.

He'd one-upped me again.

The chips hadn't fallen from his fur as he ran to hide. No, they fell from the pile after pile he somehow carted through the bathroom and stuffed into the toilet. I let out a war cry that would have made Braveheart cringe. And there he stood, posing in front of the blocked porcelain bowl: Mother Fucking Kipling. Taunting me in that piggy way of his. In my frenzied rage, I lunged, scooping him against me like a football.

Dripping wet and coated in wood chip litter, Little Satan and I took a trip to the garbage disposal. I was done taking chances with the tiny bastard. I shoved him through the black rubber sphincter into disposal limbo and turned on the water full force. Seemingly unbothered, he continued to root around in the tiny space.

"Adios Asshole," I said and flipped the switch. The disposal grumbled to life. I heard the squeals of mechanically separated pig. I laughed at my joke. Mechanically separated. I leaned my head into the sink, up against the gurgling hole.

"I'm in the mood for a pulled pork sandwich," I sang, laughing like a lunatic. With my head that close, I saw some blood spatters that had flown up out of the death chamber. He was dead. Had to be. I turned the switch off and grabbed an SOS pad.

I had just finished mopping up the bathroom floor when Jack brought Cooper home.

"What stinks in here?" my brutally honest—for once—ex asked.

Before I could explain, my son, the dear heart, who had already taken off to his room returned just as abruptly to give a missing pet report.

"Well, I know he's alive," I said holding up the chewed freezer cord which answered both of their concerns at once. That was enough to appease Cooper.

"Yeah, he's kind of a bad guinea pig...but I still love him," Coop, ever the good-hearted optimist, declared.

"Ugh. Well, good luck with all this," Jack chuckled and left without another word.

"I know, Bud. We'll find him tomorrow. We always do." I said half-heartedly while sending eye daggers through the closed door. "Go jump in the shower and I'll be up to tuck you in."

I showered before bed as well. I felt like I was covered in microscopic blood spatters—a forensic scientist's wet dream. I fell in to bed and off to sleep with a clear and unburdened conscience.

At 3:33 am, an itching on my nose awoke me from my slumber. It was that feeling you get in bed that some bug is crawling on you. I reached up to scratch and bumped into a furry lump sitting on my chest. I flipped on the bedside lamp and screamed, lashing out and slapping at the hideous thing parked on top of me.

"What the…" I got a good look at him then, the undead pig. "Oh shit, what the fuck?"

Kipling had huge patches of naked, bloodied skin exposed where his hair had been torn out by circulating blades. He was missing half his left front paw and his right rear foot was gone entirely. The stump was covered in dried blood. His lower lip protruded and hung loosely in a perpetual pout. He looked like Frankenstein's monster if Victor Frankenstein was a med school dropout with no access to adequate parts…but Kipling wasn't dead. Somehow, *he was not dead*.

Without breaking eye contact—because I feared the thing would come lumbering toward me and tear my face off—I reached for my phone and dialed Jack. Damnit, he was about to take some responsibility for this. I'd had it.

Kipling's nose twitched. Don't let him smell your fear or outright disgust for that matter.

"'lo?" my good-for-nothing ex slurred into the phone after the eight or ninth ring.

"Jack! You need to come get this guinea pig. It's all mangled up." I loathed to touch the nasty thing but Kipling was not going to get away. Not again. I pinched the sheet like a hobo's bindle around the monster.

"It's 3:30 in the fucking morning, Lori. You can't be serious."

"I have no idea what happened to him," I lied, "but we can't let Cooper see him like this. The poor thing is suffering. You need to come here and put it out of its misery."

"What? I can't do that. No, Lori. That's awful. Just make up a comfy box for him for the night and as soon as Cooper gets to school, I'll take Mr. Kipling to the vet."

"OK, OK." I gave in, defeated and then I thought, but would anyone be surprised if poor little innocent Kipling passed away before Jack could get him to the vet. "Why don't you get Cooper to school instead and I'll try to clean up some of those cuts and whatnot before you take Kipling in?"

With the plan in place, I hung up. Carrying my bloody booty around in the ruined sheet, I found a cardboard box and dropped him in without even unwrapping the sheet. I did not want to see the half dead thing ever again. I put the lid over the excess blanket and then threw a hardcover off the shelf on top. I laughed when I saw the title King's Pet Sematary.

As soon as the guys left, I grabbed the meat mallet from the kitchen drawer. Kipling was still inside the box, sleeping. I laid the blanket back over him and whacked him in the head with the mallet. Not hard enough to crush his skull. I was just hoping for a nice heavy internal brain bleed. I picked him up sheet and all. His body hung limp and lifeless but felt warm in my hand. Perfect.

When Jack got back, he found the rodent laid on a pillow case in the box as if I'd taken extra care to keep him comfy on the way to the vet. I kicked my feet up and waited for the call telling me that Kipling was dead.

Two hours later, the damaged demon returned wrapped with bandages in several places but decidedly NOT dead. Frankenpork lay in his boot box, watching me, always watching. He needed to die.

I had a brilliant new plan though and this one would work. What Kipling needed was to go one on one with someone more his own size. The last time I bought food for him at the pet store, there was a man buying frozen rats for his pet snake and lamenting how much the snake preferred live prey. He'd put up a sign on the community bulletin board offering to take any unwanted small mammals off people's hands.

I had to "run some errands" I said, asking Jack to care for the broken Kipling and to pick up Cooper from school.

Sitting in the parking lot of the pet store, I called "Mike" and offered up a sacrifice to the snake god, Thor. Mike sounded morbidly excited at the prospect and agreed to come by the house to pick up the ailing pig sometime the following day.

Jack and I had decided to not tell Cooper about Mr. Kipling until we were sure the beast was going to make it. Spoiler alert: the pig was most decidedly not going to "make it". I told Coop that I'd seen and chased Kipling around the house earlier, but couldn't catch him. Cooper seemed fine with that because it meant his guinea pig was still alive but my son could not be expected to do any of the responsible owner chores that came with having a pet. Meanwhile, the undead wonder stayed in his Pet Sematary prison beside my desk.

The following day, a middle-aged beer bellied biker named Mike came and went with his boot box full of snake food. And that evening, came back. Cooper answered the doorbell—I assumed it was the UPS—until I saw Mike standing there.

"Cooper!" I yelled. He jumped. "Sorry, buddy, but ah, I'll get the door, can you go check to see if the washing machine is done?" He gave me a puzzled look. I had never asked him to do that before. But he did, completely disinterested in the stranger holding a boot box on the front porch.

"Hello?" I said. What was this guy doing back at my house? I had no more demonic rodents to offer. He shoved a box at me.

"Here. Take your fuckin' rabid, fuckin' Cujo pig," he stammered over his angry words "Fuckin thing killed Thor."

"What?" I asked shocked. "How? I mean, the thing is half dead as it is." I glanced in the box and there he was. Kipling's head popped out from under the blanket, peering at me with unholy, demonic eyes, his lip bloodied and torn even more. One edge was now transected away giving him an asymmetric sneer. Something was different about him. His gaze was cloudy and unfocused, his chest rose and fell in rapid succession as if panting. If a pet could be possessed, this one had reached Regan MacNeil stage.

I shivered disgusted but I took the box. "I…I don't know what to say. I'm so sorry. That was obviously not my intention"

"Yeah, whatever," he said and left.

"You are really the devil, aren't you?" I shook the box.

"Mom. The washer is still…Hey! Is that Mr. Kipling?" he asked pulling at the box. "Oh no! What happened?"

"Oh, Coop. I was trying to keep this from you," I said thinking furiously "but, he ran out the front door this morning and got hit by a car. That man at the door—he hit Mr. Kipling. He felt so terrible that he took him to the vet. They did all they could for him." I laid a hand on Kipling. The little creature glared at me.

"Is he dead?" Cooper asked.

He didn't know! He didn't see the thing breathing. This was my chance. I pulled the blanket over Kipling.

"Yes, he is. I'm so sorry honey." I put the box under my arm so Coop couldn't see the mangled but still somehow living creature. "Do you want to help me bury him?" My sweet Coop nodded. He sniffled once but I didn't see any tears. He was trying to be strong.

The devil pig never moved. He lay on his side, his lip sagging, his little chest panting in and out impossibly fast. I dug deeper than I ever would have for any other backyard grave, but this was no ordinary pet. I placed the box in the hole silently willing Kipling not to move. He didn't. I scooped up as much dirt as I could get on the shovel and dumped it right on him. One after another, I tossed soil into the void until it was more or less even with surrounding ground.

The reign of rodent terror was over. Finally, I was free of the evil thing. I walked Cooper back to the house.

That evening, Jack called to see how Kipling was making out. Coop told him that his pet had died and we'd buried him. His sad little voice broke my heart but really, it was for the best. The beast was demonic or rabid or something. I made a mental note to never let Jack leave another living thing in my home again. If he wanted to get freakish pets for cheap, they could stay at his house.

"Dad wants to know if he can take me to breakfast tomorrow to help me feel better about Mr. Kipling. Is that ok, Mom?" Coop asked. Of course. Jack was the hero who bought the defective thing and now he'd be the hero helping to mourn it. I was just the big evil pig-murdering mother.

"That's fine. You'll just have to get up early." I said but Coop had already given Jack the answer and hung up.

The phone rang almost immediately and I answered without checking the caller ID.

"What now?" I said.

"Uh, hey, uh, is this the lady I got the guinea pig from? The one that killed my snake?" The husky voice at the other end of the line was decidedly not Jack.

"Oh, Mike? Yes. This is Lori. Again, I'm so sorry. The guinea pig must have had some sort of infection. He died right after you dropped him off. If there is anything I can do to—"

"Yeah, so I went to bury Thor tonight and when I put him in the hole, he started kinda squirmin' around. Like he came back to life or somethin'. I went to grab him up and he bit me. Never did that before. So he tried to get away and I managed to catch hold of him and he bit me a few more times 'fore I had to let go and he got away. Fuckin' hurts. Anyway, Thor ain't acting right that's for sure. So, guess I'm just letting you know. Must be some weird disease that pig's got. Make's 'em look dead. Probably ought to check yours out before you bury him."

"Oh, well that's done already. We buried him this morning." I said wanting nothing more than to forget about that damn pig.

"I was just thinking you ought to maybe ask your boy if the thing bit him though, cause these bites of mine are swelling up pretty good. Whole arm feels like concrete. Probably have to go to the walk-in clinic. Anyhow, I'm still pretty pissed about what happened but I thought I'd warn you. Something is seriously wrong with that pig of yours."

He hung up. I peeked out the window. The freshly dug dirt was undisturbed. I shook the thought of a giant snake coming back from the dead away. A guinea pig was bad enough.

"But I beat you this time, Kipling." I whispered.

I trudged upstairs and washed the day away with a nice long bubble bath before calling it a night.

The following morning, Jack was a half an hour late to pick up Cooper. I was just about to call his cell when I heard a car pull up. Fearing perhaps Mike had come back yet again to cry doomsday, I sent Cooper to his room to gather up his dirty clothes for laundry day.

Thankfully, Cement-arms was nowhere to be seen. Instead, an irritated and tardy father was walking across the lawn.

When he saw me, Jack shook his head. "I don't know what's going on down town. It's like all Hell broke—" He stepped in a hole and fell. Cursing on the way down.

Before my mind could recall why there was a hole in my yard, the scene in front of me played out in slow motion.

Jack pushed himself onto his knees and rubbed his ankle. At that level, he must have seen some movement in the bushes and leaned back down on the ground to peek through the foliage. It occurred to me just then that I had dug the hole that Jack fell into, except that I had also filled it back up so there shouldn't have been a hole to trip over.

"Hey buddy," Jack said, leaning further toward the shrubbery.

"Jack, wait." I stepped out onto the porch.

Mr. Kipling, covered in blood clots and mud, lumbered out of the bushes, right up to Jack….and bit him. Jack yelled. Holding his bleeding right hand with his left made him vulnerable to attack. Kipling, having tasted human flesh, seemed intent on another bite and lunged for Jack's face.

"Oh shit," I whispered.

The devil pig looked at me. His beady black eyes had turned dead gray but the stare and nose twitch was the same I'd seen many times before. There was only a split second of acknowledgement between us before he tore into Jack's face as if guinea pigs have always been apex predators.

I slammed the door. Nope. No thank you. Mr. Kipling was Jack's problem now.

"Mom, what's happening?" Cooper asked.

"Dad had an emergency to take care of. He can't take you to breakfast after all." I said, bolting the door.

"But, was that him?"

"No, it was the mailman letting me know there wouldn't be mail today." I said. Thank God Cooper didn't understand that Sunday mail was never a thing.

I heard sirens in the distance and thought about Mike's snake coming back to life and biting him. I thought about the mass chaos Jack had seen downtown before getting bit himself.

"You know, I think we should have an inside day today," I said as I led Cooper to the kitchen. Even a bad mom could see that it was not a good time to send the kid out to play.

"Ok." He agreed forgetting about the missed lunch date. "Mom, since Mr. Kipling's dead now, can I get a ferret?"

✗

OFACTORY SPECTRA OF THE UNDEAD

Robert Borski

Depending on which stage the stricken are in,
a variety of olfacta may be sensed by the tuned
nose. Hexanal, for example, one of the very first
byproducts of decay, smells of freshly-cut summer
grass, but in the beginning, you may also catch
heady whiffs of paint thinner and nail polish remover;
only later, as things inevitably begin to ripen
(and keep in mind that apart from rain or snow,
these things never shower), do indoles and esters
come to predominate—whence the more robust
notes of pineapple, cherry, blackberry, and grape
you're likely to encounter. In fact, given a large
enough concentration of infectees, you might
easily think you were in proximity of an orchard.

Alas, tertiary smells, arising anywhere
from two days to three weeks post-transition,
depending on the temperature, are not nearly
so plummy—as well might you expect given
names like cadaverine and putrescine.

Unfortunately, though no less redolent to them
than they to us, our own pungency falls well
outside the olfactory range of pleasantness.
And if fear (itself part pheromone, part condiment)
has an aromatic signature, we must fairly reek,
just not—since meat does not grow on trees—
of grass or sun-drenched apples.

Hence, when it comes to our own olfactory
profile, think abattoir—not arbor.
But Heaven help you if you're also best
described as low-hanging fruit.

arousing dark energies that lie dormant in the night,
an eerie fog rolls in, the bokor turns,
and without warning lays a hex on you.
The light in your eyes fades to a dim, unfocused haze,
your tongue grows bloated and thick,
your limbs slow further in their movement
until they are no longer under your control.
The dead man's penance has been paid
in full, the exchange now complete; the bokor's
new captive has come to serve his sentence
in the invisible prison of the damned.

LIFE UNWORTHY OF LIFE
Stephanie Ellis

The order lay on the table in front of him. Another hysterical command from Himmler. Standartenführer Anton Kaindl let out an exasperated sigh.

"Sorge, do we have enough to carry this out?"

Hauptscharführer Gustave Sorge, Sachsenhausen's record keeper glanced down at the camp's weekly figures. "All able-bodied prisoners have been distributed between the brickworks and the shoe factory *and* the counterfeiting centre. We have none to spare at present."

"What about those who have been selected?"

"Sakowski is preparing them. One hundred Russians, fifty Polish priests, fifty Roma and … twenty homosexuals."

Kaindl thought for a moment. It was going to annoy the hell out of Sakowski who hated any disruption to his routine but better that than facing Himmler's fury. "Get the prisoners back." He paused for a moment, it wouldn't do to return them to the prisoner's barracks. As far as everyone else was concerned they were already dead. Best they stay that way. "Put them in the Leichenkeller. They're all dead one way or another. Heil Hitler!"

Sorge stood and saluted. "Heil Hitler." Yet he did not leave.

Kaindl raised his eyebrows in query.

"Standartenführer …" Sorge hesitated, he did not want to anger his superior but he had to know. "Standartenführer, we have our own doctors. They have contributed much to our knowledge of Aryan superiority. Their papers have been published in the leading journals, so why has this, this Doktor Heim been sent to us?"

Kaindl had asked himself the same question. His staff were amongst the best as Sorge had stated. Dr Baumkötter would not take kindly to being asked to perform a subordinate role.

"We do not question orders Sorge. Especially when they come from Himmler himself. Dismissed." He turned his attention to the file on his desk ignoring Sorge's repeated salute. He only looked up again when he knew the man had gone.

From the office window he could see night had already begun to fall. Winter was drawing in and there was a shortage of food. Rations would have to be cut—again. The prisoners would survive if they could and if not

... well Sakowski always had room for more customers. Hitler had a rather apt phrase for them he remembered. What was it? *Life unworthy of life*. That was it. Useless eaters. Described them all exactly.

He pushed the file away from him. He did not want to read it yet in case it spoiled his dinner. It could wait until tomorrow. Kaindl shrugged on his greatcoat and walked out of his office, pulling up the fur collar as he stepped out into the cold night air. The short stroll to his house sharpened his appetite.

Below, amongst the corpses, the reprieved prisoners sat in silence. Nobody spoke for there was nothing to say. Nobody thought about what might happen next because they knew it would still involve their deaths—one way or another.

Anton Kaindl entered his dining room, enjoying the aroma of his evening meal as he did so. His initial delight changed swiftly to irritation when he saw two additional places had been laid.

"Rosa," he called. "Rosa."

The kitchen door opened and his housekeeper appeared carrying the cognac he normally insisted be drunk on special occasions only. Rosa followed his eyes to the bottle.

"You have guests Herr Kaindl. Dr Heim and Dr Romberg. They told me they have come straight from Himmler. I thought you would approve ..." she faltered.

Kaindl nodded an abrupt dismissal. He knew it was wise to offer such guests *every* courtesy. Whilst he *had* been expecting both doctors he had not expected them until tomorrow and almost certainly *not* at his own house so late in the evening. With a sinking feeling he realised they were probably there to talk about matters which could not be discussed in the camp. Paranoia was setting in with depressing regularity amongst the more senior members of the Reich.

He took a deep breath and entered the sitting room. His unwelcome guests rose to greet him.

"Doktor Heim, Doktor Romberg. What an unexpected pleasure." Kaindl made sure both received the warmest smile he could muster. He knew every word, every gesture would be reported back up the chain of command. He had to tread carefully.

"Standartenführer." His guests clicked their heels smartly and gave a slight bow of the head. "We hope you don't mind our somewhat earlier arrival but our ... our visit has taken on some degree of urgency." Doktor Heim's eyes gleamed as he spoke, keenly aware that despite his lower rank he was able to command Kaindl as he wished.

Doktor Romberg laughed. "Excuse my esteemed colleague's enthusiasm but we achieved rather startling results in an experiment carried out at Dachau. Both Hitler and Himmler are *very* excited and have asked we refine and improve our work as a matter of some necessity. It was Himmler who very kindly put Sachsenhausen at our disposal."

Himmler, thought Kaindl grimly. He was forever trying to undermine his position as Camp Commandant. "Of course gentlemen and naturally you will stay in my quarters as my guests." He smiled again at them.

The door opened behind him. Rosa came in quietly and waited until Kaindl gave her permission to speak.

"Dinner is ready, Herr Standartenführer."

"Gentlemen, I suggest we eat and then perhaps we could discuss the reason for your visit a little more. I can already confirm I have the prisoners you requested."

"Excellent, excellent," said Dr Heim, rubbing his hands together although whether in anticipation of the coming meal or at the thought of the prisoners awaiting him, Kaindl couldn't say.

The meal passed pleasantly enough. Conversation was kept to small talk about the latest films in Berlin, which actress had caught the Führer's eye, which car was the best to be seen in. All trivial matters.

Kaindl only half-listened. He had no interest in such banalities so he nodded and agreed in what sounded like the right places whilst he tried to think about the real reason for their visit. As if reading his mind, Heim refilled his glass and stood up.

"An excellent meal, Kaindl. Your hospitality is, as always, second to none."

"You are most kind, Heim. Shall we adjourn to the sitting room?"

The three men settled themselves around the fire, the last of Kaindl's cognac in their glasses. He swirled the auburn liquid ruefully. He would have to send Rosa to get another bottle and there was only one left.

"So, Heim. How can I aid you during your stay."

Dr Heim smiled. "Don't worry about the details, we can discuss those later. First I think it is important to explain to you *what* we hope to achieve."

"Naturally, everything we tell you is confidential," interjected Romberg.

"Naturally," agreed Kaindl smoothly. He took a sip of brandy, allowing its molten warmth to spread pleasantly through his body. There was a moment's silence whilst his companions followed suit. The brandy, the fire, a full stomach—all leant themselves to the congenial atmosphere.

"Kaindl, have you ever read the story of Frankenstein?"

Kaindl looked at Heim. "Yes, it's a classic of gothic literature. A genre I particularly enjoy as a means of relaxation."

"And the biblical story of Lazarus, raised from the dead?" asked Romberg.

"Yes, yes," said Kaindl somewhat puzzled.

"In fact," continued Heim. "There are many stories recounted through the ages that tell of the dead being brought back to life. I'm sure you could think of a few more."

"But that's all they are," said Kaindl. "Stories."

Heim lifted his glass, pausing to admire the reflection of the lead crystal in the glow of the fire. "Not any more," he said.

Kaindl stared hard at the man, looking for a hint this might be a joke. The seriousness of his new colleague's demeanour assured him it wasn't.

"For some time now I've been receiving reports back from parts of Africa and even as far afield as Haiti," said Heim.

"Haiti? But isn't that country neutral?"

"Yes but that doesn't stop some of our … um … researchers visiting," said Heim.

"Himmler has a team of anthropologists and other scientists studying the culture of the lesser races. So far everything that has been received has done nothing except prove the superiority of the Aryan stock—as we expected," interrupted Romberg.

"Within that information however have been accounts of what are called in Africa *nzambi* or the risen dead. What is particularly interesting is those who have 'risen' are totally subservient to the person who has brought them back. In addition, they require little, if any sustenance," said Heim. "This is a concept which quite naturally has great appeal to our Führer."

Still Kaindl could not believe what he was hearing. The Reich needed workers it was true. Those they had were troublesome, tainted. They needed feeding, clothing, they were a drain on the limited resources Germany was currently suffering from. He could see how Hitler had become attracted to these strange reports.

"So how did you manage to create one of these 'risen'?" he asked.

Romberg pulled a thin report out of the briefcase at his feet and handed it to Kaindl. "As you know we have been testing the effects of various toxins on the human body," he said. "Our usual practice is to introduce the poison to the body in an open wound. This was done to a particular patient as part of our research into tetradotoxin. You may have heard of the drug?"

Kaindl had, and only recently at that. Himmler had sent him a paper written by Dr Yoshizumi Tahara, the scientist who had first identified the poison and its effects. From what he could remember, anyone unfortunate enough to ingest the toxin went into a catatonic state from which they eventually emerged albeit somewhat mentally deficient. It had been noted that in terms of potency it was 100 times more toxic than potassium cyanide.

"But from what was stated in that paper, the test subjects didn't actually die."

A smug expression swept over Heim's face. "Well I can assure you, ours did—and they came back." Heim gestured to Kaindl to read the report handed to him by Romberg.

Kaindl glanced down. It was dated 1st September 1943. The subject name was left blank, the only identifier was a reference number 'TTX1'. The report stated an open wound on the patient's leg had been swabbed with tetradotoxin and then stitched up. A nurse had logged details of the patient's vital functions, appearance and behaviour. Initially the subject suffered some sort of fit, random twitches and jerks had lessened in violence until after 24 hours they had ceased. The heart had stopped and the doctor on duty had declared the patient brain-dead. Due to an emergency the body was left where it was and was not approached again until porters went to collect it the next day. What they found however was not what they expected. TTX1 was still lying on the bed, the restraints held him in place but the 'corpse' was now moving, twisting from side to side in an attempt to free himself. When the subject turned his gaze to the porters they fled.

A passing doctor entered the cubicle and observed the patient in an acute state of distress. TTX1 could not speak although he tried, managing only a low moan. When the doctor removed the restraints, TTX1 lunged at him, biting his hand in the process. By this time other nursing personnel and security guards had arrived and were able to restrain the subject once more. Unfortunately certain *injuries* meant this time the subject died again and remained dead. The doctor who had been bitten had been admitted to hospital but there was no other reference to him in the notes. Kaindl still had his doubts about the first so-called death of TTX1—after all mistakes could be made. He continued to read.

He flipped over a communiqué which Himmler had sent to Heim in response to his report on TTX1. It instructed him to apply the same toxin to two patients. The first, TTX2 was to be a living, healthy human; the second, TTX3 was to be a dead body, well-preserved but proven as deceased for at least three days so there could be no room for doubt. The results shocked Kaindl. TTX2 died and came back. TTX3 revived within 24 hours.

"Where are the subjects now?" he asked.

"Unfortunately they had to be destroyed," said Heim.

Kaindl waited for him to elaborate but no further information was forthcoming. Nothing else had been entered onto the report except a reference to a classified document. That document was not amongst those he had been handed. "You intend to use the prisoners you asked for in order to repeat this experiment?"

"Yes. Himmler feels not only would these creatures make excellent workers but they could also be used to break through the Russian forces. Cold seems to have little effect on them."

"You tested that?"

"Yes, before things got a little … difficult. You have heard of our freezing experiments at Dachau?"

No reply was necessary.

"TTX2 and TTX3 showed remarkable resilience to extremes of temperature. Remarkable, truly remarkable." Romberg was smiling at the memory but then the smile faded.

Perhaps it was after that that the difficulties arose, thought Kaindl. "Well I suppose I will have to believe what you have told me," said Kaindl. "But I am sure you will understand when I say I need to see it with my own eyes."

"Of course," said Heim. "First thing tomorrow we will tread the path of your enlightenment … together."

At six o' clock the next morning, Dr Heim began his work. It was still dark yet he insisted the prisoners be brought into the parade ground for inspection. Floodlights shone down on them to allow the initial examinations to take place. Even those who had died whilst waiting had been brought out and these too were examined.

"Excellent, excellent," said Heim. "These," he indicated the prone bodies, "take them to the infirmary. Dr Romberg will give further instruction there. The rest," Heim paused and turned to Kaindl. "I take it you have prepared the special barracks?"

"Yes, as you instructed," said Kaindl.

"The rest," Heim continued. "are to go in to the barracks."

The prisoners shuffled slowly between the guards. There was nothing much different about their new sleeping quarters except each patient had their own bed and each bed had sturdy leather restraints fitted.

"They are to be taken to the infirmary in groups of ten every two hours and then returned here and strapped down," said Heim. " You will have guards placed at intervals of every four beds."

"Kapos?" asked Kaindl thinking of the drain on his resources.

"No, no. Not this time. There must be a strict security blanket applied. If it looks like a problem we have authorisation to call on additional support from local SS units."

Kaindl nodded. He was curious though about the need for so many guards when the prisoners would be restrained.

"Come, Standartenführer. I think it is time you saw the dead rise …"

Inexplicably the hairs on the back of his neck started to rise. Kaindl had seen many things, atrocities some would call them, and had remained unmoved. For the first time, he felt uneasy.

They made their way to the infirmary where the relief he felt on entering the brightly-lit wards proved to be short-lived.

Heim wasted no time and led him to where the corpses were receiving their 'treatment'. Each body was restrained on a trolley. So far three had received the cuts to their lower legs in which the toxin had been swabbed. These were now neatly bandaged and a nurse stood at the foot of each one making notes. Dr Romberg was busy on the fourth, slicing open the flesh with a practised ease, an assistant applying the toxin and another on hand to stitch up. When all was complete, Romberg moved on to another and repeated the procedure. Kaindl noticed each subject was also stamped with an ID number on their forearm.

It was strangely silent. The dead can't talk, thought Kaindl, they suffer no pain. It would take longer with the living subjects he knew. He looked at the faces of his infirmary staff, barely visible behind surgical masks. He wondered what they were thinking. Their eyes showed no emotion. That was one of the first rules of self-preservation in these desperate times, betray no emotions, no thought, no opinions. It would improve your chances of survival. He prepared to take his leave.

"If you don't mind, Herr Doktor, I have camp business that needs my attention."

"Of course, of course, my dear Kaindl. I have everything I need. I look forward to showing you my results shortly. Heil Hitler."

"Heil Hitler." Kaindl clicked his heels and made his way swiftly back to his own quarters. He had work to attend to but first he felt the strong need for a shower. He did not see Heim again until mid-afternoon.

"How is it going?" he asked.

"Half-way through," said Heim rubbing his hands in satisfaction. "I thought you might like to come and see our first results."

Kaindl nodded in reluctant agreement and followed him to the Special Barracks. The dormitory was dark, low moans occasionally escaping from different corners of the room.

"We returned our untreated patients to the Leichenkeller. I thought it would be disturbing for them to sit with the patients we brought back."

Kaindl thought waiting amongst corpses was just as disturbing but said nothing.

"Come," said Heim. He led Kaindl to a bed on which a body writhed and moaned. "TTX4. This subject was the first to undergo the procedure."

Heim switched on a lamp to allow a better view. TTX4 moaned louder, twisting his head to escape the light.

"Have you noted that?" asked Hem of a nurse. "Aversion to bright light."

The nurse nodded and hastily scribbled a note on her clipboard. "They don't seem to feel much pain either." Heim flicked the light to focus on the flesh around the restraints. It was hanging limp and torn around its leather bounds where the subject had tried to free itself. "Watch this," he said, pulling a small dagger out of his waistband. Without warning he plunged it into the chest of TTX4. The subject did not even flinch.

Another nurse came over with a glass of water. Again the patient ignored it.

"See. No desire for drink and we get the same response towards food. Just think. Workers we do not have to feed, clothe or keep warm. No useless eaters."

"When will you be able to put them to work?" That was something their discussion of the previous evening hadn't addressed and he was curious.

"Shortly, shortly," said Heim dismissively. "Once they've all been treated, we'll begin their training. They'll be docile by then."

Docile? That implied an earlier violence. Another batch of prisoners was wheeled in as they spoke. Their bodies were lifted onto the beds and the thick leather straps tightened around their wrists and ankles.

Kaindl left Heim to his work once more. Thankfully the rest of the camp was quiet. The counterfeiting workshop was a particular favourite of his. The forged banknotes they produced were real works of art. He ignored the workers themselves, they meant very little to him—unless they weren't doing a good job in which case they were … disposed of. After he had completed his afternoon rounds, Kaindl made his way back to his house. He hoped to enjoy a quiet hour listening to Wagner before Heim and Romberg reappeared. Sometimes even the Camp Commandant felt the need to escape. A gentle tap on the door roused him. He realised he must have nodded off as the needle was stuck at the centre of the record, going round and round with a repeated quiet crackle.

"Dinner is ready, Standartenführer," said Rosa. "Dr Heim and Dr Romberg have just gone through."

Kaindl threw an annoyed glance at Rosa.

"They asked … they *told* me not to wake you," she said quickly heading off any admonishment. "They, they also brought Dr Mugowsky and Dr Baumkötter with them."

Kaindl refrained from any comment. He might be Standartenführer but for now Heim was able to do as he pleased. Any objections would surely reach the ears of Himmler and was something to be avoided at all costs. He put on his most welcoming smile as he entered the dining room. His four guests were already seated.

"Hope you don't mind Kaindl, but I invited Mugowsky and Baumkötter along as a thank you for all their hard work today. With their help we completed our treatments in half the time," said Heim.

"All subjects are safely tucked up and under observation in the barracks," added Mugowsk smugly.

That was something at least, thought Kaindl. "So how do we proceed to the next stage?" he asked.

"Carefully," said Heim. "We will start with some gentle exercise tomorrow but I must insist the subjects are hobbled—they do have a tendency to wander."

Kaindl was thoughtful. Although he had only read the reports of the three earlier TTX subjects it was beginning to sound as if Heim had in fact done a more in depth study involving greater numbers.

"And you are sure they need no sustenance?" Kaindl could still not believe feeding the prisoners was unnecessary.

"Obviously a body needs fuel of some kind. Our subjects have rather *specialised* diets. They will not however make any demands upon your supplies at all. You may rest assured on that," said Heim.

"Then what *do* they eat? Do they graze like sheep?"

"No, no," replied Romberg. "As we said they have a specific requirement which we cannot at present divulge. Please do not dwell on it, we will give you more detailed information in due course."

"There is one thing however you need to be aware of," said Heim looking Kaindl in the eye. "On no account approach a TTX subject unless they are shackled and gagged."

"Gagged?"

"I have observed an unfortunate tendency to bite or attack any human close by. This can be disastrous. Once bitten, the victim starts to display the same characteristics as their attacker."

Kaindl swallowed hard as the realisation of what they'd said hit him. "These creatures are dangerous and you have made them *here*, amongst thousands of prisoners! What sort of mad man gave such an order?" From the expression on Heim's face, Kaindl knew immediately he had gone too far and sought to back track. "Please forgive me, Doktor Heim. I know the creation of such a race is a logical step in the furtherance of our war effort but it is such an amazing concept. I can barely grasp it at present."

"I understand, Standartenführer, perhaps another glass of your excellent cognac would steady your *nerves*."

Kaindl made no objection, allowing Heim to pour a double measure which soon restored some sense of well-being, a sense that was to be shattered yet again when a siren started to wail across the camp shortly followed by the sound of aircraft overhead. Outside he heard the shouts of guards as they ran to take cover.

"I have a bunker gentlemen," said Kaindl calmly. "I think we should go and take cover until this little emergency is over."

"I need to check on my patients first," said Heim, slightly nervously, thought Kaindl.

"I'm sure they'll be fine," he said, just as an explosion rocked the camp. They ran outside and discovered a bomb had hit the Russian prisoners' barracks and the survivors were pulling themselves clear. Other barracks caught fire as flames leapt easily between buildings.

"The prisoners in the special barracks," shouted Kaindl at a passing SS guard.

"Don't worry sir, they're being evacuated," came the reply.

"No, no. Dear God *No!*" shouted Heim.

They were near the entrance of the special barracks. Already the inhabitants had stumbled their way outside. Some had been injured by the explosions, two had lost arms, a third had his chest ripped open with his entrails slowly snaking down his front. Yet still they walked. Kaindl started to back away but was unable to tear his eyes from the horrific sight in front of him. Another explosion from behind roused him slightly. He looked for Heim but the smoke obscured his view. Only when it started to clear could he see the doctor. He was almost surrounded by his patients who grabbed at him as he sought for a way to escape.

Kaindl wanted to run but the thought of Himmler's disapproval somehow managed to stop him, instead he sprinted over to Heim's side, firing at the creatures who still kept coming. By now one had locked his teeth into Heim's arm whilst another was ripping at his chest. Already it was too late. Kaindl fired again only to hear the empty click of the barrel.

A pain shot through him as he felt something pierce his back. Warm, wet liquid was trickling down his skin. Looking round in desperation, he could see no way out. More of the creatures attacked him. As the pain became more overwhelming he found himself slowly becoming detached from his body. Kaindl felt as if he were floating outside of himself, looking down at his body which lay there, slowly being devoured by the hordes created by Heim; strangely he felt no pain.

His last thought was *life unworthy of life*. But the question as to who exactly was unworthy remained unanswered as the darkness claimed him.

✗

MORE BLOOD
Carson Ray

Brandon Jones kept his head down as he crossed the road and stepped into the graveyard, a large book under his arm and the handle of a small cage clenched tightly in one fist.

Truth be told, he knew he could have shouted and danced his way past the headstones without anyone realizing he was there. It was half past midnight and Fairhill Cemetery was positioned back against a small forest, the empty church across the road being the only structure within a mile. Brandon had spared the church only a cursory glance, the dark windows doing little to convince him that this was all a good idea. He inhaled the smell of fresh-cut grass in an effort to steady his nerves, remembering how his father had loaded up his jimmy-rigged mower and made the short little drive out this way. Brandon had stayed home that day, and his father had not pressed him into coming to help. Some things simply had to be done alone. His father had resumed his night shift position at Chart three nights ago, and this was the first night Brandon had mustered up the courage to come back to the cemetery.

Brandon had never visited a graveyard at night before. He expected a thin layer of fog to cover the ground like in all of the movies, but it was a clear spring night, the stars twinkling like dusted crystal around a crescent moon. He would have preferred a bit more light to aid in navigating around the plots and marble benches, but the blanket of darkness would help tremendously in seeing any headlights coming around the bend in the road. He did not think anybody would be out this way so late at night, but he was willing to hunker down and army crawl if he had to.

Sighing softly, Brandon continued to make his way towards the grave near the edge of the forest. He wondered to himself if there was some bizarre rationality to what he was doing or if he had lost his mind at the ripe age of thirteen. He was currently leaning towards the latter.

While Robin Jones had been alive, she never hid the fact that she was a practicing witch from her children. Brandon could not fathom how many times he had walked through the living room to find her sitting in a circle of candles and other various trinkets. He'd always ask what she was doing, and she'd always respond the exact same way.

"Just making sure we are all protected."

Brandon reckoned that her powers had not been strong enough to protect herself. Cancer eats the body as fast and deadly as it wants to, and no amount of muttered incantations was going to stop it. This fact had not stopped his mother, of course. Though she could not leave her bed during those last few days, Brandon would come in to find his little sister, Ava, lighting candles with puffy eyes and glistening cheeks.

Brandon ground his teeth, his right hand clenching the little cage's handle so tightly his knuckles popped loudly in the stillness. He had never once taken witchcraft seriously. He had never seen any direct results of his mother's endless babbling about hidden spirit worlds and the crucial alignment of the stars. But he had never argued with his mother while she was still one of the living, though he had cursed her many times under his breath during the last few days.

It was hard seeing the person who had brought him into this world slowly wither away.

Fairhill Cemetery was like just about every other cemetery Brandon had ever seen, though his knowledge of them was admittedly limited. Maybe it was his mother's perverse fascination with the darker aspects of life that made him resist anything in the same ballpark. Regardless, it was impossible growing up in the southern United States without visiting the garden of bones. You'd sit in a hot Baptist church and listen to the preacher drone on and on about how lucky the person in the casket was for having been saved decades ago, and then the pallbearers would lift said casket and shuffle their way towards the hearse outside. More often than not, the drive was a brief one, oftentimes taking just a handful of minutes. Where there is a small church standing quietly on the side of the road, clusters of headstones were not far away.

Brandon did his best to avoid looking at the names on the marble as he passed on by. He needed to focus on only one name tonight, and the surnames of the dead only conjured up old memories. Old regulars suddenly not sitting in their usual spots on the church pews. Elementary school teachers dead and in the ground, living on only in the memories of those they taught. Don, his childhood barber, was somewhere around here, his family having enough love and money to give him one of the more ornate slabs to mark his passing.

He could not seek out those reminders of a life once lived, no matter how much he desperately wanted a distraction.

The night was quiet and still. The only sounds Brandon heard were the soft rustling of the manicured grass beneath his feet and his own labored breathing. While the coolness of the night was greatly appreciated, Brandon would still have loved to feel a faint breeze against his clammy skin. It was too quiet a night to go roaming through graveyards. It was too quiet to do what he had to do to the rat locked up in the little cage he carried.

It was too quiet to raise the dead.

Brandon muttered an apology under his breath as he stepped over the rock pebbles adorning someone's grave and cut across towards the forest, trees standing like scorched skeletons beneath the crescent moon. The location of his mother's grave, he thought, was entirely appropriate for her. When his father insisted they go to church, Brandon's mother would always go with them, even if they all knew she hadn't the faintest interest in her husband's religion. Even the church folk treated her differently, though they certainly knew nothing about her fascination with witchcraft. So a plot at the end of the graveyard—part of the whole but still outcast—was very fitting, and Brandon felt his mother would have approved.

His foot caught against a granite flower vase, sending him stumbling forward with a startled cry. He righted himself before slamming his knees into any headstones, but the thick book beneath his arm clattered loudly onto a solar light emitting a feeble green the color of glass Coca-Cola bottles, the blow dimming it even further. Brandon cursed under his breath and started to place a hand atop a headstone before thinking better of it. He did not know if chiggers even came out at night, but he knew the little red menaces crawled across the marble in the sunlight like demented dots of doom. Itching like crazy for a few days was something he'd like to keep on avoiding.

Brandon stood upright and tried to get his breathing under control, his shadow twisting in the faint green light. What he was doing was crazy. He knew this just as definitively as he knew there was nothing he could do to help turn his family's luck around. Shaking his head as if denying murder accusations, he finally allowed his gaze to settle on the book, its thick spine resting against the lopsided solar light.

Truth be told, Brandon had no idea what the book was called. There was no title stamped onto its leather cover, which was the color of burnt coffee and riddled with cracks like serpentine bolts of lightning. While the words inside were handwritten in English, there had never been a title page that he could find. The book had been a constant presence in his house as long as he could remember, so he had been provided with ample time to peruse its contents over the years, his mother never once trying to hide it from her children. Brandon was not the best when it came to understanding what he was reading, so he was never honestly that much interested in what the book had to say. That was more in line with his little sister's interests, who almost always had a book under her nose and could retain what she read like it was some sort of supernatural power.

In that moment, Brandon wished he were more like his sister. If he could have memorized all nineteen words of the ritual, he wouldn't have had to lug its considerable bulk to the cemetery. He had to be absolutely certain tonight and he didn't even trust himself to write down the words on a sheet of paper.

Brandon bent down, lifted the book with shaking hands, and closed it without glancing at the open pages and its flowing script. He had doge-ared the page he needed tonight, so there was no need in getting further confused by reading more than he had to. Knowing that everything he was doing would all be for nothing did not matter to him in the slightest. He had to try.

Placing the thick tome back under his left armpit, Brandon resumed his journey past the graves and towards the woods.

With each step bringing him closer to his mother's plot, Brandon wres-tled with the guilt of having left his little sister alone at the house. Though he had no doubt that Ava was sleeping, the thought of her waking up and discovering that she was by herself had almost been enough for him to turn back before he had made it to Fairhill. In the end, he had convinced himself that Ava would be fine either way. She was smarter than he was, after all, and was not likely to panic if she discovered his absence.

Brandon had always been more than a little jealous of Ava's close re-lationship with their mother. As long as he could remember, the two had seemed joined at the hip, sitting on the couch and reading a book togeth-er or browsing quietly through two different books. While he never once sensed any hostility from their mother directed towards him, Brandon's guts would always turn whenever she painted a forced smile on her face whenever he babbled on about whatever video game he was playing at the time. More than once Brandon tried to please her by reading a few books, never finishing a single one and leaving the whole experience feeling even dumber than when he started.

Though he was not proud of it, Brandon had taken to ridiculing his sister for her interests, hobbies, and general braininess a year or two before their mother fell ill. Sometimes meanness grows like weeds when loneli-ness needs to grow into something else. To her credit, Ava would only of-fer him an uncaring shrug, her attention hardly wavering from the book in her hands. The fact that she could not even be bothered to get mad at his insults tended to throw him into a tantrum, his bedroom door slamming to punctuate his aggravation.

In all the years they had lived together under one roof, Brandon didn't think he ever managed to get under his sister's skin until their mother was nearing her end.

A chill crept up between Brandon's shoulders and he stopped walking. He squeezed his eyes shut and tried to will his mind to outrun the terrible memory that was always at arms-length from him, ready to whisper in the back of his mind the second he felt like he was on the cusp of having a good day. It never worked. His eyes slowly opened, his shoulders sagging with the weight of his guilt. He saw that his mother's resting place was just a few plots away, little more than a dark smudge beneath the trees.

She had been little more than a dark smudge herself when he had cursed her for being the way she was.

It had been a bad day at school. Word had spread like the cancer itself that his witch mother had messed up a particularly complicated spell and had given herself the disease, which had been ravaging her body for just over two months at that point. Even now, Brandon did not know who had started the rumor or how they had found out about his mother's unsavory hobbies. When he could not find a face to direct his anger and embarrassment towards, Brandon had regrettably settled on his mother.

When he had burst into his parent's bedroom after walking home from school, his mother was little more than a pale bag of bones. Thick blankets covered her shaking body, skin stretched tightly against her skull as if horns were trying to sprout from her forehead. She had looked upon him with tired eyes when he stormed in, clammy sweat dripping from her nose like tears. Ava sat in a chair beside the bed, having skipped school that day to sit with their mother while their father had been out running errands.

Brandon had screamed at her. He cussed and shouted about how he had been cursed with an insane mother who had chosen nonsensical fantasy over normalcy her entire life. He stood near the edge of the bed, tears streaming down his face as he shouted things so hurtful that a more rational part of his mind mercifully allowed him to forget exactly what he had said. Regardless, that small blessing did nothing to help him forget the look on his little sister's face. Though his mother appeared adrift in her own little world, Ava had looked at him with a biting coldness that Brandon would not have previously thought possible from the little girl. The accusatory anger in her eyes had brought his screaming rant to a stumbling halt. Brandon had left the room with fists clenched tight, never knowing if his mother had comprehended anything he had said. That night, as he cried himself to sleep, he prayed that she hadn't.

Either way, less than three days later she was dead.

The guilt clawed at Brandon's chest as he stood less than twenty feet from his mother's plot. Guilt, he had decided, was just about the worst thing in the world. It is born from your own personal mistakes and it haunts you most in the moments when you do your best to move on. How could you fight something like that?

Brandon was not sure if what he was doing now was moving on, but it was all he could think of. Dragging out his mother's nameless book and trying to find a way to bring her back was an idea he never would have considered if the grief had not drained him of all of his tears and worries about being called crazy. It wasn't as if there was anybody around to stop him. His father worked more than ever, having returned to his job the day after putting his wife in the ground. He barely said anything when he was home, his dead eyes scarcely leaving the flickering television. Ava would not even look at Brandon anymore. He couldn't blame her.

But this was going to fix everything. Brandon held up the small cage and looked at the rat inside, which squeaked on cue. The ritual in the book called for a blood sacrifice, and catching this rat had been the hardest part of the whole ordeal. For the better part of two days, Brandon set traps near his father's tool shed in the back yard and had checked them regularly every half hour or so. About an hour before one of the traps finally sprung, he had seriously been considering stealing one of the neighborhood pets.

The rat squeaked and scuttled around the cage in little circles, its yellow teeth occasionally gnashing out in a panicky rage. Brandon checked again for the Kershaw pocket knife clipped to the front pocket of his jeans, his trembling fingers sliding across the dispassionate coolness of the clip. He had bought the knife a few years ago with his allowance, using it every now and then to carve sticks or open a package.

Brandon had never once considered killing anything with it.

Though he was young, Brandon knew that life was little more than a string of things you didn't want to do but still had to in order to get to the next disappointment. He knew his life had many, many more disappointments to come, but there was a chance he could do this right. This one thing—bringing his mother back to them—could right so many things, from the life-altering event of restoring his family to the small gift of being able to apologize for the last words he had said to her. If anything, he hoped that he would feel a small measure of peace even if the ritual turned out to be useless simply due to the fact that he had *tried*.

Brandon stomped the rest of the way towards the grave, making no effort to remain quiet. Only the dead were here, and the dead were sleeping. Hopefully, only one would wake in just a few moments. All he had to do was cut the rat, have its blood adorn the dirt sitting atop his mother, and read the words aloud from the nameless book. After that was done, he'd have to—

Dig her up.

Brandon cursed aloud, his voice carrying over the still and silent graves. He hadn't thought to bring a shovel. Before he could stop them, Brandon felt hot tears of frustration sting and blur his vision. He could remember to bring all the crazy bits—a supposed magic book, a live rat, and a blade to spill the rodent's blood—but he hadn't been smart enough to remember something as logical and *normal* as a shovel. He shook his head, tears spilling down his cheeks and onto his t-shirt.

He'd have to turn back and get one of his father's shovels from the tool shed. There was no way around it. He'd never know if the ritual had been a success if he could not see her with his own eyes. The thought of her waking up in a casket below the earth would have been enough to drive him to tears if he wasn't already crying.

One thing was for sure. There was no way he was going to lug the huge book there and back again. Adding a shovel into the mix was an obvious recipe for aggravation, and he already had plenty of that to spare. He'd just leave the book and the cage next to the plot and run home for the shovel.

Brandon glanced up at the sky, the stars still twinkling without a cloud in sight. Never hurts to be sure, even if he had checked the weather channel before picking the night to do this vile work. Being able to put it off no longer, he slowly lowered his head and walked the last few feet to his mother's plot, which was the freshest grave in the cemetery and had not yet been adorned with a headstone. He knew looking at the recently turned earth would likely make him lose his nerve, but he had to—

Brandon dropped the book and cage, his entire body suddenly feeling like a hollow sack. The rat squealed angrily from its prison, the cage itself making little more than a few quiet thuds as it bounced onto the grass. Brandon felt his mouth go dry as cold, sick fear twisted through his veins and curdled his blood.

His mother's grave was a destroyed ruin.

The dirt had been blasted outward in all directions as if ripped around by a small cyclone. Brandon could see swirling patterns in the turned earth as it had billowed up from the plot and spread some ten feet from the grave. For a brief, maddened second, Brandon imagined a gigantic hand bursting up from the dirt, gray and purpling fingers sticky with blood and rot. As he leaned over the torn hole in the ground and looked into the darkness, he felt a pang of thankfulness that they had not yet finished his mother's headstone.

The casket had been shattered. Jagged shards of wood glittered beneath the pale moonlight like the teeth of some ancient behemoth someone had tried to bury and leave forgotten. The once-pristine white lining that had softly caressed his mother's form had been torn to shreds and stained black by dirt and filth. Brandon looked dumbly off to the side and saw a large chunk of the casket's lid resting atop a nearby grave, the flowers left there knocked over and scattered as if by an ill wind.

Brandon sniffed and was seized with a terrible coughing fit, causing him to back quickly away from the hole in the ground and bury his nose into his elbow. A revolting charnel stench had risen from the grave—one part rot and moldering decay, one part bitter iron, and one part harsh sulfur—and assaulted his nose like a living, spiteful entity. Brandon leaned over, nose still dug into his left elbow while his right hand rested on a knee, and tried to regain some semblance of composure. He heard a strange clattering sound and was dismayed to discover it was coming from his teeth. He reached down deep, his eyes snapped shut and squeezing more tears down his cheeks, and again attempted to right the ship as it threatened to go down a whirlpool of madness and misery.

Almost a minute had passed before Brandon was able to stand up straight. He felt like a used washrag, twisted and drained by the hands of forces he did not begin to understand. The rat continued to squeak from the cage as if in a blind panic, causing Brandon to feel an all-too-familiar pang of guilt. As he walked over towards the shuddering and jumping rat, he figured that he'd take guilt over stark fear any day.

His fingers continued to tremble as he fiddled with the cage's latch. Once opened, the rat burst from its prison, scuttling away from the yawning grave and back the way it had been carried. Brandon tossed the cage unceremoniously into the dark woods, regretting it instantly as it clanged loudly against a twisted trunk. He kept low to the ground as he neared the grave again and picked up his mother's nameless book, which had landed closed. Brandon frowned, feeling a warm wetness oozing through his fingers as they gripped the back of the book.

Blood. Of course it was blood. On a night like this one, what else could it have been?

Brandon stared at his red hand and took a small step to the side as if trying to wrap his body as well as his mind around the strange predicament he had landed himself in. A sticky squelch announced itself from beneath his shoe, causing him to jerk backward with another yelp.

A cat lay on the manicured ground, a slit carved from throat to belly. Blood had oozed from the convulsing animal in a wide spray, peppering the grass like a busted water hose. Its eyes—vibrant yellow speckled with a deep orange—stared blankly off towards the desecrated grave of Robin Jones, possibly the last thing it saw before it had departed for more mysterious pastures.

Brandon shuddered and turned on his heel. He had to leave this cursed place before the police came. The blood he was trying to wipe on his jeans was still warm, so whatever had happened here had not been long ago. Though he did not think it likely that the few houses he knew to be on the other side of the woods had heard the commotion that must have been kicked up by an exploding grave, Brandon nevertheless knew he had to leave. Fast. In that moment, as he geared himself up to run as fast as he could, he finally believed everything his mother had said about the book and her strange hobbies. This was somehow all her doing, likely the result of some dark spell she had cast upon herself in the hours before she had died.

Brandon made it three steps before the sounds of faint singing drifted softly from the dark, jagged trees of the forest.

The singing was faint but clear, the voice one Brandon knew far too well. He stood petrified a few feet from the foot of his mother's grave, his entire body erupting in gooseflesh as the melody grew louder as if the singer was aware they finally had an audience. A barrage of terrified and confusing thoughts battled in Brandon's mind as he tried to make sense of the voice while listening to the words of a song he had known since he could barely talk.

"Pat-a-cake, pat-a-cake, baker's man..."

Turning to look back at the woods, Brandon saw a small pale shape in the gloom he had not noticed before. The nameless book tumbled from his hands for the last time, the boy whispering under his breath that he would never touch it again. Brandon stepped cautiously forward and never took his eyes off the figure, which was little more than ten feet into the line of trees that marked the end of Fairhill Cemetery. Though he had known who the voice belonged to the second it had reached his ears, Brandon did not fully believe it until he had crossed over into the shadow of the forest.

His little sister, Ava, was sitting with both legs crossed and staring up into the dark. She wore a light denim jacket and gray sweatpants, making her more prepared for the cool spring night than her older brother. As she continued to sing the nursery rhyme, she twisted in place in a vague dancing motion, the detritus of the forest floor crunching softly beneath her. She lifted blood-smeared hands as if in rapturous prayer, her long brown hair shielding her face from Brandon's line of sight. Despite this, he knew good and well that his sister was grinning from ear to ear.

When a twig snapped like a popped bone beneath his shoe, Ava slowly turned and looked at him with wide bespectacled eyes. A tiny sliver of moonlight managed to find its way through the treetops and flash across her glasses, the two white circles reminding Brandon how dark the forest really was. Ava smiled as she saw him coming closer.

"Brandon," she said in that same singsong voice. She lifted her red hand back towards the darkness away from him. "What a pleasant surprise. You were the last person I expected to see here tonight."

Brandon stood there a moment, painfully aware of his mouth hanging stupidly open. "A-Ava. What are you doing out this late?"

His little sister winked at him as she raised her hand higher. "Isn't that kind of obvious?" Then a pale hand snapped out of the darkness like a snake and slapped her palm, the sound a thunderclap in the stillness.

Brandon squealed and lost his footing, his backside landing painfully atop a cluster of snapping twigs. He was convinced in that moment that his goosebumps had sprouted goosebumps of their own. He crawled backwards a few feet like some demented crab, his voice a pitiful sputtering.

"Ava…w-what the hell have y-you done?"

He might as well have asked Ava if she wanted any ice cream judging by the radiant smile she gave him. She made a vague gesture towards the darkness from where the bony hand had sprouted and returned.

"I brought her back," Ava said simply. "She told me not to, but I had to try." She turned away from him and leaned towards the darkness. "Mommy. Come say hi to Brandon."

There was no sound for several heartbeats after Ava's words died away. Brandon sat moving his tongue, trying to find some spit in the desert wasteland that was his mouth. He did not understand how it could be so silent in the forest. It was as if all the living things had retreated below ground to hide themselves away until some shambling predator had passed by for newer, more bountiful ground. Even his own ragged breathing scarcely reached his ears with all the blood pounding in his head.

Then the forest beyond Ava's outstretched hands stirred. Hideous snapping sounds like jangling bones drummed in the darkness. A faint wheezing floated through the air like his sister's voice had done previously, but this was certainly no song. It was surely the sound of the herald of death; a rattling flute fashioned from the femur of some forgotten cadaver. Slowly, Brandon could see a pale shape moving unnaturally towards his sister, his voice having fled away—possibly where all the living things had gone—and making it impossible to warn her.

In a symphony of dry snaps and pops, Brandon's pale mother stepped into the dull shaft of moonlight. Her skin was a sickly paper white, large blotches of blackened rot mottling her thin arms from her wrists to her shoulder blades, which jutted harshly upwards with each step she took. Small patches of brown hair clung to her scalp like ivy beginning to grow onto an abandoned house. Her legs moved erratically beneath the long green dress she had been buried in as if an unseen puppeteer was tugging on her strings from above the treetops. Veins glowed from beneath her skin like hellfire, the lines a fiendish road atlas growing brighter with each jerking step. Bony cheeks stood out sharp on her sunken face, the whites of her eyes turned an alien blackness. A dry hiss escaped her throat as she shambled forward, her mouth opening and closing repeatedly.

Ava smiled up at their mother. "Something went wrong with the ritual. I am positive I said the words right, so it must have something to do with the cat's blood."

Brandon sat frozen, his mind too scrambled and stupefied to allow him a single coherent thought.

"She's already decomposing at a rapid pace, and her bones seem to be growing and twisting beneath her skin," said Ava, her voice once again resuming a singsong quality. "She's becoming something…else."

The resurrected corpse of Robin Jones shuffled past Ava—once her daughter in life—and reached a thin, pallid hand towards Brandon. Though he tried to stand and run, the boy would have been more likely to sprout wings and fly out of the black woods and over the empty church across the street, its windows dark as rotten teeth. But Brandon could not fly, and he certainly could not run. He could only stare up as his mother lumbered closer.

At the end, Brandon heard his sister's voice drift above the rasps and rattling bones.

"Mommy, do you think it would work if we had more blood?"

✗

SOMETHING WAKES
David C. Kopaska-Merkel

The fungus enters you with every breath,
It swiftly makes its way into your brain,
And hyphae worm into your inmost parts,
More intimate by far than love's embrace,
Receptors in your head have felt no pang,
Your body functions well enough for now,
But your volition's gone; you do just what
You're told, and stagger through what's left of life.

Now this unconscious thing controls your moves,
While deep inside what's left of you just screams,
Up to the highest roof you climb and cling,
Shouts from below you might have heeded once,
Your final thoughts leak from a crumbling corpse,
Co-opted flesh upon the wind is cast.

THIS CREEPING COLD
Kevin Rees

As I plummet from the second-story window onto the mottled pavement, I possess no instinct to brace myself and strike the ground with a sickening force. A fall from so high a place should have electrified my whole being with excruciating pain, yet I feel nothing except for this damnable cold. I haul myself upright ignoring the shards of glass cutting ruthlessly into my flesh and stagger blindly away, not once turning to see if I am being pursued.

Fortunately, given the early hour, the streets are deserted as I search desperately for sanctuary and come upon it in one of the lesser parks. With undisguised haste, I make for the thickest bushes that ring the perimeter and take refuge amongst them. Once I am certain my camouflage is adequate, I try to rest amongst the leafy branches and wrap my arms tightly around my quaking body.

As the morning moves inexorably on the nearby residents descend upon the park to take their morning constitutionals. Fearing someone will stumble upon me, I press deeper into the undergrowth and covertly explore my surroundings. Whatever small luck was due to me, it shows its hand and I come upon a moss-carpeted wall standing level with my crown. Like a starving man finding food on a desert island, I caress each stone with my dulled, glass punctured fingers. I follow its arcing curve until I find a point where it dips sufficiently for me to haul myself over. My transit to the ground is longer on the other side than anticipated and I fall heavily for the second time making the ungodly sound a sack of wet sand might make if too were dropped from the top of this wall. Thankfully, amazingly, incredibly, whichever adverb is appropriate there is no pain.

I raise myself to inspect these new surroundings and discover I have landed in a patch of wild, untended plants that spread out in a disorderly fashion along the wall which, I discover, forms a boundary on one side of a graveyard. The weathered stone is covered in a network of brittle vines that at one time would have displayed a vibrant green zigzag of strands but now clings to the wall like dried cordage. It isn't the only evidence of flora, which has changed the surroundings. The unkempt grass forming irregular islands amongst the tombstones was once, I imagine, manicured and kept to a reasonable length when the church was prosperous. Now I observe, it has thrived without regular attention and left to grow in wild, uncut clusters, some dead, some not, condemning the uncomplaining occupants beneath its creeping stems to perpetual anonymity. From these few clues, I deduce the church is poorly attended and the Sunday collection plate hardly rings with the sound of enough coins to pay for the upkeep of its grounds.

My situation, however, has improved thanks to the poor state of the graveyard. I may have fallen blindly from the top of the wall but now I am safely cocooned in a clump of dry briar and dead dog roses whose mildewed petals disengage with the slightest movement and dapple my clothes in faded pink. Ignoring this minor discomfort, I continue to map out my surroundings and see to the left a useful cluster of Silver Birch trees. I decide they would provide more than adequate succour from my *would-be* executioner and allow me to hold up with a little more comfort while I take stock of my dire situation. I disengage myself from my thorny protectors and crawl slowly towards the trees. I tuck myself in tightly beneath the gently waving branches that appear devoid of any wildlife and settle once more. Something else I am conscious of when I look up into the sky — no bird has flown near me since my escape. Dismissing the observation, I fumble in my pockets for a pencil and something to record what I suspect is to be a final communiqué with my fellow man before this black curse does its worse. Now, with fingers that barely remember how to hold a pen, I recount this morning's events and my last weeks in Egypt.

* * * *

Two months earlier I was in Cairo determined to make my fortune with a discovery so incredible not only would I return to England wealthy, I would become a person of historical interest—much like Carter and his Tutankhamen. To achieve this, I made a gamblers decision to stay and contend with the fierce heat of an Egyptian summer. I knew by then all the other academics would have abandoned the dig sites and retreated to their comfortable universities to write papers on the insignificant discoveries they made. With a clear field, I began negotiations with the unemployed diggers eager to earn extra money from a mad Englishman who wanted to explore the desert west of the old capital of Memphis.

The following morning I charted a boat with enough supplies onboard for three weeks and set sail. We travelled on the Nile for four days until I came upon a formation that appeared from our vessel to resemble a huge dune edging closer to the water. It was no accident I chose this destination. An old professor of mine once took me into his confidence after drinking half a decanter of a very decent Port and recounted his exploits as a young man digging for treasure in precisely this spot. His expedition was hampered by sandstorms and a cholera outbreak that forced them to abandon the site. He never returned. However, through slurred and sometimes incoherent rants, he assured it was the place to excavate for intact tombs of high value that hadn't been robbed out.

I set up camp and after a week of making exploratory probes amongst the scarred hillside; it was Ahmed, the water boy, who stumbled accidentally into a crack on one of the low-lying belts of loose sandstone. I called out to John (as he liked to be addressed), my head digger, and pointed to the blind scar the boy had found. He drove a team of men with guttural utterances and excited hand gestures over to the discovery. I lay under a rough canvas shade with my canteen and watched them dig methodically in the searing heat. It took several hours of hard labour in a rotation of three men before the corner of a huge block of dressed stone was revealed to human eyes for the first time in several millennia. I ran over as they cleared away more debris. My excitement, however, turned to doubt as I got closer and observed the amount of shattered rock the workers had shifted. I made a fleeting (and miscalculated) assumption there must have been a landslide sometime in the last century that could have destroyed whatever secrets lay undiscovered on the other side of the enormous block of sandstone built to resemble a doorway. Had my knowledge of geology been more astute, I would have dismissed this notion immediately and realised whoever had constructed this tomb had dug into the side of the hill for a length and cleverly angled the shaft down sharply into the stable bedrock.

"You want us to clear more, boss?" John said, his wide, permanent smile rendered lop-sided by an old crescent-shaped scar bisecting his cheek, which had turned white over the years with age and the sun.

I nodded.

The diggers sang as they worked, each chorus brought a rush of spades clashing in the still desert air. The hot hours passed while I slumbered fitfully in my hammock until a scream so terrifyingly piercing broke across the camp. I leapt to my feet and shot a glance towards the workers fearing the stone they were uncovering had shifted and crushed one of them. John ran over to me with an expression I never thought I would witness on such a robust man. Something had petrified him.

"Boss, we must go from this place... we all must leave!" pointing over his shoulder his voice cracked. "The stone, it has a curse on it!" John turned on his heel and directed the workers back to the tents without waiting for me to bark orders and demand they return.

I despaired at the superstitious nature of some of these men who would not hesitate to pull a knife on an unsuspecting tourist and demand their valuables.

"Insufferable," I muttered to myself. Turning, I walked over to the sandstone block aware every eye in the camp was on my back. I reached the perfectly exposed stone and saw what I can only describe as the biggest cartouche I had ever seen. It was wider than two of me and as tall again, and I stood a little over six feet.

"My God," I could utter nothing more intelligent than that.

I was not a great scholar of hieroglyphics although on inspection some of the symbols were easier to decipher than others. What I was looking at was one huge image dominating the surface while other, smaller glyph's formed a frame around it. The main object, carved and painted in shades of black with a delicate precision I had only witnessed in the tombs of royalty, was a depiction of a snake poised ready to strike. I was later to learn it was Apep — a dark god of the ancients.

I should have heeded John and returned to camp with some humility but my sense of superior intellect undid me. I also couldn't overcome my baser need for recognition amongst my peers, which is what moved me to press my weight on the stone. Without the slightest forewarning, the whole thing moved with an unexpected momentum as if it were mounted on a fine pivot. As the great stone shifted, it released the vacuum that had been building up since the priests sealed the tomb. A putrid cloud of four-thousand-year-old air rushed out and engulfed me. I clamped my mouth shut and masked my face with my hands but it was too late. My legs lost all strength, and I crashed to my knees retching. A maelstrom of swirling blackness overcame me as I fought desperately to stand. As I was flailing blindly around for a handhold on the door, I felt the unmistakable penetration of two fangs entering the flesh of my left forearm. I recoiled—fearing the worst. An overpowering coldness, so profound, took hold of me. I can only liken it to having ice water injected forcibly into my veins. My knees gave way once more, and I collapsed onto the sandstone cobbles where I fell into a deep chasm that went to the core of this world. I recall nothing else until I woke up on a steamship heading back to England.

Onboard was the British doctor who oversaw my care from the moment John and several of the diggers put aside their fear and saved me. They returned my wretched carcass back to civilisation and made sure I was cared for. I will always be grateful to those men for their loyalty, although the chest containing almost five hundred pounds and a few of my valuables didn't return with me.

"How are you feeling today?" Doctor Long enquired as he peered down at me through round, gold-rimmed glasses, which magnified his eyes alarmingly.

"I think I've turned a corner," I replied, somewhat groggily. "Except for an infernal sensation of being trapped inside an ice cave." Not having risen from my bed since coming aboard, I enquired further of the good doctor. "Are we sailing near the Arctic?" I didn't mean it as a jest, but Long took it in that spirit and chuckled instead of answering. "Doctor, what happened to me?" I pressed.

"Too much sun I suspect, old man. Mad Dogs and Englishmen and all that. Most sane archaeologists returned to Blighty weeks ago. Maybe a lesson learned, eh?"

I sat up, watched him pack his small Gladstone, and bade him farewell. I never saw him again.

I returned to my apartment in London and questioned if the capital was experiencing the turmoil of a new ice age even though the evidence of my own eyes disputed my physical extreme. The blooms were as colourful as I had ever witnessed, yet my body refused to acclimatise to the seasonal warmth. I spent a week in bed under mounds of the thickest woollen blankets I possessed and yet my body quaked and shivered with such intensity my heavy brass bed moved across the floor judging by the exposed time-worn wells impressed into the carpet. I reasoned I was still suffering from the severe malady that saw me leave Egypt. Reluctantly, I shuffled out of bed cloaked in the weight of eight sturdy blankets and made an appointment with my own trusted doctor.

"How long have you felt like this, Peter?" My doctor pressed his stethoscope against my quivering chest. I could smell the overtones of brandy on his lips. No doubt medicinal to quell the slight tremble in his hand. Still, he had been my physician since I was eleven and I had complete faith in him.

"Since disembarking from that blasted boat in Liverpool," I chattered. "No matter how much clothing I wear, I still feel as if I'm immersed in a barrel of ice water. You can see by my pallor the tanned glow I possessed in Egypt has turned to skin that has the appearance of being rolled in flour."

The doctor dropped his stethoscope clumsily down on the desk with little thought and sat down. "Did you keep up with your malaria treatment?"

"Every day, Doctor Goode. In fact, I made sure I had double the supply in case any of the diggers helped themselves."

"I can't seem to find anything wrong with you," Goode said turning his chair absently away from me. I noticed the slight tremble had become more pronounced. "Your temperature is quite low, but not unreasonably so and I'm certain it isn't malaria. I've performed the gamut of tests an old quack like me keeps in his bag. I'm… truly baffled, Peter." He stumbled over the last few words while fighting to avoid my eyes, which I didn't question.

"There must be some ailment that is preventing my body from absorbing the heat it requires to make me comfortable? Perhaps another round of tests? I'll submit to anything."

"Let me make some enquiries on your behalf," Goode promised.

A few days passed when one morning I received a summons to attend an appointment with a *David Carstairs* in Harley Street at the odd hour of five in the morning. I readied myself by dressing for winter on what *they* forecasted to be a clement morning. As I stepped out of my door, a light fog swirled balletically around my head forcing me to exercise caution along the pavement. By the time I found his rooms I was already gelid.

"Please come in Professor Ellis and sit." Carstairs manner was inviting and pleasant as he directed me to a chair.

I had never been in a more elegant room. The vaulted ceiling was adorned with a beautiful rose where a chandelier of exquisite crystal hung down. It glimmered majestically even though very little light was forthcoming from the two large sash windows situated behind a magnificently polished mahogany desk. I shuffled over to the chair and sat down heavily. By now my teeth had taken on a staccato rhythm of their own.

"May I suggest you sit nearer the fire I have prepared for you? It may at least give you a little comfort in these moments."

I followed his outstretched hand and shuffled the chair towards the welcome flames.

"It isn't that I don't feel the heat, Dr Carstairs," I explained if explanation were needed before Carstairs questioned me. "I can appreciate the sensation a fire should have upon my skin except that experience is neutral. I feel nothing. Layers of clothes and blankets have been my only comfort in the weeks since my arrival back in England. Though now I have observed in the last day or so they are also becoming ineffective."

"May I ask what brought you back?" Carstairs enquired.

"I suffered a severe reaction to something that bit me… a snake—maybe."

"And when did you notice your body becoming deathly cold?" Carstairs picked up his fountain pen and held it poised toward me like a conductor waiting to begin a concerto.

I gave a moment's consideration to my answer, as I didn't want to offer an observation that wasn't perfectly correct to account for my strange affliction. "When I regained consciousness onboard the ship everything was much colder, especially when we stopped to refuel in Gibraltar. It was the first time I felt the need for a second vest. Then, as we neared the home port, I wore almost all the clothing packed in my case. I've tried to formulate a cogent reason why I am suffering this way and can only conclude I was back in England still in a state of recovery and the weather wasn't as salubrious as it was in Egypt. I've known fellow academics take a few days to become readapted to the weather. However, I have not known it to be as acute a problem as my experience."

Carstairs nodded and noted my reasoning in a small notebook before addressing me. "Professor Ellis, I gather you are familiar with the superstitious notion of a Pharaoh's curse as absurd as that must sound to a man of science," Carstairs said with little emotion disarranging his lean features as he rested back into his chair. Without waiting for me to reply he continued. "I have seen other men, explorers and archaeologists mostly, with a similar condition that appears to defy the laws of medicine. Men who have trespassed into the past and wilfully robbed the graves of those at rest." Carstairs held up his hand, as I was about to interject. "I am not making a judgement upon you, Ellis, pray. However, I find the disturbance of someone's resting place a little unpalatable. It is merely an observation I hold. Yet—rightly or wrongly—there is an element of reprisal in the symptoms you are presenting. May I inquire if you are suffering from any stiffness that feels as if it is emanating from the very marrow of your bones?"

It hadn't struck me until Carstairs mentioned it. When I rose this morning what little heat had been captured by the heap of blankets on my bed dissipated within moments of starting my ablutions. By the time I finished, I was thoroughly chilled and starting to experience a numbing ache that ran like a procession of ants through my limbs and up my spine. A few drops of morphine I had been given by Long took some of that annoyance away.

"I believe that symptom has begun. Does it mean you have some idea what ails me? It baffled my physician. Then he is no expert in tropical medicine like yourself."

Carstairs looked up from his writing with a frown carving heavy lines in his brow. "Why do you associate me with a specialism in tropical medicine, sir?"

"Why… I presumed Dr Goode referred me to you given I have just returned from abroad. Have I made the wrong assumption?"

Carstairs regarded me strangely before speaking. It was when he brought his fingers to rest beneath his chin I noticed something peculiar. As his cuffs rode up, I saw dark patterns on his wrist that appeared to snake up underneath his shirt. I had seen enough Egyptian diggers to know what I glimpsed were tattoos. My intake of breath was sharp enough for him to brush down his frayed sleeves and hide his wrists. A gentleman with such common practices was beyond my understanding. On closer inspection, I found the veil that was cast over my eyes by the opulent grandeur of the room didn't match with the man seated across the desk.

"Who are you, sir?" I demanded.

"Professor Ellis, it appears you are suspecting I am not who you first perceived me to be and you would be correct. You see, a few like you get through our mostly efficient process whereby we can correctly determine who has, by their own foolish actions, contracted what we in the government like to term, *Mortui Ambulantes Syndrome*. Incidentally, Dr Goode was duty-bound to send you here."

"*Mortui Ambulantes Syndrome,*" I repeated in a quiet whisper and struggled to remember my Latin. "And Dr Long?" I demanded.

Carstairs smiled thinly, "Yes, he's one of ours as well. Allow me to elucidate. You opened a tomb guarded by Apep — The Snake God of darkness and chaos. In doing so, you received his judgement."

"What judgement? I don't understand what you are talking about, sir," I said, shakily as a profound shiver ran the course of my body.

"You are the victim of a curse placed upon the tomb you were intent on defiling for your own gain. As a punishment, you received a bite from its guardian, a God whose gift is now confined within you, Professor Ellis."

"Do you expect me to believe that nonsense," I snarled through clenched teeth. I brought both hands up to my face and tried to close them. I saw they had turned a milky white like the rest of me. I glared up at Carstairs who had risen out of his chair and was taking off his jacket. He rolled up his sleeves and for the first time, I saw the extent of the markings he had inflicted upon himself. Most I recognised as protection symbols, but some were the darkest of hieroglyphs. He brought his hands up to the side of his head and chanted in perfect ancient Egyptian.

I gasped loudly as if no air were reaching my lungs, "Am I dying?"

"His Majesty's Government regrets to inform you," he stated formally while drawing all his attention upon me, "that you have been on the cusp of death for several weeks. Without my intervention, the process you are experiencing would have concluded soon. All I am doing is closing the circle as they say. Therefore, it is with sincere regret, Professor Ellis, I am tasked with having to dispose of you before the curse renders you a cannibalistic corpse."

With a scream that came from the depth of my soul, I moved with little grace and launched myself towards one of the windows. Carstairs, stricken by my action, made no move to stop me.

* * * *

Now this day's hours are spent and the lonely night entwines itself around me. The testament I have tried to record on the few scraps of paper about me have become wild, indistinguishable scrawls. From here on I will be forced to conceal myself from those who seek to bring about my demise. Yet, the slim hope I cling to is I am a patriotic Englishman. That surely must be worthy of some consideration? However, if I am to believe Carstairs, even God Almighty has already forsaken me and condemned my soul to *Perdition's Flame*?

Something ghastly unfurls within me as I sit woefully contemplating my situation, I am experiencing a ravenous hunger. I try to quell this urge but it is stronger than any will I once possessed and physically drags me to my feet. For the first time since the voyage, I become aware the creeping cold, which has plagued me since Egypt, has transformed into an empty, inhuman hollowness. It leads me to surmise I have transitioned with no conscious resistance in the last hours and now I have no control over myself. This curse, this act of diminishment is complete. My legs won't walk at my command and my arms will not rise — they refuse me. I have become an unwilling captive who gazes out through my own, dead eyes in sheer horror. The implication of this truth means I will be forced to bear witness to murderous acts driven by an unholy lust for human flesh. My strangled utterance goes unheard contained as it is within this prison of skin and bone. Already, I fear the madness has begun.

Oh, Dear Lord, I whisper the words in my mind as an unoiled hinge announces another's presence; *it appears the time is already upon me.*

Approaching from the North side of the churchyard I hear with the utmost clarity the click-clack of rapid footsteps approaching. The hunger surges with an unstoppable want. I try to open my mouth and scream a warning only to discover my jaw locked and my lips drawn back over bared teeth that drip with saliva. Above my head, the trees scrape their limbs over one another as the gentle breeze of a few minutes ago grows to a strengthening wind as dusk approaches. On its tentacular swirls, I detect a potent scent, which sends this thing I have become into a frenzy. My body is forced to crouch down amongst the dampening tufts like an animal and I shamble towards my unsuspecting victim.

Her intoxicating aroma dances wildly on the chilly night air eliciting a tension, which squeezes this repellent flesh cage into readiness. I lope dog-like on all fours, stopping after ten paces to listen and sniff the air before moving again. From inside this corrupted shell, I wish for a bright moon to illuminate the sky and provide the wretched woman with *some* warning of my silent approach; alas the approaching darkness is all prevailing tonight.

I am so close now I hear her heart beat with a strong, unsuspecting rhythm. Eerily, my hands open and contract into tight fists keeping time with each engorged pump and I am further assaulted by a sickening image of an organ pulsing. All that is happening exceeds torture and feeds this dreadful thing I have become in an effusion of bloodlust. Crouching beneath the crumbling bell tower poised to strike, I am subjected to grotesque imaginings of my hands tearing at her innocent flesh and my teeth clamping onto her delicate throat, whose skin parts easily and gifts me her charging blood. Once I have drained her I will squat beside her corpse and gorge on mouthfuls of warm, bloody meat.

Before I am forced to kill, I pray if there is a place left inside me where an atom of humanity still exists I want it to forever scream these words for the rest of my cursed existence — *In God's name I beg you to forgive me as I cannot stop myself!* ✗

MUMMY'S CURSE
Colleen Anderson

The dead wrapped tight for the journey
through the inscribed tomb's long passage
shadowed pyramid's end the underworld's start
where Osiris took his time to judge all deeds

Centuries meandered in virtual solitude
the bound minded their moldering business
when grave robbers dug deep, cracked doors
where souls slowly sought the underworld

Thieves ignored reverence and taboo, all the signs
gave only cursory thought to durable hides
preserved against the test of time, living
forever slumbering in the ancient hidden troves

The eternal sanctum stripped of gems, glass
purloined gold, weapons, priceless chattels
did not incense Maat's gauzy dreamers
placid still, they sustained their long voyage

Until the sand pirates pried amulets free
uprooted and pocketed talismans
cracked hieroglyphic seals asunder
winding back the ka from its everlasting rest

Denied the Field of Reeds, water's rebirth
bodies not the lush fruit they were expecting
incensed zombies cracked wood and stumbled forth
to wreak forestalled havoc in the world they left

Exploring scholars secured their spot in history
not for discovering long gone Pharaohs
but for becoming victims of the denied sleepers
searching for flesh vessels in which to pour their ka

They now move among us, speeding, cursing
drivers, looking to go back to the underworld

THE BODY I USED TO BE
Scott Edelman

The question I used to ask myself most often, back when I still thought a correct answer could make everything better, was—

Are you happy, Mo?

And if not—what do you plan to do about it?

But the only question I ask myself now, the only one that has any meaning, is—

How many I have killed?

How many?

How many I have killed?

My answer, which, sadly, unlike my ongoing answers to that other question, won't be able to make anything better, is—

This many:

So many I can no longer remember how many.

Stumbling through the forest, blood from a fresh kill dripping down my face and onto my shredded blouse—and how odd to suddenly remember it was once one of my favorites, worn the day this all began because it was also one of Sean's favorites, and I thought it might help put our pieces back together—I'm still uncertain how it's come to this, while at the same time all too certain how it's come to this.

How many dead?

So many dead.

I once would have thought that to lose track of a trail of the dead behind me would have been impossible. But that's because I once would have sworn the count of my kills would have remained forever at zero.

I am not the kind of person who kills.

Correction: I was not the kind of person who kills.

No—

No.

I was right the first time. I do not kill. This isn't me. None of it is my doing.

And yet—

I *have* killed men. Many men. I've killed women. I've killed children, too, children which as they screamed—and I'm surprised I haven't been driven mad by those screams and the way I'm forced to endure them—reminded me of the children I will never have. That Sean and I will never have.

Sean who I hope I will never see again.

Sean who I fear I will never see again.

I've killed dogs as well. And cats, too. And even horses.

And then, after those killings, I have eaten them.

And not just the animals.

I don't want to do that, not any of it. Not the killing, but especially not the eating, which somehow seems worse. Not that the dead can care. But I care.

I don't want to go on this way.

But I can't control these urges.

I don't think anyone could in this situation, not really, and I doubt they'd claim they could, not if they were being honest.

Would you believe me, Sean, if I told you that choice itself is beyond me—if I had the power to tell you? Would you understand that?

The worst part, if there can be said to be a worst part, is—these desires, and the actions which follow them—they're not even mine. Would you accept I'm just a passenger. A witness? A bystander to my own crimes?

Oh, many people have claimed that, Sean, and how well we were both taught that. Our lives before we found and rescued each other weren't the best. I remember from before, how murderers, and abusers, and even those only complicit with them would blame, oh, lousy childhoods, or drugs, or alcohol, or the simple "look what you made me do." Or the Devil.

But there is no Devil.

There have been many times since we last saw each other, Sean, that I've thought—maybe *I* am the Devil. Because if I weren't, wouldn't I be able to stop? Wouldn't I be able to choose, to lie down, to make this all go away?

I thank God each day you have no idea what's happening, Sean, no, not really, not all of it, even though you probably think you do. Then as soon as I'm done with those prayers of gratitude, I switch to cursing God instead because you have no idea what's happening.

And yet ... if you knew ... what then? If you knew who I am now when looking into my eyes—if you ever have the chance to look into my eyes again—it wouldn't save you. It would not save ... us.

There's no longer any us to save.

Our friends, though, they thought they could save us. Not from what was out there, not from what was coming for us, not from *them*, a them which before my new life began was only hints and echoes and whispers, hints and echoes and whispers which have now given way to a truth I know too well. No, *that* them our friends didn't know about. What they thought they could save us from was ... each other.

And so they lent us their cabin in the woods for a long weekend get-away. They wanted us to have a space where we could try to save each other from each other. And though we tried those first few days, each in our own way, we could not. It was never even possible. All we ended up doing by escaping the city was delaying briefly what was waiting for us all.

I guess I should have known we were truly lost as soon as I heard your cellphone ring. What I would give to hear the ring of a cellphone now, anyone's cellphone, but oh, how I cursed that intrusion then. We'd made a promise, you and I, before we even began the drive north out of the city, that you'd leave yours with mine locked in the car parked down the gravel drive from the cabin. And how I raged to have that promise broken. Oh, the thoughts that exploded in my mind!

How could you? Didn't you get it? Couldn't you even have pretended to try? All that swirled within me. I felt betrayed. And that betrayal in a place to which we'd traveled so we could heal all past betrayals was hard to bear. Knowing what you'd become though, what we'd allowed ourselves to become, it was easy to believe.

We were sitting together in the porch swing when it happened, a spot which in a short time had quickly become my favorite on the property, and at that far too familiar sound, I dug my feet into the dirt, jerking us to a stop. You flinched and turned away when I glared at you, and how I wish I could take that glare back—even though you deserved it.

I don't want that to be your last memory of the real me.

Too many glares like that from me had given birth to too many looks like that from you for too long, and our time alone together was supposed to put a stop to that, remember?

I hope you do. I hope you're still out there to remember. But not like the way I now remember.

I hope you escaped that.

The ringing, coming as it did a couple of days after we'd arrived, had already seemed unnatural. I'd gotten used to hearing nothing more during our time there than the rustling of leaves, the buzzing of insects, the rush of a nearby waterfall, and at night—after the squeak of bedsprings—the hooting of owls, calling one to the other, echoing my heart. How I wanted your heart to answer then, as it once did!

But on that morning, at that moment, all those sounds were forgotten, buried by the muffled electronic one coming from your shirt. As I contin-ued to stare at you, you stared off into the woods from where we sat on the deck, motionless, wordless, until the ringing stopped as the call rolled to voicemail. Only then, after the natural world had risen up once more to fill the void, did you speak, apologizing with too few words, looking at me only briefly, then turning away again. I wanted you to look at me, look without me having to ask, but you wouldn't, not until it was too late for you to see me.

I'd never before seen you appear so interested in the squirrels which leapt among the tree limbs.

I was angry, oh, how I was angry, because this trip, it wasn't just my idea. We'd both of us agreed we needed a vacation. And of more than one kind. A break from our jobs, a break from the world, a break from screens, a break from everything which came between us.

A break from anything else but each other.

Even our friends could see we needed that, especially the ones who'd pushed us into leaving the city for the weekend. I am so grateful to have such friends.

I wonder what happened to them.

I hope they're OK.

I held out my hand, and after only the slightest of pauses, you pulled the phone from your shirt pocket and dropped it into my palm. I turned my back on you then, stomped down the drive, unlocked the car, and tossed your phone onto the seat. And as soon as I slammed the door and looked back up at you, I could hear the phone begin to chirp again, its volume tamped down by the glass. It was a sound I'd hoped not to hear until the weekend was over, and it stole the peace I was starting to feel settle over us there. I was furious—at you, at them, at everyone.

I couldn't imagine who would be calling us anyway, then, there, that weekend. All our friends knew where we were, and why. They'd never have interrupted what we all thought might be our last chance.

But now ...

Now I know why, now we both know why, what they were calling to warn us was happening. But then, as I looked at the phone, then back up at you, I felt such anger toward you, too great an anger, recognized it could push me to say things better left unsaid, and so—I decided I should go for a walk.

Alone.

I turned away from you, not knowing it would be the last time you'd see me as I really am. I walked slowly along the trail we'd discovered our first day there, that trail which meandered through the woods, and which I knew if followed until its end would lead me to the bottom of the waterfall, one so loud it would block all thought. I needed to go there, to let the white noise of water hitting water calm my rage.

I thought I knew what rage was then. I had no idea.

I kicked at the leaves as I walked, wishing I knew the names of the trees from which they fell. But we'd never left time in our lives for knowing things like that, did we, having plotted a course which kept us chained to our desks, chained away from each other.

How could we have chosen to work, work, work, instead of working on *us*? But we *had* chosen it. We were fools.

I was a fool.

Because I know now what I knew then but wouldn't admit—that on a different day, it could just as easily have been me hanging on to my phone on that porch swing when I should have been thinking of you.

These days I have nothing but time to think of you.

I sat within the white noise of the water until I felt suitable for human company again, and then started back. As I moved along the winding trail, and the roar behind me began to fade, I could hear you approaching—at least, that's what I thought—and I was so happy to think I would come around the bend and find you there, come to make peace, that I was nearly in tears.

And we *would* make peace, right there on a bed of leaves, I knew it.

But no, it wasn't you coming round the bend. It was a man who was no longer a man. He—it—was a walking corpse, its clothing tattered—its skin tattered, too. It moved quickly toward me, its jaw snapping at the air in preparation for snapping at me.

I turned.

I ran.

I tripped.

I fell.

And then a great weight pressed me to the ground.

And then I smelled a foul stench as teeth bit into one side of my neck.

And then I felt my blood pulse, first spurting away, then seeping away, then ...

Then ...

Then there was you.

You were looking down at me, I was looking up at you, with nothing above you but a ceiling of leaves, and I was never so happy to see you. But you were not happy. You were horrified, and fell back from me, as if what was revealed to you when I opened my eyes was a punch in the gut.

I'd never seen an expression like that from you, not even during our most difficult times. You stood up, backed away. And I—

I followed.

Or ... the thing I had become followed. I felt myself clumsily rising to my feet and begin moving toward you, staggering as I stepped, but my steps seemed not my own. I felt disassociated from my body as I moved, as if it was acting on its own, outside my control, and at the time, at first, I thought—surely this is because of a fall.

Had I fallen and hit my head? Did I have a concussion?

But though that might explain the way I felt, it wouldn't explain the way you were behaving.

You called my name, again and again, and I cried out yours, or tried to anyway, but it wouldn't come. All that left my lips—lips I could not feel—was a growl. No matter how much I willed the words to come, they wouldn't.

I wanted to tell you I loved you. I wanted to tell you I forgave you. I wanted to tell you to please, please forgive me. But most of all, I wanted to tell you—it's me, Sean, it me, why are you backing away, can't you see?

But I could tell you nothing. No matter how I tried to assert control over my body, I was nothing but a passenger. And as my fingers clenched and jaw snapped, and my hands reached toward you, and I saw my fingers—which were not grasping because of me—my pale, gray, grasping fingers ... I remembered.

I remembered how I had died.

I remembered that terrible, terrible bite.

And I knew in that moment the shell I now wore, the shell that had been made of me, that I could no longer control, wanted you to die as well.

I knew what would happen next, and I couldn't bear to live through what was going to happen next.

I tried to shout at you to run. I tried to tell you it was still me, but not me. I tried to force myself to turn away, to let you live. I could only watch, be a witness, as you continued retreating from me until you backed into a tree, and froze.

Run! I screamed where only I could hear. *Don't let me do this to you.*

But my thoughts could not reach you, so all you did was weep while repeating my name. And the face you made, crumpled in pain, a face I'd only seen before when we'd shared out pasts and made ourselves real to each other, oh, how I wanted to hold you then, to make it all right, as the weekend was meant to do, but it was beyond me now, and I could do nothing but scream, scream silently, as I kept moving.

You slid down the tree until you could drop no further, and grabbed the leaves by your sides as if they were a blanket you could pull over your head. And then I dropped on top of you, even as I struggled to pull away, struggled as I'd never struggled to do anything before, but could not stop myself, my body disobeying. But as my face neared yours, an instant before my teeth could rip into your cheek, you screamed and rolled to one side while kicking out, knocking me back.

I tumbled, grateful of how awkward death made me.

That's the first time I'd thought that word—death. But that's what I was—dead. Along with so many others we and the world had been trying to ignore.

By the time I staggered back to my feet, you'd vanished.

I knew where you had to have gone, back to the cabin where I hoped you'd immediately jump in the car and take off. But though I knew that, whatever I had become did not. The I that I am now had no idea where to find you, no way to deliver another to death, and so stumbled in circles before moving deeper into the woods. I couldn't figure out where I was going, or if I was going nowhere at all and just wandering aimlessly, but at least I wasn't heading toward you.

I was glad then. Glad I wouldn't have to live trapped inside this thing with the knowledge I'd caused your death. Glad you had gotten away and saved me from that.

But as I shuffled this way and that, happy in that strange gift the world was giving me as it was ending, I suddenly became filled with an intense fear.

What if, having escaped me, you *weren't* running away? What if you'd only gone off get a weapon, so you could kill the thing you thought I had become, not knowing I was still inside?

I couldn't let them happen. I didn't want you to live with the knowledge you'd killed me, even if you didn't know I was still me.

I had to get away quickly. But I couldn't. I was only a passenger trapped in a vehicle I could not steer. So I shuffled with agonizing slowness, and had to hope it was fast enough to escape you.

I had no idea where I was going, but I went anyway, leaving the familiar behind. The places Sean and I had walked as we tried in our own imperfect way to heal vanished, and what came after all looked the same to me. I was raised a city girl, so to me, woods were woods. Forest was forest. Trees were trees. I could have been walking in circles for all I knew of nature. And with no control, no agency, I had nothing to do but think. And I wondered ...

If I'd let Sean answer that call, or had answered his phone myself instead of locking it in the car, would we have been warned? Could we have avoided this? Was that why our friends had been calling, to tell us the mystery had been revealed, and what had been revealed was *this*?

I would never know.

Eventually—and I lose track of how long that eventually is—I hear a rustle in the leaves, and want to turn my head to the source of the sound, but cannot. I—or the body I wear—does not care that something, maybe even someone based on the volume, is nearby. Does not fear. Does not pray like I do the noise comes from anything, anyone, but Sean.

Does nothing but want.

When my head tilts and the maker of that sound comes into view, I see it is another walking corpse, as horrific to me in aspect as I must have seemed to Sean. Wet blood is smeared across his face, which means he has succeeded in doing to someone what I had been saved from doing. I flinch at the sight, but it is a flinch only in my mind, for the walking corpse I inhabit neither cares nor registers it. The two of us come together as if pulled by gravity, and stumble off.

As we shamble on through no choice of our own, with him coming into view from time to time depending on random twists of my neck, I realize—

I am alone. But I am not alone.

We are each alone together.

For he must surely now be nothing more than a passenger, too.

I wonder who the hidden rider is beside me. I see no sign anyone is in there whenever our eyes unintentionally meet—but I know he must be.

Was he out camping the day everything went wrong for him? Or did he, already gone, wander in from the city?

Does that blood mean he killed his partner? Or his child? Or was it only a stranger?

Only.

Could he have been the one who killed *me*? If so, I do not blame him. I wish I could tell him that.

Is he screaming inside? Or is he surrendered? One more thing I will never know.

From now on, I never will know—or be known. For the only one who ever truly knew me is lost to me now.

We move on, weaving together and apart, remaining bound together for no reason I can discern, other than that like calls to like, the way those nightly owls I would hear back in more hopeful times did, back when I still thought Sean and I had a chance. We move on, prisoners in straightjackets of rotting flesh, until I see a flash of orange ahead.

A hunter, his gun tucked under one arm, its barrel pointing skyward.

We see him before he sees us.

He starts to turn at the sound of our approach, but not in time. He manages to spin and get off one shot, which passes through my arm and out the other side. I feel no pain. I think I would have preferred to feel pain. I think I would like to remember what it was like to be fully alive.

He does not get a chance to fire a second.

Together, my companion and I do to this man what I was spared by chance from doing to Sean. I try to close my eyes to avoid what must come next, but cannot, and so am forced to watch.

I'm not sure how my new companion had attacked, but as for me, I bite through the poor man's clothing, bite into his stomach, chew organs I can't identify. I taste nothing, and in that instance at least I am glad I have no connection with this body I now wear, the body I used to be.

But the sense of sound is still mine, and so I can hear the screaming. I am grateful when it stops, even though it stops long before we are done.

Our feasting finally over, we rise, turning from the body, and leave it behind, unmourned by any but his murderers. I wonder how long it will be before he—soon to be it—rises as well.

How long was it, I wonder, before Sean stumbled upon me, before I woke to whatever this is? Hours? Days? I don't know. I wish my sleep had been longer.

I wish I was still sleeping now.

Because then what came next could have been a dream, instead of what I have to live with until ...

Until what?

Until I rot?

Or until I'm lucky enough that someone takes me out for good?

But this is not a dream. And so I've had to watch as two became four became a dozen became a horde.

As we assembled, I would try to look in their eyes—as I'd tried from the first moment I encountered one of my kind—to tell if anyone was home. But I had no control over my gaze, and we—whatever we were— rarely bothered looking at each other. I could not choose to turn my head from whatever it is my body desired. And so it was only chance that gave me glimpses from which I sought clues to build lives. The eyes of the others were blank, as blank as my own, I imagined, but still, I used what I saw to make an imaginary history in place of the memories which we trapped souls could never share.

This one an artist. That one a banker. And those other two, who likely had never met, I pretended had been lovers.

What else was I to do with my time? How else could I stay sane?

If sane is what I was even staying ...

Eventually, we broke from the forest into the nearby town, and it was a relief at first to see something other than trees, until we killed what survivors remained from those who had been kind to us when Sean and I first arrived and bought the supplies we'd need to keep us through the long weekend. A weekend which would now never end.

And so I wished I was back in the forest again, far from the new world that had been made and was being destroyed. But if that is to be my future, it will not be up to me.

Occasionally, one of our group would die at the hands of one of the living hopelessly defending herself before we devoured her, and I would wish it were me. I would wish this all were over.

And then, one day, this day—it almost is.

As I stumble along railroad tracks at the back of the pack—wondering as we do so if my body somehow knows where those tracks will lead (for I do not)—the head of the corpse beside me explodes, and what remains drops and falls still. I—the me that still is—makes no movement which shows curiosity or fear. I do not turn to see the source of the shot behind me or shamble more quickly away from where the next might come. If I were now my old self, I would have already sought safety by tossing myself down the ravine which parallels the tracks. But I did not. I do not. I cannot. I keep moving forward as others beside me fall and I wonder—frantically at first—whether I will be next.

And then I find I no longer care what happens next.

Which is when a hand slaps against my back, and I am spun around, and I see it is Sean, with a rifle in his hands. Sean, who has never held a gun. None of my kind turn to see what we are doing as he waves it before him in a circle. His clothes are filthy, for he, too, is wearing what he was when we last saw each other.

Before I can futilely attempt to shout at him to run from the inevitable, he pushes me off the tracks, and into that ravine, and I tumble, growling instead of calling his name, grasping at the spinning air between us, snapping my teeth at nothingness. I roll and flail and finally stop on my back, and see him sliding down toward me, with an expression I cannot read.

It seems blank, which puzzles me at first, because he has always been the more animated one of us. There is no love, no hate, no anger, no fear ... no recognition. As he gets closer, I see it isn't a blank expression after all, but one of determination. To do what, I cannot tell. But the gun which above was pointed at the others, is now pointed toward me, and that tells me enough. The body I wear, though, pays no mind, does not even seem to recognize the threat, and struggling to rise, is hungry for him in a way I never was.

What do you see in me, Sean? I wonder, and laugh maniacally, not in a way you can hear it, because it is a question I've often asked before.

But you couldn't know to listen anyway, even if I could make myself heard, because you don't know I'm still here, you don't know, how could you know, how could you even imagine it? You're going to kill me, and not know you killed me, because you think I'm already dead.

Why did you have to follow? You could have left my fate in the hands of another. I had been so glad you wouldn't be the one to kill me. It was the one thing I hung on to in the midst of all the horror. I didn't want you to have to live with this, and you wouldn't have to live with this. But, no ... you had to decide you don't want me to live like this either.

And now, as I rise up even as I tell myself to stay, and begin to close the distance between us, your gun rises as well. Your finger wraps around the trigger. And as one shuffling step is followed by another, I see your expression of determination tremble, turn to one of hesitation. That finger quivers as you let me grow closer, too close.

Run! I shout to myself within the thing which wears my frame.

Run! I shout again as tears fall from your eyes and the rifle falls by your side and you say my name as if that will stop me.

Run! I shout for the final time—with no frantic motions saving you the way they did the last time we were this close—as I bite into your neck.

Not a love bite like in the old days, but one which rips out your flesh so that blood spatters against my face.

No matter how much I want to ... I can't even cry.

Oh, Sean! You love me enough to want to kill me, and also love me enough *not* to kill me. And you have made a choice. But I don't get to choose.

I drop to my knees beside you, tearing at your flesh, glad we're in a ravine by the side of the tracks rather than on the tracks themselves, because it means we can't be seen, and I don't want us to be seen. I don't want us to attract the attention of the others. We are alone, which is as it should be. It's just the two of us now, and no one else is here by my side to do what I am doing. Or what the flesh suit I am wearing is doing. It would be wrong.

I love you, Sean.

I love you, and I guess ... I guess ... that is why I had to be the one to kill you.

If it wasn't me, it would have been someone else, right? Of course it would, as such a fate is inevitable now. So it had to be me. I wouldn't have been able to live with myself had it been another.

Well ... I can't live with myself now. But I had no choices. I have no choices. But at least now I know how this all ends. Now I know ...

No.

I step back from you body.

Wait.

I get one final glimpse of you, your belly—where I had once so often rested my head—broken and bloodied—and turn away.

Wait!

But I am unable to wait, to stay for what I now realize will happen next—the moment you rise and join me again. How could I have been so foolish not to understand this?

I want to stay to see it happen, but I do not. I cannot.

I am but a passenger.

I crawl back up to the tracks and walk on toward where the horde has vanished, not knowing if what should happen next actually does happens next. I care terribly, though this shell which carries me does not.

Perhaps you are on your feet already, joining us, a prisoner in your body as I am in mine, realizing that because you are somehow still here, I must be still here. You now know that I live. I live!

And you live, too.

We are together. And just like we wanted.

No more staring into screens. No longer lost in our jobs. The world which once came between us has faded away. I guess our weekend getaway worked after all, Sean, huh?

I can't turn my head to see if you are there behind me, but I hope that you are. I hope someday you will be beside me, and I will catch a glimpse of you, perhaps as we both bend to feed.

We are nothing more than passengers now. But as long as we are passengers together, that's all that matters.

And as I shamble forward, and imagine you shambling closer to me, I again ask myself the question I have always asked myself ...

Are you happy, Mo?

And I answer:

I have never been happier.

STIRRINGS

David C. Kopaska-Merkel

By day we're stacked like wood where beetles dwell,
At dusk we're roused to work if we still can,
We dig the beetle larvae from our flesh,
Do what we're told to do; our will is gone.
I stagger through the gelid nightmare hours,
A clumsy robot just this side of death,
A cog of limited utility,
But one that needs no fuel, repair, or rest.

I clutch at tatters in my rotten brain,
They're fragments of the life that once was mine,
A woman in a dress I think was blue,
My mother, lover, daughter? I don't know.
A scream is rising to my shuttered lips.
I fumble at the twine that holds it in.

QUEEN OF HEARTS
S.E. Lindberg

"Does this coffee smell right, Lady?" Retired detective Samwell Edison held out the mug before the Labrador retriever's head gracing his lap. His other hand patted his heart to ensure it still beat. Too bad the soft pajama T-shirt that doubled as daywear did not bestow any superhero powers or heal his aging.

Ironically, the *City Tribune* had just nicknamed him 'Heart Attack Sammy' since the legendary gangster Al Cappo suffered cardiac arrest as Samwell captured him. Few knew that the detective suffered a similar condition. That case closed his career. Damned doctors had prescribed a caffeine-free diet years ago, but Samwell didn't try it until after he saw his nemesis collapse.

This decaf smelled like car exhaust. Samwell coughed as he imbibed. The Cap-faux-ccino brand came highly recommended but tasted like a soup of cigarette butts.

"Come on, Lady, convince me this isn't coffin varnish? You must smell the chemicals used to suck out the caffeine."

The sniffer dog assessed the drink, whimpered, then put her head down.

"Nothing?" Samwell asked. Lady once alerted the location of narcotics by scratching the ground; not doing so indicated the target was nontoxic. "Huh, this is safe?" Samwell glowered. "Well, I'm not drinking anymore."

From the kitchen, a wolf-howling ringtone resonated from his smart phone. It was a standard, and obsolete, phone issued from Police Head Quarters—a retirement gift from the Chief. The relic recharged via three daisy-chained adapters, coiled in a heap. To reach the device, Samwell would have to shift Lady's head from his lap. "Move over, now. We still need to pay the rent. My pension will barely pay for air conditioning, and that could be our first client calling." Lady sprawled onto the couch cushions, releasing Samwell. She shed a lot, but the cream-colored linen hid it well.

"Huh. Not even a real call. Just a notification. Cripes, it's the emergency broadcast for the whole district. Figured they would get me off that list already."

The phone read: "ALERT. Military Law imposed over the French Quarter. Rabid dogs infect the East Ward. All units report."

"Oh, I get it. The Station is messing with me. Real funny. Well, I ain't responding to that." Samwell tossed the phone back onto the counter. "I could go for an espresso right now." The declaration drew a raised eye from the dog.

"Easy, Lady. I know my body is showing wear. Dammit, Chief said I'm too old to work a real shift. Pat on the back for ol' Sammy, here's a Key to the City for taking down Al Cappo's drug-trafficking ring. Al goes down with a broken heart, and half his South River Gang minions are in jail. And just in time, they said to me, since I'm getting' geriatric. Go home, they said. Want to stay busy? Become a PI. Want to keep health insurance? Stop drinking coffee."

He petted the dog to calm down. "A few weeks off the Force, and I already feel imprisoned."

The phone howled again.

"Cripes." Samwell shuffled into the kitchen.

A silhouette of a cat and dog flashed on the screen beside the answer/ignore button.

"Oh, Lady. It's your Vet's office calling. Doctor Katz likes you a bunch for saving her from Al Cappo." Marge Katz was an unmarried debutante. She was smart, petite, and full of spark. Her mane of natural hair was the real stuff, a blonde roast with wisps of creamy whiteness—not bleached, nor neon-streaked, as was the fad now amongst hipsters. Her brother ran a café in the French Quarter near port; he served great eggs there.

Samwell accepted the call and unleashed a deep showman's voice. "Samwell Edison here. Private Investigator."

Lady lifted an ear to eavesdrop, as if she could hear better from across the room than Samwell could up close.

A soft-spoken female spoke, "This is Kelly from Dr. Katz's office. Is this Lady's guardian?"

"Yes. No worries, she is recovering fine. Removed the cone-of-shame a day ago." The dog had sustained cuts when they confronted Al Cappo and his men at Marge's Katz's clinic. Lady wore a protective collar for twelve days.

"Sir, did you give her heartworm pill recently?"

"As scheduled," Samwell lied. He knew enough about drugs not to trust pharmaceuticals blindly. He hadn't even taken his own calcium-blocker meds today, nor his cholesterol and blood-pressure pills. Samwell had too many tablets to account for.

"Well, sir, you didn't log that into our system," Kelly explained.

"Ah, crap. You mean that new phone App? Allow me some time to figure that out."

"So, no odd behavior?" The receptionist paused, choking up on some emotion. She continued, "Bleeding from the eyes?"

"Cripes, no. What kinda questioning is this?"

"Just doing due diligence, sir. We are in crisis mode right now. Dr. Katz asked me to call you specifically."

Samwell replied, "Listen Honey, you're going to have to put the Doc' on the phone. I don't like talking to middle men ...women, whatever."

The receptionist started to cry.

"Hey, Miss Kelly, no need to freak out. I'm not yelling at you. Just get the Doc' online. Hello?"

She sniveled. "I am trying. It's just that… they are all swaying. Staring at me."

"What the heck? Don't put me on hold."

Jazz Muzak suddenly poured out of the speaker and hit Samwell like a pulsating, cold shower. He sighed while pacing, Lady decided it worth standing on all fours. She heeled beside Samwell in the kitchen to eavesdrop.

"Samwell Edison?" Marge Katz labored to breathe. "Detective?"

Her voice made his ears tingle. Even if distressed, her voice aroused him. Samwell spoke fast, "Doc' Katz, I'm retired now. You know you can call me Sammy. What the hell is going on? Your receptionist was freaking out."

Marge panted. "I am not sure who to turn to. The authorities won't help. They wouldn't understand my condition."

"Hold on Marge. What are you talkin' about? You in some kinda trouble?" Samwell was ready to save her from any enemy, even if he was still in his pajamas. "Is some remnant of the South River Gang after you?"

"No. It's a disease. A mutant form of *Dirofilaria immitis*. The police are quarantining the entire French Quarter, Sammy. They won't let me out of my building, and I'm not sure if I should stay either."

"Hey, that's a lot to take in. Slow down." *Guess that alert wasn't a joke.*

"Can I trust you to help me in confidence, Sammy? Please, come."

Samwell's cholesterol plaque melted. "Of course."

Click.

He threw a button-down over his T-Shirt. "Lady, hired or not, we got a woman to save. Let's go." As he rushed to dress, his subconscious mind digested the news. Samwell decided to medicate Lady. "Given the circumstances, you better take this pill, right now." She spat out the heartworm capsule and looked up defiantly. "Look, I don't trust voodoo prescriptions either, but Dr. Katz is the last dame to take me seriously. She healed you up nicely after the Al Cappo takedown. If it wasn't for her brave tip, we wouldn't have knabbed him as he picked up his dog. She is a trustworthy gal, and… she hasn't broken my heart yet."

Lady relented when peanut butter slathered the pill. Samwell updated the App, lest Kelly berate him again. Then the PI grabbed his Smith & Wesson .38 Special, the Key to the City, and his smart phone. He headed out with his partner.

* * * *

Samwell hummed inharmoniously, rocking his head while tapping the steering wheel and mumbling: "It don't mean a thing… ba… da… bada… if you ain't got that swing…"

He headed south in his retro-styled, black Chevy HHR on an empty lane. Blue emergency lights decorated the median of Route A40, evenly apart. Cars packed the northbound lanes. Two cruisers beside orange-striped barricades stopped him on the outskirts of the French Quarter. An overcast sky covered the downtown port, like usual. It would rain soon. It always rained. Samwell pulled up to the makeshift waypoint, rolling his window down. "Damn, you're just a cadet, kid." He flashed his emeritus badge. "Where's your Sergeant?"

The green-as-a-fresh-bean cadet stepped to the window. "Pull over, sir."

Samwell Edison parked his car and stayed seated. In front of him, a crowd of dogs stood in portable kennels.

"Show us your paperwork."

The old detective lifted his lanyard, showed the Key to the City.

"Impressive, but I know you are, Heart Attack Sammy. I need to see her papers."

"Oh. I just got an App for that." Samwell pulled up his phone, clicked on the button for Katz's Veterinary Clinic. Lady's records opened, and he handed the phone over.

"Your dog's shot and pill schedules are up to date." The cadet's own phone buzzed. After inspection he said, "Sergeant just gave me your clearance, but you'll have to park the car here. Streets are all set for outbound right now, all the tourists evacuating. If you want in, you are not taking your car."

Sammy exited the HHR. His old compatriot Sergeant Willis greeted him, sipping coffee while eating a beignet. Confectionary powder speckled his mustache.

The Sergeant asked, "Why are you here? You need to stay away." He indicated the cages. The dogs stood on their hind legs, remarkably keeping their balance as their heads looked skywards. Each had one black eye with necks frilled with red, swollen buboes—some of which popped and leaked blood.

"Cripes, they look like zombie-clowns!" A helicopter flew overhead. Over the rooftops of the French Quarter, toward the river, streams of smoke issued from large fires. "What'd you guys do? I'm gone two weeks, and my ol' playground is a military zone?"

"Jeez, Sammy, you got out just in time. Sure, you caught a real dirty one. Al Cappo is dead, and his gang locked up in the East Ward. Thanks to you, everyone is drinking 'Al Cappuccino's personal inventory of coffee confiscated after your raids. But we've got bigger problems now, Sammy. You and Lady are not needed for this."

"Then what do ya need, Sarge'? Another beignet?"

Sergeant Willis gulped down the pastry and brushed off the powdered sugar from his hands. "An army of doctors. And a vaccine or something. Otherwise, a larger crematorium." Sergeant Willis's neck and face look puffy. He stood awkwardly, with his feet close together so that he seemed top heavy.

Stress must be taking a toll. Perhaps he needed more coffee to soften up those pastries? Samwell replied, "What's the cause?"

"Heartworm. It's only contagious to other dogs who haven't had their pills, it seems. We are still working on details. There are too many un-knowns, so we had to quarantine. Why are you headed south? Are you working this case?"

Samwell did not have to explain himself to Sarge anymore. Anyway, Marge had asked him to be hush about meeting her. He obscured his mis-sion. "Headed to my afternoon snack at Fat Jacks." This was mostly true. Jack was Marge's brother and his café only nine blocks from her office. Sergeant Willis glared, since he was not that naïve. Samwell continued: "Gotta check on my buddy. You're making me walk the last mile?"

"At least you can go through. Hey, take these."

Samwell sighed. "Evidence bags?"

"You can say they are for Lady's poop."

"I can bring 'em back to you, Sarge. You know, to maintain the chain of evidence."

"They're yours to keep," Sergeant Willis said. "More importantly, take this." He handed an emergency-yellow, plastic poncho. "It'll designate you as a first responder. Without it, you'll be rounded up."

* * * *

The clouds rained and flickered from within. Thunder grumbled from somewhere. Yellow-coated Sammy and yellow-furred Lady strode the sidewalks toward Fat Jacks. All the buildings were less than three stories tall, decked with floral-patterned, cast-iron balconies. Pastel lemon, blue-berry, and peach paint covered the brick facades.

The sky offered a dreary sunset. Long shadows cast from neon bar signs beside historic gas lights; clearly, the city didn't know if it was evolving or stuck in the past. The crime fighting duo stepped in and around puddles, as well as the homeless with their dogs curled up beside them. Phil was at his usual sleeping spot under an awning on St. Paul Street, garbed in fatigues which he did not earn in battle—but he had received from a soldier who did. Sammy instinctively reached into his pocket to throw a dog treat toward Molly, but he halted abruptly. Molly, Phil's scrawny mutt, stood to attention. She swayed, propped on two legs. Her head rolled like a bobble-head doll, with swollen eyes. Red buboes encircled her neck. *Jeez, she was a goner.* Too bad. Phil deserved better. He was a good informant, one of several locals who tipped Sammy off about Al Cappo's drug trafficking through the port's coffee bean distribution.

Pungent clouds of smoke hovered near ground. It smelled of a curious mix of burnt coffee and garbage. Lady dealt with the stench like a professional. She didn't seem too concerned yet.

The door chimed as Lady entered Fat Jacks with Samwell. Jack was only one hundred pounds, skinny as a rail. His face looked his age with a grubby white bearded. He only had two uniforms. Each had a unique coffee-stain. Today he sported the one with a right-shoulder-spot.

A set of three dragon-tattooed, college-aged women spilled away from the bar. They had colored hair with streaks of fluorescent orange and cyan. The gals were slow to wake from last night's endeavors, had stumbled in from the adjacent hotel, and grabbed some grub. They were aware enough of the current situation to skitter around Lady. Dogs were getting rabid out there. They should have left town yesterday.

"Heart Attack Sammy? Come in."

"Lady scared off your customers," Samwell snarked. "She tracks down Al Cappo, and instead of being praised, folks fear her."

Jack grumbled back, "Oh, not all my clients can be heroes. And most dogs aren't healthy now."

"True. But Lady isn't diseased. Your sister prescribed her ketchup and eggs. Can you set her up?"

"Marge thinks my restaurant is a pharmacy. Helps me get customers," Jack said. He cracked two eggs over the griddle behind the counter. Then his hands flashed like he worked *teppanyaki* on a Japanese grill. Despite the hot surface, a butcher's knife mixed the eggs homogenously within seconds, and then folded them to perfection. Jack cooked everything—pancakes, hamburgers, eggs, steak sandwiches, you name it—with that knife which served as a spatula, cutter, and ladle. Watching him work magic on the griddle was a key reason to order food here. The cook collected his thoughts. "You have bags under your eyes big enough to hold my laundry.

I know what you need: an 'Al Cappuccino'." Before Samwell could stop him, Jack offered a mug topped with whipped cream. Something was odd about the lathered milk. It popped and undulated as if energized.

Samwell declined. "No need to honor that bastard."

"It's sourced from Al Cappo's warehouse. After the cops seized all the contraband, they distributed the abundance of coffee beans to all the restaurants here in the Quarter. It's good stuff. Columbian," Jack explained.

"Can't accept it, anyway. Not good for my heart."

"Ha," Jack said. "I have an IED for you folk now. Apparently, that's code after Al Cappo's fall."

Samwell noticed the automatic external defibrillator newly mounted near the fire extinguisher. "You mean AED, Jack. IED's are 'improvised explosive devices.' That first vowel is important."

"Whatever, Sammy, you know what it is. Truth be told, I hate coffee. Anyways, if you stay here, you may not live long enough to care. Cap-faux-ccino, instead?"

Sammy gathered his resolve, answering sarcasm with resigned affect. "Yes."

"Ok, cup 'o Faux coming up." Jack raised an eyebrow in disbelief. "Things haven't been the same since you've been off the beat."

"Cripes, Jack, it's only been a few weeks. I can see you are worried though. Why the glum face?"

"It's my sister."

"Marge? She's a real hero."

"A nerdy recluse too. She's not a people person, but she should be responding to my texts during this crisis. And I'm stuck here. I must watch the store because of looters. Not sure if I want to stray out there anyway. I want to know if Marge is ok. She has to be bombarded with sick dogs."

"Well, you are in luck, Jack. Her office phoned me this morning. I talked to her. I'm taking Lady to an appointment, just stopping on my way through. I'm sure she's fine," Samwell fibbed, partly to shore up his own denial. Both men worried equally.

Lady ate her eggs in a single gulp. Samwell downed his Faux with displeasure. As they left, a wolf-howl called from his pocket. He gulped as he read the police notice: "ALERT. Disease now expressed in people. Wear Personal Protective Equipment."

"Jack, lock the door. It's getting even more dangerous out there. I'm going to get Marge."

The cook raised his trusty butcher knife in a salute.

* * * *

Samwell and Lady walked eastward on Market Place, with the touristy boutiques to their left and the riverbank to their right. Full lockdown was in effect. The streets resonated an eerie white-noise from rain pattering rooftops and pavement; no street musicians pounded drums, nor did live jazz spill out from every café, bistro, and bar. Owners had shuttered the doors usually left open year-round to allow tourist traffic. Typically, cinnamon and sugar scents masked the garbage, but now the latter saturated the air. Crushed beans and maggot-like worms littered the streets and puddles. Lady was scratching all over the sidewalk.

"I got it, Lady. You don't need to signal the entire walk." He tugged her leash.

They reached the river. No sailboats or shipping vessels perturbed the water. A few barges docked along wharfs, apparently abandoned. Historically, coffee sacks would break when mishandled. Beans, roasted and green, would spill and then boots and forklifts smashed them. Plumes of powder would waft across the streets. Other times, one could smell beer and piss. That was the city for you: beauty and horror mixed up and displayed simultaneously.

Lady sniffed the air, the scratched the ground a bit. She wasn't liking the current recipe.

"What are you gettin' at, partner?" Samwell asked. "No, we can't head over there now. Gotta go to Marge's." He pulled on the leash. "I know, something ain't smelling right again." He breathed deep through his nose. He savored the aroma, even if was smoky. Lady nudged him. "Don't judge me. I'm allowed to breathe. Not like I can get much caffeine from it."

Samwell surveyed the riverscape for the source. Silhouettes of three burning hills blended into the river's edge. Packs of stray dogs roamed atop. Red and blue emergency lights flashed, illuminating a dozen men in HAZMAT suits. One donned a flamethrower that belched fire.

"What in tarnation?" Samwell watched for a moment, intrigued. The men were shifting strangely. Smoke obscured the scene. Some figures suddenly disappeared. Did one jump into the fire? Did the flamethrower just fry several dogs? He shook his head. That couldn't be happening.

Samwell's phone howled. The screen read: "ALERT. East Ward Jail overrun. South River Gang prisoners are infected and have escaped."

"Let's find the Doc' and get out of here."

Smoke drifted into the city streets, enshrouding the storefronts. They avoided dozens of stationary zombie dogs. Finally, they made it to where Burgundy Street intersected Rue Saint Dominique. Marge's Veterinary Clinic sat near the corner. Fence rails of historic, cast-iron *fleur de lis* ornamented the first-floor columns and upper balcony.

They were welcomed by jazz playing on speakers: "Puttin' On the Ritz" by Irving Berlins. Samwell started singing off-key: "If you're blue, and you don't know where to go to, why don't you go where... Harlem flits ...."

Kelly stood behind the counter, her nametag still clinging by one pin. Her head rested on her left shoulder. The receptionist was a goner. A cup of coffee at her desk had tipped over. Either her cream had curdled, or maggot-like crawlers soaked in the spill. Three master-less dogs, a German shepherd, chihuahua, and a poodle, rocked with Kelly to the Muzak. *How long until they collapsed?*

Samwell and Lady avoided the sick attendant and patients to survey the joint. Each examination room was clear. Lady found Marge in the back room, squirreled away in a kennel.

"Hey, Marge. Who locked you in there?"

"Oh, Sammy!" Marge Katz turned to greet him. She stood in her lab coat with just an inch clearance in the cage. *Damn, she had nice hair*. Her eyes showed her true sadness. She looked down as if a guilty kid. "I did."

"Were you trying to protect yourself from the sick?" Sammy shook the door to jar it open, to no avail. "What the hell is going on, Doc'? Where is the key?"

Marge held her hands over her heart. "Had to lock myself in. To protect others." She became silent as he stared from the other side of the cage. She suddenly extended her hand through the bars, grabbed his lapels, then brought him close. She kissed Samwell, lips closed.

"What was that for?" Sammy pulled back slightly.

She kissed again. Sammy soaked in the moment. Then, her tongue penetrated his mouth. It was more pointed, and cold, than he expected. He retreated to have a look, but her tongue recoiled into her mouth.

Lady wedged herself between them and the kennel grate, scratching the ground and growling.

Sammy broke Marge's hold. "You need to come clean."

She got glazy eyed. Her eyes twitched rapidly, as if she was negotiating some conversation in her head. She stared unfocused, through Samwell, and whispered, "Whatever I do, don't let her... me... out." Marge's voice croaked. "And do *not* kiss me again... you can't..."

Samwell reached through the pen to slap her. "Snap out of it." Marge rolled her head back cackling. He continued, "Explain yourself. Why did you call me here, if not to save you?"

The doctor shuffled to the far side of the cage, two yards from Sammy and Lady.

"I thought you may be able to help. But it's too late." Marge shivered. "You know that I cared for Al Cappo's dogs. They came down with a type of parasitic infection, which is how I learned about it. It's how I contracted it."

"What craziness are you talkin' about?"

"I didn't figure this out until my symptoms expressed today. Al Cappo was smuggling more than just drugs. He bootlegged bioweapons too. The coffee beans were not for covering up cocaine—they were infected with a strange parasite. I had called him in to discuss the prognosis of his dogs. I shouldn't have confronted him."

"But you did the right thing, Marge. You involved the police too. You enabled us to capture him here!"

"Well, I still failed. Before you and the SWAT team arrived, I told Al Cappo what I knew about the parasite. About how it was a dangerous, socialized version. How it may be contagious even to humans. He didn't care. He just forced himself on me. He kissed me. Long and hard." She paused to reflect. "I didn't fight back. Guess I deserve my fate."

Samwell was suspicious. Was she in on the criminal activity with Al Cappo somehow? Guilty? "Were you more than his State-side vet?"

Marge cried and shook her head 'no.'

"Then, what does Al Cappo's crimes have to do with you? Let me get you out of there."

"He… the She inside him… transferred into me with that kiss." Marge's chest heaved. "Her presence came on strong the past day. I thought I was crazy. I didn't know whom to tell. Then the police quarantined the whole French Quarter. I wish you could save me now." She swooned, collapsing in the corner.

Sammy sobbed, bent to her level, trying to open the door. He couldn't open it or reach her. "Don't leave me, Marge. Hang in there."

On her back, she spasmed and murmured, "It's not me anymore…it's *her*. She controls me." Marge's eyes rolled back, body shaking. "It is too late."

Samwell shook the cage. "Marge!"

Eventually the seizure passed, the possessed doctor sat upright. She frowned deliriously as blood leaked out of her nose to roll over plush lips. "Al Cappo was just doing the queen's bidding. He had a plantation in Columbia where he experimented and got infected. His entire crop got infected by her larvae."

"We all thought the coffee was used to disguise his shipments." Samwell was still processing the situation.

"A maternal entity controls all the offspring. She was inside Al Cappo, feeding on and controlling his body. She implanted her eggs into the beans. Her brood is everywhere… and she has been calling its babies to her. The colony of heartworms are coming to us."

Outside, police sirens echoed. *What is going on out there?* Sammy thought. Lady heeled and growled. "Why are you telling me this?"

Marge spoke, her tone a deeper octave than prior. "You deserve special attention. Once Al Cappo sensed his entrapment, the queen left him. That's why his heart failed. He died right here as you and the police entered. The city donated Al Cappo's inventory of beans to all the restaurants in the Quarter. Roasting hatched her larvae. Every Al Cappuccino consumed puts a person at risk of infection."

Cripes, the beans were weaponized. Everyone is drinking those—except me and Jack. Guess my heart condition has a benefit.

Marge continued. "I am the queen's host now. Al Cappo's kiss transferred her into me. You must end me, since the queen, is inside me. Wrapped around my heart." Blood rimmed her eyes as she held onto the cage for support. "She made me try and kiss you. She senses a trap again. She controls me, which is why I locked myself in. You must shoot me!"

"I couldn't do that to you." Samwell held out his .38 Special, his finger trembling. He took two steps back.

Marge's head snapped back.

Her ribs cracked suddenly, her shirt tore open.

Blood doused Samwell's yellow poncho.

Marge's ruined body lay inside the kennel, emptying of blood.

The queen emerged from the fractured chest, stretching vertically, her three-pronged, pharyngeal maw begging for a kiss. At three-feet tall, the mother worm appeared as a skein of thin, knotted tubes, skinny as a snake. The queen sensed the location of Samwell, and directed her attention to a fresh heart outside the cage.

Dear Marge, what the hell killed you? My heart is no better than Al Cappo's. He held his chest with his free hand.

Through the kennel, the entity lashed out, whipping about Samwell's right arm, pinning his fingers and preventing him from shooting his revolver.

The queen's white form stretched from the cage as Samwell stumbled backward toward the reception area.

Lady bit into the distal end of the heartworm. The dog back-peddled to pull the mass away from Samwell's face.

The zombified German shepherd, chihuahua, and poodle manning the entry snapped from their idle state and hobbled to aid their master. They growled with blood-filled throats as they clustered atop their prey. Kelly reached forward to bearhug the detective; the receptionist put her fingers into his mouth, trying to draw it open.

Samwell dropped his hips, rolled out the exit. The bunch of zombie-dogs-worms-and-humans rolled with him. The assembly shot onto a congested Burgundy Street, splashing in a puddle. His gun was lost in the chaos.

The pleasant Muzak of the clinic diminished under the chaotic din of helicopters, sirens, and a screaming herd of sick animals. Sergeant Willis, frothing with saliva thickened by powdered sugar, fought side-by-side with the possessed South River Gang members. Homeless Phil and his dog Molly joined in. The Port Authority donning HAZMAT suits, respirators, and flamethrowers surrounded Marge's clinic. City cops joined with riot-gear to battle the infested mob. Giant clear shields pounded the doomed into groups, while flamethrowers set them afire. Rain sizzled against the burning masses.

The queen was desperate for a host; her skin could not handle the exposure to heat, rain, and air. Her parasites, and their host bodies, received a final order: *protect your queen*. Until she found a heart she would surround herself with her offspring—they could sacrifice themselves to buy time. The zombies responded, even as the police battered them. Bodies shook. Worms shot out of their fleshy shells, exploding bloody fragments as they all became exposed. Countless minions flagellated their way to join with one another, seeking their mother, wrapping and bundling into thicker and thicker ropes.

Each drop of rain turned to steam as it ate away at raw parasite flesh. The queen's minions wrapped about her thin body. Reinforced, she went after Samwell. Lady bit into her form and pulled oppositely.

Spotlights from helicopters highlighted them. The duo tugged and stretched the queen into a tug-of-war. Lady's legs bled a new; her mouth too, where a tooth was pulled out.

"Hey, that's Heart Attack Sammy!" a cadet yelled.

Samwell's heart panged like a hammer on anvil. "Back, everyone!"

Police lights strobed. The muddle appeared a as drugged-crazed disco, though the dance was to the death and the floor a bloody mess. Armed authorities were too afraid to shoot their infected friend. The throng collectively decided to root for their heroes, hoping Samwell and his dog could break free without aid. Shouts called out, cheering: "Sammy! Sammy!"

Detective Edison drew away from the crowds. His heart beat like a broken clock. *The queen could have it,* he snickered. He opened his shirt, exposed his chest. His heart would be a trap. He laid down, closed his eyes... *she can die in me...*

The queen took the bait. She latched her mouth onto Samwell's chest. Started to burrow...

"IED coming!" Jack's voice penetrated the skirmish, clambering atop the dead as a berserker, the defibrillator strapped over his shoulder. "IED!"

Everyone scattered, except Lady who wrestled with the ropey queen.

Jack brandished his butcher blades. He began dicing the mass atop Samwell, slicing twice as fast as any worm could lunge. A mound of writhing, white carcasses suffered his secretive martial arts.

Then the queen's body was exposed, though her head was just immersed into Samwell's clammy breast—most of her was vulnerable. Samwell's heart was not beating, so the fatigued worm strained to determine where to go.

Jack removed the foil from the AED electrodes, placed one on the right breast—keeping the queen locked into to flesh; the other went on Samwell's left side. A robotic voice spoke from the device: "Continue CPR as the sensors check…," Jack pressed a button, "… Manual override accepted. Delivering shock…"

Zap!

Samwell's back bent. The jolt straightened the queen's serpentine form into a rigid rod; then it relaxed. Still the parasite's mouth remained embedded, and Sam's heart failed to beat.

Jack charged again, overriding the AED console, and forced another shock.

Zap!

The queen shot out of Samwell's body. Lady jumped on the thrashing form, chewing until the giant parasite severed into segments. Sundered tendrils squiggled uncontrollably. The Labrador retriever gnawed the thing to pieces.

A pasty white Samwell remained quiet.

Jack frantically prepared the AED again. Zap!

Samwell inhaled, curling forward, hyperventilating.

Lady licked his cheeks as he caught his breath.

A camera flash illuminated the scene. The exhausted heroes thought it was just lightning, not a *City Tribune* photographer's camera. After publication, all would see the prized snapshot capturing the end of the Burgundy Street melee.

* * * *

Samwell and a collared Lady sat at Fat Jacks bar. A young officer was with them too—he looked even greener than he had yesterday morning at the A40 barricade.

Sammy said to the cadet hunched over beside him, staring inches away from his smart phone's news feed. "What are you reading, kid?"

The young officer craned his neck further, then showed his screen. "See this? *City Tribune* got a shot of all of you."

Jack and Samwell gathered around the snapshot. Samwell sat in mud, freshly resuscitated. Lady's blood-soaked legs reflected in the puddles. Jack stood with a ruined uniform. Before them all, was the deceased queen—an intricate briar patch of white, fleshy fibrils.

"Not quite the photo to hang in a restaurant," Jack said. "We'll have to pose for another."

Outside, a barrage of trumpets and trombones blared. Musicians warmed up in the street. It was just 9:00AM, two days after the incident, but the public was ready to celebrate. The parade would start around the corner on Market Place. They were due to lead it in half an hour. "I'm starting to appreciate Faux," Samwell said sipping his decaffeinated cappuccino. He spoon-fed Lady some fresh eggs-n-ketchup. "The solvents in this hellish cocktail must kill larvae."

Jack wore his last and only uniform—the one with a coffee stain on his left breast. He admired his new butcher's knife, looking forward to breaking it in. "Aye, everyone is switching to Faux now. Maybe in a few months, we'll all learn to move on. Today's celebration will help. Let us first pay respects."

Samwell, Kid, and Jack raised their mugs of Cap-faux-ccino in salute. "To Marge."

Lady whimpered.

The 'kid' added, "And Sergeant Willis."

"Hear, hear." They gulped down their Faux coffees.

Samwell swallowed his heart meds, with a Faux chaser. The pills were insufficient for his broken heart, but he needed all the help he could get. *Damn, Marge is gone.* "I really do need to retire one of these days," Heart Attack Sammy grumbled as he stood. "But first, another beat needs walked. Come on Lady, up you go. We've gotta get you out front."

They exited Fat Jacks into sunshine, humidity, and the screaming crowd of celebrants.